CROSSFIRE

CROSSFIRE

Miyuki Miyabe

TRANSLATED BY
Deborah Stuhr Iwabuchi and Anna Husson Isozaki

KODANSHA INTERNATIONAL
Tokyo • New York • London

The translators gratefully acknowledge our perceptive readers Wallace Paprocki and Pamela Uchida, the valuable input of our editor Ginny Tapley, and the undying patience and support of our families, especially our better halves, Ken Isozaki and Ikuo Iwabuchi.

Originally published in Japanese in 1998 by Kobunsha, Tokyo, under the title *Crossfire*.

Distributed in the United States by Kodansha America, Inc., and in the United Kingdom and continental Europe by Kodansha Europe Ltd.

Published by Kodansha International Ltd., 17–14 Otowa 1-chome, Bunkyo-ku, Tokyo 112–8652, and Kodansha America, Inc.

First edition, 2005
12 11 10 09 08 07 06 05   10 9 8 7 6 5 4 3 2 1

Library of Congress Catalogue-in-Publication Data available.

www.kodansha-intl.com

1

The abandoned factory appeared in a dream. The chilly rust-colored ceiling, the corroding metal pipes scattered about. The cavernous room, uncared for and uncleaned, filled with machines still connected complexly to each other and linked with a steel-colored conveyor belt. Everything silent and unmoving.

Somewhere water was falling in steady drops. Even in the dream, the monotonous sound was soporific. Just like the faint heartbeats of someone dying, a dark sign pointing to impending death. The water dripped onto the bare floor, forming a small puddle. Walking over to it, the surface ruffled as though startled by the approach of a human shadow.

Reaching out to touch it, the water was cold. And black, like night. It looked like oil, and was sticky, clinging to her fingers. Scooped up, it coagulated in her cupped hand to make a new little puddle. Ceiling pipes were reflected in the dark surface.

Cold. The chill was refreshing. Even in the dream, it felt good, passing the water back and forth between her hands.

But then the liquid began to take on body heat, becoming lukewarm. She could feel the change distinctly. Fingers spread to let the water spill out, her palm suddenly grew hot. Looking down, she saw that the black water was on fire. The flame seemed alive, raising its head to confront her. The next moment, with a whooshing sound, it jumped to her sleeve and raced up her arm—

She woke then. She snapped wide awake, as if her sleep had been switched off. She could see the white ceiling in the light of her bedside lamp.

Junko Aoki jumped up from her single bed. She lifted up her warm quilt and patted it over with the palms of her hands. She pulled out her blanket from under the quilt, and patted that, too. Next she pulled both the quilt and blanket off the bed and patted the mattress over from end to end, checking.

The bed seemed okay. Junko hit the wall switch to turn on the ceiling light and got down onto the floor. Blinking in the bright light, she inspected the room. The curtains? Carpet? Sofa? The half-knit sweater, newspapers, and magazines in the wicker basket next to it?

Everything intact: no smoke, no flames. No burning smell, either. Okay here.

Junko jumped up, left the room, and went into the kitchen. The metal bowl she used for washing the dishes was sitting in the sink. As usual, she'd filled it to the brim with water before going to bed. Now there was steam rising from it. Holding her hand over it, she could feel the heat. It was about the temperature of a hot bath.

Junko sighed.

She felt a surge of relief mixed with tension, not a compatible combination. Unable to relax, Junko glanced at the clock. It was ten after two in the morning.

Guess I have to go.

She'd last been to the factory less than ten days ago, and yet she'd already dreamed about it again. Her body seemed to be needing it.

She needed it as a place to radiate and release. The cycle was speeding up, dramatically so in the past six months. She was having more dreams, too. And in those dreams she was releasing spontaneously, against her will. At least she had unconsciously chosen somewhere with water she could use as a cooling agent, but still . . .

Were her powers intensifying? Was that why she was starting so many fires involuntarily? Or was she gradually losing control over the power?

Just thinking about this wasn't going to help. Junko shook her head, then passed a hand over her unruly hair, and got busy changing her clothes. Outside it was close to freezing. The north wind was rattling the windows, a typical December night.

Tayama, Arakawa Ward, Tokyo. Tayama 1-chome was a twenty-minute bus ride north from Takada, the station after Arakawa. East of it was Tayama 3-chome, a long and narrow old residential district marred by the new Tayama Garden House development with "Condos on sale now!" Up until about ten years ago, this area had still been dotted with modest-sized farms, but they had almost completely disappeared, replaced with a wide variety of housing. Just across a bridge not far from Tayama was neighboring Saitama prefecture, now a mere continuation of the seemingly endless residential sprawl.

Farmland had started to disappear during the period of rapid economic growth from 1960 to 1965, when the population of the metropolitan area began to leave the city center for the suburbs. Later, the land grab during the Bubble Era of the 1980s snuffed out the few remaining farms. Within the boundaries of Tayama there was only one piece of property that could still be called a farm, a place about five minutes on foot from Junko Aoki's apartment building. Sasaki Gardens was about the size of a football field, and was cut into little chunks that were rented out as kitchen gardens on a yearly basis. As a plot of three square meters went for the modest price of twenty thousand yen a year, applicants outnumbered lots, and there was a waiting list of prospective "farmers."

Many long-time Tayama residents had operated small or medium-sized companies in a variety of industries such as printing, bookbinding, construction, shipping, or the manufacture of moldings for plastic goods. This, however, had been prior to the rapid growth period when most of Tayama was still zoned as a second-class residential district, and their fate, too, had been determined when Arakawa Ward assumed the role of a bedroom town to the metropolitan area. Any attempt at nurturing local industry had been abandoned, and about half of those little neighborhood factories had been either closed down or moved by Tokyo district planners to light industry parks. The remaining factories and workshops stuck out here and there like objectionable outsiders. There was a lot of friction with neighboring residents over issues like noise and waste disposal, and their future was not bright. The wave of an economic recovery or another housing boom would wipe them out completely.

Junko Aoki had moved to Tayama in the late fall of 1994. She worked for eight hundred yen an hour, slightly more than the minimum wage, as a waitress in a local café called Jeunesse. It was unusual for a single woman of her age—twenty-five, still in her working prime—to choose this kind of part-time job, all the more so because her résumé listed Toho Paper, a major manufacturer, as her last employer. Her coworkers had questioned her, "Why'd you quit such a good job? What made you take up waitressing?" but Junko's answer was just silence and a smile. She left them to decipher an answer to their questions in that smile, knowing full well that they would never come up with the truth.

In fact, she had applied to work at the café after finding an apartment she liked. She had wanted a job close by that would not require a lengthy commute, and she'd decided that waitress work would allow her to keep complicated interpersonal relationships to a minimum.

She chose to base her living arrangements in the north end of Tokyo because she had already lived in the eastern and central areas. She wanted to be in a place she'd never lived before, so she simply got on a northbound train and got off at each station on the line, dropping in at real estate agencies near each of them.

When she'd picked this apartment, the decisive factor had been the view she'd caught from the window of the real estate agent's car when he took her to see it. She had spotted a small pond at the end of a narrow one-way street after they turned off the main road. She'd leaned out the window and murmured, "A pond . . ." and the real estate agent had grimaced. "Looks filthy, huh? It's a breeding ground for mosquitoes in the summer, a real hassle."

He'd probably come out with this opinion without thinking, and he quickly added, "But the place I'll be showing you is pretty far, and of course they spray it in the summer, so it's nothing to worry about."

Junko had smiled. "I don't mind."

Never mind the bugs, she'd be happy as long as there was water nearby. She'd considered living by a river, but the wide, walled riverbanks were something that drew people. If there was even the slightest danger of her being seen by someone, it was no good for Junko. What if she were out in the middle of the night releasing energy towards the river, and a young couple saving the cost of a hotel room caught sight of her—now *that* would be bad.

"Is the pond on private land?"

"That's right. That's why the city can't do anything about it."

"So it won't disappear any time soon, will it?"

"I don't think so." The real estate agent glanced at Junko. His eyes were questioning.

And so it was that Junko decided to rent the apartment, not in spite of but *because* the problematic pond was only a ten-minute walk away. Ever since she'd moved here, until about June this year, she'd used it as a place to release. But with summer, just as the agent had said—no, worse than the agent had said—hordes of mosquitoes took over the pond, and there was no way she could stand still for even five minutes. It wasn't likely the owners were doing any spraying. She'd had to give up and walk around the area, searching for another body of water.

What she'd found was an abandoned factory on the edge of Tayama.

Junko dressed in a thick sweater and slacks, and pulled on her coat and mittens. Then, slipping a flashlight into her pocket, she left her apartment. It was on the second floor, number 203. Stepping as softly as she could, she descended the outside staircase, unlocked her bike and rode off.

The nighttime street had lights here and there, but it was deserted. Nights in this residential area were quiet; night owls partied elsewhere. On top of that, it was Tuesday—to be precise it was Wednesday now—and although it was the busy December season, there still wouldn't be many people out past midnight. On the streets of Tayama, she was passed by exactly two taxis heading in the opposite direction—one out of service, one without a fare.

The way to the abandoned factory was nearly straight. Partway there, where the condos were up for sale, was a three-way fork, but all you had to do was keep heading in the same direction along the middle street, and you'd be fine. She'd taken this route so many times since the beginning of summer that she could probably travel it in her sleep.

Soon the familiar shape of the abandoned factory loomed in the dark. The factory consisted of a steel-framed structure, with sheet-metal walls holding up a roof of galvanized iron tiles. A small three-story building nearby had probably been used as the office. Set in between the two buildings was a large parking lot that could have been used for transport trucks.

A chain link fence encircled the buildings, and at the front was an iron barrier set on wheels so it could be pushed aside. Junko passed by that gate, which was chained and securely fastened with a substantial padlock, and headed around to the back.

When she'd first found this place, she had walked around it once and given up on finding a way in. But it looked too good: it was big, deserted, and no homes were immediately adjacent. Narrow roads ran along its east and west flanks, and on the north side stood a dilapidated warehouse for some transport company. The south side was vacant land that, according to a notice board, belonged to the Tokyo Metropolitan Government. Perhaps irritated that the city was leaving the land unused, the local residents were using it as a place to dump garbage. No one came around for any other purpose; children didn't play there either.

It fit the bill perfectly. But it was no good if she couldn't get inside.

She couldn't bring herself to give up on it, and she'd come again looking more closely for a way in. It had turned out to be unexpectedly easy. The steel door facing the single-lane street on the east side—what would have been something like a back door on a regular house—was, as expected, chained and padlocked. But both hinges were off, and when pushed, it opened about fifty centimeters. It was so wobbly that leaving the door as it was seemed downright dangerous, but since hardly anyone passed by this way, nobody had noticed it or complained about it. On the opposite side of this street was a public housing block, but the side of the building overlooking the factory was windowless, and a water tower was planted between it and the road. As for the street itself, after passing between the abandoned factory and the housing block, it quickly turned into a dead end, not connecting to anything or anywhere else.

Junko wasn't from the area and wasn't familiar with Tayama's history, but judging from the decrepit fence and the rusty padlock, she guessed that the factory had been abandoned quite some time ago. She had no idea why it hadn't been razed, rebuilt, or sold for its land. There could be complex issues of ownership rights, a license to operate the factory hadn't come through, or any number of other factors—not to mention the economy, now at rock bottom.

Counting tonight, how many times had she been here? She was sure it was at least ten, but the place still gave her the creeps.

To avoid attracting attention, she left her bike behind the factory and walked back to the door. Slipping through it, Junko quickly switched on her flashlight so she could see where she was going. Having done that, she summoned the strength to shove the door shut, the way it had been.

The smell of mud and rusted iron engulfed her.

She'd never been here in the daytime, so she still didn't have a grasp of the full layout. When she came in the back entrance, though, she'd figured out that she was positioned to the left of two big machines connected by a conveyor belt. On her left were huge shelves fixed to the factory wall, covered with a thick layer of dust. Hammers, wrenches, and giant Phillips-head screws about thirty centimeters across were scattered here and there on the shelves. There was a disc resembling a large turntable fitted onto the machines linked by the conveyor belt. When it had been in operation, it had probably done something like cutting or polishing iron. For Junko, who didn't know much about manufacturing, there was no way to figure out what this factory had made so long ago. She got the vague impression that whatever it was, it must have taken up a lot of space, been very heavy, and working on it had probably made a lot of noise. Maybe rails, or steel cables.

Junko passed by the machines and headed for the center of the factory. The bare ground of the factory floor had unused parts and garbage strewn everywhere; before she'd gotten used to it she'd often stumbled and scraped her hands or bruised her shins. Over the course of her visits she'd gradually cleared a path, cleaning up and moving small things off to the side, so it was easy to walk through now. She still used her flashlight to light the way ahead of her, although she hardly felt the need anymore.

The entire factory was about the size of a school gym. The ceiling was high, too, about the height of a normal three-story building. Catwalks ran lengthwise and crosswise overhead, with a number of pulleys attached. There was also a walkway about a meter in width crossing the factory from east to west and a ladder that reached up to it. Workers must have had to climb up there, but Junko had never gone up—she had never liked heights.

Junko's goal was a little to the right of the factory's center, near the main entrance. It was a big water supply tank and a concrete holding pool that could fill from it. The supply tank was about twice the size of the tanks one saw around town loaded onto trucks. Tapping it to see if there was still any water inside didn't help—the only sound was the dull thud of her palm hitting something hard.

But there was water left in the holding pool, which came up to Junko's chest. It was filled to the rim with black water. When the factory had been abandoned, someone must have forgotten to flip a switch or pull a plug or something, and it had been left just as it was.

It might have as much water as that mosquito-infested pond. Well, maybe not. Junko really didn't know. But this water, from which the smell of oil wafted and which looked black as mud, was just what Junko needed. Even if she happened to lose control and released her energy at full power, it would still be difficult to dry up *all* of this water. If she just used it for regular releases to let off steam and relieve the pressure, it looked like it could last her for about ten years. Which meant that as long as this factory stayed abandoned, Junko wouldn't have to go searching for anyplace else.

As always, Junko began by switching off her flashlight against the awful chance in a thousand that she'd be spotted and questioned.

Pocketing the flashlight, Junko stared at the pool's black water. She tried to remember the coolness she'd felt in her dream. When it came, the lingering recollection of power she'd released in her sleep acted as a primer to call up the power of the real Junko, now. It quickly welled up inside her, ready to pour out.

Had it been a moment later, the euphoria that came with release would have taken over and Junko probably wouldn't have been able to hear anything. She shut her eyes, about to give herself over to the surge of power, when she heard a sound. The sound of something heavy being moved.

Followed by a person's voice.

Junko opened her eyes wide. The power was boiling up. All that was left was to turn to the black water and hurl her energy towards it. But she sucked in her breath quickly to halt the power before it could burst out. Just then, she heard another voice.

"Over here. Hurry up."

A male voice, accompanied by the indistinct sounds of a number of people. Someone was coming.

2

Junko checked her surroundings quickly. She had to hide. Luckily the heavy darkness acted as a natural screen for her.

"What the hell are you doing?"

"Shh! Keep it down, stupid!"

The voices became clearer. The beams from two flashlights flew up and down, crisscrossing each other. She could make out heads moving in the light. It looked like there were three, maybe four of them. They were trying to get in through the same unhinged steel door that Junko herself had come through.

She ducked her head down and, in a crouch, slipped in behind the water tank, pressing herself against the wall. Junko's power, the lid slammed on just before release, had settled down quietly inside her, but her heart pounded at the sudden intrusion. Who the heck were these guys? What were they doing here? And at this hour?

The cluster of human shapes was still in a confused knot around the door. It looked like they were having some trouble getting in. Junko strained to see them. She could hear something thumping against the door.

Soon the black silhouette of the first figure became fully visible. In the light cast by an unsteady flashlight beam she could make out that his back was to her, and he seemed to be moving backwards. It looked like they were carrying something—

Junko's breath caught in her throat.

They were lugging in a human form. Dead or unconscious, it was stretched between them, hanging limply. The first guy grasped it under its arms, and another carried its feet. The thumping sound she'd just heard must have been its shoes hitting the door.

Behind them came another two figures carrying flashlights and nervously jerking their heads back and forth, checking the street outside, and hurrying the others along. The flashlights they were holding seemed to be much larger than Junko's, and the beams were stronger. Still crouching, she put her hands on the wall to guide herself as she inched along, retreating further into the shadow of the water tank.

"Hey! Hurry up and shut it!" someone ordered. In response, the unhinged door was closed with such a violent shove that it listed slightly to the side, opening a narrow crack through which light from the street outside poured in a thin diagonal line. The only other light in the abandoned factory was from the two flashlights held by the intruders.

Now that they'd gotten through the door, their progress was faster. One of the guys holding a flashlight led the way, coming in Junko's direction along the path she had cleared. His footsteps were getting closer.

As they got to the center of the factory, Junko could make them out a little more clearly. She couldn't see their full bodies in the capricious light of the flashlights, but she could discern their builds. And voices.

"About here okay?"

A young guy. Younger than Junko. Twenty? Were all of them so young?

"Let's put him down. He's heavy."

There was a thud as something heavy hit the ground. The way they'd been carrying the body was rough, but the way they set him down was awful. Even so, there was no grunt of pain as he landed and the wind was knocked out of him, no groan of protest. He seemed completely helpless. Was he dead?

Junko clenched her fists. Her palms were sweating. Whichever way she looked at it, this was clearly no friend of theirs. They didn't look like trouble-making high school students who'd been on a spree and were bringing in one of their friends who'd drunk too much and passed out, or a motorcycle gang who'd come in to lay low and hide a member injured during a police chase. This had more of a grim, ugly look to it.

Junko rigidly observed the proceedings. It seemed that none of the four youths had noticed her at all. One of the two holding flashlights yawned loudly.

"Man, I'm beat."

"What *is* this place? It stinks."

The beams of the two flashlights started flicking around the factory. Up, down, left, right. To avoid being caught in one of the circles of light, Junko crouched as low as she could, and kept her head down.

"Asaba, how'd you find out about this place?"

"My old man used to work here a long time ago."

"Oh, w-o-w," came from the other three, their voices a mixture of respect and derision.

"Hey, I thought you said your old man didn't have a job."

"Yeah. He was fired when this place closed down."

"But that must have been years ago, right? He hasn't had a job since?"

"*Whatever.* Who cares?"

They burst out laughing. Hearing their laughter confirmed for Junko that they really were young. They had to be teenagers. Unrestrained, youthful laughter. It was so totally out of place that it raised goose bumps on Junko's skin.

"Whadda we do? Bury him here?" asked one of them.

"Yeah, it's just bare ground, huh?" replied another, flashlight in hand. He was kicking at the ground with the toe of his shoe.

Bury? Then that guy was dead after all? They'd snuck in here to dispose of a body?

"But the ground's hard. You gonna make us dig a hole here?"

"Why don't we just dump him?"

"Yeah, and what if they find him?" came the voice of the one they'd called "Asaba" just now. "We've got to hide him right."

"Then why not throw him in the river like I said before?"

"Sooner or later, someone's gonna find him," said Asaba. His tone was admonishing. It sounded like he was the leader. "As long as they don't find a body, no one runs around screaming. That's the way it's worked so far. Just as long as we do it right, like I said."

"Shit. It'll take all night."

Asaba silenced the discontented muttering with a terse, "You've got a shovel, right?"

"Yeah, got it."

"Then dig around here. This is a good spot. Nobody'll come poking around behind these machines."

Junko thought that Asaba must be on the other side of the factory from her, somewhere by the conveyor belt. One of the flashlights was shining over there. But the second flashlight started moving around the interior of the factory again. Worse, it wasn't aimed at the ceiling at all anymore, but instead was carefully going over the area from about waist height down. Junko held her breath and shrank deeper into the crevice between the water tank and the factory wall.

She heard the crunch of the shovel hitting the ground.

"What the fuck is this? It's too hard for this shovel."

"Just shut up and do it."

The other flashlight was still shining here and there. The beam landed on the water tank Junko was hiding behind, the wall next to it, skimmed the rim of the holding pool, went to the conveyor belt—and suddenly flicked back in her direction.

"Hey," the guy called to the others. "Looks like a pool or something."

The round beam of light from the flashlight was on the holding pool, just a few steps from where Junko was hiding. Sandwiched in between the water tank and the factory wall, Junko's ribcage was squeezed painfully and breathing was difficult, but she controlled herself, remaining absolutely still. They might catch any inadvertent movement.

"What're you talking about?"

"Over here."

The sound of the shovel ceased. The guys came closer to the holding pool, and one of them leaned over the rim. Junko could see his silhouette reflected on the water's surface.

"This water's putrid!"

"It's oil, isn't it?"

"That's what I mean! It's perfect. If we toss him in here, no one will ever find him. Looks good and deep, too."

"It might work . . ."

There was a splashing sound, as if someone had plunged their hand into the water.

"It'd be better than burying him, right, Asaba?"

Asaba didn't reply right away. Junko thought he was the one who'd plunged his hand into the holding pool. After a few moments, he pulled his hand out of the water and answered.

"Water this filthy could be okay."

The other three cheered. Junko closed her eyes. What *was* this? They'd come searching for a place to hide a dead body, and now they were all excited to have found her holding pool. What *were* these guys? Were they human beings?

Human.

Junko opened her eyes, and shivered from a different kind of tension than she'd been feeling until now.

These four. These four creeps . . .

They left the side of the pool and headed back toward where they'd been digging. Moving with purpose. Were they seriously planning to throw a dead body in there? Dead body? Dead *person*?

Not just dead—these guys had killed him, she was certain. And they were planning to dispose of him here. And worse, from what she'd heard Asaba saying, this was not the first time they'd done this sort of thing.

That's the way it's worked so far. Yes, that's what he'd said. They must have killed before.

Could their type be called human? Or was it stretching the word too far? Well, they could be called anything—people were free to say what they wanted. They were human, they were wild and aimless youth, they were victims of society . . . they could be called whatever people wanted. But she, Junko Aoki, didn't think a group like these four were human. And furthermore—

She wouldn't mind getting rid of them.

Her heart started to pound painfully fast, and Junko had to pace each breath to slow down the mounting tension. *I can do it. For me, it's no trouble at all. It would only be a matter of letting out the power I just sucked back down inside. That's all. There's no point in hesitating.*

Because I'm not normal; just the way they're not human.

Their feet scuffed along against the dirt—they were coming back over, dragging the body with them. What should she do? Where should she start? Who to aim at first?

If they were too near, there was a risk of danger to Junko herself. And the position she was in now wasn't to her advantage. It would be better if she could get out for a clearer view, to get a good fix on the positions of the four of them.

"Here, you take his feet." It was Asaba's voice. "Sink him as far towards the middle as you can."

"Chuck him in headfirst," laughed the voice of another.

Junko moved her head forward ever so slightly to bring them into view. They were separated from her only by the pool. The two closest to her were holding the body by the trunk and legs, starting to lift him up over the edge of the tank. The flashlights were shining from both sides. Thanks to that, Junko could now see their faces clearly.

They were surprisingly good looking, and their cheeks and foreheads still had the soft skin of children. One was strikingly tall, wearing a loud checkered shirt. His protruding Adam's apple gave him a slightly uncivilized look. The other had his hair fashionably long, just brushing his shoulders, and the tips that fell into the flashlight's circle of light shone reddish brown.

From her vantage point, Junko could only see part of the body and the back of its head as the youths attempted to drag him up and over the side of the holding pool. She could see that it was a man and that he was wearing a suit. His necktie was dangling, touching the surface of the water.

She couldn't see the faces of the two in back. But when the one holding the flashlight on the left, perhaps nervous at the surroundings, turned partly around, she could see the words "Big One" emblazoned on the back of his jacket.

Junko made a snap decision. She'd aim for the one with long hair. Hair burned well, and the light from it would be of use. First she'd set his hair on fire, and while the others were distracted, she'd jump out. She knew this abandoned factory a lot better than they did. Once she'd left her hiding place, she'd run around behind the conveyor belt and then target them one by one as they came chasing after her. Even if they tried to run away, the only escape route was through that one steel door. She'd be prepared, positioned to burn them.

"Ready? In he goes . . ." As the two in front were hoisting the body up to the edge of the holding pool, the "corpse" suddenly groaned.

"Shit! He's still alive!" Long Hair yelled. The flashlight beams flew up and circled around. Junko jerked in surprise, too, bringing her within the circle cast by one of the flashlights.

Uh-oh, damn!

The instant she realized they'd be able to see her, the youths were already yelling.

"Someone's here!"

"What?"

"Someone's there! Behind that tank!"

Junko tried to leap out from the space between the water tank and the wall, but she had wedged herself in too tightly to move quickly. Those moments were enough for the flashlight beams to return and shine directly on her face. Reflexively, she shaded her eyes with a hand.

One of them yelled in surprise, "It's a woman!" and the voice of Asaba ordered, "Hurry up and get her, asshole!"

They moved fast to cut off Junko's escape route. The one closest to her stretched out his hand to grab her and latched onto her sleeve.

Stumbling as she was pulled forward, Junko managed to steal a glance at the "body" they had lugged in. They were right. He *was* alive. His face was covered with cuts and bruises, his eyes were only half open, but he was holding onto the rim of the pool with both hands.

I've got to make sure I don't hurt him.

Then she settled on her target. She shifted her gaze back to the guy pulling her towards him. She saw that he was smiling. *A woman. A woman in here!* he was obviously thinking. Oh, yeah—these guys weren't scared of a woman. *They're going to die. I'll barbecue them. It'll be just like turning on the garbage disposal; simply grind them up and wash them away.*

Junko let loose.

The one tugging her sleeve suddenly flew back. The flashlight flew from his hand in a graceful arc, hitting the metal ladder connected to the catwalk and smashing its glass. Junko watched it go, but she was the only one. The others had their eyes glued on their buddy. His hair, shirt, and pants were spewing flames as he hit the highest point of his own arc through the air. He was a ball of fire by the time he hit the factory floor. He didn't even scream. Junko could sense how powerfully her strike had connected. The energy had flown like an arrow and it seemed to have broken his neck before it had turned to fire.

Now the others were screaming, all three rooted to the spot. Unable to move or even wipe the leers off their faces, their shock was almost comical.

Junko took her time stretching, then turned her head to stare their way. The one with the checkered shirt was closest to her—almost within arm's reach. Next to him was Long Hair. And then the one holding the second flashlight. He was small, wearing a bright red sweatshirt, and he had an earring in one ear.

Junko took one step towards the line of petrified youths. They all stepped back. The one in the sweatshirt took two steps. His mouth was quivering and he looked about to burst into tears. Junko could see this clearly in the light of the flames from the burning body. The stench was starting to close in around them.

"What did you do to him?" asked Long Hair. His voice was trembling. His eyes shifted uneasily, looking Junko up and down. "What've you got?"

Junko kept her gaze fixed on them in silence. *You want to know what I have? You mean, do I have a weapon? If that's what you mean, yes, I do. But searching me won't help you find it.*

My weapon is inside my head.

She smiled slowly and calmly, and took another step forward. This time they all retreated two steps in unison. They'd reached the center of the factory.

"What's with her?" continued Long Hair, shaking like a leaf, his eyes riveted on Junko. "What's she doing? Do something, Asaba!"

He was calling to the tall one, Checkered Shirt.

I see, so you're Asaba, huh?

Junko looked him in the eyes. His were the most clear and steady. He was clearly shaken, but in his eyes she could see some kind of passion rising. Was it fear? Or—

Junko brushed some stray hairs from her face, then jerked her head to mow down all three.

The power flowed out smoothly. Her control was perfect, like an experienced animal trainer cracking a whip with precisely judged distance and strength. She could even see the lash of heat.

But Asaba moved to dodge it. His effort was clumsy, but he succeeded in avoiding the fire and was only flicked backwards and thrown on top of the conveyor belt. The two others were enveloped in flames the moment the heat struck them. Faces, hands, hair; all burning. Even their screams were on fire. Asaba flailed atop the conveyor belt, his eyes wide and fixed on the other two as they burned. The hems of his jeans were smoldering.

Now it's his turn.

Junko settled her aim on Asaba. He looked back at her. He didn't move to run. He just shook his head slightly and put one hand out as if to hold her off. One hand. Not both.

Put out both hands. Cry out for me to stop. That's what you probably made that poor guy do. Grovel and beg for your life just like he had to.

Her power was still pumping. It had been a long time since she'd let off so much, but there was still more ready to come. It had been waiting for this.

Junko lifted her chin and riveted her gaze on Asaba, readying herself to hurl out the next wave of energy. Asaba's hand reached for his back pocket. Yelling incoherently, he pulled something out and pointed it at her.

A gun—the instant she saw it, her shoulder seared with pain.

The impact of the bullet was tremendous. Junko felt her body lifted into the air and flung backwards. An emotion resembling wonder flashed through her mind. *So this was a gun. This was the power of a gun.*

Her back hit the ground first, then the back of her head, and she saw stars. Her left shoulder was on fire with pain. Something warm was running down her arm. Blood. She was bleeding.

Junko fought desperately to stay conscious. She could not pass out. She had to stand up. *Get Asaba!* The life of the poor man by the water tank depended on her. She had to help him. Junko scrabbled at the ground with her hands, struggling to get up and frantically trying to suppress a wave of nausea.

Another shot rang out. Then she heard footsteps—Asaba's—running away. At first Junko thought he'd shot her again, but she felt no new impact or pain. Where had Asaba pointed that gun?

Supporting herself on one elbow, Junko was finally able to raise the upper half of her body. Simultaneously, she heard the steel door being dragged open. Looking toward it, she could see Asaba's shadow cutting across the oblong of light streaming in from the streetlamp. Not turning back, not bothering to close the door, just legging it out of there.

Fires were burning red all around Junko. But they were no longer blazing— rather, they were getting smaller and weaker by the second, as the clothes, the hair, and the bodies of her victims were completely burned through. Junko counted them. One, two, three. Only Asaba had gotten away.

Junko managed to get to her knees and move closer to the holding pool.

The poor man who'd been draped over the edge was now lying beside it. In the flickering red light of the flames, she could see that his body was curled up as if to protect himself. His shirt was torn and his side was wet with blood. So he was the one Asaba had shot; Asaba had wanted to finish him off before he escaped.

His cheek was waxen, even in the reddish light. His eyes were shut. Junko crawled closer to him and reached out to touch his hair. She tried stroking his head. She touched his cheek. There was still some warmth.

"Hang on," Junko told him. She slapped his cheek, whispering, "Please." As she repeated it she heard her voice breaking. "*Please*, open your eyes!"

To her surprise, his eyelids moved. His eyelashes fluttered. Looking at him up close like this, she could see he was young, about her own age. He was older than Asaba and his burnt buddies, but still a young man. Too young to die. "Hang on!" She gripped his shoulder and shook it. His head lolled and his eyes opened. Halfway. They were unfocused. Junko put her face close to his.

"Don't give in, you can't die. I'm going to call an ambulance. Hang on."

His lips moved in response to her voice. He managed to open one eye fully. Junko moved so that her face was almost touching his, and then he was able to see her.

The opened eye was bloodshot and wet, swimming in its socket as though he'd seen things he could not and did not want to believe. Junko took his hand with her good one and gripped it tightly, speaking louder.

"I'm on your side. It's okay now, those guys are gone. Just don't move. I'm going to call an ambulance."

She moved to leave, but with surprising force, he returned Junko's grip, stopping her. Junko's left arm was drooping uselessly at her side, so when he pulled her right arm, she lost her balance and crumpled down next to him.

Her face was against his, as close as a lover's. Junko looked at him. Blood trickled from the corner of his parched, mud-splattered lips. It was dripping from his nose, too.

His lips moved, and his voice came out. "H—help!"

Junko nodded. "Yes, I'm going to help. It's okay now, just relax."

The man's eyes closed, opened, and ever so slightly he shook his head to say no.

"Please . . . help—"

He released her hand and grasped her shirt, pulling hard and repeating, "Please . . . go . . . help . . ." His lips trembled. "Her."

Junko gasped. "Her? There's someone else?"

His eyelids moved, twitching convulsively. From his wet eye, a tear fell.

"Someone you know? Your girlfriend? Where is she?"

Her face up next to his and questioning him loudly, Junko felt herself freeze with an unbearable premonition. She had a feeling that even if she didn't get it from this dying man, she knew the answer.

A woman. So this young man had not been attacked alone, he'd been with a woman. Guys like Asaba would not just let a woman go free.

"Where is she?"

His face contorted and pulled painfully. The edges of his mouth twisted pitifully as he struggled desperately to speak.

"Took . . . her . . . away—away . . . with them."

"Those guys?"

The man nodded.

"Do you know where they went? Did they take you, too?"

Another tear fell from his eye. Blood spilling from his mouth, he clung to Junko's shirt.

"C—car."

"A car? Whose? Theirs?"

"M—mine."

"Those guys took it?"

"She—"

"With her still in it? And they took you off somewhere else to kill you? That's what happened?"

"H—help."

"Got it. Of course I'll help. Do you remember anything about where they took her? Have you got any idea at all?"

His breathing slowed. Junko could feel the hand gripping her shirt weaken little by little. He was dying. "Please, hang on! Do you know where they took her? Tell me!"

The young man's head sagged. His eyes blinked and his mouth opened and closed, gasping for breath.

"Na—Natsuko," he said in a faint voice, and his hand fell limp. His half-open eye lost its focus. He coughed up more blood and shuddered. The flames around them were dying down, and the factory began to fall back into darkness. In that darkness, Junko felt the life leave the young man's body.

"Poor guy . . ." Junko murmured.

Sitting up, she managed with her good hand to lift his head onto her lap. Junko was now the only living being in the factory. The three charred villains were indistinguishable in the dark. Around their bodies, low, flickering red flames clung tenaciously, like hungry insects swarming around a dead body to see if there was anything left to consume. Those flames were Junko's loyal disciples, assassins who never misjudged their target. But she'd been unable to help this young man.

And worse, there was another person captive; his girlfriend.

"Na—Natsuko." That must be her name. *Natsuko*. What had happened to her tonight? What was she being put through right now? Junko shut her eyes tightly for an instant as a chill ran down her spine.

I've got to stand up. I can't pass out. I've got to rescue Natsuko before it's too late.

In the light of the remaining flames, the blood that flowed from the man whose head she held on her lap and the blood from her own left shoulder were the same deep, dark, painful color. The young man had bled much more than she had—his body was soaked.

Junko quickly searched him, hoping to find some clue to his identity. There was nothing in his suit jacket or trouser pockets. Most likely he had been stripped of his wallet and driver's license by Asaba's gang. But then she found a name sewn inside his jacket collar: FUJIKAWA.

"Fujikawa." Junko said his name out loud.

She gently lowered his head to the ground and stood up. Next to the sooty lump of the body nearest to her was a flashlight. The glass was cracked, but the light was still on. Junko picked it up and flashed it around her. She began searching, straining her eyes to examine the three bodies and their surroundings as closely as she could, looking for any hint that might help her figure out where they'd been headed.

The bodies were so badly burned that she could no longer distinguish one from the other by the clothes they had been wearing; and in this state, they all looked about the same size.

Junko was once again conscious that she'd released her power full force. Fleetingly, she recalled the last time she'd done it, two years ago. That time, there'd been four and she'd got them all.

Junko inspected the three corpses, kicking them over with her toe. The pain in her left shoulder was no longer searing, but the loss of blood was making her cold and dizzy. Her stomach heaved in nausea.

She didn't feel a trace of guilt. As far as Junko was concerned, the only human remains in this factory were those of Fujikawa. The other three were no more than unidentifiable vermin.

If she'd had her wits about her, she would have wielded her power more carefully to make sure some clues were left behind, but the situation had left her no choice.

She shone the flashlight in the direction Asaba had fled. Nothing to see but the black floor and the factory equipment. Wasn't there anything for her to go on? Junko lifted her head and listened hard. Had someone in the neighborhood heard those two gunshots and called the police?

For the moment, there was no change in the hush of the night enveloping the abandoned factory. Surely someone had heard the gunshots, but to the people of this neighborhood, used to peaceful nights, connecting a sound they had only heard in movies or on TV to something in real life would be difficult. Even if awakened by a loud noise, they would probably assume it was a car backfiring, or they'd frown, thinking it was neighborhood kids again, and burrow back into their beds.

That's what set Junko apart from other people. She knew that this city was a battleground. *Looks like it'll be my job to call the police*, she thought, lowering the flashlight. Just then she felt something under her foot. When she stooped to pick it up, she saw it was a matchbook, with the name "Plaza" printed on it. A bar. There was a phone number and address along with a simple map: Komatsugawa, Edogawa Ward, Tokyo. The closest station was Higashi Ojima.

Only one match from the book was gone. Otherwise it looked new. Maybe Asaba had dropped it.

Junko pocketed it. With an effort, she straightened up and steadied herself, then went back over to Fujikawa. She bent down and stroked his disheveled hair. Struck by a thought, she pressed her palm against his blood-soaked suit, then pressed it to the wound on her own left shoulder. She prayed for their blood to mix so that her body would never forget the horrible way he had died.

"Because I'm definitely going to get them back for what they did to you," she murmured in a low voice. Then she stood up.

As Junko left the abandoned factory, the clear cool night air washed over her like water. She felt like she was waking from a nightmare. She couldn't ride her bike—it was impossible for her to lift her left arm at all, and she was too unsteady. Somehow pushing her bike along with her right hand on the road home, she stopped at the first public phone she set eyes on and picked up the receiver. Junko spoke in as low a voice as she could to the clipped-voiced police officer on the other end.

"There are some dead bodies in an abandoned factory next to the public housing block in Tayama 3-chome."

"What? Someone's died?"

"A teenage gang broke in. There were gunshots."

"Hello? Where are you calling from?"

Junko ignored the hurried questioning and continued her purposely toneless report.

"One man was killed, and one woman was kidnapped. One of the guys who did it is a teenager named Asaba. The murdered man's name is Fujikawa, and his car was stolen, too."

Having communicated that much, Junko cut the connection without waiting for a reply. She started shivering in the cold air.

The police had their know-how, their mobility, and their manpower. Would they be able to hunt down Asaba and rescue Natsuko, or would Junko get there first? She didn't care which it was. Junko didn't think that by going it all alone she could do everything, but she had to do all she could to make sure that Natsuko had a chance of being rescued.

The police had their organizational power on their side, and Junko had her wits on hers. And even if the police caught Asaba first, in the end what Junko had to do wouldn't change.

Sooner or later, she'd kill Asaba.

While pushing her bike back to her apartment, she felt tears well up in her eyes. She trudged on without the energy to wipe them away, and drops started spilling down her cheeks. Soon, still stifling her sobs, she let loose and wept.

Those tears were from the unexpected battle and carnage tonight, with indeniable terror mixed in. Her knees were shaking, and she was in pain from the gunshot wound. But she couldn't acknowledge that. *It's Fujikawa I'm grieving for,* she thought. For him and for Natsuko, who she had yet to meet. At least that's what she told herself.

The police reached the scene in under ten minutes. The officer in the first squad car was almost overcome with nausea from the smell that engulfed him as he set foot in the abandoned factory.

Just as the caller had reported, there were dead bodies. One was that of a young man who'd apparently been shot. The other three—who could be counted only because they were spaced apart—could not immediately be identified as human remains due to their condition and the meager light of the factory.

All three had been burned through.

Some of the equipment in the abandoned factory was still hot—not hot enough to cause a burn, but hot enough to convince the police that shortly before, an enormous amount of heat had been released there. Next to one carbonized body, an officer found an old metal bar, twisted and partially melted.

"What the hell is this?" he muttered to himself. "Did they use a flame-thrower or something?"

Junko heard the sirens as one, then another and another squad car raced to the scene. When she got home, she removed her clothes to appraise the wound on her left shoulder. The ribbons of flesh and congealed blood made her head spin.

But she'd been lucky. Cleaning it up with gauze dampened with disinfectant, she gradually saw that the bullet had missed its mark and was just a graze.

Junko frowned. When she'd been shot it had felt like being hit with a hammer and blown backwards. And for no more than a minor wound. There was no way a little gun could have done that. It must have been a more powerful, high-caliber gun. How had Asaba, a minor, managed to get his hands on a gun like that?

Once Junko had managed to clean the wound as best she could, she found she was unbearably thirsty. She walked unsteadily to the refrigerator and drank straight from the first thing that came to hand, a carton of orange juice. She gulped it down, but her stomach rebelled and she had to race to the bathroom, where she vomited it all up. Still hanging onto the sink, she passed out.

When she came to with a start, water was still pouring from the faucet. She hurriedly splashed some on her face. She didn't think she had she been unconscious for very long.

Standing up, she felt a little better than before she'd passed out. When she moved her left arm, though, the pain shot right to the bone. She pulled an old scarf out of her dresser and set her arm in a makeshift sling. It improved things considerably.

She switched on the TV. As she'd expected, most of the stations were off the air and none of the others were broadcasting news. They probably wouldn't start reports on what had happened at the factory until much later in the morning.

Junko searched the pockets of the clothes she'd shed, and pulled out the matchbook from "Plaza." They were open until 4 A.M. She checked the clock. 3:40 A.M.

She'd never make it in time.

But it was still worth trying. Natsuko's life was hanging in the balance. Junko got moving.

3

Chikako Ishizu had just finished clearing up after breakfast and was getting ready to go to work when her cell phone rang.

Hurriedly rummaging around in the pocket of the jacket she'd left hanging on the back of the chair, she pulled it out. It was Captain Ito.

"Where are you now? Still at home?"

"Yes, I was just on my way out," answered Chikako. Catching her reflection in the mirror on the wall next to the phone, she realized she had only applied lipstick to her upper lip before she was interrupted. No wonder she looked so odd.

Ito's voice sounded urgent and she refocused her attention. "Listen, there's a crime scene I'd like you to check out. Can you get there right away?"

Chikako felt her heart jump. "Yes, of course. What kind of case is it?"

"Something just like *that* has come up again."

Chikako knew exactly what he was referring to, and she tightened her grip on the receiver.

"It's happened again?"

"Yes. This time there are three bodies. I haven't seen anything myself, but I was told they're burned to a crisp. It sure sounds like that other case."

"So, it's just the bodies? Nothing else at the scene was burned, right?"

"Very perceptive. That's why I want you to go check it out. I contacted Shimizu, too. He's already on his way, so you can meet up there."

"Okay. Got it."

Ito gave Chikako the location, traffic access information, and other details. She jotted it all down and hung up. Shoving her arms into her jacket sleeves, she looked at her face in the mirror once more. Rubbing her lips together, she coaxed a little color onto her bottom lip. Satisfied with the effect, she slung her bag over her shoulder and ran out of the house, excitement bringing a flush to her cheeks.

Sergeant Chikako Ishizu would be forty-seven this year. There were only two officers older than her in the arson squad of the Criminal Investigation Division at the Tokyo Metropolitan Police Department, and they both did deskwork. At crime scenes, Chikako was often the oldest, and the other arson squad detectives called her "Mom" in a mixture of teasing and respect. Even Captain Ito, the squad leader, was fully five years younger than Chikako. Kunihiko Shimizu, her usual partner, was only twenty-six, not much older than her own son.

But Chikako herself wasn't particularly worried about the age issue. Indeed, it had its advantages. Chikako had started out as a patrolwoman in the traffic division and had been shuttled from one undistinguished post to the next. When she was unexpectedly promoted to detective and assigned to the Metropolitan Police Department, or MPD, three years ago at the age of forty-four, it had been a favorite topic of conversation in police stations throughout Tokyo. The truth was that there were a number of reasons for her transfer, none of which were related directly to Chikako herself. The MPD had been under pressure to appoint more female detectives. At the same time, the opinion that "you can't count on a woman to fight with you in a tight spot" was still prevalent. Complicating things further were awkward differences of opinion between the top brass over which of the younger women maneuvering for the position to bring in, and it became a battle of wills. When it became clear that the situation could not be resolved without winners and losers, uncontroversial Chikako was chosen to reap the reward of the prestigious assignment.

Chikako knew about all of this, but did not let it bother her. She figured growing older ought to have some compensation, and whatever the backstage maneuvering had been, she was the one who had got the job and she was determined to do it well.

Just once, soon after she had transferred in and Captain Ito had taken her out drinking with a few other squad members, she had laughingly brought up the subject with her colleagues.

"You're all *so* lucky I'm a middle-aged woman. No nasty rumors, no unhappy wives, and my son's all grown up. Pretty handy, don't you think?"

Most of the men smiled wryly at this half-joke, but one sergeant, the longest serving member of the arson squad, was up front with his hostility.

"*L-a-a-dy*," he had said, "just do what you're told and try not to get in the way. The only reason you're here is to balance out personnel. Do two years here, you'll get a transfer to the PR Center, and that'll be it, you know."

Chikako had brushed this off with another laugh. "Yes, sir!" She knew it was a waste of time to get drawn into an argument with men with attitude problems.

Chikako had lost her father in a work accident when she was seventeen. He was an on-site construction engineer and had fallen from a scaffolding three stories high. Death was instant, and it was his family's sole comfort that he had not had time to feel fear or pain.

Without their father, Chikako became the anchor of the family. Her sister was barely thirteen, and her mother had chronic health problems that kept her in and out of the hospital. So Chikako decided to become a policewoman—mainly because she'd heard that civil servants had job security, and police work sounded more exciting than being a clerk at City Hall. She thought it would make her all-female household feel safer and more secure, too.

She went to the police academy, became a patrolwoman in the traffic section, sent her little sister to high school, and looked after her mother. They had her father's pension and insurance and were able to make ends meet. Chikako's main worry was that her mother was prone to depression. She had always been dependent on her husband and was unable to get over losing him. Year by year, she grew further from reality, falling ever deeper into a world of dreams and grief.

Even so, Chikako would often tell her little sister, "In this world, whether life's easy or hard depends on how you take it. It's better not to think about some things too much." Her sister was more like her mother and often wondered how her elder sister could be so easygoing while dealing daily with illegal parking and drunk driving, probably seeing only the disorderly, lawless, and mean side of the world. Whenever she mentioned it, Chikako smiled and replied, "Of course there are plenty of total losers in the world.

But they're just trying to get through life, too. And besides, it's not like we serious types always lose out. Somewhere the accounts balance out."

Chikako didn't know whether or not this optimistic theory was universally applicable, but it turned out to be true for her family. Her little sister married one of her teachers not long after she graduated from high school. He was a steady, reliable man, and the match was everything Chikako could have wanted for her sister. And it had a bonus thrown in. The teacher was the only son of an old, landowning family in the countryside and was hugely wealthy. As he was the sole inheritor of the family fortune, there was little conflict with troublesome relatives, and the couple soon sent for Chikako's mother to join them so they could look after her.

For Chikako, two big worries were suddenly gone, but her motivation went with them. With police work, which she'd chosen to be able to support her family in the most efficient way possible, she began to feel that she had reached something of a dead end. She continued to work, albeit cheerlessly, day in and day out and seriously considered quitting the force.

And then she happened to pull off a great piece of work. While she was giving a warning to the driver of a car with a broken brake light, which she had spotted and stopped while out on patrol, she became suspicious of his behavior and decided to do a search of the car. What did she find but a child, bound and gagged, in the trunk. In short, she had halted a kidnapping in progress and had caught the kidnapper red-handed.

Chikako's heart was warmed by the joy of the reunited parents and child and their gratitude to the police. Thoroughly encouraged, the incident helped Chikako see police work in a new light, and she felt as though she had rediscovered her reason for living.

On top of that, Chikako received a marriage proposal out of the blue from a childhood friend who'd come to congratulate her on her big success.

"I knew you'd never listen to me before," he said, "but now that your sister is married, I thought maybe I had a chance."

Soon after he proposed, the two were married, and before a year had passed they had a son, Takashi.

This old friend, now Chikako's husband, was Noriyuki Ishizu. He'd majored in civil engineering in college and had then been hired by a big construction firm, so his work involved a lot of long business trips. But he kept in touch, sending picture postcards or learning the local dialect and using it when he called home. He was a truly good-hearted man and always made Chikako smile.

Ishizu was now president of the branch office in Kobe, dedicating himself to reconstruction work following the huge earthquake that had flattened much of the city and claimed upward of five thousand lives. He had a place to live there and only made it back to Tokyo once every ten days or so. Takashi was in college in Hiroshima, not so far from Kobe, and would sometimes meet up with his father for dinner or drinks, but Chikako had to be satisfied with infrequent telephone conversations with her son.

In her oft-absent husband's place, Chikako had had the job of caring for Ishizu Senior, her father-in-law—an old-school craftsman who was short-tempered and headstrong. Until his death just last year, he'd demanded a great deal of care and attention from Chikako. He kept up a steady stream of complaints when she was around, but he was lonely the minute she left his sight. Chikako had been equal to the task of caring for a man like that and consequently had no difficulty putting sarcastic or hostile police greenhorns in their place with a single snort.

Now that Chikako was thus unencumbered, her claim to being "a handy middle-aged lady" was pretty close to the truth. All the same, Chikako's position in the arson squad was tenuous. It was lucky that Captain Ito and she got along well, the captain valuing Chikako's character and ability. Thanks to his occasional back-up, she was still visiting crime scenes—otherwise she would have been assigned to a desk and equipped with a key to the copy machine long ago. In return, Chikako was determined to do good work and to ensure his expectations of her were not disappointed.

And now this case. Another burned-body homicide had turned up.

Chikako was deeply grateful that Captain Ito had informed her right away. Two years had already passed since that first time, when Chikako had adamantly insisted that the arson squad should have been more involved in the investigation, and as a result had been shunned for some time within the squad. Even so, she hadn't been able to give it up. At every opportunity, she'd reminded the Captain that since they hadn't caught the perpetrator, something like it was bound to happen again—and when it did, the arson squad would really have a job for itself. The Captain had remembered her prediction and now he was giving Chikako a chance. That said, his meaning was clear: "And now it's up to you to take the ball and run with it, Mom."

The crime scene this time was in Tayama, in Arakawa Ward. Apparently the location was about twenty minutes by bus from Takada station, one stop past Arakawa. Chikako thought hard while checking the map she'd dashed into a neighborhood convenience store to buy and now had spread out in the taxi. This time the murders were much further north.

The original case had happened in the autumn of the year before last, in the early morning hours of September sixteenth. A burned-out car had been discovered by the Arakawa River. There were three bodies in the car, and another about ten meters away. All been murdered, all burned beyond recognition. The condition of the four made it impossible even to determine their gender, although skeletal analysis revealed that three were males and one was female, and that all four were in their teens or early twenties. It truly was a ruthless mass homicide.

As the investigation progressed, however, another facet of the case began to emerge. For one thing, the car turned out to have been stolen from a Tokyo parking lot. Also of interest was that a fingerprint found on an unburned section of the car—that parts of the car remained undamaged was in itself problematic—proved to belong to the prime suspect in a series of murders of high school girls around Tokyo some years before.

This suspect had still been under twenty, the age of legal responsibility, so both the investigation and the news coverage had been restrained and cautious. They were never able to get a single confession but they had detailed information obtained from highly reliable informers and, according to Captain Ito, the investigation team was confident that their prime suspect was indeed the ringleader, and that he and his gang of juvenile delinquents had committed all the murders.

Unfortunately though, they were short of forensic evidence. Nor did they have any eyewitness testimony. Usually with horrendous serial crimes like this, while the criminal piled up offenses, a victim of an attempt would turn up—someone who had made a lucky escape from the clutches of the criminal. Their testimony would become the conclusive evidence, firming up a case. But in this series, there'd been no survivors. As far as they knew, all of the girls targeted were dead.

These homicides had a striking difference from other vicious crimes committed in Japan in the past. By all appearances, they were committed for the sheer joy of killing. It wasn't that the killers were after money or had started out bent on sexual violence. The prime suspect and all his suspected accomplices had police records for sexual assault and blackmail, but in these cases their goal had been expressly to kill.

Their method was simple. On an otherwise deserted street, they would target a girl in school uniform on her way home and chase her down in a car, finally running her over and killing her. But circumstances were rarely just right, with a girl walking alone on an empty street. So the gang began luring or forcing their targets into their car, and taking them off to a more suitable location for the "death race." Police had learned that although the punks had also stolen their victims' belongings and beaten them up, that had just been an extra: their ultimate goal was to kill, that was all. What's more, they delighted in killing their victims as they tried desperately to flee, screaming and pleading for their lives. As the whole picture of the crimes became clearer, the mass media went into hysterics, reporting that what in America was referred to as "sport killing" had now surfaced in Japan.

The ringleader and his gang took full advantage of the combination of media hype and the lack of material evidence. They proclaimed themselves sacrificial victims of false charges, insisted that they were innocent, and declared that they would stand up to police abuse of authority to the very end. A couple of human rights groups and some sections of the media sided with the suspects, lending them support and starting up campaigns. The prime suspect even became something of a celebrity. At that time Chikako had just transferred into the arson squad, and observing the case as a bystander, she thought that things would have turned out differently had the prime suspect been less charismatic. He possessed a kind of star quality.

The accusations against the gang began to lose their intensity, and the investigation, which had been on shaky ground from the beginning, began to falter. News coverage petered out, and six months later, the investigation team was dissolved. The case was eventually listed as "pending"—in other words, it was shelved. Everyone in the criminal investigation division could hear the investigation team grinding their teeth in frustration. But at the same time, they were demoralized, and little by little everyone managed to push the memories of the murdered girls back into the recesses of their minds, back beyond their guilty consciences, and finally into the fog of oblivion.

The Arakawa homicides occurred after the high school girls' killings had been more or less forgotten. Once again, however, that prime suspect was back in the news—only this time because it was he who had turned up as a grisly corpse.

Because the murder method was fire, arson squad members were pulled in as advisors to the investigation team, and were involved in inspections of the scene and team meetings. Chikako wasn't included and only saw what was on the news and the photos of the crime scene. But the moment she heard the gist of the case, it hit her. *This is a revenge killing.* Call it a mother's intuition. She knew immediately that this was a work of vengeance against the girls' murderers.

She was even more intrigued because the case was so utterly bizarre. She argued that the arson squad should be more deeply involved in the investigation and not just stand by as "advisors." But she was given the cold shoulder for her trouble: detectives were very territorial and abhorred stepping on each other's toes. It was part of the competitiveness that men seemed to bring to every aspect of life and it drove Chikako mad.

The case of the Arakawa riverside murders had never been solved. They hadn't even been able to identify what the murder weapon had been. A blowtorch had been discovered stolen from an ironworks in the vicinity of the crime scene, and the media hailed it as the murder weapon, but there was no way one blowtorch could emit sufficient heat to burn four humans into charred lumps. The police would have known that, but the mistake was left uncorrected as the investigation began to stall.

Chikako still wanted to know what on earth the murder weapon had been, and she was convinced that the police should thoroughly check out the family members of the murdered high school girls. Which is why when she found that Captain Ito held the same interest in and frustration over the case, they had continued talking it over between themselves. They were certain the same killer would show up again some day.

While the prime suspect in the girls' murders was dead, some others allegedly involved were still alive. The three other burned bodies at the Arakawa riverside were all identified as those of youths with violent pasts and criminal records, but they were apparently not involved in the murders of the girls. In other words, during an evening of troublemaking with the prime suspect, they had been caught in the crossfire when the killer had managed to track him down. And if Chikako's and Ito's theory was correct, this killer with his mysterious weapon would surface again to take care of the remnants of the gang.

Now their prediction seemed to have come true. The Tayama case would almost certainly resemble the Arakawa murders. Heading for the scene in the taxi, Chikako pressed her lips together in determination.

4

Junko Aoki stood stock still at the end of a dead-end alleyway and hugged herself as best she could to keep warm.

It was five-thirty in the morning and dawn was still a way off. The surroundings were dark, and the doors and windows of the lined-up houses and apartments showed no signs of opening. Sleepy quiet still reigned.

She was facing a neatly leveled plot of land enclosed by a chain link fence. Set approximately in the middle was a sign: *Land for sale—Daiko Real Estate Corporation.* There was a phone number printed under the company's name. Junko read it and re-read it, imprinting it in her mind.

This was the address written on the "Plaza" matchbook she'd picked up at the abandoned factory in Tayama. On the other side of the narrow street was a small white-walled apartment building, and next to it a dingy looking two-story house. Both of those had their addresses clearly posted, and there was no mistaking that this plot of land was where Plaza was supposed to be. In other words, Plaza no longer existed.

It wasn't really hard to imagine what kind of place it had been. This vacant lot wasn't big. Scanning the area, Junko saw that it was crowded with houses, apartment buildings, and little shops. There was no way that "Plaza" alone had been a classy bar in a shiny new building. It had probably been an ordinary house with a section converted into a small bar—a shabby sort of drinking establishment that would be cramped if there were more than ten customers.

But it was pointless wasting energy imagining what it had looked like. Plaza was not here. What she had in her hand was the matchbook of a place that no longer existed. On the chance that it had moved elsewhere, she tried dialing the number printed on the matchbook, but she got a recorded response saying the number was no longer in service.

Junko's only recourse was to call this Daiko Real Estate with a plausible excuse and get them to tell her how to contact someone connected to Plaza, but for that she'd have to wait until business hours began.

It was terribly cold, her wound was throbbing, and her spirits were at rock bottom. She felt like she was running a fever, too—her cheeks were burning, and she was heavy with fatigue. She pulled herself together, stood up straight once more and slipped quietly out of the alleyway.

Junko headed out onto the main street and walked back towards the train station. On her way she took the matchbook from her coat pocket and tried looking it over in the light of the streetlamps.

This matchbook is still new.

A torn-down bar and brand-new matches. What would that mean? The person who'd run the bar still had a stock of these matches on hand. If that was the case, and Asaba had access to the matches, that meant he must have had some personal connection to Plaza. He was not just a customer, but was probably related to the owner.

Junko blinked.

If this were correct, it would give her something to go on. If Asaba was nothing more than a Plaza customer, it wouldn't do her any good, but if he were close to the owner, and she could locate this person, she might be able to pinpoint Asaba's whereabouts.

Junko looked up at the dark sky. Wouldn't dawn *ever* come? Why couldn't real estate offices be open twenty-four hours a day?

Right now, time was her greatest enemy. It was passing quickly and she still had no idea where Natsuko, the girl she was trying to rescue, was being held. Where was Natsuko now? She might already be dead. Asaba and his gang could be shoveling dirt over her still-warm body at this very moment. The pressure of time and her welling anger made her head feel as though it would burst, and she clenched her fists. Her wounded shoulder throbbed in protest, and she grimaced in pain.

Returning to the train station would bring no new discoveries. It was just that it was open, bright, and warm; like a mother in a kitchen before her family gets up, busy with preparations for the day.

At the newsstand in front of the station, newspapers were piled up, still in bundles. Their presence made her suddenly realize that the television stations would have started broadcasting by now. Would they be reporting what had happened in Tayama on the news? What position were the police taking on it?

Junko turned on her heel in front of the station and began walking through the town with a clear goal in mind now. She was looking for a cafeteria or coffee shop; some place with a TV switched on.

This was her first visit to Higashi Ojima. The streets ran in an orderly grid pattern and the layout of houses and stores was easy to follow. She came to a big bridge, built high up, and she had to climb a set of stairs to get onto it. She held her aching shoulder and climbed until she could see the wide expanse of the river below. On the embankment she saw a sign that read, "Nakagawa River."

She stood motionless for a while, gazing down on the black surface of the water. She recalled the map of this area, which she'd checked before leaving her apartment. Nakagawa River—it was a tributary, wasn't it? Didn't it merge with the Arakawa River a little further downstream?

The Arakawa River. That was a name she'd never forget. It was on its broad floodplain that she'd carried out the executions that made her what she was today.

I got rid of four that time.

The memory was vivid. She could instantly recall it at any time. And reliving it in her mind did not torment her. Nor had she ever been disturbed by nightmares of that night. She always slept deeply and peacefully.

Junko had a vague notion that this might actually be a dangerous trait, so she'd tried reading memoirs by murderers or books about the psychology of death-row criminals. According to these, your average murderer without Junko's intentions or methods—who'd killed in passion, for gain, or in self-defense—was tormented by horrible nightmares, imaginary voices, or hallucinations, regardless of whether or not they regretted the crimes. Junko suffered nothing of the kind.

Junko's killings were always done in the course of battle; battles which she considered her duty to fight.

She'd been born with a power few others had, which meant it was something she was *supposed* to use. This was the correct path in life for her. *I am a loaded gun. My mission is to hunt down monsters who live only to consume and destroy innocent lives.* For Junko, this conviction was a sanctuary, its foundation solid in a special place in her heart. Her only regret was that this loaded gun did not come equipped with either navigator or radar. Where was the enemy at whom this loaded gun should be pointing now?

The biting wind that came off the water let fly at Junko's cheeks. She let out a sigh, and had started descending the stairs when she saw something white out of the corner of her eye. It had been off to the right. Looking down over the rows of streets, she could make out white steam rising from the corner of a tight cluster of buildings. She couldn't see a chimney anywhere—what was it?

At any rate, the steam was proof that there were people awake and working beneath it. Junko ran down the stairs and jogged in its direction. The pain from her shoulder made her gasp, but she pressed on it with her hand and hurried on.

As she rounded a second corner, she saw the steam drifting thickly over the street, a commercial area lined with narrow-fronted shops. Amidst the closed shutters and rolled-up awnings, the door of just one shop was open; its ventilation fan on and people bustling in and out. The white steam was flowing out from the front of this shop.

Junko stopped and stood looking up at the sign—"Ito Tofu." *Oh, a tofu shop*, she laughed to herself. Yeah, they *would* be at work early.

A woman wearing a white smock came out carrying a metal frame. She had a mask on, and her hair was covered by a white scarf. Junko dropped back a little and stood partly hidden behind a utility pole to avoid being noticed.

Ito Tofu was slightly larger than the other shops lined up here. Though the sign indicated it was a shop, there was no place to display its wares. It could be that they sold it wholesale.

A small truck was parked just in front. Loaded on it were drums filled to the brim with a damp, white substance. *Okara*—the dregs from tofu-making. They must be about to deliver it somewhere. Junko moved quietly out from behind the pole and closer to the truck. She could feel the warmth from the steam. There was a medicinal smell, too.

The woman put the metal frame in a large bucket into which a long hose

41

was feeding water, and began scrubbing the frame with a brush. Junko craned her neck for a better look into the shop; there were two more people, outfitted in the same white smocks, busily moving back and forth between machines.

Junko approached the woman, whose back was turned to her, with the first words that came to mind.

"Excuse me . . . Good morning."

The woman, startled, looked around at Junko, dropping her work to face her. The hose in the bucket slipped and water came flying at Junko.

"Oh, sorry!" The woman hurriedly redirected the hose downwards. The water splashed off the sidewalk and droplets splattered Junko's coat. "Are you okay? You didn't get wet, did you?" The woman had on aqua blue gloves, and boots of the same color. As she took a step closer, the boots squeaked wetly.

"I'm fine. I'm sorry for startling you like that."

The woman's face was half-covered by her mask. Even so, judging from her voice, she wasn't all that young. There were a number of fine wrinkles, too, around her eyes.

Junko continued. "I just wanted to ask for directions."

"Yeah? Where to? "

The woman's manner had turned brusque. She shoved the hose back into the bucket and stood up again, hand on her hip. She obviously wanted Junko to hurry up so she could get on with her work.

"Is there a bar around here called Plaza?"

The plot of land she'd just checked, where Plaza had been, was quite a bit closer to the station than this tofu shop. But even so it wasn't that far, and businesses in neighborhoods like this often had local associations or some kind of union, so she thought it possible that the woman might know something.

"Plaza?" The woman cocked her head.

"Yes. At least I think it's a bar."

"Do you mean the one that was in the alley next to the station?"

She *did* know it!

"Yes, that's it."

"Well, if that's the one, it's gone out of business. The building's been torn down too, and it's a vacant lot now."

"You wouldn't happen to have any idea where the owner is now, would you?"

The woman jerked in her chin and looked Junko over warily, clearly on guard. Junko gave her a friendly smile.

"The owner there helped me out once . . . Since I was in the neighborhood, I thought I'd try to drop in and say hello, but this area seems to have changed so much, I guess I lost my way."

Thinking about it objectively, the lie didn't sound very plausible even to Junko's own ears. It wasn't even six in the morning yet. It was way too early to be dropping in on an acquaintance. But Junko didn't have the leeway at the moment to cook up a good story. What with her joy at finding the one and only shop with people already up and about in this sleeping neighborhood, exhaustion from the night before, pain from her wound, and impatience at her thread of investigation unraveling, her concentration was starting to flag.

And there was this steam, too. She liked tofu, but the smell of it being made wasn't exactly pleasant. Enveloped in the medicinally-scented steam, the dizziness and chill she'd felt after being shot came back again.

"Well, Plaza's gone," the woman said bluntly. "I don't know what the owner is doing now. We didn't have anything to do with them."

"So when did it go out of business?"

"Maybe a month ago. I don't really remember."

"I wonder if the owner lives anywhere around here?"

"I wouldn't know."

The woman turned her back on Junko and bent down to the bucket. She twisted the faucet noisily to shut off the running water. Then she yanked the metal frame out of the bucket and began walking away, carrying it to the back of the shop.

"Um, excuse me—"

The woman looked over her shoulder. "Now what do you want?"

Junko's words got stuck in her throat. Somehow she seemed to have angered this woman. It had been a mistake to give in to impatience and approach her without planning first.

"Nothing, sorry. Thanks very much for your help."

Junko bowed politely, as deeply as she could. Then as she lifted her head, the abrupt movement combined with a sick feeling made her head spin. She lost her balance and reached out to grab onto something for support.

Her hand met thin air. The next moment she felt something cold splash over her; she'd fallen into the bucket the woman had just been using.

"Hey, you!" The woman came running towards her, boots squeaking. Junko struggled to get up. The water was seeping into her coat, the cold from it coursing through her body and making her shake. The dizziness got worse and worse, and the smell from the steam was making her nauseous.

"Hey, what's wrong with you? Get hold of yourself!"

I'm fine, sorry—she meant to say, but instead she passed out.

When Junko came to, the first thing that met her eyes was a face peering into hers.

It was a girl. She was cute, with a pointed chin, upturned nose, almond eyes, and lips in a slight pout.

Junko tried to speak, but before she could, the girl turned her head and directed her voice back over her shoulder.

"Mom, it looks like she's waking up!"

Junko moved her eyes to take in her surroundings. A wood-paneled ceiling, a simple lamp hanging from a cord. She was warm and lying on something soft.

I've been set down to sleep somewhere—

The girl bent back over her. "Are you okay?"

Junko couldn't find her voice, so she nodded. The movement reminded her of the ache in her shoulder.

"Good," the girl murmured. Her face was taut and unsmiling. "We were going to call an ambulance if you didn't come to pretty soon—we were really worried."

Junko tried to get up but her body refused to move. She moistened her dry lips and was finally able to speak.

"I'm sorry for causing all this trouble. I guess I fainted."

The girl narrowed her eyes slightly. It was if she were weighing Junko's words on a scale and straining to make out the reading. Then she said, "You're injured, aren't you?"

A chill washed over Junko. "Yes . . . kind of."

So they'd noticed. Apparently they hadn't called a doctor, though. Good.

If she were examined by a doctor, the wound in her shoulder would quickly be exposed as a gunshot wound, and the police would be notified. That would lead to all kinds of complications.

"But it's nothing much. I've just got a cold and I'm a little unsteady, that's all. I'm okay now."

To lend credibility to her words Junko roused herself, supporting herself with her right arm when she got halfway up. She looked around.

The floor was covered in tatami, with a low table in the center around which were placed some flat-bottomed chairs. Junko had been laid next to that table. Her coat and shoes had been removed, and she'd been covered with a blanket. It was soft and smelled nice.

Speaking of smells, the smell of that steam was hanging faintly in this room, too. This must be the living area behind the tofu shop. A sliding screen partitioned this room from the next. There was a TV next to the girl, and a clock set on top of it was ticking away. It was close to seven o'clock.

That would mean she'd been unconscious for almost an hour. Since being shot, she'd kept going on sheer willpower, but the wound had taken its toll. She'd made a mistake. Junko bit her lip.

The girl was eying Junko dubiously. Junko noticed that she was wearing a white smock. She was outfitted exactly like that woman she'd met outside, except for the mask and the hair cover. This girl must have been one of the people she'd seen working inside the shop.

Once again the girl raised her voice, directing it back over her shoulder. "Mom, would you come here a minute?"

Then she turned back to face Junko, her face stiff, and said, "Look, you came here to ask about Plaza, right? That's what my mom said."

So the woman she'd just met outside the shop was this girl's mother.

"Yes . . ."

"What for?" the girl asked straightforwardly. "Are you . . . did you . . . But you're a little older than me, so . . ."

The girl looked questioningly at Junko as she voiced these half-questions. Junko stared back at her in confusion, and the girl dropped her eyes slightly and then asked resolutely, "Did you get dragged into some trouble with Asaba? Did something awful happen? Is that why you're here?"

Junko's eyes widened. The girl, seeing her face, nodded as if comprehending.

"Oh, so that *is* it. I thought so. Because there wouldn't be any other reason to come looking for Asaba."

"You *know* a guy called Asaba?"

The girl gave a slight shrug.

"Well, yeah. We were friends from nursery school. We were together in elementary and junior high school, too."

"He's from this neighborhood?"

"Yeah. He used to live at Plaza. There was an apartment on the second floor."

"Do you know where he's been living since Plaza closed?"

"I've no idea. I can't even guess."

Outside the shop, the girl's mother had said with cold indifference that they had nothing to do with Plaza. But if their children had been nursery school playmates, the parents on both sides must have done a certain amount of visiting back and forth. That this girl's mother had been lying was clear enough, but the question was why. Did she want to protect the Asaba family? Or did she want to avoid any involvement with them?

Judging from the girl's clouded expression and close questioning of Junko, there was a good chance that it was the latter. Women who were having trouble with Asaba might have come calling here in the past.

"So other women have come here before, like me, looking for Asaba?"

The girl nodded.

"Not just women, either. Debt collectors have been around, and so have the police."

"The police?"

"Yeah, plainclothes detectives. Asaba must have done something and got found out."

"When was that?"

The girl's gaze flew over to the calendar on the wall and she looked at it, momentarily lost in thought. "Hmm. About six months ago, maybe? Plaza was still open then, and Asaba's mother was there."

"I wonder what he did?"

"I don't know. Detectives never say anything unless they have to." The girl's voice took on a slightly conspiratorial tone as she added, "If they suspect you once, they never leave you alone."

Junko studied the girl's small-featured face closely. She wasn't wearing makeup, and her shoulder-length hair was neatly combed and smoothly pulled back behind her ears. Junko noticed that both ears had a number of piercings.

"I came here by chance," said Junko. "But the other people—and the police, too—why did they come to *you* about Asaba?"

"As if you didn't already know!" laughed the girl. When she laughed, her almond eyes narrowed to lines, making her face look much younger than she probably was.

"I don't understand."

"I know you're lying. Well, whatever. Everyone lies. Not just you."

Junko listened without commenting.

"It's because I ran with Asaba and the others until about a year ago."

"You were in their gang?"

"Yeah. But not anymore," said the girl as her eyes bored into Junko's. "I quit. Now I don't have anything to do with them at all."

It was a forceful denial. Junko sensed there was strong fear underlying it. It wasn't that the girl was irritated at being questioned, neither was it just that she wanted to make it clear that she wasn't like Asaba and his gang—it was more like she had fled something that had terrified her and she still had to remind herself that she was safe now.

This girl had escaped from Asaba and his gang. She must have had experiences that still made her tremble when she recalled them.

Junko ran the scene at the factory in Tayama back through her mind. *I know what you must feel, and I believe what you say, because I saw what they did there,* Junko thought to herself.

"My name's Junko Aoki," she said, nodding her head in an attempt to be formal. "I'm really grateful for all the help you've given me."

"It's nothing—no big deal," the girl hurriedly waved her hand as though to brush aside the thanks, and perhaps to cover her embarrassment, she quickly twisted around backwards and yelled loudly. "M-o-m! Can't you hear me?"

"I can hear."

Just as Junko realized the voice was coming from close by, the girl's mother showed her face from behind the sliding screen.

"Hey, you were right there all along, huh?" the girl pouted. "Eavesdropping?"

The girl's mother didn't answer, but stood protectively behind her daughter and glared at Junko. She had taken off the mask and the white scarf, and now looked like a completely different person.

If she were the girl's mother, she was most likely in her forties. When Junko had met her in front of the shop, her complexion and the energy in her voice had given the impression of someone younger. But now, without the mask and scarf, Junko thought she looked well over fifty. Her hair was almost shockingly white. It might be that she had a natural tendency to early graying, but considering the girl's admission, Junko suspected that her mother's hair was evidence of the anguish she had suffered over her daughter's relationship with Asaba.

"Now that you're awake, would you please leave?" she said cuttingly. "Whatever you're up to, leave my daughter out of it."

"Mom! You really shouldn't talk like that," the girl protested.

"You be quiet."

"I can't keep quiet—it might have something to do with me, too, right?"

"It has nothing to do with you anymore!"

It was painfully evident that the mother was at least as frightened as the daughter. Junko didn't know what had transpired, but her daughter's involvement with Asaba had had awful consequences, and she had finally got her back safe and sound. Naturally enough, she wanted no part of anything to do with that gang again.

"I have no intention of involving your daughter," said Junko slowly and clearly. "Thank you very much for letting me rest here."

Junko tried to stand up. The girl quickly reached out a hand to help her.

"Are you okay? You should lie down for a little longer. And go to a doctor, too."

"Nobue, stay out of this!" her mother scolded. "She should leave now. I've had enough."

"Then leave us alone! I'm worried about her."

So the girl's name was Nobue. Junko smiled at her.

"Nobue, your mother's right. Like I just said, I didn't come here on purpose. It really was just by chance. You've already helped me enough."

Junko found her sneakers neatly set on the narrow step separating the sitting room from the shop. Nobue's mother went and brought her coat and wordlessly thrust it under Junko's nose. Junko thanked her politely, put on her shoes and walked through the shop towards the street door.

Nobue didn't know where Asaba was, so there was no point in sticking around. Junko was strong in battle, but she was an amateur at hunting someone down. She also realized dispiritedly that her body was weaker than she thought.

A third white-smocked person was still in the shop working—it had to be Nobue's father. He was watching as a machine sealed packages of tofu and sent them with a clatter down in a line, from right to left, in front of him. He lifted the sealed packages with a practiced motion and lined them up neatly in a box next to him.

"Thank you very much. I'm sorry for having disturbed you."

He glanced toward Junko as she spoke to him. His face was hard and his eyes were angry. Without saying a word, he quickly averted his eyes. Junko was sure that his hair, too, was probably white beneath his cap.

Junko left the shop and started walking in the direction of the station. Here and there the rest of the neighborhood was starting to wake up. There were more people out on the street, on their way to work. They passed Junko with hurried footsteps. If anyone bumped into her she'd probably lose her balance again, so Junko carefully kept to the inside edge of the sidewalk. It might be better to take a taxi rather than the train. She wasn't sure if she had enough money on her, though.

"Hey! Wait!"

Just as Junko was wondering if she'd heard a voice behind her, something blew past her and stopped with a squeal of brakes. It was Nobue, mounted on a bicycle. She'd taken off the white smock and was wearing jeans and a blue sweater.

"Just a minute. Where are you going?"

Junko smiled despite herself. This girl really was nice, she thought. "I'm going home."

"Really?"

"Yes, really."

"How are you getting home? Can you walk?"

"If I take it slowly, I'll be fine."

"What are you going to do about Asaba?"

"I'll start over again. I can't do anything until I know where to find him."

Holding on to the handlebars, with one foot on the ground to support herself, Nobue considered this.

"What did you come looking for Asaba about?"

"Something that has absolutely nothing to do with you, Nobue."

"I don't know that. I won't know unless you tell me."

"Don't worry. I know what I'm talking about. And besides—" Junko turned back in the direction of Ito Tofu. "If you don't get back to the shop, your mom and dad will be furious, and I'm more worried about that. I don't want you getting into trouble because of me."

"It's okay," Nobue returned flatly. "My parents have no sense of gratitude."

"No gratitude? Your parents?"

Nobue's accusation seemed incredible, given what she had said to Junko earlier. Junko was pretty sure Nobue was the one who should be thanking her parents.

But Nobue reiterated, "Yeah. They're ungrateful. When Asaba and the others almost killed me, it was a stranger who helped me get out alive. But they won't help other people in trouble. They won't even help people in trouble with Asaba. Wouldn't *you* call that ungrateful?"

Nobue's serious tone and the unmistakable words "almost killed me" hit Junko like a slap in the face. She took an unsteady half-step back and looked Nobue over carefully.

As if conscious of the effect of her words, Nobue nodded, adding, "Yeah, they were going to kill me. That's the kind of guys they are. So I don't know what kind of trouble you're having, but I think it must be big, and I wouldn't want you to face Asaba alone for anything."

Near the station was a small open area with a neatly planted garden and benches set around it. Junko and Nobue sank down on one of the benches.

"You're white as a sheet," said Nobue. "Aren't you cold? How about if we go into a coffee shop or something?"

"I'm fine. And we don't want to be overheard, right? If we stay here, I don't think we'll need to worry about that."

Indeed, the two were completely alone in the morning bustle, with the roar of car and motorcycle engines swirling around them. It made Junko feel a sense of kinship with Nobue. This girl was growing on her.

"Like I said before, you seem a little older than the usual girls who get mixed up with Asaba and the others."

"Yes, I remember."

"So who's in trouble with them? Is it your little sister or something? Because those guys don't usually go for older women. At least that's how it was. Asaba told me that they wouldn't be able to use their *excuse* if they had anything to do with an adult."

"Excuse?"

"Yeah. If their target is in high school or someone about the same age, everyone'll say it was some kind of inside fight. Even if they use threats and blackmail, the target is usually too scared to talk to the police. Asaba said no one would notice, even if you did something right in the middle of town. If a girl is stupid enough to go along with them, and then they turn on her, then even if the police come they think they're in it together. But if you target an adult, it's a different story, right? If Asaba and his guys surrounded a middle-aged man or pulled some lady into a car, everyone'd make a big deal out of it."

Nodding, Junko closed her eyes. It was true; what Nobue said made perfect sense. But it seemed that Asaba's policy had changed since Nobue had fled from the gang. And in a big way.

Those guys have killed an adult, you know. Last night they attacked a couple, killed the man, and took off with the woman. They still have her somewhere. And not just that, it looks like they've killed others, too.

The words rose as far as her throat, but Junko swallowed them back down. She couldn't tell Nobue. There'd be no way she could answer if Nobue asked her how she knew about that. The dead bodies of the three from Asaba's gang who she'd torched were still at the scene, in that dark factory in Tayama. Or they might be getting cleaned up about now. This thought brought back a faint sense of victory to Junko's discouraged heart.

She opened her eyes and looked at Nobue.

"I'm afraid my little sister is hanging out with Asaba's gang these days."

"I thought so." Nobue clucked her tongue. "She must be pretty. Like you, huh?"

"Hmm, I don't know about that . . ."

"Asaba goes for looks."

"Yeah, you're cute too, Nobue."

"Not cute enough," Nobue snorted. "That's why they tried to kill me. So, you want your sister to get out, right?"

"That's right. My sister . . . she's getting in deeper fast, so I'm worried. She talks about Asaba and Plaza a lot, and I found a matchbook from Plaza in her coat pocket, so I thought I'd come and check out what kind of place it was."

"This early in the morning?"

"I thought it was a bar, so I didn't want to go there at night. And I was actually on my way to work, anyway."

Nobue gave Junko's clothing a quick up-and-down glance.

"You're going to work like that?"

"Yes—it's a small company. But I guess I'd better take today off. My cut hurts anyway."

"The cut on your shoulder, right? How'd you get that?"

"Oh, it's nothing—it's no big deal."

I'm a lousy liar, Junko thought to herself, and when Nobue said in a low voice, "I'm sorry, but I don't think you're telling me the truth . . ." it almost came as a relief.

"The part about being caught up in something bad and that it involves Asaba, and that you've got to do something about it, so you came looking for him—I think that much is true. But the rest doesn't add up."

"Sorry," said Junko and gave her a little smile. Maybe Nobue would understand that.

It seemed like she did because she smiled back.

"Mind if I smoke?"

"Go ahead."

Nobue got up from the bench and trotted across the street towards a vending machine. Thrusting her hand into her jeans pocket, she pulled out some change and bought a pack of cigarettes, then, searching through her pockets again, she returned.

"My lighter . . . Oh, here it is."

She settled back down on the bench and tried to light a cigarette. But there was a wind, and even after several tries it wouldn't light.

Junko judged the timing of the lighter's sparks and blinked lightly, concentrating on the tip of Nobue's cigarette. It required fine control over her power, constricting the wave of heat down smaller and smaller, then, ever so gently, sending it over.

There wasn't a flame on the lighter but the end of the cigarette was burning. Nobue, a little flustered, took the cigarette from her mouth.

"Hey?" She looked from the cigarette to the lighter and back.

"Nobue, how old are you?" Junko asked.

"Huh? Me? I'm eighteen." Nobue waved the hand in which she was holding her cigarette. "But it's okay because I'm already working."

"Yeah."

"Anyway, I've been smoking on the sly for years. But now it's okay by my parents, too. My dad bought me this lighter for my birthday."

It was a fashionable lighter designed for women, decorated with cloisonné enameling.

"It's beautiful. Could I have a smoke too?"

Junko didn't need to use any sleight of hand this time because Nobue lit the cigarette for her from the tip of her own. They sat together, smoking. Junko coughed a little at first, but the smoke soothed her nerves.

"If you're eighteen, Nobue, then Asaba must be eighteen too, huh?" said Junko.

"Yeah. But he quit high school."

"Mmm, so he's not a student."

But either way, he was still underage, a juvenile. When she'd seen him in the abandoned factory, though, she'd thought he was about twenty. He had a good build.

"What's Asaba's first name?"

"Keiichi. It's written with the characters for 'respect,' and the number 'one.' You didn't even know his full name?"

Kei-ichi, huh?

"His father named him that, hoping he'd become the most respected man in the world. Ironic, isn't it?"

While speaking, Nobue tossed her cigarette butt down by her feet, grinding it in with her heel.

"How about I show you what he did to me?"

Before Junko could answer, Nobue turned her back, pulling her sweater out away from the back of her neck.

"Have a look here."

The wind was ruffling the fine hairs at the nape of Nobue's delicate neck. Junko looked down at her back. What she saw made every hair on her body stand on end. Somebody had cut a huge "X" there. The scars showed that two cuts had been made starting at each shoulder, crossing her back, and ending at her waist on either side.

After a pause, Nobue turned back to Junko. "They were pretty deep." Nobue's hands were steady as she pulled her sweater back into place. "They used a long knife with a serrated tip."

Junko had leaned in slightly towards Nobue while listening silently to her. She was quite close to Nobue's face. If she wanted to, she could probably see right though her eyes and into her mind.

Her eyes were a shining dark brown. But in her right eye there was one tiny point of jet black that looked like it had been made with the point of a needle. It occurred to Junko that maybe the wounds Nobue had suffered and the terror she had felt had all condensed into that one spot. If that black spot were analyzed, would they catch a whiff of still-fresh blood drifting over that gruesome scene?

"So was that attack your chance to get out?"

Nobue gave a deep nod.

"If you don't mind my asking, why did you get involved with them in the first place?"

"No special reason." Nobue shrugged. "I guess I was bored."

Nobue clasped her hands behind her head and leaned back, surveying the sky.

"On the weekends . . . it would be Saturday. By that time Asaba'd already dropped out, but I was still going through the motions, so I'd be really happy when Saturday night came around. School was so boring."

"Were you and Asaba in the same high school?"

"No, I went to a girls' school. Asaba went to an all-boys' school in Shinagawa Ward." Nobue gave a laugh. "All of us were so dumb we could only get into the schools for total losers."

Junko did not laugh along with Nobue. Instead she looked down abruptly and stared at the cigarette butts at their feet. Nobue had the two things mixed together in her mind, but grades in school and actual intelligence were completely different things. There was also no connection between whether a person had good grades and whether they were decent human beings. The Keiichi Asaba that Junko had encountered in Tayama was vicious, but he wasn't stupid. And *that* was the most frightening combination.

"How many were in the group?"

"It was kind of loose—it wasn't like there was a set number. We picked up kids around town, too, sometimes."

"I see. But Asaba was the leader?"

"Yeah. Him, and Takada's older brother."

"Older brother?"

"Yeah. There were two Takadas. The younger one was our age, but the older brother was twenty by then."

"So the older Takada brother had a car?"

"Yup. That's what we got around in. When we had too many people to fit in one car, some of us would sneak off with our parents' cars."

"Without licenses?"

"Right. Pretty crazy, huh?" There was a barely perceptible tone of defiance in her voice as Nobue stole a look at Junko's face.

Junko was busy calling up her memory. At the abandoned factory in Tayama, had these Takada brothers been among the three she'd burned? Had she seen two faces that looked alike—like brothers—in the flash of light illuminating their final moments?

"Were these Takada brothers from your neighborhood, too?"

"No. I don't really know where they were from. They were Asaba's friends. I think the younger brother was in his class at school. His name was Junichi, but we all called him Jun. His older brother we just called Big Bro—come to think of it, I never heard anyone use his name."

"Were they there when your back was cut up, too?"

"Yeah, they were there." The corners of Nobue's mouth went up in a grimace and she laughed mirthlessly. "While Asaba was on my back with the knife, Jun held my legs down. Big Bro just sat there smoking."

Without thinking, Junko lifted her eyes and looked at Nobue. Nobue was pulling out a new cigarette.

Junko said slowly, "You know, it sounds like that older brother could have been the leader."

After a number of flicks of the lighter, the flame took and Nobue drew deeply on her cigarette. "I don't know . . . I always thought Asaba was the leader. That time with me, I just thought Big Bro was too scared to join in. They were all scared—except for Asaba."

"But—"

"When I was crying and screaming, and there was blood everywhere, Jun lost his cool. 'That's enough!' he said to Asaba, so Asaba got pissed off and started after Jun with the knife. That's when I jumped up and ran away."

Nobue's voice was toneless.

"I just ran and ran. I didn't know where I was going even—I just wanted to get away. Asaba came running after me, then turned back and went for the car. I thought he was going to come after me in it. If he'd caught me, he'd have killed me for sure. The cuts hurt like crazy and I was too dizzy to stand up straight, but I couldn't stop, so I just kept running. Then a truck came along, and I waved my arms to get him to stop—"

"Where was that?"

"Do you know the Wakasu River landfill?"

"In Tokyo?"

"Yeah, not far from here, in Koto Ward. You know, near the Island of Dreams."

"You guys were *there*? What were you doing?"

"There are huge rats there," Nobue spread her hands about thirty centimeters apart to demonstrate. "With their tails, they're *this* long. We were chasing them around, killing them, shooting at them—"

Nobue clapped her mouth shut. Junko kept her eyes fixed on her, not looking away.

"Someone had a gun?"

Nobue didn't answer.

"They had one, right? It's okay. It's too late to surprise me. I already thought it was something like that."

Now it was Nobue who seemed surprised. "Why?" Then her eyes widened and her mouth fell open. "Did you . . . that cut on your shoulder—did Asaba shoot you? Is that it?"

Junko was silent, pressing against the wound in her shoulder with her hand, and then persisted, "Asaba had a gun, right?"

Nobue nodded.

"He had it when he hurt you, too."

"Yeah."

"That's strange, isn't it? A truck driver helped you out—so the police must have been involved. But then why didn't they do anything about it? You're right, Asaba shot me. And he's still got a gun. You said this happened a year ago. Why didn't anything happen?"

Nobue was visibly flustered, and Junko realized the truth. She was shocked. "You didn't report it to the police?"

"Umm . . ."

"But . . . *why not?* The driver who picked you up must have tried to take you to the police or to a hospital. Didn't he?"

Nobue let out a little, helpless laugh.

"That truck driver was there to dump stuff he wasn't supposed to. He would have been in hot water if the police had gotten involved."

Illegal dumping.

"So, there was no way he could go to the police or anything, right? Hospitals could be trouble, too . . . But he stopped when he saw me screaming and waving. He didn't just ignore me and drive by. He was a nice old man. And he brought me all the way home, but then he took off fast. Everything else my parents took care of."

"Didn't your parents want to go to the police?"

Nobue looked as though an electric current had run through her, and her face was dead serious as she turned to face Junko.

"I begged them not to," she said flatly.

"Why?"

"Because I knew that if we did, all three of us would be killed for sure."

Junko looked again at that dark spot in Nobue's eye. She thought she could see something seared into it.

"Do you think that was the right thing to do?" Junko asked quietly.

"I'm glad," Nobue said in a low voice. "I don't know if it was right or not. But I'm glad. We're still alive, anyway."

She gave a little shrug, and continued. "After I got away, and was home sleeping, Asaba called. It was the next day, or two days after, I think. My dad told him then to leave me alone. He told him that if they left me alone, he wouldn't go to the police."

To Junko's eyes this bargain was extremely dangerous. All the power was on Asaba's side. He could go along with the agreement, or break it. When he broke it, it would be just as Nobue feared—all three of them would be killed. Their silence did not secure their safety.

"Asaba laughed like a maniac at that," Nobue continued. "He knew who was stronger. And I'd done a lot of stuff that I didn't want the police to know about. With Asaba and the guys."

"Your father knew about that, too?"

"Yeah. That's why he didn't want to tell the police. 'It'll ruin your future,' he said." Nobue laughed out loud at this. "As if I had one."

"Sure you do. And you're working now, with your parents."

Nobue dismissed this roughly with a shake of her head. "That's not what I want to do all my life."

"Yes, of course it's too early to tell . . ."

"Whatever way you look at it, it's *boring*." Nobue ran her fingers through her hair. "Work, eat, sleep, and work again. Nothing to make you feel really alive. And it's not like we'll ever get rich, either. There are lots of cool things to do in the world, and there are lots of people out there getting what *they* want."

"I'm not so sure about that—"

"Somehow it feels like I'm the only one who got the short straw. It pisses me off, y'know?"

Junko suddenly had an idea why this girl had spent time running with Asaba and his gang, feeling the same way they did, doing the same things they did, sharing the same forms of entertainment. She felt she could see part of the reason Nobue had been drawn to Asaba and the others.

Ennui and anger.

Yeah. That group of four that Junko had taken care of at the Arakawa riverside had said the same things. *The world's boring. I want some excitement. It's a free country, so we can do whatever we want. Why do some assholes have it all and my life sucks?*

Nobue had felt the same way, and she still did. Not much had changed for her. The only thing she had learned was that *Asaba* was scary. Now she knew enough not to get involved with him, but that was all.

Whether she knew it or not, if she ever met someone else like Asaba, she might be induced to slide back in a direction that would endanger herself and her parents and bring harm upon society.

Was this girl merely a victim? Junko continued thinking hard. *Would I want to wreak revenge for this girl?* It was the first time she'd run into a situation like this. In the past, she'd known a man who didn't have enough courage to carry out revenge—

His face crossed her mind. Junko blinked hurriedly, and tried to pretend to herself that she hadn't seen him and hadn't remembered him.

"Around here, neighbors are pretty tight with each other," continued Nobue. "Everyone knows that I was hanging out with Asaba and all. So even if you hadn't collapsed in front of our place, if you'd gone around asking about Plaza, you'd have found me in the end. 'Oh yeah, the tofu makers, the Ito's—their girl Nobue was one of them.' But all our customers are local, so it's not like we can move away. I'm hoping to get out someday soon, though."

If this girl were still with Asaba—even with the cuts on her back and even though she is truly afraid of him—I'd probably torch her along with him without a second thought. Anyone who sticks with evil of their own free will is evil themselves. That was the way Junko saw it. If this girl was with Asaba, that made her as bad as him.

But on the other hand, it would be a pity. Nobue had been kind to her. She'd worried for Junko's sake, too. So Junko spoke in spite of herself.

"Nobue, you don't want to get back together with Asaba, do you?"

Nobue nearly fell off the bench. "No way! I'd rather die!"

"Doesn't it make you mad? Don't you think about getting back at him for scarring up your back like that?"

Nobue turned her head to the side and looked at Junko seriously.

"How can normal human beings get revenge on the devil? If the devil does something to you, the only thing you can do is run." She stood up.

Junko smiled. "Yeah. Well, thanks for everything." She stood up.

" . . . You're going home?"

"Yes. What else is there to do? I'm just a normal human being, too."

A bald-faced lie. *I'm not even human. I'm a loaded gun. Always searching for a target. The right target.*

"But before I go, could you tell me if you remember anything about places Asaba might go? I know it's been a year since you were with him, but I bet he still hangs out at some of the same places."

"Would you go there?"

Junko flashed her a smile. "No, I won't go. Didn't I just say? There's nothing I can do."

Nobue looked dubious. It looked like Junko was beginning to scare her.

"Those guys just hung out at Plaza. So I've no idea where they'd be now that Plaza is gone. Other than that, they ran around in cars and stopped at convenience stores and all-night restaurants . . ."

"Could you make a guess about who Asaba might be hanging out with now? Like the Takada brothers you mentioned?"

Nobue shook her head. "No. I told you, I know their faces, but I don't really know who they are or where they're from. That's the way it was with us. In the group, my relationship with Asaba was different from the others because we'd always known each other."

"How'd you get in touch with each other?"

"At night or on the weekends, if you went to Plaza, someone would be there."

They knew each other's faces, moved together, and could contact each other. But they didn't know each other's names or any other details. They stayed anonymous, and there was no connection to other parts of their lives. You couldn't even call it friendship.

"But Nobue, you must have called some of the others, sometimes, didn't you?"

"Yeah, I did—but when I got hurt, my dad got rid of my cell phone and threw out my address book, too."

Junko gave a cluck of regret, and Nobue's eyes widened. She was catching on to Junko's change in attitude towards her.

"Don't get angry . . . I'm just telling the truth," said Nobue in a small voice.

"And you don't know where Asaba's mother is living now, right?"

"No idea. I know where his dad's grave is, though."

"Grave?" *So Asaba's father was dead?*

"His father died when he was thirteen. He hung himself."

"Suicide?"

"Yeah. The factory where he'd been working closed down, and he lost his job."

With a start, Junko recalled what she'd heard the guys saying at the abandoned factory. Was this what they had been talking about?

Asaba, how'd you find out about this place?

My old man used to work here a long time ago.

But that must have been years ago, right? He hasn't had a job since then?

Whatever. Who cares?

So that had been about Asaba's father, had it? She had to tell the police about that. Junko was an amateur; she'd never be able to follow the thread from the former employee of the abandoned factory to Asaba. That was a job for the police. Time was passing, and she still had no idea where Natsuko was being held captive. She would have to pass on what little information she had.

"Do you know what Asaba's father's name was?"

"Wasn't it Asaba?"

"Where's the grave?"

"At a temple in Ayase called Saihoji."

"How do you know that, anyway?"

Nobue flinched a little at Junko's aggressiveness.

"Because I went there a bunch of times . . ."

"To do what?"

"I don't know. Asaba went in alone, and I waited. It's an old temple and during the day anybody can go in and out."

"Thanks." Junko turned on her heel to leave. *A phone. She had to find a phone.*

Nobue got up from the bench, and called out after her.

"Hey! Junko!"

Junko just waved goodbye and kept on walking.

"Who are you really? What are you going to do?"

It was better if Nobue didn't know. So Junko didn't answer and walked on, quickly putting distance between them.

It would be better if she never ran into Nobue again. It would be better, in fact, if Nobue found a way to be happy living a quiet life with her parents.

Junko also wished that Nobue would realize that although those cuts on her back had been made by someone else, she'd brought them on herself, and that was what had changed her life. But Junko wished more than anything else that Nobue would realize that she still had Asaba in her heart.

I hope you figure it out, Junko pleaded silently. *Because I know the fate of those who sacrifice the lives of innocent people for their own ennui, discontent, and greed. At least if I, Junko Aoki, get them in my sights.*

The Tayama factory had been roped off and "No Entry" signs posted. Behind them a noisy crowd of curious onlookers had gathered.

Chikako Ishizu was standing just inside the rope, her arms folded on her chest, looking up at the old walls of the factory. Here and there the steel was cracked, the paint was peeling, and part of a gutter had broken and was hanging loose from the edge of the roof. The run-down building brought to mind an old man without a coat to cover himself, looking cold and hunching his back against the freezing air.

No one saw any fire. Chikako chewed this over in her mind.

The site inspection continued and blue-uniformed forensic staff worked briskly. The bare ground where Chikako was planted, in a corner just inside the fence, had already been carefully combed for evidence, and a final inspection had just been completed. No other areas were open; even the forensic team stayed on a narrow taped-off path.

The four bodies were still inside the factory. The police were hampered by the darkness and lack of electrical power, and it was taking a while to do the necessary photography. Forensics had unsuccessfully tried high-speed film, and now they were bringing in generators and special lighting equipment for a second try.

But there was proof that either the attacker or the victims had been aware of the lack of electricity. A flashlight had been discovered next to one of the bodies—somebody had been prepared for whatever it was they'd intended to do here.

Only one entrance to the building showed signs of breaking in, a steel door on the east side with no hinges. This was the only way in or out. There were no signs of tampering at the padlocked front gate.

Now, however, both the front gate and factory entrance had been thrown open, and police guards were standing beside them. A blue plastic sheet had been hung inside the doors, impeding the view from outside, but every time the sheet was buffeted by the north wind, the small crowd of onlookers stood on tiptoe jostling each other to catch a glimpse.

Chikako looked up at the factory wall again. The building itself was about the height of a three-story building, and there was a window with broken glass right about where the second floor would be. Part of the window was gone, and the remaining cracked glass had been clumsily repaired with masking tape, but that must have been some time ago judging by how dirty the tape was. Chikako noticed what looked like a bird's nest on the upper part of the window frame. It, too, was gray with age. When the factory had been in use, the noise and commotion would have kept birds away. Little birds like sparrows, swallows, or brown-eared bulbuls must have arrived to build nests after it had shut down. But even the birds had deserted the factory. And now there had been a homicide here.

That window . . . thought Chikako.

Flames of a fire that had burned human bodies completely through must have been reflected in that window. But the police had not received any reports from residents in the area, nor had the local fire department been alerted. Nobody had seen a fire.

This meant that the fire must have flared up suddenly, instantly reaching a high temperature that quickly consumed the bodies, and then, just as suddenly, gone out.

The police wouldn't know any details until after the autopsy. Without checking the extent to which the skin, organs, and bones of the remains were burned, how long they burned, and what the highest temperature reached at the time was, they couldn't begin to speculate. But Chikako knew after one glance at the scene that it had been carried out by the exact same method and means as *that* case—the Arakawa riverside homicides. The similarities were chilling, including the fact that the bodies didn't smell. The smell of roasted meat, of course, hung in the air. What was missing was the smell of a flammable liquid.

Anything would suffice. Gasoline, paint thinner, kerosene. Without something to start a fire, it was impossible to burn a body in such a short period of time. And all known varieties gave off distinctive odors.

Chikako was not an official member of the investigation team in this case. She was just an observer dispatched by the arson squad. She was supposed to stand by until inspection of the site was concluded, but because it was essential to understanding the case, when she arrived she had overstepped her authority and ventured to ask that she be allowed to go inside, get close to the bodies, and check for any odors.

They couldn't be certain that some sort of flammable liquid hadn't been used until samples from the scene had been analyzed, but it was important for investigators to use their noses in these cases, too. Arson squad veterans could identify what had started a fire by smell alone, and Chikako detected no tell-tale odor in the factory. Veteran or not, she was sure that the results of the gas chromatography would support her conclusion. That's how it had been with the Arakawa case, too. Neither the investigators nor the subsequent analysis had detected an accelerant.

"Ishizu."

Chikako turned around to see Kunihiko Shimizu coming through the rope towards her. He'd just put in a report to Captain Ito.

"They still haven't called us?" Shimizu asked in an aggrieved tone. "How long are they going to keep us waiting?"

"You do hate to wait, don't you?"

"But we have a right to be in on the investigation, too!"

This case was under the jurisdiction of the Criminal Investigation Division, under a squad led by a captain in his mid-thirties named Shinagawa. Chikako wasn't directly acquainted with him. Ito had mentioned that he was quite sharp—so sharp, unfortunately, that his confidence in himself kept him from granting credence to the opinions of others. Before Chikako had come to the arson squad, Ito had worked with him on a case in Minato Ward in which a financier and his family were robbed and murdered, and he had repeatedly run up against Shinagawa's bullheaded attitude.

"Now don't get all bent out of shape," Chikako soothed Shimizu. "It's just because this case is less 'arson' and more 'homicide' with fire used as the weapon."

"Yeah, I *know* that!"

"What did the Captain say?"

"He said that we should concentrate on collecting information."

Chikako nodded. Shimizu fell silent, still looking disgruntled. It wasn't that he didn't understand, he just wanted to complain. Actually, he'd arrived slightly ahead of Chikako and had put in a list of details they wanted the forensics team to check for the arson squad.

"Since Shinagawa hasn't been telling us anything, I did a little digging myself just now," Shimizu began again. "The first report that came in was from a woman, a young woman. If she hadn't called in, it would have been a long time before anyone noticed four dead bodies in there."

Chikako nodded. "Yes, and we can't say for sure that she saw it from the outside. I heard from the neighborhood people that none of them noticed any fire."

"I wonder when this place closed down?"

Chikako pulled out her notebook and began flipping through her memos. "Originally it was a company called Isayama Steel. It went bankrupt and the company president ran off, sometime around the spring of 1991, as they recall. Right around the time the economic bubble burst."

"Seven years ago . . ." Shimizu said thoughtfully, then raising his eyebrows, looked at Chikako. "Detective Ishizu, have you been questioning witnesses?"

Chikako shook her head. "There are locals in that crowd, and I just listened to them talking. Without checking it out, it's not solid information, but local people often have surprisingly good memories."

Shimizu shrugged his skinny shoulders. "Isn't it risky believing the rumors old ladies pass around?"

"I heard this from the old men," Chikako replied. "Oh yeah—and for a while there were some yakuza-looking types going in and out; they might have been the creditors for Isayama Steel. They were probably the ones who broke the hinge on that door."

"Oh . . . yeah?" Shimizu's face returned to its unhappy expression.

Just then the blue plastic sheet was pushed aside and one of the detectives stuck his head out. He waved Chikako and Shimizu over.

"All yours!"

They stepped onto the taped-off pathway and hurried over.

On the other side of the sheet, the lights the investigation team had brought in had made the building's interior almost glaringly bright. There were a number of detectives there, but Chikako's eyes were drawn to the four bodies on the ground. She made her way over to them almost as if they were calling her.

The one on the right was slumped down by a pool full of dark, stagnant water. The other three had fallen to the other side, near a conveyor belt and something like storage shelves, with their heads all facing the left wall.

These three were in different positions. One faced up with his arms outspread, one was in a crawling pose. One looked like he had been sleeping and was about to roll over; the side of his face was pressed into the dirt.

There was another striking difference between the three bodies on the left and the one on the right. The former were burned black, but the latter was untouched by fire. Though parts of his skin and clothing appeared blackened, closer examination revealed that he was only covered with soot.

That body also showed signs of recent injuries and bleeding. Shimizu came over to nudge Chikako, who was so absorbed in observing the bodies that she was ignoring the other detectives. He got excited, however, when Chikako pointed out the injuries.

"That's a gunshot wound, isn't it?" he said.

Chikako wouldn't have been able to judge that with her naked eyes. She was looking at the face of the dead man. He was young. His face was handsome, but distorted from beating and pain.

Chikako offered a short, silent prayer for his soul and walked over to the detectives who were standing in a knot, talking in undertones, precisely halfway between the bodies on the left and the one on the right. In the center of the men was a short but well-built man—Captain Shinagawa.

"We're Detectives Ishizu and Shimizu, from the arson squad." Chikako bowed her head in greeting, and he nodded curtly in return.

"I heard about you from Captain Ito. We'd like to ask for your cooperation in determining what was used to burn the bodies." His tone was unexpectedly soft. "At this stage, I don't see any point in having you added to our team. The forensics analysis will take a while, and there have been no autopsies yet. We've been told that there was a previous case in which a similar method might have been used. Would you please check into that for us?"

"The Arakawa riverside case."

At Chikako's words, a thickset man standing next to Captain Shinagawa muttered in a low voice, "Kinu is in charge of that." The detective was referring to Sergeant Kinugasa, who was part of another squad at MPD.

"It's been classified as a continuing investigation in Arakawa precinct. Actually we considered the connection immediately."

"You shouldn't go jumping to conclusions," interjected the thickset detective. "I remember that too, but there are a lot of differences this time. There wasn't a gun involved that time, for one."

Shimizu, not to be left out, added, "Yeah, you can see the gunshot wound on the victim who wasn't burned."

The detective's eyebrows flew up and then down again, and he commented sarcastically, "Hey! You could tell that just by looking?"

Shimizu opened his mouth to retort but Chikako stepped forward slightly to restrain him.

"We'll have the documents on the Arakawa case for you in time for the investigation meeting tonight. And may we have about thirty minutes before the bodies are removed? We'd like to record our observations of the scene."

"Be my guest," Shinagawa answered indifferently. "Higuchi, you stay here. I'm going back to the car."

Two of the others followed Captain Shinagawa outside. Left behind were Chikako, Shimizu, and the thickset detective—the one he'd called Higuchi.

"Well, do as you please. But hurry up with it, would you? We'd like to get on with the autopsies."

His meaning was clear: *you won't find anything we haven't.* Chikako yanked Shimizu along with her and began examining the corpses. She could feel Higuchi's eyes on her back.

They wrapped up their observations and informed Higuchi, who sauntered over to the sheet and stuck his head out to call the forensics team in to remove the bodies. They carried them out and Higuchi went with them to supervise.

Chikako gave him a brief nod, and holding back Shimizu, who'd been waiting for Higuchi to leave to explode with anger, pointed behind him.

"Did you notice this?"

Shimizu spun around. He was standing in front of a row of shelves that must have been used to store tools. Of the three charred corpses, the one in the middle had fallen just in front of it, and the body's right hand had touched its base. White tape on the ground outlined where the body had been.

"So what is it?"

Chikako squatted down. She pointed to the base of the shelves.

"*This*. Get down here and take a look."

Shimizu did as he was told. Immediately, his eyes widened.

"It's melted . . ."

The base of the shelves had melted and warped. Without close inspection you would never notice it, but the straight edge had caved in to form a gentle curve.

Eyes still wide, Shimizu looked up at the shelves and knocked on the blackened part with one hand. It made a metallic sound.

"These shelves are steel, right?"

Chikako nodded. Whoever had done this had used something that emitted temperatures high enough to melt steel.

"Okay, what shall we do? Go unannounced to Arakawa precinct, or return to MPD and talk to Sergeant Kinugasa?"

"I know Kinugasa," said Shimizu. "Compared to Higuchi, he's a real gentleman. I used to work under him when we were in the same precinct."

"Well, that settles it."

Chikako and Shimizu left the building. The distraught expression on the face of the body that had not been burned had pierced her to the heart, but now she felt adrenaline rush though her and make her shiver.

"They really don't want us here, do they?" Shimizu muttered bitterly as they were passing through the noise and activity outside.

"That's because we're playing different roles."

"If it were a straight-off arson case, the positions would be reversed."

"God forbid. Don't even say that and bring it on us. If someone really is walking around starting fires with a weapon this powerful, it will be a real mess."

"Detective Ishizu, have you got any idea what the perpetrator used?"

Chikako shook her head. "I couldn't begin to guess."

"A flamethrower . . . ?"

"You can't get your hands on one of those easily, and even if you could, it would never have *this* effect. As you well know."

In the Arakawa case too, some of the weekly tabloids had taken up the flamethrower theory and had clung to it tenaciously, but it was actually a laughing matter for the police—that theory had been discarded during the very first stages of the investigation.

"I know. I was just saying it. But can you think of anything else? Like a microminiature laser gun or something?"

"How many years have you been on the arson squad now, Shimizu?"

"Come on, don't rub it in! It's only been a year—nothing compared to you, Mom."

Chikako grinned. "No, I'm still a novice, too. Let's get back to MPD, meet Sergeant Kinugasa, and pick the brains of the arson veterans. At least Captain Shinagawa asked for our cooperation, so let's keep our heads and get on with business."

Shimizu sighed and raised his hand to hail a passing taxi.

There were still too many things that neither Chikako nor Shimizu knew at this stage, and too many things they hadn't been told. They didn't know that the woman who had called in the incident had said that someone named Asaba had fled the scene. Nor did they know that the man who was shot and killed had a girlfriend who had been abducted. Finally, they had no idea that just now, as Captain Shinagawa had been leaving the scene, MPD had radioed in that the same anonymous woman had called again, informing them that Asaba was the son of a man who had worked at that factory, that his permanent address was in Higashi Ojima, Tokyo, and that he was an eighteen-year-old with a record of criminal violence.

5

Just as Nobue Ito had said, there was a temple called Saihoji in Ayase. Checking the phone book, Junko found that it was part of the Rinzai Zen sect and had two phone numbers listed. She had no idea what rank of temple it was, but this meant it must be fairly large.

She called one of the numbers from her apartment and asked for directions. The woman who answered was clearly used to such requests and responded in an efficient, practiced manner. Junko had prepared an explanation for her business at Saihoji, but there was no need for it.

She took the train to Ayase and followed the directions to the temple gate. No wonder they were used to visitors—the compound itself was large, and there was a nursery school on the premises. It was just past noon when she arrived. Either the children were inside having lunch or they had left for the day, but at any rate the playground was quiet. The main temple was positioned to overlook the nursery school. It was a square, gray building that looked more like a gymnasium than a place of worship. Even the main gate was made of the same gray concrete. A wooden plaque engraved with "Saihoji" was the only item that looked even remotely worn. Junko stood in front of the gate for a few moments, convincing herself that she would probably not meet up with anyone who would question her presence there, and then walked through it.

The gray box-shaped temple was in front of her, and the nursery school was to the right. The cemetery must be to the left. The grounds were paved over in a dry, tasteless way, the only patches of color supplied by flowers in planters placed here and there. Junko didn't recognize the blooms; they were all bunched together by the cold wind that was blowing.

The cemetery was smaller than she had imagined. The neatly-arranged rows of gravestones were of every possible shade of gray. The path leading to them was paved just like the rest of the temple yard but slightly higher and with narrow drainage ditches on either side.

Junko hesitantly moved forward, when suddenly an old woman appeared from the row of graves on her right. The woman had apparently finished her own graveside visit and was making her way back to the entrance, close to where Junko stood. Junko had brought a small bunch of flowers along to lend an air of legitimacy to her presence there, and when the old woman saw it, she stepped towards her and said, "It's awfully cold to be out visiting graves today, isn't it?"

Junko returned the pleasantry, to which the old woman bowed. She passed Junko slowly: the bucket she was carrying looked heavy, and water left over from tending the grave splashed up to the edge with every step she took.

Junko felt a sudden pang of conscience and waited until the woman had returned the bucket and left the cemetery before moving on. Now she was ready to get back to the matter at hand. What had Keiichi Asaba been up to in this cemetery where his own father was buried?

Nobue said that she had been here with Asaba on more than one occasion and that he had left her outside while he'd gone in by himself. Junko thought it unlikely that Asaba had carried a bucket of water to refresh the flowers or wash down the grave of his father, who had deserted his family by committing suicide. Nor could she imagine him stopping to visit the temple priest.

If only she could find the grave, she was bound to find some kind of clue. Alone at last, she felt free to lift her head and examine her surroundings. Asaba was not a common surname. Surely it would not be too difficult to find it on one of these gravestones.

She decided to look at each stone in order, starting with the first row on the right. It was a weekday and very few of the graves had fresh flowers to indicate a recent visit. Most of the flowers were wilted, the water in their vases dirty from decomposed foliage, and other offerings to the souls of the deceased were dried out and covered in dust.

She came across the grave that the old woman must have visited. The flowers there were new and the incense was still burning. Junko noted the brand-new *sotoba* board indicating a recent death.

Junko continued inspecting all the graves on the right side of the main path without finding the name Asaba. As she returned to the center and prepared to take on the left-hand side, she came across a large statue of Buddha. Surrounded by flowers and other offerings, it sat enshrined, its hands folded and a faint smile on its lips.

Once again, Junko felt a twinge of guilt, and she carefully avoided the statue's gaze. It seemed to be asking her what she was doing there, and Junko knew there was nothing honorable about sneaking around looking for the grave of someone else's family. But she also knew that she had nothing to fear as long as it led her to Keiichi Asaba. She would incinerate him, right down to his bones. Junko would ensure he was so thoroughly destroyed that not even an almighty god or a merciful Buddha would be able to provide him with the comfort of an afterlife.

Pulling herself from her reverie, Junko returned to her search, carefully ignoring the Buddha whenever she was in range of its gaze. Finally, she found the Asaba family grave. It was in the sixth row on the left-hand side. If she had started out on that side she could have saved herself so much time. *Oh well*, she shrugged.

She stood in front of the black granite gravestone and let out a snort of laughter. It was a neglected, sad-looking grave. The built-in vase was completely dry of water. There was not a crumb's worth of offering laid there, either. The only thing the Asaba grave boasted was dead flower petals that had blown over from neighboring graves.

The small plaque erected next to the gravestone revealed that four people had had their cremated remains laid to rest there. The most recent was Shuji Asaba, age forty-two. That must have been Asaba's father. Junko squinted as if trying to find something else written between the tiny characters of the inscription. So this was all that was left of Asaba's father, the man who had given his son the name Keiichi in the hope that he would grow up to be a man others respected. This was the man who'd lost his job and any hope he may once have had, and who'd hung himself. Junko had no idea if he had considered what that would mean for his wife and son. If he had known his son would grow up to be a murderer, would he have done anything differently? Would he have put a rope around his son's scrawny neck before putting one around his own?

Junko slowly let out her breath and murmured to the spirit of Shuji Asaba, "I'll soon be sending your son to wherever you are. I've come to clean up the mess you left behind."

Having said that, Junko realized there was nothing more for her to find here besides her own growing indignation. It was clear that Asaba had not come here to pay respects to the soul of his dead father. She suddenly felt cold. She took one more long look at the name Shuji Asaba engraved on the plaque, and turned to leave, disappointed that this was all there was to see.

Just then her eyes lit on a small can. It was placed beside the metal frame holding the *sotoba* boards behind the grave. It was a Peace cigarette can, blue with a silver border, a design recognizable to almost anyone. The lid was closed, and it was positioned behind the grave in a way that would not be noticed in passing.

It was not an uncommon practice to place an offering of cigarettes at the grave of someone who had loved smoking, but it would be placed in a prominent position, surrounded by flowers and incense. It wouldn't be hidden like this. On a hunch, Junko picked up the can. It was light, but something rattled inside. She opened the lid and found a key.

The single key was attached to a key holder with the number 1120 printed on it. It looked like the key to a coin locker, but where would it be? Junko found a scrap of paper at the bottom of the can and spread it out to read what was written.

Call me as soon as you get it. Tsutsui.

A number for a cell phone was written underneath the name.

Junko grasped the key and looked up at the gravestone once more. So that was it! Keiichi Asaba used his father's grave as a place to carry out trans-actions—most likely illegal transactions. Junko thought it was terribly un-original, like something you might see in an old movie, but she had to admit that it had worked for him. When Asaba had come to the cemetery with Nobue, it must have been to retrieve messages and keys, or whatever else may have been left for him.

Call me as soon as you get it.

When you get what? Junko wondered if it was a gun—like the gun he had shot her with. The gun he had used to kill Fujikawa. She felt a twinge of pain from the bullet wound in her shoulder—it was almost as if it were responding to her discovery.

Junko whispered a word of thanks to the gravestone and put the key and the note in her coat pocket. She turned quickly to leave the cemetery, but looked back once to glance at the statue of Buddha.

She no longer felt guilty, not even a twinge of conscience.

Nobody answered when Junko tried calling the number on the note.

A cold wind raged around the phone booth as she called the number over and over. She hung up every time she got the recorded message, but she kept on calling. Why have a cell phone if its owner couldn't be contacted wherever they happened to be?

After about ten times, she found herself dialing and hanging up almost automatically, and she had to catch herself when a man's voice finally came on the line.

"Hello? Hello?"

There was a lot of noise in the background, and she could barely hear the scratchy male voice that answered.

"Yeah. Who is this?"

Junko was overjoyed. She felt like a hunter who had finally spied the footprints of her prey in a snow-covered meadow.

"Is this Mr. Tsutsui?"

There was a brief silence before the voice responded.

"Who are you?"

"Keiichi, I mean Keiichi Asaba, asked me to call."

"What'd he say?"

"He told me to go to Saihoji and open up the Peace can."

"And?"

"He told me there would be a key to a locker and asked me to bring it. I just got back, and he's not here. He's not answering his cell phone, either. This key is important, right? I can't just sit here and do nothing."

She tried to sound chatty and breathy. *I'm Asaba's girlfriend*, she told herself. *He's got me wrapped around his little finger, and I do whatever he tells me.*

"Are you the one that's been calling over and over?"

"That's me."

"Why isn't Asaba calling himself?"

"How should I know? You're the one that wrote the note. I'm just follow-ing instructions!"

"Who *are* you?"

"Hey, you've got no right to talk to me like that! Who are *you?*"

"There's no way Asaba would've asked you to do this for him."

"Why? How do you know that? I went to Saihoji, didn't I?" Junko felt her palms getting sweaty, but she did her best to keep up an aggressive tone of voice. "You're the one that left the note to call right away! *I'm* the one that should be complaining!"

"Okay, okay. Wait a second." The man on the other end of the line began to back down. Junko got the idea that he was changing his position, either sitting down or standing up. His voice became clearer. "I don't know who you are. But I've got nothing to say to anyone but Asaba himself."

"Even though he asked me to do it?" Junko closed her eyes and did her best to sound like she was pouting. *Use your head!* she told herself. *What can I say to trick this guy into talking?*

"You know, Asaba's been acting weird . . ."

"Weird?"

"Yeah. When he asked me to go get the Peace can, he was in a hurry. Come to think of it, he was talking to someone on the phone. He didn't say anything about going out, but he was gone when I got back." Junko lowered her voice. "Is he mixed up in something bad? He's pissed off all the time and I keep hearing stuff about the police."

The man was silent. Junko waited for him to speak. She thought fast about what she could try next if he didn't begin to cooperate.

He began to speak slowly, like he was making sure of something. "So, have you got it with you now?"

"What? The key?"

"Yeah."

"I've got it. It's right here."

"And Asaba told you to get it, but he was gone by the time you got back?"

"Uh-huh."

"And you don't know where he is?"

"No idea." Junko kept up her act. "You're Tsutsui, right? Look, I'm really worried. Was he supposed to call you right away?"

There was another silence before the man spoke.

"It looks like you and I will have to get together."

Junko held her breath and her eyes opened wide.

"I'd better get it back from you." His voice was beginning to sound hoarse.

"Get what back?"

"What was in that can."

He seemed to be avoiding mentioning specifics. Was he trying to make her prove she had it? He was either very careful or a coward.

"You mean the key, right? The one I have here," she supplied quickly. "It's for a coin locker, isn't it? Where is it?" What Junko really wanted to know was what was behind the door that the key unlocked.

"Look, sister, it's better if you don't know what that key is for." Tsutsui must have pulled the receiver away from his mouth because Junko couldn't hear his voice well anymore. Soon he was back. "You got something to write with?"

Junko didn't have anything, but she didn't want him to stop talking.

"Yeah, go ahead," she said.

"Do you know the Aoto intersection of the Mito Highway and Kannana Avenue?"

"Yeah, I know it."

"Turn left at that intersection—left with your back to Shiratori, got it? There's a place called Currant that's right before the first signal you come to. It's a coffee shop. Bring the key there."

"Okay, I've got it, but there's one problem."

"What now?"

"I can't give you back the key without telling Asaba first—you know that." There was another silence, so Junko continued. "I've *got* to talk to him first. Are you *sure* you don't know where he is?"

"If he's not in his apartment, I don't know."

"Yeah, but which one?"

"Look, you're his girlfriend. How come you don't know where he lives?" Junko could tell he was starting to get nervous about her, so she took up the sulky routine again.

"The only place I know is this dirty little apartment called Onishi Heights in Ochanomizu. But he said something once about another place he's got. There's hardly any furniture here, and there are other guys who sleep here, too." Junko had to come up with some sort of name, and Onishi Heights seemed to do the trick. *Come on!* She willed the man with the hoarse voice to tell her what she needed to know. *Tell me where he lives! Tell me where he might have that girl!*

"Onishi Heights? Ochanomizu?"

"Yeah. It's a real hole behind the station."

"So when you got back from Saihoji with the key, you went back to that Onishi place?"

"That's right."

"I've never heard of it."

"That just proves it! I *knew* he was really living somewhere else!" She clicked her tongue and did her best to sound as though she was mortified. "He's just been leading me on. He must have other girls. That's why he won't give me his real address!"

"Calm down!"

"Come on, tell me where he lives! I need to talk to him myself. Then I'll go meet you at that Currant place. Wouldn't you rather see him, too, and not just me? I don't know what this is all about, but you need to see him, don't you?"

She said this all in one breath, and before she had a chance to inhale again, he'd turned her down flat.

"If Asaba hasn't told you where he lives, there's no way I'll tell." There was a trace of a jeer in his tone. "I don't want to get involved in his girl problems."

What a shithead!

"Come on," Junko begged.

"No way!"

It was no good. Junko sighed and said, "Okay, I'll meet you there."

Café Currant was a squalid little place.

It wasn't so much that it was uninviting as that it positively rejected any potential business. Any customers it did have must be like the place itself: without means of economic support and in no hurry to find any. The doorknob at the entrance was sticky to the touch. As Junko walked in, she checked the knob and the lock, noting that they were made of brass.

The floor was filthy and arranged on it were chairs upholstered in red plastic set around several cheap plywood tables. A woman in a flashy-colored apron sat behind a counter just inside the entrance. A man was sitting at the counter, laughing and talking loudly. The woman did not greet Junko as she walked in, but the man's laugh turned to a salacious grin. He wore a white shirt and slacks, but no tie. In its place, Junko could see a thick gold chain at his collar.

Junko quickly looked to her right, at the tables by the window. A small, middle-aged man sat there. He wore the gray work clothes of a laborer and a cap of the same color. He was hunched over a racing form, which he lifted slightly as he looked up at Junko. Junko went over and sat down opposite him. The red plastic seat was dirty, and stuffing stuck out in places where the plastic had split. It was extremely uncomfortable, and Junko was afraid ticks would crawl up her pant legs.

"You're Mr. Tsutsui, right?"

"That's right."

"I knew right away," Junko laughed for effect.

Right behind his seat was an obviously fake rubber tree, complete with faded plastic leaves that sprang out right next to his face. Maybe that was what made him look like a monkey hiding in the jungle. An ugly old monkey that even his friends had abandoned.

"You got the key?" he asked.

"Can I order something first?"

Tsutsui was drinking coffee. At least Junko assumed that was what the coal-black liquid in the coffee cup was.

She wasn't thirsty, but she wanted to stall for time so she could figure out the layout of this shop. She was still hopeful that she could get the information she needed from this man. The only thing she wanted to avoid was a fuss. How many people were in here? Did it only have the one entrance?

Fortunately, the windows were tiny, and they were covered over with stickers that were meant to give a stained-glass effect. They even had dusty curtains over them. If she could manage not to burn the curtains, there was no reason why anyone walking by would want to peek in.

"I'd like iced coffee."

Tsutsui lifted a hand towards the woman at the counter.

"Iced coffee over here."

The woman looked annoyed and did not even bother to answer. The man she had been chatting with used the magazine in his hand to hide his face as he stole another look at Junko.

"And some water, too, please!" Junko addressed the woman at the counter. "Where's the restroom?"

The woman looked offended at Junko's question and wordlessly waved her left hand in the general direction of a screen door. It must have originally had a plaque on it that read "restroom," but only the rectangular outline remained. Junko stood up and headed for it. As she walked past the counter, she could feel the rude stares of the man and the woman. Junko glanced quickly behind the counter. There was a large refrigerator behind the woman and a sliding door that most likely led to the back of the shop. *Too bad,* she thought. *A regular door would have been quicker.*

Then she turned deliberately towards the man at the counter and gave him a winning smile. He continued to leer at her.

The restroom was filthy and the smell made her feel sick. If I wash my hands here, I'll just make them dirtier, she thought. Junko closed her eyes to think.

That man wouldn't be leaving for a while. She'd have to get rid of both him and the woman, but first of all, she had to cut off their escape route. The filth and stink impeded her concentration, but Junko forced herself to focus. She mapped out her plan and then left the restroom.

When she opened the door, the waitress was plodding back to the counter after leaving a glass of water at the table by the window.

"Thank you!" Junko called out with a smile. "Oh, and could I have some matches, too?" As she turned back to the counter, she could feel Tsutsui eyeing her backside.

The instant the woman bent down behind the counter to grab some matches, Junko bit down hard on her back teeth to shoot her energy directly behind her, towards the entrance of the shop. Energy as sharp as a dagger flew to the brass doorknob and lock, melting them instantly and welding them shut.

There was a sharp ringing sound as the door, under pressure from the melted lock, was almost pulled off its hinges.

"What was that?" The man at the counter turned to look at the door. "Hey, there's smoke coming from the door!"

The waitress leaned forward.

"What?"

Black smoke came billowing from the doorknob. It stank terribly, but Junko didn't pause. As the customer turned his back to her, Junko shot another flash of energy to the right side of his head. This time it was in the form of a whip. It flew from Junko in an arc, and when she leaned her head to the right, it hit the man precisely where she intended it to.

Without a sound, the man fell over, dropping from his seat to the floor.

"Hey! What's the matter with you?" the woman screamed at him.

The whip of energy Junko had unleashed made a half circle and headed for the woman. The whip groaned as it set its sites, bashing into one of the counter supports and bending it in half before it hit the woman hard, knocking her backwards.

Her body hit the sliding back door and fell. She was out cold. Junko sent another whip of energy towards the refrigerator; it took a hit to one side and began to fold over. As it dissolved, it started to tip right over the woman.

Just at the moment the refrigerator toppled over, Tsutsui began running towards Junko.

"What do you think you're doing?"

She immediately turned and hit him in the stomach, sending him flying. He crashed to the floor, his arm extended as if to block her path. Junko was careful to step over rather than on it.

Her heart was pounding so fast she could hardly distinguish one beat from the next. Her temperature was high, and there was sweat on her brow. But it was not because she had used her energy. She had not used anywhere near enough to affect her physically. It was the high from showing her true nature as a loaded gun, and of clearly demonstrating who had the power, who was stronger. The pleasure was startling.

"There's no need to worry, Mister." Tsutsui was flat on his back, doing his best to lift his head and turn it towards her.

"I won't kill you as long as you listen carefully and answer my questions. That's all you have to do."

"D-d-d-d . . ." The edges of his mouth were twitching and he drooled as he tried to speak. "D-d-don't kill me!"

"Didn't I just tell you? I won't kill you. Those two over there aren't dead. They're just unconscious."

Tsutsui was unable to move. He was trying desperately to slink away from Junko, but only his head moved. Junko smiled at him.

"Looks like your back is broken. Sorry about that, I didn't mean to be so rough. But it's your own fault, you know. None of this would have happened if you had only told me where Asaba was."

As Junko took a step towards him, he began to cry. "Now, answer my question. Where can I find Asaba? Where do you think he is right now?"

His lips began to shake. Saliva mixed with blood began to drip to the floor.

"Come on!" Junko urged him. "Give me some answers. Someone's life depends on it." She crouched down to look at him. His eyes flickered in fear and his eyelids twitched, but he couldn't take his eyes off Junko as she stared down at him.

"Sa—"

"Sa?"

"Sakurai."

"Sakurai? Someone's name?"

"It's a s-s-s-store." He gulped and then spit out a whole phrase. "It's where they—Asaba and the gang—hang out. That's all I know. I don't know anything besides that."

"Where is this Sakurai place?"

"U-u-u-u—"

"Hurry up!"

Tsutsui looked like he was trying to shrink into himself. He closed his eyes. "Don't kill me!"

"I won't kill you as long as you talk. Come on now, where is it?"

"Uehara, near Yoyogi Uehara Station. It's a liquor shop. There's a sign in front of the station. You can't miss it." He had a fit of coughing. His body was twisted in an unnatural position as it lay on the floor. His torso was jerking, but his legs were perfectly still, just as they had landed. They must be paralyzed.

Junko reached out and patted Tsutsui on the shoulder. He was startled, and his bloodshot eyes looked up at her.

"Now you wouldn't lie to me, would you?" she asked.

"No! I swear!"

"Sakurai is a liquor store, and Asaba and his friends hang out there, right?"

He nodded his head so emphatically that it looked like he had a spring in it. "Asaba's mother runs the store. I went there once. I didn't think he was good for the money he promised, so he told me to see his mother."

Junko narrowed her eyes again.

"Money? What money?" Does it have something to do with this key?"

She took the key she had found at Saihoji from her jacket pocket and held it up to his face.

He nodded furiously. "Yeah. That's right."

"This key opens a coin locker, doesn't it? Where is it?"

"Shi-Shibuya Station. The lockers at the north entrance."

"What's in there?"

He shook his head, his face begging Junko for mercy.

"Please! I don't know! Don't kill me! Please! Please!"

"Answer my question," Junko insisted, shaking his shoulder. "What's in the locker? If you can't say it, shall I say it for you? It's a gun, right?"

Tsutsui's mouth trembled and spittle drooled out. She looked at his hand extended on the floor. It was large and rough, the fingers had hangnails, and they were black. *That's probably machine oil.* She continued staring at his hand as she questioned him some more.

"You work in a factory, am I right? And I bet you're good at your work."

"Come on, sister . . ."

"Do you make guns? Do you make them and sell them on the side?"

"I don't know anything!"

"It's just like I told you. Tell me what you know, and I won't kill you. Don't try to hide anything. You make guns on the black market, and you've been selling them to Asaba and his gang. Right?"

Tsutsui looked like he'd given up, and his head dropped to the floor.

"If anyone finds out, I'm dead."

"Who's going to kill you? Asaba?"

"Not Asaba. He's just a second-rate punk." He began to gasp for breath.

"All I wanted was some extra money."

Junko understood what he was saying. "Now I get it. You work for an underground gun maker. And what the others don't know is that you've been selling some on the sly. Is that about right?" Tsutsui's silence was her answer.

"I see." Junko stood up slowly. He looked up at her imploringly and reached out to grab her ankle.

"I told you everything, right? I talked. I told you what you wanted to know."

"Yes, you did. Thank you." With a faint smile, Junko yanked her leg back. Tsutsui's hand touched the toe of her shoe as it fell back to the floor. "Now I'll tell you a secret."

"Call an ambulance . . . please! I won't tell anyone about you."

"A gun you sold—last night it was used to kill someone."

"Listen, sister!"

"I was there. And you know what? I got shot with that gun, too."

Tsutsui was no longer listening to her. He inched sideways, trying to grab her foot. Junko thought he looked like a disgusting worm.

"I said I wouldn't kill you if you were honest with me," she said.

He nodded with an absurdly relieved smile on his face. Junko mimicked his expression and looked down at him.

"I lied." With that, she let her energy fly. She aimed for his dirty, wrinkled neck and let it go with a roar. Tsutsui's neck broke instantly. The residual power broke the floorboards. His hair went up in flames, and Junko quickly stepped back to keep her own clothes from catching fire. She turned back to the door, stared at the lock that had been welded shut, and it promptly began to melt. The knob fell to the floor. Junko walked over, gave the door a light push, and walked outside. A burnt smell wafted out into the street, but there was no smoke; nothing to raise the suspicions of passersby.

Junko closed the door gently to make sure it stayed in place. If someone were to look closely, they might notice that the lock was not quite right, but otherwise no one would notice anything amiss. Then she flipped the "Open for Business" sign around to "Closed," and walked off.

At the Aoto intersection, waiting for the light to change, she asked a young woman which subway line to take for Yoyogi Uehara. The woman unhesitatingly supplied her with directions. When she was finished, she gave Junko an apologetic smile and added, "Excuse me, but you've got something black on your face. It looks like a piece of ash."

Junko raised her hand to her cheek. The black ash rubbed off on the palm of her hand.

"Thank you," she smiled. "I was just cleaning out the kitchen vent."

6

Just as Junko Aoki was leaving Café Currant, Detective Chikako Ishizu was talking to Sergeant Kinugasa in the corner of an office in the MPD Criminal Investigation Division. Kinugasa's section was in charge of investigating a robbery-homicide that had taken place in Akabane a week ago. He was spending much of his time at Akabane North precinct, so Chikako was lucky to catch him on a visit back to MPD.

Kinugasa was fifty-two years old, and small but solidly built. He was known for being diligent and careful in his work, but the way his eyes drooped at the corners gave away his warm personality. Chikako had never been formally introduced to him, but she had heard much about the reputation of this sergeant who was affectionately nicknamed "Kinu" by the men who worked under him.

Kinugasa was drinking a cup of instant coffee sweetened with several spoonfuls of sugar. Chikako thought he looked tired, and she noticed that the collar of his shirt was stained from prolonged wear. She was sure that he had not had a good night's sleep or even a bath since the homicide had taken place.

"I heard about that Tayama incident," Kinugasa said as he sipped his coffee. "Of course, I've been busy with my own case, so I've only heard a comment here and there; none of the details."

"It's similar to the Arakawa riverside case your section handled the year before last," Chikako responded. "I've heard that the Arakawa precinct has it on pending status. On the chance that it might be the same offender, I'd like to ask for their help. Who do you think I should talk to there?"

She would have liked to ask him more about the older case, but she couldn't bring herself to bother him about it right now.

Kinugasa squinted, thinking for a moment. He took another sip of coffee and answered, "There's a detective named Makihara. He's young, but he knows what he's doing. I'm sure he can help you out. I'll let him know that you'll be contacting him."

"That'd be great," Chikako smiled in satisfaction.

Kinugasa gave her a quizzical look and then added in a lower voice, "As far as I know, Tayama isn't under your section."

"That's right," said Chikako. "Arson is on observer status."

Kinugasa laughed. "That can't be easy. They ought to just turn over arson cases to the arson squad."

"It's just that they're not sure whether it really is simple arson. Isn't that what happened with the Arakawa riverside case, too?"

Kinugasa nodded slowly. "It was strange. On the face of it, the four victims were burned to death. The burns were clearly fatal, but . . ."

Chikako knew the rest of the story. The autopsy revealed that the necks of each victim had been broken, and it had been impossible to judge whether the injuries had been inflicted before or after they had caught fire. The arson squad was familiar with victims with head wounds indicating blows with a blunt object. This initially gave the impression of murder followed by arson, but they were generally found to be caused by the brain expanding and exploding in the skull due to the high temperatures.

A broken neck, on the other hand, was a very different story. There were no known cases of broken vertebrae caused by heat. This meant that the victims at the Arakawa riverside must have been killed first and then set on fire. This assumption, however, was refuted by contradictory evidence that the victims had been burned alive.

The coroner's autopsy report read "Death by Fire," but it also stated the opinion of the medical examiner that the weapon used had emitted powerful impact waves which broke the victim's necks at the same time it set their bodies on fire. In other words, the fire and the injuries occurred simultaneously.

But there was a wrinkle in the impact waves theory. The windows of the car containing three of the victims had been shattered. It appeared, however, that the windows had been broken before the victims had been burned. This was based on the fact that several pieces of glass scattered around the victims had melted in the heat. The way the glass had spread out led police to believe that some form of "power" outside and to the right of the car had shattered them.

Did such a weapon exist?

To start with, what sort of heat medium would be small enough for a criminal to carry around and yet have enough power to carbonize human bodies so quickly?

There was another problematic aspect. Three of the four victims in the Arakawa case had been burned to death as they sat in the car. Only one was found lying on the ground outside. The weapon—whatever it was—had therefore incapacitated the victims before they knew what had hit them. None of the three in the car had their seat belts fastened, nor were there any marks to indicate they had been tied up or otherwise restrained. Since they were free to move, and assuming that they would have done so had they noticed that one of the others was on fire, the three had almost certainly been hit by the weapon at exactly the same time. The car doors were securely shut, which made it only natural to assume that the one victim outside the car had left it before the attack. He too had died on the spot.

"Everything about the Arakawa incident defied common sense. Tayama also goes against everything we've ever seen before. The perpetrator might be different, but I think it must have been the same weapon," Chikako mused aloud.

She told Kinugasa about how the steel shelves in the abandoned factory had been partially melted. "Since the place hasn't been used for years, we don't know much for sure yet. We'll have to check to see if any other machinery or equipment has been destroyed or melted. As far as I could tell, there was no broken glass this time."

"The important thing is to find out whether the victims' necks were broken."

"Right. But did you know that this time one of the victims was killed with a gun?"

Kinugasa blinked. "One was shot?"

"That's right. A young man. The gunshot wound was almost certainly fatal. All of the bodies were in the same location, but he was the only one without a single burn."

Chikako sighed and examined Kinugasa's expression. "That matches the Arakawa case, too, doesn't it?"

Kinugasa stared off at some point over her shoulder, recalling aloud, "Yes, the burned area was extremely limited."

"Right!" Chikako quickly agreed. "Even though the Arakawa victims in the car were burned through, the seat belts were still there. When the bodies were removed, the seats they were sitting on were relatively undamaged. Isn't that the way it was?"

That was not all. Kinugasa went on to describe how the clothing of the body in the back seat had been left partially unscathed. His body had been completely carbonized, but the collar of his shirt and his pants below the knees were not. That was how they had known beyond a doubt that the victims had not been bound.

Chikako's eyes revealed her surprise. Kinugasa looked at her.

"Was there any trace of an accelerant?" he asked.

"We couldn't find any. No smell either."

"That matches, too." Kinugasa crushed his empty coffee cup in his hand and stood up. Chikako followed suit.

"But this time there was a shooting . . ." Kinugasa muttered and shook his head wearily. "This case I'm on now; the victims were shot during the robbery."

"I heard there were two fatalities."

"They were employees at a pachinko parlor; they exchanged pachinko balls for prizes. Both of them were killed while they were working and just minding their own business. It's hard not to let it bother you. We've got to get gun laws with teeth in them—we're always a step behind and struggling to catch up."

Chikako knew that Kinugasa had come back to MPD to file a report with the Special Committee on Firearm-Related Crimes.

"Anyway, get in touch with Makihara. Since you're just an observer, it means you can do whatever you like. It would probably be a good idea to look at the facts with a completely open mind."

"Open mind?" Chikako looked puzzled.

Kinugasa laughed and explained, "What I mean is, take a look without thinking too much about how strange it all seems. Put your preconceptions on hold, and start over from zero. Oh well, who am I to tell you what to do?"

Chikako thanked him for his advice. Kinugasa walked towards the door of the office, and Chikako sat back down again. Despite what he'd said, no matter how you looked at it, it *was* a strange case. From every angle. Strange. And she thought again about Kinugasa's use of the phrase "open mind." She didn't think he had given her his complete assessment of the case. He had left something unsaid.

She frowned, concentrating. Which was why she didn't notice Kinugasa giving her a long, hard look as he turned around to toss his paper cup into the wastebasket before he left the room.

7

The shiny, brand-new sign for Sakurai Liquors was large and in a prominent spot outside the exit of Yoyogi Uehara Station. Junko walked right up to it for a closer look. The sign included the address and a simple map, noting that it was a ten-minute walk from the station. Junko memorized the route.

So this was the store owned by Asaba's mother. That's what Tsutsui had told her anyway. And it was where Asaba and his friends hung out.

From the looks of the sign, Sakurai Liquors was doing well. At the very least it was doing better than the ill-fated Plaza. If what Tsutsui had said was true, it meant that even though Asaba's mother had failed to make it with Plaza she was now involved in a more profitable business.

Junko frowned as she walked. It seemed unlikely that Asaba's mother would be able to make such an amazing turnaround, and it didn't make sense that she would own a store bearing someone else's name—Sakurai. Why a liquor shop and not a bar like Plaza? What exactly was Asaba's mother's position at Sakurai? Did someone hire her to run it? It was hard to imagine that her son and his pals would hang out at her workplace if it was owned by someone else, though. And why would a gang of punks choose to hang out at a store— even a liquor store? A bar would make much more sense.

Junko had battled in the past with similar types and had become acquainted with their thought processes. Fugitives like these didn't have the presence of mind to check into a motel they had never seen before or steal a car the police would not be looking for. To be blunt, the sort of fugitives that Junko was after usually didn't have the brains. They would go back to their nests, covered in blood or dragging in their kidnap victims. It wasn't that they were unafraid of getting caught, but rather that it never occurred to them that it might not be the best plan of action. They never considered that what they were doing might be dangerous. This was especially true right after they had murdered someone. They were intoxicated by slaughter and thought they were superhuman.

But the main reason they chose to return to their cozy little nests was to take their prey somewhere they could enjoy it at their leisure. And that was why Junko made it her practice to look for these nests.

Asaba and his gang must know by now that what had happened at the Tayama factory was already in the news, so they would know enough not to drive around in Fujikawa's car with Natsuko still in it. They must be hiding out somewhere. There was at least a ninety percent chance that they had holed up somewhere that was both familiar and comfortable.

She'd thought she was onto something, but a *liquor store*? Suddenly she caught sight of a sign on a utility pole: "Sakurai Liquors—turn right here." Junko turned right and then stopped in her tracks facing a three-story building.

It wasn't so large maybe, but a purpose-built commercial building nevertheless. The Sakurai Liquors sign topped a large entrance on the first floor. Next to the door was a vending machine for beer, which a small woman in an apron was refilling.

From where she stood, Junko could only see the side of the woman's face. She clearly wasn't young, but she wore a bright red apron over a pair of jeans, and her short hair was a shade of red almost as bright as her apron.

Sakurai Liquors was flanked on either side by private homes. The entire area was largely residential, with small shops and three- or four-storied apartment buildings here and there. Junko noted a dry cleaner's and a small apparel shop. This was a neighborhood you might see anywhere in Tokyo.

Sakurai Liquors looked newer than its surroundings. The walls were still pristine. There was a much older building of about the same size directly behind it, and that made Sakurai look even cleaner and whiter. The effect was enhanced by the reflection of the sun shining on it.

The first floor was the liquor shop and the second and third floors appeared to be apartments. The second-floor balcony was filled with laundry hung out to dry. The third floor balcony was empty except for a separating panel in the middle. Junko could see cheap-looking yellow curtains hanging inside the windows. She had seen curtains like that before while apartment hunting: landlords often used them in empty apartments to keep tatami and wallpaper from being bleached by the sun.

The woman in the red apron had her back to the street as she stocked the vending machine. Junko walked a little closer and decided that the second floor must be the home of the liquor store manager, while the third floor apartments were for rent. Junko couldn't see it from where she was, but she knew that there must be a separate staircase or an elevator for the third-floor tenants.

The partition on the balcony indicated two separate apartments—most likely only large enough for a single person to live in, and the curtains meant the apartments were currently empty. Maybe that was where Asaba was hanging out. This made more sense than the liquor store—this was a kind of nest.

But where did Asaba's mother's fit into the scheme of things?

He told me to see his mother.

Asaba had clearly talked to his mother about getting the money for an illegal gun. So she must know he carried one. Remembering what Tsutsui had said and looking at Sakurai Liquors, Junko decided that there was a good chance that this was where Asaba had brought Natsuko. Her heartbeat quickened.

Junko decided that all she had to do was ask his mother about it. If she didn't want to talk, Junko would make her. If Asaba was here, her job was almost done. If not, at least she could get information. Junko yanked the corners of her mouth up into a pleasant smile and walked up right behind the woman in the red apron.

"Hello!" she announced herself cheerfully.

The woman turned around, shocked to find herself almost eyeball to eyeball with Junko; she leaned backwards hurriedly.

"Hey, what do you want?" she rasped in response.

Junko continued to smile but did not back off. The woman tripped as she retreated and fell against the vending machine.

"You startled me. Are you looking for something?"

"Hi," Junko repeated. "Would you by any chance be Keiichi Asaba's mother?"

The woman's eyes opened wide, and she looked Junko up and down. She lifted a hand and absently began scratching her cheek. Her nails were long, and bright red.

"Yeah," she said defensively. "And you?"

Bingo! Junko's smile grew even larger.

The woman furrowed her thin eyebrows. They were drawn on in a reddish-brown color. "What do you want? Who are you?"

"I've got something to discuss with you." Junko walked purposefully towards the store entrance. The inside looked small, probably due to the poor layout. There were refrigerated showcases to the right and left, and a counter in front. Beside the counter was a propped-open door leading behind the shop. Junko could see into a hallway covered with mats.

There was no one in the shop, no customers or other employees—at least as far as she could tell. Junko marched right up to the counter, and the woman hurried in after her.

"Look, what do you want? Who *are* you?"

Junko turned around to look the woman full in the face. She appeared to be in her mid-forties, but she was wearing so much make-up that Junko couldn't be sure. She had a small nose, a somewhat pointy chin, and the mouth of an underfed rabbit. She might have been pretty in her younger years, and she probably thought she still was. Junko caught a whiff of strong perfume.

"So *you're* Asaba's mother," Junko began slowly. "What I want to talk about is personal. Do you mind talking here, or should we go somewhere else?"

The woman frowned and glanced toward the entrance. "I'm the only one here. My husband is out making deliveries."

"Husband? Oh my! So you've remarried, have you?"

The woman's frown deepened. Ugly wrinkles formed at the corners of her eyes. She made no answer.

"Well, that's beside the point. I'm here because I'm looking for Keiichi Asaba. Do you know where he is? I heard that he's often here with his friends. Is he in one of the upstairs rooms right now?"

Hearing the name of her son, the woman jutted her chin out defensively, and Junko could see a flash in her eyes.

"*Who the hell are you?* What do you want? What business do you have with Keiichi?"

Junko continued to smile. "Is he here or not?"

The woman grabbed Junko's arm and tried to pull her out of the store. Junko grimaced in pain.

"Hey, don't be so rough!" she protested. "My arm's been injured."

"You're the one that's rough," the woman shot back. "Coming in here bothering me while I'm working!"

"Ow, that hurts! Let go of me!" The pain wiped the smile from Junko's face. "Your son shot me!"

The woman looked as if Junko had slapped her in the face. Junko looked her in the eye and repeated, "He shot me with a gun he bought on the black market." The woman dropped Junko's arm as though it was a piece of excrement, and took several quick steps backwards.

"What are you talking about? I don't know anything about any gun."

"Oh yes you do." Junko took a step closer to her. She kept an eye on the woman's face while cautiously checking the street. Nobody was there. No passersby. "You know, all right. Asaba talked to you about getting money to pay for it, didn't he? Don't you remember meeting that guy who sold it to him? He told me all about it."

"You . . ." The woman's lips began to tremble. "Who sent you?"

Junko laughed. "Forget about that, and answer my question. Where is Keiichi Asaba? Your idiot son. You can't pretend you don't know. Out with it!"

The woman glared furiously at Junko. She brought her face right up to hers and spat, "Forget it!"

Junko laughed back, "Is that all you have to say?"

"I don't know what sort of game you're up to, but I won't play it with you. Get out!"

"Are you sure?"

"Listen, you'd better leave while I'm still in a good mood!"

"*Good* mood? What's *good* about you, you made-up hag?"

The woman's expression stiffened as if someone had pasted it with laundry starch. Junko couldn't restrain a chuckle.

The woman could barely contain herself—the make-up could no longer hide the red hue her face had taken.

"Who are you calling a hag? Just you try saying that again!"

Junko sounded bored. "I'll say it as many times as I like, you stupid slut."

The woman's red lips opened and closed like a fish's. She lifted her arm and swung it at Junko's face. In the next instant, her arm was on fire.

The flames looked like they'd sprouted from her skin. Her fingers, wrist, and arm were enveloped in a cloak of smooth, red flame. The woman stared at it in horror before drawing in her breath to scream.

But before she could, Junko hit her cheek with a whip of energy. To Junko it felt like no more than a tap, but the woman's head was flung sideways, throwing her whole body off balance. Junko deftly caught the woman's arm and shook it up and down. The flames disappeared as if by magic. The remains of her thin sweater were no more than a film on her skin. The smell of cooked flesh hung in the air.

"Don't try to scream . . . Next time it'll be your hair." Junko smiled brightly and grabbed the woman's shoulder. "Let's go on inside. We've got a lot of talking to do."

Junko dragged her to the back of the store and into a tiny room containing a desk, a telephone, and a sink, that probably served as an office. Cases of beer were piled up in one corner, partially hiding the stairway to the second floor.

There was another door. Keeping her grip firm, Junko jerked her chin at it. "Where does that lead?"

The woman was incoherent. The corners of her mouth were flecked in foam.

"You can talk!" Junko grabbed her by the throat. "I didn't hurt you enough to damage your voice. That was no more than a nudge. Speak!"

The woman pursed her lips, and did her best to get her jaws to open. Saliva dribbled out of her mouth as she spoke. "Sto-storage room."

"There's a storage room? Okay, let's go in."

Junko shoved the woman through the door and then closed it. It felt heavy and secure. The room was full of cardboard boxes and bottles of beer and saké. The floor was bare concrete. Junko yanked the woman upright, and pushed her up against the wall.

"Okay, lady, I'm after your stupid son." Junko spoke in a calm, reasonable voice. "He's a murderer and he's kidnapped a young woman. I've come to rescue her, so I can't afford to be too nice. Do you understand?"

The woman had tears in her eyes, and her nose was dripping. "He-e-lp!"

"I don't have time to listen to your problems right now. Tell me: is he here? Or somewhere else? Which is it?"

"He's no-no-not . . ."

"He's not here? Are you sure? If you're lying, you can guess what will happen next. I know you're proud of that face—you've made it up so beautifully. You want to be able to wear make-up again one day, don't you? Skin care, all that stuff? You don't want that beautiful face to turn into roast pig, do you?"

Tears black with mascara trickled from the woman's eyes.

"Just goes to show that when you have a black soul, even your tears turn black. Learn something new every day, huh?" Junko laughed and banged the woman's head against the wall. The woman squeezed her eyes shut.

"So Asaba's someplace else?"

The woman nodded, her eyes still closed.

"Where?"

"I don't know!"

Junko took a step back from the woman. "Open your eyes, bitch."

She opened her eyes. This time, the toes on her right foot were on fire. The woman screamed and tried to run. Junko stopped her and pushed her back against the wall.

"It's just your sandal. There's no need to make such a fuss."

The woman managed to shake the sandal off her foot. It flipped over and emitted a stench of smoldering rubber. Then she covered her face with both hands and slid to the floor. Junko folded her arms across her chest and stood there watching her.

"Come on! Is he upstairs? Is that it?" The woman shrank further away, shaking her head.

Junko looked around. Keeping her eye on Asaba's mother, she backed carefully into the office. She found what she was looking for in the bottom desk drawer: some plastic rope. "Well, looks like I'll have to tie you up." Junko walked after the woman, who retreated farther and farther into the storage room. "You're wasting my time. I'll have to check for myself whether Asaba's upstairs, since I can't take your word for it."

"It's true!" The skin on the woman's cheek was red where Junko's energy had hit her; it looked sunken in. Maybe that's why she was having trouble talking.

If Asaba wasn't here, she'd need his mother for more information, so Junko wanted her alive for now. She'd tie her up and then weld the door shut. She'd better hurry too, before the husband got back or some unsuspecting customer wandered in.

Junko was frustrated by Asaba's mother's lack of cooperation, and her head was throbbing from the effort of holding back her power and using it in tiny spurts. It wanted full release. As for Junko herself, she wanted to blow the whole store off of its foundation and burn it to ashes.

She told herself that she could do that just as soon as she rescued Natsuko. She only had to hold it in until then.

Junko was about to gag Asaba's mother when she heard it. It was faint, but she was sure she heard someone scream. A woman. It was gone the next instant, and Junko almost thought she was hearing things until she looked down at her captive's face. Her skin was muddy with streaks of make-up, but her eyes were glittering with fear. Both of them knew that she had been caught in her lie.

Junko looked up at the ceiling. Asaba was definitely up there.

8

In that instant Asaba's mother, eyes glittering, flung herself at Junko in a frenzied attempt to escape. But simultaneously an old memory flashed into Junko's mind: it was so vivid that the scene inside the liquor store seemed to move in slow motion. Junko lost all sense of reality. She watched from within her memories as Asaba's mother came at her as if through a sea of oil, moving at half speed.

Junko, why did you do that? It was her mother's voice. *How could you do that to the neighbor's dog? The poor thing. I thought you liked it!*

But, Mama, it bit me! It came over to me with a strange look, and then jumped up and bit me. I was scared. I was scared of it, and that's why . . .

Asaba's mother crashed into her, and they both fell to the floor. Junko landed painfully on her back and elbows, and she felt blood coming from the reopened wound on her shoulder. That was it! That dog had the same look in its eyes as this woman. It looked like it had gone mad.

That's why I burned that dog, Mommy!

Now Junko remembered. *That was the first time I killed a living thing. But why am I remembering it now?*

Her mother's voice came back to her. *So anytime something or somebody bothers you or refuses to go along with you, are you just going to kill them, Junko? What about your father and me? If we scold you or spank you, or do something you don't like, are you going to burn us like that dog?*

Asaba's mother scrambled over Junko, stepping on her in her haste to reach the door.

If you do that, there won't be anyone left for you. You'll be all alone. Is that how you want to live, Junko?

The memory of her mother's harsh questioning cut rudely into her reverie, and reality returned to its normal speed. Junko sat up. Asaba's mother had just reached the door and she was grabbing for the handle. Junko aimed a flash of energy at her back that sent her flying forward and the door with her. With her arms and legs spread-eagled against it, she looked like she was riding a magic carpet. The door hit the automatic glass door at the entrance to the store, shattering it to pieces. Then it caught fire.

Junko stood up and went out to view the remains of the door and Asaba's mother as they went up in flames. Only her legs were visible, and Junko was surprised to see the left foot was still wearing its sandal.

The crashing sounds and flames would soon bring in the neighbors. Junko moved quickly out of view, and looked for stairs leading to the upper floors. They didn't take long to find because she could hear someone running down them.

"What's all the noise?" a male voice called out.

Junko ran to the foot of the stairs, almost colliding with a thin, pale-skinned young man. He had long hair and was wearing nothing but a dirty pair of boxer shorts.

"Where's Asaba?" Junko demanded.

The youth stopped in his tracks.

"Who the hell are you?"

"Asaba—where is he?" Junko put one foot on the stairs. "And get out of my way!"

He stepped back, missed a step and stumbled, grabbing onto the handrail to keep himself from falling.

"What the fuck's with you? Whaddya want with Asaba?"

People were gathering in the store and calling out for the owner. The voices were getting closer. Junko knew she had no time to spare.

She looked up at the longhaired youth, and let out a lash of energy that sent him flying backwards. He slammed into the wall of the second-floor landing and burst into flames.

"You should have moved," Junko muttered as she ran up the stairs. The door to her left opened just as she reached the second floor. Through it she could see a sofa and matching chairs, and for an instant she saw a male head peeking out from behind the door before it slammed shut again.

Junko didn't think that was Asaba either. How many were there? She had killed three of his group at the abandoned factory. Had he called more of his friends here? Why?

Junko heard the cry of a woman from behind the closed door. There was no mistaking it this time.

Suddenly she realized why Asaba's gang was here: they had come to take turns with Natsuko. Junko broke down the door. As her rage grew she could feel her power howling to be let loose. It only took one hit to break the door into splinters, and the remains burst into flames that reached the ceiling. Junko could feel a few of the embers falling on her head and smell them burning her hair.

Through the smoke, she could see that this was a living room. There was an armchair and a glass table piled high with clothes, and the floor was littered with socks and underwear. The flames from the door began to spread through the room.

On the left-hand side of the living room was a single sliding door, typical of the type used for a tatami-floored room. Despite the commotion, nobody ventured to open it. Junko was sure that Natsuko was in there. And Asaba, too.

Junko stepped towards it, when suddenly she heard a voice.

"Stop! Don't move!" A guy was crouching in the corner on her right. Both hands were raised, holding a gun aimed at Junko.

Junko turned her head slightly to look at him. The clothing on the glass table was smoking and making her eyes smart. She blinked to clear the tears.

"I said don't move! I'll shoot!" He pulled the trigger. The bullet whizzed past the right side of Junko's head and made a hole in the wall behind her.

Junko ignored it, looking straight at the youth instead. He was young, had a large, stocky build, and was just wearing a faded pair of khaki pants. His bare feet were already blackened from the ashes of the door.

He seemed surprised that the gun had gone off, and his hold on it loosened. Junko took a step forward, and he shrank back against the wall.

"S-s-stay away!" His finger searched frantically for the trigger. Junko squinted, squeezing out a fine line of energy aimed at the gun.

"Ouch!" The youth dropped it. Both of his hands had been burned red, and the soft skin of his palms was swelling into blisters before his eyes. He screamed and tried to soothe his hands by brushing them against his pants leg.

Junko smiled and said, almost tenderly, "Sorry, that must have been hot. But don't worry; I'll make sure you don't feel anything anymore." As she spoke she unleashed another lash of energy. He went up in flames still crouched down against the wall. Junko watched as his open eyes began to melt in their sockets and then she moved towards the sliding door.

It was open a few inches but slammed shut the instant she looked towards it. Junko had to smile.

The room stank of smoke, and the temperature was rising. She knew that the heat did not come from the burning door or from the bodies on fire, but from herself. Her anger burned. The more she tried to control her rage, the more it tried to escape from her body and was generating heat.

Junko realized that if she saw Asaba now, she would incinerate him on the spot, and that would most likely be the end of Natsuko, too. She took a deep breath and shook her head lightly. The lace curtains in the living room instantly went up in flames.

Junko carefully put her body up against the sliding door. Her back felt the heat from the burning curtains. Then she flung open the door.

It was a small tatami room. There was hardly any furniture other than a pile of crumpled bedding in the center. She had heard a woman sobbing as she opened the door, but she couldn't see anyone. Junko stepped inside.

A window opened onto a metal fire escape. It was typical of the sort used in small apartment buildings: all you had to do was jump over the window ledge. From the open window, Junko could hear the siren of a fire truck approaching.

The sobbing. Junko looked back. Opposite the window, in a corner next to the closet, she saw a young woman with her arms clasped to her chest and her legs folded beneath her. She was naked except for the towel she was covering herself with.

"Natsuko?" Junko drew closer. The woman tried to make herself even smaller, hiding her tear-streaked face with the towel.

Junko ran to her and put her arms around her. "Don't worry, I've come to rescue you. Fujikawa sent me to find you."

As soon as she heard the familiar name, the woman lifted her head.

"Fujikawa? Is he okay?"

Junko tensed. Her energy fed on her rage; it was like a high-speed breeder reactor creating new waves of power. But the battle had narrowed Junko's field of vision and her mind felt worn. She didn't have the concentration to spare for a convincing lie to Natsuko's sudden question.

"He's fine," she said, but her pause had been too long and her expression betrayed the truth.

In a trembling voice, Natsuko asked, "Is he dead?" And then added, "Please don't lie to me."

Natsuko grabbed Junko's arms. Up close, Junko could see that she was covered with bruises and had been badly beaten. Her lips were split and swollen, and there were cigarette burns on her arms.

"Yes," Junko nodded. "They killed him. Just before he died, he asked me to find you."

Natsuko's face crumpled and she began to sob, heartbroken. Junko was surprised she still had that much strength left in her.

The living room was in flames and the fire had spread from the curtains to the ceiling.

"Come on, we have to get out of here."

Junko pulled Natsuko to her feet and tried to lead her to the window, but Natsuko recoiled in fear.

"We can't go out there! *He* went up that way!"

"The guy who kidnapped you?"

Natsuko nodded. "There was a crash, and he looked out to see what was going on. Then he climbed out the window and went up those stairs!"

"I've got to follow him."

"He'll kill you!"

"Don't worry. I'm stronger than he is," Junko assured her confidently. "Was he the one that did this to you?" Junko pointed to the blisters on her arm. Natsuko nodded.

"Then I'll give him something even hotter to think about. Come on, let's go! This place is burning down; you can't stay here."

Junko couldn't see anything for Natsuko to wear. Her head began to ache just thinking about how long Natsuko had been left exposed like this. She could feel the power inside struggling even harder to get out.

Junko held out her coat. Natsuko put it on and stepped out over the window railing. As she did so, Junko caught a glimpse of dried blood from cuts on Natsuko's thigh. Her temples throbbed.

Junko followed Natsuko out onto the fire escape. In the narrow space between buildings, she could make out a group of neighbors looking up at the flames. She saw them pointing up at them and yelling. She could also make out a red fire truck and the silver-colored uniforms of the firefighters.

Natsuko gasped, "I'm scared!"

Junko held firmly onto her left arm to steady her.

Then she saw that they wouldn't be able to descend the fire escape. The lower flight was piled high with old beer cases, cardboard boxes, and wooden crates. *Stairway storage, huh?* thought Junko grimly. There was no way to move the trash and get down, and it would be impossible to climb over it. That was what the people below were making noise about.

It was too far to jump from the second floor. They would have to go up to the third floor to escape the flames. As they climbed, Junko saw that the fire escape extended all the way up to the roof. If Asaba had come out onto the fire escape, he must have reached the roof by now.

Junko was about to continue climbing, when she heard a thump from somewhere inside. She tensed and waited. Could it be Asaba?

She opened the fire door to the third floor, but everything was perfectly still. There were two doors, and Junko tried each knob, but neither gave way. At the end of the hall there was a tiny elevator.

She pressed the button, but the door didn't open; the electric wiring had probably been damaged in the fire. Smoke began to seep up to the third floor, and the smell of burning filled the hallway. Junko ran back to Natsuko's side.

"He's not here. Come on, we've got to get up to the roof." She helped Natsuko back out onto the fire escape. There was less than a flight of stairs to climb.

The "roof" was no more than a tiny patch of concrete with a water tank in the middle. Junko looked around, and her eye caught something strange. A small pile of shredded tobacco—not cigarette butts or ashes, but whole cigarettes torn to bits. The paper had been peeled off the cigarettes, and the contents were being blown about by the cold north wind. Was Asaba's gang into smoking dope or something?

Behind her, Natsuko had curled herself up into a ball and was sneezing. Junko turned back and rubbed her shoulder to reassure her that everything was under control. She looked around again.

She saw that there was a tiny room built on one side of the roof, with a "No Entry" sign on the door. It was probably the control room for the elevator. If Asaba had escaped to the roof, it was the only place he could be hiding.

Junko motioned for Natsuko to stay put and crept over to the water tank. She could use it as a shield. She circled the water tank noiselessly, then stood up straight and moved towards the control room. She placed her hand on the door knob, and turned it slowly to the right. She pulled it gently. It was heavy. She opened it a crack and waited to see what would happen.

Nothing. Junko tried to keep her heart from pounding and carefully closed the door. Then she took a deep breath and yanked it open. It took more effort than she expected. She braced herself so that she would be able to fling out her energy if Asaba suddenly appeared.

She heard the sound of the wind mixed in with the sirens of fire trucks, ambulances, and the noise of the gathering crowd. Despite the tension, she was momentarily distracted by the vague thought that sound rises. Junko pulled herself ever so slightly away from the door. It took a tremendous amount of strength to have her energy at the ready and still keep it under control. Her teeth were tightly clenched and her temples throbbed.

She stooped down, steadying herself with her right hand, and all but crawled through the open door. As she crouched forward, a black shadow fell on top of her.

It was a human body. Unable to support its weight, Junko fell forward onto the concrete. She could smell blood.

Behind her, she heard Natsuko scream. Junko struggled to free herself of the body. It was naked except for a pair of pants, and its upper torso was drenched in blood. As it lay face down, Junko could see that the back of its head had been blown away. She reached out and grabbed the short hairs of its bangs, and lifted its head.

It was a young man. Both of his eyes were open, and blood was flowing into them from a reddish black hole in the middle of his forehead. Junko could have fit a finger into it.

Natsuko screamed again. This time she continued hysterically, and Junko knew the people on the ground would be able to hear her. The rescue workers would be more panicked than necessary. Junko ran quickly to Natsuko's side.

"It's all right! Please! Try to be quiet!"

Junko tried shaking her, but she continued screaming. Junko slapped her across the cheek.

The cheek that had been pale from the cold quickly reddened from the blow. Natsuko stopped screaming and began to gasp for air, trembling as she did.

"Is that Asaba?" Junko asked, indicating the half-naked body with her chin. "You recognize him, don't you? He was the one who did that to you and your boyfriend, Fujikawa. He was the one who was holding you prisoner until I got here, isn't he?"

"Ye-e-es."

Junko turned back to look at Asaba's body. She had a good view of his bare shoulders, and the pale skin looked disconcertingly white in the wind. Junko noticed a scar on his left arm. It looked old; the remains of some deep cut that had been sewn back together. Maybe it was a childhood injury.

His mother must have been sick with worry when it happened. She'd probably picked him up and run to the nearest doctor's office, held him tight to comfort him while they stitched him up, and then praised him for being such a good boy. Asaba's mother could never have guessed then that her son would grow up to be a monster who enjoyed hurting and killing people.

When did he set out on that path? If there had been a sign pointing in that mistaken direction, why didn't anyone warn him? What had gone wrong?

How should I know? Junko shrugged.

"It's all right now. You're safe. He's dead." Junko hugged Natsuko tightly. "He did terrible things to you, but he finally got what he deserved."

Natsuko's throat began making a sound as though air was leaking from it. She had been weeping soundlessly, but now she began to moan. It sounded as though something had broken in her and she was crumpling in grief.

Still holding her around the shoulders, Junko turned and squinted into the cold wind. Something occurred to her: how did Asaba die? Was it suicide? Did he shoot himself? Nobody else was there—it was the only possible explanation.

Natsuko began to speak.

"It was . . . it was . . ." She could hardly get the words out. "It was . . . our first date."

"You and Fujikawa?"

Natsuko nodded convulsively. "Today . . . we had a day off. So we decided to take a drive. It was the first time. We worked together . . ."

Junko rubbed Natsuko's back. "You don't have to talk yet." She got to her knees, stood up, and went over to Asaba's body. She looked him over carefully, but there was no gun. It must be in the control room.

"Why? What did we do to deserve this?" Natsuko continued hoarsely. Junko stepped over Asaba's body and into the control room. She closed her eyes for an instant and thought. *You just had bad luck. You were in the wrong place at the wrong time. You made the mistake of running into Asaba.* That was the only answer there was for Natsuko, but it was just too heartless to voice.

Inside the control room there was a strong smell of oil. Stepping carefully, she searched the floor and behind objects in the room.

There it was!

The gun had fallen behind a squashed cardboard box. The top of the box had been torn off and she could see the cut ends of cable peeking out. As she reached out to pick up the gun, she scraped the palm of her hand on the end of one of the cables. It was just as if Asaba had planned this final feeble resistance.

Some people find it hard to give up, thought Junko, as she bent over to pick up the gun. A drop of blood the size of a pinhead appeared on her hand. She licked it off, and tasted metal.

In most of her battles up to now, criminals had pleaded with her to spare their lives. They treated other people's lives as playthings, but when it came to their own, they cried their eyes out. Some had even crawled up to her and licked her toes, begging for mercy. None of them had been able to admit their own crimes—they always blamed them on someone else. Usually someone who had died first—someone Junko had already punished with his life. *He was the one who made me do it! He threatened me to make me help him! I didn't want to do it—believe me!*

None of them had committed suicide. Not one.

Was Asaba different from the rest? Was he especially bad? No, there had been one guy who was worse and who wanted to die even less. That punk who had chased high school girls around in a car. He'd killed them as if he was a hunter and they were his prey. Right to the end, when it was his turn to be the prey, he refused to admit what he had done. As Junko prepared to destroy him, he had looked at her and screamed, *Don't think you can get away with this!*

Junko found it hard to believe that Asaba had shot himself.

She turned around to leave, tightly gripping the cold gun in her hand. The weight of it felt good.

Just then, she heard Natsuko's voice.

"Who's that? Is someone there?"

Junko quickly stepped through the doorway. She could see Natsuko curled up just as she had left her. Asaba's corpse was there, too.

Natsuko was looking to the right, questioning someone hidden behind the water tank.

"I know someone's there. Oh, it's *you!*" Natsuko's eyes were wide with surprise and her next words died on her lips. Junko ran, leaning forward, flying across the short distance to Natsuko. She felt everything shifting into slow motion, drawn out, inching along frame by frame.

As she leaped over Asaba's body, a gunshot rang out and Natsuko's body was blown backwards. Her neck snapped back, with her eyes wide open and her arms thrown out. She looked like she was swimming through space, ready to clasp someone to herself. She fell to the ground in that position, her arms spread out and her head facing the sky.

"Natsuko!"

Junko tried to lift her up, but her body was lifeless. There was a hole in her forehead—just like Asaba's. Junko could smell the gunpowder.

She turned to look in the direction Natsuko had been facing. There was nothing, just the darkening sky. Junko stood up, grabbed onto the roof railing, and looked frantically around her.

The buildings on each side were two stories. Over the roofs of each spewed black smoke from the windows of Sakurai Liquors. What the people gathered below could not see, however, was that behind the store was a two-story house with a flat roof. Just as Junko leaned out over the guard railing to look at the house, she thought she saw someone leap from the roof down to the ground. She tried to look more closely, but the smoke obscured her view.

Could someone jump off that roof? Who? What was that person doing there? Was that the person who shot Natsuko? But *why?* Who would do such a thing?

Was there someone other than Asaba who she should have been chasing? But Asaba had been the leader of this group, hadn't he? Junko walked unsteadily back over to Natsuko, lost in these questions. Suddenly, she felt something hard under her feet, and automatically bent over to pick it up. She knew what it was right away.

It was the cartridge from a gun, still hot. Junko squeezed it in her hand. She went back to Natsuko's body, walking quietly even though she knew that nothing could disturb her now. She had been through hell since the night before, and who knew what she had been subjected to. Junko didn't want to bother her with any more noise.

Natsuko's eyes were open. Junko laid Asaba's gun down at her feet, reached out her hand, and closed them; they were most likely already dry. In her place, Junko felt her own eyes grow suddenly hot.

For just a few moments, Junko cried for Natsuko. *I'm so sorry. I couldn't help you. A few more seconds and you would have been safe. I must have missed someone or something , and now you're dead.*

Junko looked back at Asaba's corpse. He was undeniably dead, no longer a threat to anyone, just a harmless lump of meat. As Junko looked at his mutilated head, she felt a cold shock of realization.

Asaba had not committed suicide! But who had murdered him? The person she saw jumping from the roof of the house next door—was that the person who had killed Asaba? If so, who could it possibly be?

It was reasonable to think that anyone in Asaba's gang would want Natsuko dead to keep her from identifying them. But they wouldn't kill Asaba. On the other hand, no enemy of Asaba would want to kill Natsuko. Who on earth would need to kill them both?

Supposing it was one of Asaba's gang, where had he been hiding? Natsuko had told her that Asaba escaped alone through the window.

But where would an enemy of Asaba have come from? Reflecting the confusing swirl of questions in Junko's mind, black smoke pouring from the windows below darkened the rooftop around her.

Junko was rescued from the roof by a ladder truck. A firefighter had quickly wrapped her in a blanket, putting it right over her head. Junko pretended to be terrified.

"Is anyone else up here?"

Junko had been brought off the roof before the firefighters found Natsuko or Asaba. Junko responded to the hurried question by nodding her head vigorously, but she did not speak. Somebody tried to direct her to an ambulance, but she shook off the helping hands.

"I'm going to be sick. Excuse me," she said, running to the side of the road. The whole area was swarming with firefighters and curious onlookers. Junko put her head down, mixed in the crowd, and left the scene. When she got to the edge of it, she turned around to look back at Sakurai Liquors. The smoldering building almost looked like an enormous gravestone.

Accompanying the taste of defeat in her mouth was a splitting headache. She'd collapse if she stopped, so she kept walking.

She'd lost this battle. The two people she'd set out to save, she'd seen die instead, and all she had left was a riddle. She didn't even have enough strength left to be angry at herself.

Junko walked on. Like a soldier retreating from the front line clutching the identification tags of a fallen comrade, she gripped the used-up cartridge in her hand.

9

After talking to Sergeant Kinugasa at MPD, Chikako Ishizu headed for Arakawa precinct to meet Detective Makihara, who was investigating the riverside case. There was still time before the evening rush hour began, so she decided to take a taxi. Rocked gently by the car, she was recalling the scene at the abandoned factory in Tayama when the taxi driver spoke to her.

"Tough day, Ma'am?"

Chikako was startled out of her reverie. "Who, me?" Confused, she looked up and saw the driver grinning at her in his rearview mirror.

"You're going to the police station, right? Can't be good news, now, can it? So has your kid been up to no good? There's no telling what young people will do these days."

He was a small, round man with a bald spot on the top of his head, probably about the same age as Chikako. Maybe that's why he spoke in such a familiar manner, Chikako thought, amused. This happened every once in a while when she was heading to another precinct or to the coroners' office. Taxi drivers never assumed that Chikako might be a detective. This was the first time, though, that any had gone so far as to assume that she must be some poor woman who been called down to the precinct to pick up her delinquent child. She was more interested than annoyed. She had to give him credit for having a good imagination—or had he had a problem lately with some local troublemakers? Maybe there was something more behind his comment. Chikako decided to humor him for a while. She started out with a cliché.

"You can't do anything with kids these days. They're faster than adults, and they're bigger. But kids are kids, and they're just not as clever as they think."

The driver nodded in agreement and looked at Chikako in the rearview mirror. Chikako could see his small, restless eyes.

"The other night I almost got beaten up by some kids."

It gave Chikako a kind of thrill to find out she'd been right. She encouraged him to keep talking.

"You mean you were robbed?"

"That's right. Three of 'em got in. They must all have been minors. Their hair was dyed weird colors, and they were wearing those baggy pants."

"Where did you pick them up?"

"Near the public hall in Shintomi. Do you know where that is?"

"More or less. What time was it? Pretty late?"

"Not really. I think it was before eleven. They wanted me to take them to Shinjuku, and I remember thinking that they must have lots of cash to spare if they were taking a taxi while the trains were still running."

The driver went on to describe how they had given him their destination and then began yakking loudly among themselves. From the sound of it, they all lived in the Shintomi area, and they had snuck out to have some fun. The driver had wondered what their parents were up to in the meantime.

"I'd never let my own son out after eleven if he was still in school. I'd wallop him one before I let him do that."

"You bet," agreed Chikako.

"Especially not on a weekday! But maybe they're not even in school." The driver was getting more and more worked up. "They had terrible manners! They put their feet up on the back of my seat—with their shoes on! There was a woman in another taxi when I stopped at a red light. They rolled down the window and started hollering at her. They were using words you never even hear from yakuza these days. I felt like throwing up just listening to them."

"Were they drunk?"

"No, they were sober, all right. That made them even scarier. Who could act like that when they're sober? I was sorry I picked them up. What I really wanted to do was tell them off and throw them out, but there were three of them. I figured I'd better just get it over with. Then when we got to the Kudanshita intersection . . ."

The driver described how they'd pulled up alongside another taxi with a young woman accompanied by two middle-aged men. "When those jerks saw that, they went crazy. They said they wouldn't let those old guys get away with it, and they opened the window and started shouting. The people in that other taxi looked good and scared.

"When the light turned green, the taxi took off as fast as it could, trying to shake them off. Then the punks told *me* to follow." The taxi driver was clearly upset as he told Chikako about how the youths had seemed determined to catch the men.

"They were saying death would be too good for them. Unbelievable! I couldn't take it anymore, and asked them to please get out. I told them I didn't want to be chasing another taxi. So then they turned on me: 'Who does he think he is? A *taxi driver* ordering *us* around?' I lost it and told them they'd better watch their mouths." The three had laughed and asked if he knew who he was dealing with, and he had seen something in their eyes that was more animal than human.

"I was outnumbered, but I knew there was a small police station near the Kudanshita intersection, and I couldn't just let them get away with all that. I stopped the car there and got out and gave them a piece of my mind.

"Who the hell do you guys think you are? Where do you get off acting like you own me? Living off your parents and going around throwing their money away, making fun of people who make a living for themselves when parasites like you never will? You're just trash. Get outta my cab and outta my face!

"That wiped the smiles off their faces. They went white. I've been driving for twenty years and I've seen all kinds, but I've never seen anyone lose color the way those kids did." Without a word, the three had gone straight for him. He'd turned and run, heading for the police station.

"One of them saw where I was going, and told the others to lay off. One stopped, but the other one kept right on coming—he was huge, with a bright yellow crew cut. They managed to hold him back, but then he went back and kicked my cab as hard as he could." The driver ran to the police station, told them what had happened, and stayed there until the coast was clear. "There was a huge dent in the door. He was a strong son of a bitch."

The policemen on duty chewed out the driver, telling him he shouldn't provoke delinquents like that. "There's no limit to what guys like that will do. They'll kill you to shut you up. I saw that for myself, so I told the police that I'd watch myself from now on."

Chikako thought over what the driver had told her. Those three punks must have been angry at what the driver said, but that wasn't why they blew sky high the way they did. It was because they knew that what he'd said was true and it scared them.

Who the hell do you guys think you are? . . . You're just trash.

Kids nowadays were catered to all their lives, with all their needs met. But they weren't the only ones raised like that: so were the kids next door and across the street. They were all the same. They were all raised to think of themselves as special, as better than others, and they needed to find something to prove it to themselves, to justify their sense of entitlement.

But what if they never found that "something"? All they were left with was their enormous conceit. They were like flower bulbs raised in water, floating in a transparent, colorless pool of nihilism. Surrounding the bulb was nothing—nothing that could give them a true sense of themselves.

Materially, however, they had everything they needed or wanted. They enjoyed spending money and having fun. The more fun they had, the more apt they were to forget that the only thing they had was their unwieldy conceit. It sucked in nourishment from its surroundings and put out roots that only grew longer and wilder, until they were like jungle vines getting tangled up with each other, no longer able to move freely. No matter where these youths went, those tangled, knotty roots of pride and vanity dragged along, always taking up more space than the original bulb. This made it almost impossible for them to move or make anything of themselves, so they remained lazy and idle out of sheer inertia.

That's my opinion, anyway, said Chikako to herself, as she brought herself back out of her thoughts. The taxi driver was still talking.

"What do you think about that, Ma'am?" he asked.

"Of course, I agree . . . I think," Chikako said, nodding mechanically, but it was enough to keep the driver going.

"I knew you'd agree. We just can't depend on the U.S. to take care of us forever, now, can we? We should start an army and bring in the draft. That would straighten these kids out. I mean, what would we do if a war started? Young people nowadays would sell Japan down the river if they thought there'd be something in it for them. You can just hear them: 'Seeing as we've got this far, we could always annex ourselves to America. Just think of the opportunities! I could go to Hollywood and be a movie star!'"

While Chikako had been lost in thought, the driver had gone off on quite a tangent. Chikako chuckled wryly to herself. Just as she was about to redirect the course of the conversation and comment on the heavy traffic, her cell phone rang.

"Ishizu speaking," she answered.

She felt the driver's eyes looking at her questioningly in the rearview mirror. Chikako looked down.

It was Shimizu calling her from his desk in the arson squad office. He was clearly in a hurry as he demanded to know where Chikako was. She replied that she was in a taxi on her way to Arakawa. Shimizu raised his voice.

"Great! Get to the Aoto intersection—that's Aoto in Katsushika. Do you know where it is?"

"Yes, I know it. What's up?"

"More burned bodies."

"What?" Chikako lifted her face, and she could see the taxi driver tense up.

"A coffee shop called Currant near that intersection. Three fatalities. The corpses are just like at the Tayama factory—broken necks and severe burns."

"But how . . . ?" Chikako was sure that the same person was behind both the Arakawa and Tayama murders—a serial killer, but how could he have done it again so soon? "I'm on my way," she finally responded.

"Me too," said Shimizu. "We'll meet up there."

Chikako cut the connection and asked the driver to change destination. They had just stopped at a red light when something occurred to her. "Wait, don't turn yet. Stop here for a moment, please."

She called the Arakawa precinct number and was put on hold for Detective Makihara while he was paged; the lights changed twice while she waited.

"Makihara here."

Chikako was surprised to hear a soft, almost weak voice. He sounded young. Then she remembered that Kinugasa had mentioned that he was good for his age. Chikako quickly gave him her name and briefly explained what she was doing, then she outlined the incident near the Aoto intersection and asked if he could accompany her there.

"I'm in a taxi nearby. I could swing by and pick you up."

Without hesitating, Makihara responded, "I'm on my way. Tell me where you are and any buildings in the area I might recognize."

Chikako read off the name of the intersection displayed under the traffic signal.

"Got it," said Makihara, "I'll meet you there. We'll get there faster that way."

"I'll be standing by the car—it's Toto Taxi. Yellow with two red stripes."

"You said your name was Ishizu, right?"

"That's right. I'm short and round; you'll know me right away!" Chikako said with a chuckle, but Makihara didn't return the laugh.

"I'll be there in five minutes."

When Chikako hung up, she noticed the taxi driver staring at her.

"You're with the police!"

"Yes, as a matter of fact."

The driver slapped himself on the forehead with his white-gloved hand. "And you're pretty high ranking, aren't you, Ma'am?"

Chikako had to laugh.

Detective Makihara arrived within the promised five minutes. Chikako saw a tall, thin man with unusually long arms and legs appear, walking quickly towards the crosswalk on the other side of the street. As he came into view, Chikako thought that if this was Makihara, then she and Sergeant Kinugasa must have a ten year difference in their respective definitions of "young." The man exuded exhaustion as he walked, his long, black coat flapping about his legs. His gait had no hint of drive or energy.

He must be about forty, thought Chikako. And then she wondered how old Kinugasa thought *she* was—maybe she looked much older than she really was. Perhaps that was why he'd described Makihara as "young."

She could picture her colleagues laughing at her if they had a chance to read her mind; just like a woman to spend time thinking about something like that! Meanwhile, the man waiting for the light to change noticed her standing there. He nodded slightly in greeting. So this *was* Makihara. Chikako nodded back.

Makihara ran across the street as soon as the light changed. Chikako looked down at her watch. Exactly five minutes.

"Detective Ishizu?"

"That's correct," said Chikako, sounding more formal than usual. "Detective Makihara? Pleased to meet you." She didn't ask him for his rank because he hadn't asked her. They both got into the taxi.

"Aoto intersection, please," Chikako instructed the taxi driver. The driver no longer seemed inclined to chat. He merely nodded and looked at the two of them from time to time in the rearview mirror.

"Who gave you my name?" asked Makihara as he settled in. His voice was as soft as it had sounded over the phone.

"Sergeant Kinugasa," responded Chikako.

Makihara raised his eyebrows.

"Really? That's a surprise."

Chikako looked him over and tried again to guess his age. Up close, she could see that the firmness of the skin under his eyes and around his mouth meant that he was actually young. Probably in his early thirties. So how come he looked so hunched over and old from a distance? Must be bad posture.

Makihara looked at Chikako, and she noticed that his eyes were clear and attractive.

"What did Kinugasa say about me?"

"He said that if I wanted to know more about the Arakawa incident, you could help me out."

"Is that so?" Makihara was still surprised.

"He said that you were a young but talented detective."

A hint of a smile in Makihara's eyes belied his serious expression, and Chikako half expected him to burst out laughing.

But he kept a straight face.

"Didn't Kinugasa call to let you know I'd be contacting you?"

"No, not a word."

"Then I guess I moved too quickly."

"Kinugasa said I was talented?" Makihara looked straight ahead as he spoke.

"That's right."

"He didn't say I was eccentric?"

Chikako turned to look at him. "No, he didn't say anything like that."

"Really?" Makihara finally laughed a little. When he smiled, his expression became almost childlike. "Now that *is* strange!"

After making that ironic comment, he fell silent. Chikako stopped talking too as they sped along in the taxi. Makihara twisted to face Chikako, his expression still showing surprise.

Abruptly, Makihara said, "Pyrokinesis." It sounded like some kind of incantation. Chikako gave him a puzzled look.

"Pardon?"

"The ability to start fires using willpower," Makihara said, his light-colored eyes fixed on Chikako. "That is the theory I gave the investigation team for the Arakawa incident. I told them they should deepen their knowledge of pyrokinesis in order to proceed with their investigation." He laughed again in a mischievous way. "That must make me sound pretty eccentric to you, doesn't it?"

Shimizu had told her that she should take the taxi to the Aoto intersection, and that Café Currant would be easy to find.

He'd also told her that the sign and the awning over the entrance were untouched—pretty weird, for a fire that had killed three. And it was just as Shimizu had said. The orange-colored sign was in perfect condition, and some curious bystanders were looking up at it. There were two patrol cars in front.

When she explained what they were doing there to the patrolman guarding the site, they were directed to the supervisor. He was an officer Chikako knew from a different department; he gave them a thorough run-down of what they'd found so far, but was vague about whether it was a case that they were going to formally turn over to the arson squad.

Nevertheless he let them take a look inside. The front door was off its hinges, and yellow crime-scene tape led into the dark interior. As they walked in, they could smell the sickly-sweet smell of burned plywood and synthetic paint.

Up to that point, Makihara had remained silent. Chikako had had to introduce him because he seemed unable to do even that. He followed behind her, silently and obediently. He was beginning to remind Chikako of a collie the Ishizu family used to have.

When Chikako was at home, the collie would stick to her, following close behind. He didn't make a sound, and he moved his large body fluidly in a way that made her forget he was even there. She would be reading a magazine on the couch and suddenly find him with his nose right next to her knees.

"How long have you been there?" she'd ask. Then she would scratch behind his ears until his eyes narrowed. If Chikako were weeding in the yard, he would be positioned in one corner of it. If she were washing the car, he would be in the garage. Always waiting in his quiet way. If she was planting tulip bulbs, deeply engrossed in her activity, and someone came to the door, he would slink up and begin circling her to get her attention. That was the way Makihara was behaving now.

How funny that this prickly young man somehow brought to mind her dear old collie. This was the first time she'd thought of him in years, and she almost laughed. What would he do if she told him, "You remind me of a dog I used to have"?

"Have I got something on my face?" he asked. Chikako swiftly came back to her senses. Makihara was standing in front of the overturned refrigerator in the kitchen, looking at her.

"No, nothing," she said with a faint wave of the hand. She pressed her mouth together tightly to keep from smiling and refocused her attention on the crime scene in front of her.

The positions of the victims had been marked with tape. There'd been two dead men on the unwaxed floor of the coffee shop, and the waitress behind the counter. According to the police at the scene, both the men and the woman had been seriously burned but only over small areas, and broken necks were the cause of death. One of the bodies had been lying on its stomach, with its head at such an abnormal angle that it was clear that the neck was broken. The head of another had flopped like that of a broken doll when it was carried away.

The weapon had been fire accompanied by a strong impact wave: the same pattern as with the other murders. But what *was* the weapon?

Glancing around the room, it was clear that it had not been a large fire.

Even so, she could see that it had been stronger in some places than others. The floor was scorched, but the curtains were unburned. The vinyl of the chair next to the facedown corpse had melted into tear-shaped drops. On the other hand, the table legs were unscathed. On the table next to one of the burned chairs was a glass filled with paper napkins; all of the napkins were clean and the glass showed no signs of heat.

Chikako sniffed the air. She had noticed a sickly-sweet smell when they walked in, and that was all. No trace of fire accelerant. The results of the gas chromatography would answer some questions, but she was willing to bet that no starter fluid would be found on the scene. Although, she reminded herself with an inward sigh, that only meant that it wasn't anything known to them. If something new to the arson squad had been used to start the fire, they would be unable to analyze it without a large sample.

Chikako folded her arms and looked down at the tape marking the position of one of the bodies. They had still not identified him, but she was told that he appeared to be a laborer in his late sixties. The other man had appeared to be in his forties: he hadn't been wearing a tie, but he'd had on a sports coat with a thick gold necklace around his neck. His face was severely damaged by fire, but the hair left on the top of his head had retained its perm.

This coffee shop didn't seem the kind to draw in serious-minded professional types on their lunch hour. Chikako was afraid it would take time to identify either of the men. They couldn't even guess what the motive had been or which of the victims the murderer had originally been after.

"Are you about finished here?" the supervisor asked them. Chikako headed for the door while Makihara continued to snoop around the kitchen, but by the time Chikako had taken a deep breath of the outside air, he had joined her on the pavement. His face was devoid of expression.

Chikako thanked the supervisor and told him she would be glad to cooperate if there was anything she could do for him. He accepted this formality, but he was obviously anxious to be rid of both of them. He hadn't received formal instructions to hand the case over to the arson squad. Chikako had appeared on the scene with a mere "there may be a connection with another case under investigation," and had proceeded to get in their way. And if it wasn't already bad enough that Chikako had come, she'd dragged along a detective from another department, too.

"Let's go," Chikako suggested quietly to Makihara while glancing at her watch. What was taking Shimizu so long? As she walked back to the Aoto intersection, Makihara followed silently. He was reminding her more of her dog by the minute.

"What were you looking for at the scene?" asked Makihara.

"Well, I just wanted to make sure it wasn't an ordinary fire." Chikako was honest. If there had been an odor of starter fluid or the floor had been burned away under the bodies, she would have been disappointed.

"What are you thinking, Detective Ishizu?"

Chikako laughed. "I'm not thinking anything. I can't think anything, because everything about this case is so abnormal."

"Abnormal?"

Makihara stopped walking. At the same time, a car came hurtling around the corner, screeching to a halt beside Chikako. Shimizu flew out of the driver's seat.

"You sure took your time," said Chikako in a leisurely fashion, but she stopped when she saw the expression on his face.

"There's another one!" panted Shimizu. "This time at a liquor shop in Yoyogi Uehara. What the hell is going on?"

Shimizu was so worked up that he didn't even notice Makihara. His agitation was more apparent the closer he got to Chikako, and he continued: "It's just the same! Two men and one woman burned to death. But there were also two people shot—a young man and woman. The liquor shop is three stories, and the bodies of the people who were shot were on the roof."

Chikako listened closely to what Shimizu had to say, but couldn't help wondering about his rage.

"All right, I understand. But what are you so mad about?"

Shimizu suddenly looked embarrassed and mumbled, "I'm not mad."

"Well, something has certainly offended you. What's up?"

Shimizu looked around to check if anyone was listening and noticed Makihara for the first time. He yanked his chin in, taken aback.

"Who's this?"

Chikako briefly introduced Makihara, who bowed wordlessly.

Shimizu lowered his voice and whispered to Chikako, "You shouldn't be moving around so much."

"And why is that?"

"What I mean is . . . right after I heard about the Yoyogi Uehara case, I got a call from Captain Ito. He told me that there are orders from the top for the arson squad to stay out of these homicides."

"From the top, eh?"

"Yes, the Captain is angry about it, too. But when you think about it, they're not just about arson. There are guns, and the cause of death is almost always a broken neck. We've been told to stay out of this until we're asked for our opinions on the connection between the suspicious fires and the burns on the corpses."

Makihara suddenly spoke up, cutting cool-voiced into the conversation. "But the burns were not made posthumously. The evidence shows that all of the burns in these cases were made on live victims and the neck injuries occurred simultaneously."

Shimizu was caught off guard, and his eyes flew over to Makihara and then up; Makihara was a full head taller.

"They should be thinking about the weapon—the connection between the cause of death, the burns, and the small fires. These are primarily arson cases and it's a mistake to view them otherwise."

"Well then please offer that advice to Captain Ito at MPD!" Shimizu was indignant now, and he emphasized MPD. "Or would you rather write it up for him?"

Chikako couldn't contain herself any longer—she had to laugh. Now, rather than her dog, Makihara reminded her of her son when he was small. She felt like she was witnessing a set-to between a boy who was a good student but a little odd, and one who was quick but mouthy.

"What are you laughing at?" Shimizu was angry.

"Nothing, nothing at all." Chikako tried to stifle her amusement, and looked over at the car he had arrived in. "By the way, did you get that car and come all the way out here just to pick me up? If all you had to do was tell me to drop the case, you could have used your cell phone."

Shimizu cleared his throat and mustered up a show of concern for her.

"I know you too well—it wouldn't do any good to just call and ask you to come back in."

"So does that mean we can use that car?"

"Well, yes, but . . . What do you want to do?"

"There are some people I'd like to see. If it would look bad for you to go back alone, why not come with us?"

Makihara was quicker to the draw than Shimizu.

"Who are we going to see?"

"People with no connection whatsoever to these three cases. Well, there is a very distant connection. At least, I believe there is. But it is so uncertain that we will not be in danger of contravening Captain Ito's orders."

"That doesn't sound quite right to me," Shimizu looked suspicious.

"I've visited them before. They won't be surprised to see us. Shall we go together?"

Shimizu did not appear convinced, but acted as though he were going to great pains to cooperate with his partner.

"All right then, let's go. I'll drive."

Chikako was sure that he thought he'd better keep an eye on her. She and Shimizu started towards the car, but Makihara didn't move. He thrust both of his hands in his pockets and stood there with a frown on his face.

Chikako stopped and looked back.

"Are you coming or not?"

Makihara thought for a second, looking up at the sky. Then he turned to Chikako and asked, "Since you seem to expect me to go with you, may I assume that we are going to see someone connected to the Arakawa case?"

"That's right."

"But it's not the family of any of the delinquents who were killed there. Isn't that right?" Chikako didn't say anything, but she was pleased that Makihara was so intuitive. "One of those four, however, was a suspect in the abduction and murder of several high school girls. His name was Masaki Kogure, and he was seventeen at the time."

"That's right."

"You want to talk to a family of one of the girls allegedly killed by Kogure. Am I right?"

Chikako was both surprised and gratified.

"I'm impressed," she said.

"It was just a matter of recall." Makihara finally started walking towards the car. "I met the families of those girls, too, after the Arakawa incident. I talked with them over and over. I suspected that the Arakawa murders were an act of revenge on Kogure. The investigation team did not go along with that idea, though."

So Makihara thought it might be revenge, too. She was thankful that Kinugasa had recommended she meet him.

"When I kept bringing up the idea, everyone said it was impossible—that it had not even been proved that Kogure had been behind the murders of the girls, so how could it be punishment for that? I did my best, but had to give up on that line of investigation in the end. I heard a rumor, though, that there was a detective in the MPD arson squad who thought the Arakawa murders were retaliation for the murdered girls. That detective was apparently not involved in the Arakawa investigation."

Makihara was right. At the time, Chikako had just joined the arson squad and she was the one Makihara was talking about. She had done her best to put her opinion forward within the squad, but at the time that was all she could do.

Makihara opened the passenger door and looked directly into Chikako's eyes. His eyes were smiling.

"So it was you, Detective Ishizu." He smiled broadly at his discovery. "And that means you are almost as strange as I am."

Only Shimizu looked uncomfortable.

"So where are we going?"

"Head for Odaiba," Chikako said as she looked at her watch. "Both of them should be home by now. They're probably finished with dinner, too."

Shimizu got in the driver's seat and Makihara climbed in next to him. Chikako got in the back, but grabbed the driver's seat and pulled herself closer to the other two.

"What Makihara says is true. I was interested in the Arakawa homicides, and I had my own opinions on the matter, but I was not involved in the investigation. I was not yet in a position to be. But I was very marginally involved in the case before that, the abduction and murders of the teenage girls, and that, to set the record straight, was why I was interested in the Arakawa incident."

During the days of the high school girl murders, Chikako had been assigned to the Marunouchi precinct. Her work then was mainly clerical: lost and found, issuing traffic accident reports, and so on.

"So, to tell the entire truth, I wasn't actually involved in the investigation of the girls' murders, but . . ." Before Chikako could continue, Shimizu interrupted to needle her.

"And to think you went straight from there to the detective division at MPD. Women get all the lucky breaks!"

"You can call it lucky if you like, but there was a lot of hard work that went into that 'luck,'" Chikako shot back good-naturedly.

Shimizu did not appear convinced. "It was all politics, if you ask me," he grumped with a hint of a smile.

Chikako was used to her junior partner's habit of saying something hurtful but pretending it was a joke and laughing it off as he said it, so that others wouldn't hold him to account for his rudeness. A lot of young people nowadays did that; her son included.

Makihara looked ahead without saying a word. Sitting next to Shimizu, he once again looked old for his age.

Chikako continued. "There was a chief named Tanaka at Marunouchi who used to arrange lectures once a month. The themes varied, and he usually invited an outside expert to talk to us." Chikako counted the topics off on her fingers: "'How to make a neighborhood safe from crime,' 'Crime prevention in apartment buildings,' 'How to teach school children about drug addiction.' There were some really good ones. My division was in charge of running the lectures, but officers throughout the station attended. About the fifth month, the theme was 'Psychological injuries of crime victims.'" Makihara raised his eyebrows as he turned to look at her. "An expert on PTSD came to speak. Since the Kobe earthquake and the subway sarin gas incident, of course, we know all about that, but it was new at the time."

"What's it mean again? Post-traumatic stress disorder?" Shimizu tried to recall what he'd learned. "It's what people get after they've gone through some sort of disaster or been victims of crime, and they can't get over what happened, right?"

"That's right. It affects victims, of course, but it also affects their families and friends."

"Do we really have to think that far?" asked Shimizu. "Isn't that the job of doctors and counselors? We have to deal with cases where the husband who cried so hard at his wife's funeral was actually the one who murdered her. We'd never be able to see a difficult investigation through to the end if we had to worry about the wounds of the victims and survivors."

Shimizu always had lots to say, but he still didn't have much experience to back it up. If asked what he meant by "difficult investigation," he probably wouldn't have an answer. Chikako laughed wryly to herself. Shimizu was being even more his immature self than usual today.

Makihara's tone was level as he retorted, "There are cases that require consideration for the mental damage of victims, even at the initial stages of an investigation."

Shimizu gave Makihara a sidelong glance. "Such as?"

"A good example is rape."

Makihara had clearly won the round, but Shimizu refused to acknowledge it. He tried to close the discussion by mumbling something about not knowing anything about that because he had never questioned rape victims before, but Makihara refused to let him off.

"I see. Well, I guess the arson squad doesn't handle that sort of case."

Shimizu glared at Makihara this time. It was as easy to follow his thoughts as it was to watch pachinko balls spinning around—only you never knew what holes the pachinko balls would fall through, but for Chikako, Shimizu was predictable ninety-nine percent of the time.

He scowled and said, "Precincts are always going to be limited in the cases they handle."

Makihara's expression didn't flicker, and he responded evenly, "That is true."

Shimizu was left with no option but to continue driving in silence.

Chikako tried to get the conversation heading in a more amicable direction.

"Anyway, that lecture was a great success," she picked up again from where she'd left off. "I remember that it went overtime. That's how caught up in the subject we all were. We even held a second session later on the same theme. The lecturer we invited, a psychiatrist, suggested that we hear directly from actual victims and families of victims. Of course, we had to ask if they would be willing to talk to a police study group."

"And did they come?" Makihara asked quickly.

"Yes, they did. The psychiatrist had a group of patients he had been counseling. All of the members agreed that they wanted to help out as many other trauma survivors as they could. They said they would be glad to go anywhere and talk about it if it would help the police or courts to understand people in their position better."

Four people had turned up to speak at the next session. They had either lost family members in violent crimes, or had themselves been victims. "One couple that came had lost their daughter in the serial murders of the high school girls. In fact, they were the leaders of the support group."

Chikako went on to explain that this was the couple they were going to visit now. "At the time, those cases were still under investigation. The mass media was just beginning to report on Masaki Kogure and his gang. When they spoke to us, the psychological wounds of this couple were still raw. The counselor, the psychiatrist we had invited, had told them that it was too soon for them to talk, and urged them not to. But they insisted. They wanted us to listen to them. They wanted us to hear their side while the cases were being investigated and while it was still fresh in their minds. They were both school teachers, and so they also wanted to speak from their position as educators."

Chikako's heart ached again, just thinking about that study session. The couple had been tough, and they had tried their best to stay calm, dry-eyed, and to speak in steady voices, but that had made it all the more agonizing to listen to.

"After the session was over, we saw each of the guest speakers home. That couple lived near my house, so we rode together in the same taxi, and we talked some more on the way home. Especially about the activities of their support group."

"And they made a big impression on you, didn't they?" Shimizu spoke up. "You're always being moved by *something*."

"Well, actually, we did end up becoming friends," Chikako admitted.

They drove the considerable distance from Katsushika to Ariake, by Tokyo Bay, but the roads were not too crowded. The car sped smoothly along the Mito Highway.

"So if they were both teachers . . ." Makihara narrowed his eyes, trying hard to remember, "it must have been Yoko Sada—she was in eleventh grade when she was murdered."

Chikako nodded.

"That's right. She was the second victim. She was tall, and loved playing basketball. After the first girl was killed, her mother told her to be careful on her way to and from school, but Yoko had just laughed and said that nobody would bother picking on someone her size."

The Sadas had not been able to mentally separate their daughter's memory from her love of basketball. They told Chikako that the mere sight of a basketball hoop glimpsed from inside a bus was enough to send them into tears.

"So, what are we going to do when we see these people?" Shimizu asked.

Chikako knew from Shimizu's dissatisfied expression that he wanted to ask her what the point of visiting this couple was. It was almost cute the way he said, "What are we going to do?" when what he really meant was, "What does it matter anyway?"

Night was falling, and the lights in Tokyo were coming on. Chikako spoke slowly as she looked out of the car window.

"In the initial stages of the Arakawa investigation, there were some detectives who sensed a strong link to the murders of the girls. I heard, frankly, that they even went back to the surviving family members to get their alibis for the night of the Arakawa incident. It was from the side that was investigated—the Sadas—that I heard that."

It was a logical move considering the past that Masaki Kogure had.

"That's right. We talked to everyone," said Makihara. "We spoke to all of the families and concluded that none of them seemed suspicious. None of them had the specialized know-how to carry out a murder like that, either. It was at that point that they decided to abandon revenge as a line of investigation. Just like that. They've refused to hear another word about it since."

Makihara sounded tired.

"Yes, but the Sadas have asserted all along that the Arakawa homicides were revenge," said Chikako.

Shimizu began blinking rapidly in excitement.

"So, do they believe that the murderer was a member of one of the families? Are they claiming that it was one of their own group? Do you think they might actually have an idea who did it?"

"No, not quite like that."

"But . . ."

"What the Sadas said was that it was more like an execution than an act of revenge."

"Execution?"

"Right."

Makihara was silent. Shimizu gave him another sidelong glance. Chikako continued, "If it was an execution, the person who murdered Kogure and the three members of his gang wasn't necessarily related to any of the dead girls. It could have been someone outraged that Kogure had escaped legal punishment for what he had done, and who'd decided that he and his accomplices should not be allowed to live. It could have been anyone."

Shimizu spoke more softly now. "That would make it a lynching."

"Exactly."

"There was no proof that Kogure killed those girls. He might have been innocent. He was neither arrested nor formally accused of a crime because there was no physical evidence."

Makihara sighed, and responded.

"If his murder was an act of punishment, the executioner didn't need evidence to prove anything; their own conviction that Kogure had murdered the girls would have been sufficient."

Shimizu seemed to think Makihara's sigh was exasperation at his own remark.

"I know that!" he retorted with a snort.

"As long as you know," Makihara came back.

"What's that supposed to mean?"

"My apologies."

Chikako laughed and broke in.

"Anyway, Masaki Kogure was tried, convicted, and executed by someone who believed that he was behind the high school girl murders. The members of his gang who happened to be along when the killer found him got executed along with him. That's what I believe to be the truth behind the Arakawa case, and that is what the Sadas believe, too. But I haven't told you the most important part yet."

"So, what is *that?*" Shimizu urged angrily.

"If it was an execution, that person will eventually, at least once, let the victims' families know that it was done to avenge the deaths of their daughters: to wield the iron hammer of justice. This is the belief of the Sadas."

There was a short silence that felt almost like a gentle breeze. The car stopped for a red light, and Shimizu took his hands off the steering wheel and scratched his head.

"Now that sounds like . . ." and the hint of a laugh was mixed in with the words. "It sounds like some movie script."

"I don't agree," said Makihara. "It's not an unreasonable notion. I'd say that the victims' families might not be the only ones who get a sign. It might come as a declaration sent out to the mass media; a declaration of execution rather than an admission of a crime."

"There's been nothing like that so far."

"Not so far. We have no idea what might happen, though. We only know that Kogure was suspected to be the ringleader of the high school girl killings. Some of his gang who would have been in on it with him are still alive and well. The executioner might be planning an announcement when all of them are taken care of."

"But could anyone find all of the members without some sort of organization or investigative powers?"

"We don't know about that either. The executioner might be a part of an organization or some sort of group, and not working alone."

The atmosphere in the front was getting tense again, and Chikako leaned forward once more to separate the two men.

"Shimizu, take the next left, please." Shimizu hurriedly switched on his blinker. If Chikako had still been a patrolwoman, the way he was driving would have made her want to pull him over and slap him with a warning.

Once the car had merged comfortably with the flow of traffic, Shimizu spoke up again.

"The idea of an organization of executioners is just too farfetched. Let's all remember that we're police, not scriptwriters. Let's try to stick to reality."

Again, Makihara sighed deeply and meaningfully. Chikako interpreted it as saying, "Nobody here has declared that this series of murders was carried out by an organization of executioners," and she had to laugh.

"Of course, everything we've said is no more than theory. But the Sadas did say," Chikako looked at Shimizu's scowling face and continued, "that if this theory happened to be correct, it would be a good idea to have a victims' support group that would be in charge of collecting information. What they want to say is that, if by chance the murders *were* executions, and supposing they *were* carried out by a party who at some point wanted to send a message to the families, it would be important that the message was received. The families also want to be able to get a message out to this third party executioner and ask him to send them a message."

Makihara nodded slowly, "I see."

"And just how would they make such a request?"

"Through magazines or newspapers."

"That sounds like an unreliable way to go about it."

"You're right. They do have a website. Of course, they're not coming right out with any statements addressed directly to a judge-and-executioner who fits their hypothesis. They are just asking for information about the murders of the girls and inviting families of other victims of violent crimes to join them."

Shimizu seemed to be struggling but was finally able to come to terms with it.

"So, what we're going to do is go to the Sadas and ask if they have any new information."

Chikako pointed out in front of the car. A high-rise apartment building emerged out of the night.

"That's it. I'll give them a call." She took out her cell phone and pushed the button to dial the number she had recorded for the Sadas. It rang twice before it was picked up.

"Ah! Detective Ishizu!" It was Mrs. Sada. She sounded excited. "At last we got hold of you. We've been trying all afternoon!"

10

The Sada's apartment was on the eleventh floor of a high-rise apartment building in the trendy Odaiba area, overlooking the sea. It was small, and stuffed full with furniture and other belongings, but it felt warm and homey rather than cluttered.

The family altar, the resting place for the soul of the couple's only child, was positioned in a prominent spot, facing the living-room window.

"Yo-*chan*, Detective Ishizu is here!" Mrs. Sada addressed the altar in a cheerful voice, and lit a candle in front of it. Chikako went over to the altar to look at the small photo of a girl in her school uniform. It was black and white, but one could clearly see a healthy tan on the face of the sports-loving girl. Chikako lit a stick of incense and placed her hands together in prayer.

The other two detectives followed suit. Makihara spent a long time with his hands joined, and then looked back at Mrs. Sada questioningly.

"I see there's no posthumous Buddhist name on the name tablet."

The tablet was inscribed only with "Yoko," her given name.

Mrs. Sada nodded, looking over at the altar.

"We thought she would be happier having us call her Yoko rather than a difficult afterlife name."

As they settled down on the bright cloth-covered sofa, Chikako introduced the other two detectives. On hearing that Makihara had been on the investigation team of the Arakawa case, the Sadas exchanged a glance.

"We met a number of the investigation team detectives, but I don't think we've seen you before," remarked Mrs. Sada.

"A lot of detectives came to see us around that time," added her husband.

Makihara glanced over at Yoko's name tablet and then answered.

"Yes, for a while the team went around checking up on the families of victims from the high school girl murders."

"Actually, that's why we dropped by," Chikako added. "But before that, I'd like to hear what you wanted to tell me. Did something happen?" she asked the Sadas.

"Well then, first of all we've got something to show you." Mrs. Sada rose lightly, disappearing for a moment into the next room, and returned with a sheaf of computer printouts in her hand. "We printed up the email messages that we've received since this morning's news of the murders at the Tayama factory."

Chikako accepted the bundle and ran her eyes over the pages. Most of the messages were short, at most about ten lines, but some filled an entire page.

"All the members of our survivor's support group use their real names along with their email nicknames, but we have no idea of the identity of people who contact us through the website. About half of these are anonymous."

Nodding, Chikako raised her eyes from the pages. "Did you find something in particular in these messages?"

Mr. Sada stretched out a hand, pointing in the practiced way of all teachers. "On the third page, second message from the top."

It was an email from someone using the name "Hanako." Chikako read aloud for the benefit of the other two detectives.

Hello. I've been visiting your homepage occasionally for the past six months. This morning, there was another strange murder case on the news—it seems a lot like the Arakawa case, doesn't it? To tell the truth, I used to live near the site of the Arakawa murders. I was still in school when it happened, and for a while there was a rumor going around that it was a gang falling-out, and that the leader of the group that did it might be in our school—a guy a couple grades ahead of me. I've no idea where he is now or what he's doing. But maybe you could check into it.

Shimizu, who had been minding his manners, must have begun to loosen up in the homey atmosphere of the Sadas' apartment, because suddenly his true colors came out and he broke in petulantly.

"What is this? It's just a false lead, and it's pretty late to be feeding it to us. To begin with, Masaki Kogure wasn't a student at the time, so it's not likely he'd be fighting with troublemakers at a local school."

Chikako looked over at the Sadas, about to try to smooth this over, but they were both smiling brightly.

"You're right, Detective Shimizu, this information doesn't sound reliable. But a bit further on . . ." Mrs. Sada was pointing to the next page. "It's the same Hanako, mailing us again. Now *that*—"

It was indeed Hanako again, and this message had arrived later, in the afternoon. Chikako read aloud once more.

```
I called an old friend during lunch break. She still lives
near the Arakawa site, so she remembers more about it than
I do. She said that for about a year after the murders,
a tall, skinny guy who looked about thirty years old
often came to look at the site. She assumed that he was a
policeman. But I noticed when I looked at your website
that police officers don't visit crime scenes alone, so I
thought I'd mention it. What if there were a thirtyish,
tall, thin man hanging around the Tayama site?
```

As Chikako lifted her eyes from the page, Makihara reached for it.

"A thirtyish, tall, thin man, huh?" Chikako repeated for confirmation, and Shimizu cut back in again.

"Look, Ishizu, this message isn't any more reliable than the last one. The Arakawa homicides happened ages ago. At this late date something or other about some man . . . we can't take it seriously—"

Chikako gave Shimizu a little smile. To silence him. All Japanese mothers acquire this technique to stop mouthy children in mid-sentence—at least that's the way it was up through Chikako's generation.

"So is there anything about this man that rings a bell?"

The Sadas nodded in unison. Mrs. Sada spoke, "It sounds like Tada, we thought."

Makihara swiftly raised his eyes from the printouts.

"Do you mean Kazuki Tada? Yukie Tada's elder brother?"

The Sada couple looked surprised. "Do you know him?"

"I saw his name once on a list of people whose alibis we were asking for just after the Arakawa incident. Kazuki and his father, too."

"His mother passed away soon after the Arakawa murders. She'd been in the hospital for a long time."

"Who's Yukie Tada?"

Chikako turned to Shimizu and began to explain.

"Yukie Tada was one of the murdered high school girls, like Yoko Sada. Her elder brother's name is Kazuki."

Mrs. Sada picked up the thread.

"The murder of Kazuki Tada's little sister ruined their mother's health and broke up their family. When we started our little survivors' group, we tried calling Kazuki and his father to see if they'd join us, but they insisted they just wanted to be left alone. For a while we were hearing that Kazuki wasn't doing well at all, and though we didn't want to interfere, we were worried and we kept on calling. But nothing worked . . ."

"Did you ever see him in person at that time?" asked Makihara.

"No, it was all just by phone. Kazuki had left his parents' home and was living alone. He was at work during the day and came home at different times, so even when we tried dropping in we'd miss him. But we still pestered him to keep in touch."

"But why would this Kazuki Tada be the guy in Hanako's email?" asked Shimizu. His question was perfectly timed.

"That's exactly it. Although he refused to meet us when we contacted him soon after his sister was murdered, he later went to the trouble of looking us up. It was after we'd started the website, right after the Arakawa murders. He came to see us."

"He came here, you say?" Makihara repeated for confirmation.

"That's right. But we couldn't figure him out. It wasn't that he wanted to get involved in our activities, and he wasn't looking for comfort or counseling. He just seemed to have been deeply shocked about Masaki Kogure's murder."

"Shocked? Not crowing?" Makihara's brow furrowed slightly. "He seemed disturbed?"

"Well . . . confused. When he came to visit us, the killings had just taken place and the shock was still fresh, so it was only natural, I guess."

"But it's not like he did it, right?" demanded Shimizu. "The investigation team checked up on all the families of Kogure's victims and ruled them out as suspects."

Shimizu was always like this. It was clear from his tone that he harbored no doubts that anything the police did could be mistaken in any way. Having this much belief and pride in the organization to which he belonged must make him a pretty happy guy, mused Chikako.

"No, not Tada," agreed Mrs. Sada. "He doesn't have that kind of cruelty in him. But he did love his sister, and he wasn't able to forgive her murderers, so he was suffering. If he'd been able to simply kill Kogure for what he'd done, he wouldn't have been in the kind of pain he was in."

The Sadas themselves were no different, thought Chikako.

"And then? After that visit, did you see more of Tada?" prompted Makihara.

"Well that's it—it didn't go awfully well. He seemed strange . . . We didn't know why he'd come—or what he wanted from us. As for the Arakawa killings, he said he wasn't interested in the details. He said Masaki Kogure had gotten what he deserved, and he didn't care who'd done him the favor, and that he'd told the police who'd come to question him the same thing . . . talk like that," said Mrs. Sada.

Mr. Sada added, "He certainly didn't want to go to the crime scene, he said. We had gone. Somehow we couldn't settle down until we had been to see for ourselves where Masaki Kogure and his friends had died. But you can bet we didn't leave any flowers."

"So Tada was being stubborn?" asked Chikako.

"Maybe. We were scratching our heads for a while, trying to figure out what he'd come for all of a sudden. We finally decided that probably he'd been feeling bad and just wanted to talk with us since we had all shared the same experience. But then we lost all contact again . . ."

Shimizu made a face that said, *So what?* and Chikako sent him another chilly smile.

Mr. Sada cleared his throat and continued, "Well, we were pretty slow on the uptake, but after Tada's visit we were busy meeting various people, organizing incoming information, and holding little gatherings, so before we knew it about six months had passed. Then suddenly it hit us. He had wanted information. So when the investigation of the murders was discontinued, it was our website that maintained the most information related to the cases. He knew we'd have information and letters coming in from all over Japan, and he'd wanted to access that. So he came to see us face to face. He might have been checking to see if he wanted to have more to do with us. But in the end, he obviously didn't . . ."

"What would he have done with that information?" asked Shimizu.

"I don't know. But we can make a guess. If he could get a good picture of the entire series of murders, and how they connected with the Arakawa riverside killings, and whether or not there was anyone left who needed to face judgment, and if there was, where they were . . . that's probably what he was searching for."

"That's the job of the police," snorted Shimizu.

"But it was left unfinished, wasn't it?" Mrs. Sada returned briskly.

Shimizu's face took on the expression of a stubborn child, and he replied, "But we don't really *know* what Kazuki Tada was thinking or doing. All this talk is nothing more than speculation!"

"Of course." Mr. Sada's voice reflected a teacher's ability to remain calm and still be persuasive. He took in Shimizu's protest as though he were catching a football—then threw it back. "But that's where the email message that came in today becomes a problem. Kazuki Tada is tall, and after his sister's murder, he lost a lot of weight. We heard that he'd gotten some back at one point, but when he visited us, he was nothing but skin and bones. So looking at this Hanako's message, we think the person who was hanging around the Arakawa site could have been Tada."

"I see." Makihara's answer was appropriate, but Chikako noticed that his eyes were still racing across the printout pages.

"He told us that he had no interest in going to the Arakawa site, when actually he was going there so often that people remembered seeing him. Which would mean our original suspicions were right, and that Tada was looking for information. Searching, and doing his own investigation."

"Then he might show up at the new crime scenes," said Chikako. "If he wants information. Anybody can see the similarity between the Arakawa killings and today's series of murders."

"Yes, that's why we wanted to get in touch with you. We thought that this time there might be a chance that you'd be able to find Tada."

Shimizu blinked in surprise.

"By 'find Tada,' does that mean you don't know where he is now?"

"We've no idea. Soon after his mother passed away he quit his job, moved out of his apartment, and according to his father, hasn't been home in two years. He just calls once in a while."

Chikako understood the situation immediately. "I see. I'll be careful— and if I run across him, I'll be sure to let him know that you're concerned about him."

Relief spread across the Sadas' faces.

"Oh, how rude of me, I forgot to make you all something to drink!"

Mrs. Sada jumped up, passing by the family altar and hurrying into the kitchen. The flowers set in front of Yoko's tablet fluttered as she passed. It looked to Chikako as though Yoko was waving at them—laughing and saying, "My mom's such a scatterbrain!"

As they drank the delicious coffee Mrs. Sada made for them, Chikako explained their own reason for coming. In view of the email they'd just been shown, the explanation went quickly.

If the motive of the person who killed Masaki Kogure and committed this string of new murders was punishment and execution, there was a possibility that they would somehow announce themselves—and when they did, they might use the Sada's website. The Sadas listened carefully to what Chikako had to say.

"We'll keep a close eye on our incoming email, then. You really could be right about that."

Chikako moved to temper their expectations.

"But please don't think about it too much. The murders today were in three separate locations. And the death count looks double that of the Arakawa killings. The method appears identical, but if the perpetrator is the same as the Arakawa killer, we really have to wonder what the motive was."

Mr. Sada frowned deeply and glanced over at his daughter's picture.

"You're right, it's too much killing . . ."

"Have the victims of today's murders been identified?" asked Mrs. Sada.

"No, not yet."

"When they are, there may be a number of things to reconsider. Especially if the victims were just innocent citizens who weren't doing anything wrong," Mrs. Sada noted.

The Sadas invited them all to dinner, but they declined and left. Shimizu said he needed to return the car.

"Well, then, I think I'll take that new Yurikamome monorail home," said Chikako.

"You're not going to stop back at MPD?"

"There'd be no point going back today. The arson squad's been told to pull out, anyway. I'll go home and write up a report for Captain Ito to look over."

"I'll get myself home, too," said Makihara.

Shimizu made a face that clearly said, "Nobody asked *you*." Chikako was still smiling to herself when the squad car lights disappeared from sight, around a corner.

"Aren't you glad you met the Sadas?" Chikako asked, looking up at the side of Makihara's melancholy face. The Sadas had given him the wad of printouts and it was clasped under his arm. As the winter night wind blew, his coat tails and the papers flapped together in unison.

He responded without directly answering Chikako's question.

"I wonder about Kazuki Tada."

"Yes, I wonder what he was intending to do? Getting to the bottom of the Arakawa case would be impossible to do on his own, I'd think."

Chikako started off walking. Makihara followed a half-step behind, deep in silence. Chikako assumed he would be taking the train with her, but just as the Odaiba station came into sight he spoke up again.

"Well, good-bye. Thanks a lot."

"You're not taking the train?"

"I want to walk around a little more."

"But it's cold . . ."

"I need to think about something."

Before Chikako could ask what about, Makihara said in a rush, "I can't get it off my mind—who is Kazuki Tada searching for?"

And before Chikako could question him further, he was gone.

11

Junko was tired. Her footsteps began to falter from fatigue as she neared her apartment. Her wounded shoulder had started bleeding again, too.

She let herself in, fell into bed and was soon fast asleep. She didn't know if it was three or thirteen hours later, but at some point she opened her eyes and unbearable thirst sent her to the refrigerator for a drink. Then, still dressed as she had been when she arrived home, she fell back into bed. From the dim light outside the window, she guessed it must be dusk.

The next time she woke, the sun was shining brightly. Junko got up and staggered to the bathroom. Then, thirsty again and lightheaded with hunger, she searched the fridge and found some cheese, bread, and ham. Mechanically, she prepared a sandwich and wolfed it down.

After the food had settled a bit, she began to feel human again, and at last noticed what a mess she was. Her underwear and shirt had been soaked through with sweat during her battles. She was covered in mud, and blood from her wound had soaked through her clothes and become dry and crusted. She realized her bed sheets and pillowcase must be filthy, too. She'd have to wash everything. Lost in these thoughts, she gazed out at the sunlight on the balcony, and it occurred to her to wonder what time it was. How long had she been sleeping?

The hands on her little living room clock pointed to five minutes past noon. She'd slept all night and through the entire morning.

She switched on the TV to get the noon news broadcast. The date was displayed on the screen, and Junko was astonished to see that a full two days had passed since her visit to Sakurai Liquors.

She changed channels and found a daytime tabloid show that was broadcasting from Yoyogi Uehara, right in front of the store. A blue plastic sheet covered the entrance where Junko had blown out the door. Without meaning to be she was drawn into the program, narrowing her eyes at the TV screen like a cat sighting its prey. Asaba was dead—she suddenly had a vivid memory of his body falling on her as she opened the door of the elevator control room.

Who had shot Asaba? Who else had been up there with Junko and Natsuko?

Nothing she saw in the report answered those questions. The police investigation hadn't gotten that far yet. Junko shook her head and stood up, went and got some mineral water from the fridge, and downed the whole bottle in one go.

She turned the channel back to the news. She watched for a while as it reported that other members of Asaba's group had been pulled in during a police sweep and were being held in custody. Apparently the gang had been running speed and toting underground guns, and had carried out numerous assaults and armed robberies over the past couple years. The gang members who were lucky enough not to have been at Sakurai the same evening as Junko were now murder suspects. The police were taking the view that what happened at the liquor store was the result of a falling out within the gang.

The gang's last victims had been identified as Kenji Fujikawa and Natsuko Mita. They'd been twenty-six and twenty-three respectively, and had both worked for a Tokyo computer firm.

Junko recalled how thin and pale Natsuko's shoulders had been. Regret and guilt lashed Junko like a double-stranded whip. *If only she'd gotten Natsuko out a little sooner. If only she'd stayed by her side, not letting her out of sight.*

Natsuko had been shot dead, too. Junko remembered what she had said just before she was killed. She had caught sight of somebody and had called out: *I know someone's there. Oh, it's* you!

From the way she'd said it, it was clear that Natsuko had known that "someone."

As for why both Asaba and Natsuko had been murdered, the police theory was that there had been a disagreement within the group over what to do with Natsuko once they had her confined at Sakurai Liquors, and that the tensions within the gang had boiled over into a full-fledged battle. An anchor and a reporter were discussing the incident with evident anger.

Presently, a youth with his face obscured by a pixellated mosaic appeared on the screen. He was a member of the Asaba gang, but hadn't been present at the scene, nor was he currently under arrest. His voice, answering the reporter's questions, was also modified to make him unidentifiable.

When did you begin hanging out with Asaba?
—About six months ago.
How did that come about?
—My friend brought me along one time, and I just sorta joined.
What did you do with the group?
—I dunno. I didn't do that much.
But you got arrested for auto theft, didn't you?
—Asaba made me do it.
So you did do it, isn't that right?
—Yeah, but Asaba slugged me for getting caught, so I kinda stopped hanging out there.
You got scared?
—Yeah. My friend got scared of Asaba, too. And mad—he was saying Asaba was a real asshole.
Why was he mad?
—Asaba always got all the money and when he got pissed off at you, he and the others went straight for your throat.
The money from selling speed?
—Yeah, and other stuff. Asaba always had a lot of money on him.
Did other members have fights with Asaba?
—Not fights exactly, but, y'know, they argued a lot.
Over what?
—Lots of things, I don't really remember.
You don't remember anything?
—Asaba'd go too far and someone'd try to stop him, and then Asaba'd have it out with him. I was scared so I just pretended not to notice anything.

Junko got up and went to the bathroom to run hot water for a bath. The steam felt good as it rose and touched her face. She returned to the living room, where the anchor and reporter were still talking.

"According to our teenage witness, there were regular incidents of discord within the group. We understand that police investigating these murders believe there is a connection between the internal problems and the spree of violence."

"That's right. There are still many unanswered questions, and it's too early to draw conclusions, but that does seem to be the most likely explanation."

"Similar incidents took place in three separate locations over a twenty-four hour period. First the victims, Kenji Fujikawa and Natsuko Mita, were abducted in a Tayama parking lot about five hundred meters from the factory where Fujikawa's body was found. Then there was the Sakurai Liquors store in Yoyogi Uehara, where the gang had reconvened and were holding Ms. Mita captive. About two hours preceding the fire at Sakurai Liquors, however, there was another similar fire at a coffee shop in Aoto, Katsushika Ward. There were three fatalities there. What seems to be the connection between this incident and the other two?"

"It's hard to say. The casualties in the Aoto incident were not teenagers, so it is still not clear whether there was a direct connection. But because of the similarities with the other two incidents, such as the fire and burns on the victims' bodies, the police are currently treating it as part of the same investigation."

So the police had not yet figured out that Tsutsui, the man she'd met at Café Currant, had been the supplier of Asaba's black market guns. Junko bit her lip, recalling that she'd taken out the leering male customer and the waitress, leaving no witnesses to fill in the blanks on that matter. At the time, her momentum had been stronger than any inclination to care what happened to them.

The reporter was holding a map of the area around Sakurai Liquors and was explaining something. Mr. Sakurai, a widower and the owner of the liquor store, had started seeing Asaba's mother about a year before, and they'd lived together for six months. When the mother had moved in, Asaba soon followed. He and his gang used Sakurai's home as their hangout.

Sakurai had regretted this development immediately and had tried to throw them out. When the neighbors began complaining, Sakurai had instead turned to them for advice about how to get rid of the punks, but Asaba's mother seemed to have had the final word in their relationship and his efforts hadn't gotten anywhere. He'd survived only because he'd been out making deliveries at the time of the fire, and it was reported that he was cooperating fully with police inquiries.

According to Sakurai, Asaba could do no wrong in his mother's eyes even though she had known about the majority of his criminal activities. *That's no surprise—they were doing it right under her nose,* thought Junko. *And this Sakurai had seen everything too, and had turned a blind eye. Because he was scared. Because he wanted to stay in Asaba's mother's good graces.* It really was a pity that he'd been out when she'd gotten there, thought Junko. She'd have liked to incinerate him, too.

The bath was full, so Junko pulled herself away from the TV and got in. The dried blood on her shoulder covered a crater-like wound, and she winced in pain as she submerged herself in the bath.

It was a small tub, but she stretched out as far as she could into a relaxing position, resting her head and closing her eyes. Hazy images swam through her mind, their shapes unclear but their color distinct. The color of fire: the color she was proud of, the color she loved best.

By gently moving a washcloth over her shoulder, Junko managed to remove the dried blood, and she got a good look at the wound itself. Her skin was torn up, but she couldn't see any bone. So it wasn't all that deep after all. If she took care to avoid infection, it would probably be okay. Relieved, she closed her eyes again.

The hazy images became clearer. Asaba's face, in death, floated up before her. Then his mother's face as she lunged at Junko. Whether that woman's little bar had gone under on its own or the building's owner had evicted her, she'd had to take her business elsewhere. So she'd found new prey, latching on to the owner of Sakurai Liquors. She'd put one over on him, getting her son and his friends in there; she'd basically hijacked his business and his home.

There'd probably been other victims at Sakurai Liquors before Kenji Fujikawa and Natsuko Mita. How much sweat and blood, and how many screams had been absorbed by that rumpled pile of bedding in the rooms over the store? How could Asaba's mother have been so unconcerned when all that was going on in her own home? How *could* she?

The black-market gun dealer Junko had killed at Café Currant had been the same. He only did it for the money, but he was certainly aware of what people could do with those guns. He had decided that it didn't concern him and faked his own ignorance. How *could* he?

Junko opened her eyes, gazing at the pastel pink ceiling. The room was full of warm, peaceful steam and the faint aroma of soap.

I can't understand it.

She'd seen a lot of bad things. She'd seen a lot of evil people. Keiichi Asaba's brand of evil could be found anywhere. It was unbelievably common. Guys like that were the dregs of society, and as long as society was a living, functioning organism, they could never be eradicated. They had to be exterminated when they appeared. That was all.

But the brand of evil exemplified by Asaba's mother and the gun dealer was another matter altogether. They rode on the coattails of evil—they were willing accessories to it. They brought immeasurable harm to society with their negligence and avarice. They were not purely evil like Asaba; they didn't have it in them to act independently. They were secondary evils, sticking to their primary source as long as it carried them along.

So they all had to fry, that was all there was to it.

Junko had no doubts about what she had done, no misgivings or pain. Or at least, that's what she told herself.

It was late afternoon when she finally called into work. The café manager was angry about Junko's unexplained absence and told her she was fired.

Junko didn't offer any arguments. Actually it would be better not to have to work for a while. She could use the extra free time, so it was almost what she'd have wished for.

She went out shopping and bought a pile of different newspapers at the first convenience store she happened by. Without exception the Asaba gang story had made headlines on all the front pages. Junko casually tossed the papers into her shopping basket, picked up some chocolates and boxes of cookies, and took them to the register.

She invariably craved sweets after releasing a lot of power. She could consume a box of cookies in one sitting. It seemed unbelievable that such intense energy was fueled by something as prosaic as sugar, but that was the way it was. It had been like that since she was a child.

Junko's parents had put her through grueling practice sessions, trying to teach her to control her power. Afterwards, they would always take her to an ice cream parlor or cake shop. "You can have whatever you want," her father would say, lightly stroking her head. She could recall the touch of his hand even now.

Her parents had both been completely normal. They were gentle, honest people. Neither of them had the power Junko had; it had been passed down to her by her grandmother on her mother's side. Junko's mother had told her how difficult it had made her own mother's life.

Your grandmother was a great and beautiful woman. And she was really strong, too. She was a true champion of justice. But your father and I prayed that you wouldn't be born with the same power, we knew how hard it was for her. But you were born with it, Junko. So your father and I will think very hard about helping you learn to use it right, so you can be happy. Don't worry.

"Mom . . . Dad . . ." Junko whispered to herself, as she remembered her parents.

Junko's father had died in a work-related accident when Junko was in high school. Junko's mother never recovered from the shock of losing him, and when she herself died two years later, Junko was truly alone.

Thanks to the savings and insurance her parents had left her, and some property inherited from her grandmother, Junko was able to live comfortably. She had a lawyer taking care of her assets, so she didn't have to spend time worrying about how to manage them. As long as she lived simply, she didn't always have to work.

But Junko didn't intend to withdraw from the world. In order to use her power the way her parents had expected her to, she had to stay involved with society. She had to keep herself, the loaded gun that she was, aimed in the right direction.

Back at her apartment, she heard the phone ringing as she stumbled inside, both hands full of bags. It stopped ringing before she could pick it up.

Who could that be? Junko didn't have any friends who were close enough to call her. At least not since she'd moved to Tayama.

Then about thirty minutes later, as she was making a salad in the kitchen, it rang again. This time she flew over and reached it in time.

"Hello?"

The other end was silent. *It's just a prank call*, she thought, anticipation ebbing away.

"Hello? Who's calling, please?" she asked once more, loudly. She was reaching to hang up when—

"You're Junko Aoki, right?" It was a man's voice, and there was a teasing ring to it. Junko quickly brought the phone back to her ear.

"Hello?"

"Hello, Ms. Junko Aoki." A young man, with a clear, unhesitating voice.

"Excuse me, who is this?"

"I can't tell you that," replied the man. "We don't know enough about you yet. To tell the truth, I'm not even supposed to contact you, but I wanted to hear your voice. You've got a nice voice."

Junko stiffened. *Who the hell was this?*

"What is this? What are you talking about?"

The man laughed, an unexpectedly refreshing laugh.

"It's okay, don't worry about it. I'll visit you to introduce myself properly, okay?"

"Who *are* you?"

There was a moment's pause before he answered.

"A Guardian."

"A what?"

"Guardian. As in 'protector.'" With another teasing laugh, he continued. "It's okay, you don't have to understand. You will soon enough. I just wanted to let you know that we're impressed with the way you work." Almost as an afterthought he cheerfully tacked on, "And that you're very pretty. Okay, bye!"

The connection was cut and Junko was left, astounded and alone.

12

During the two days Junko Aoki was sleeping soundly and healing her wound, Chikako Ishizu was watching the shock waves from Junko's battles spread before her eyes. Not as a participant in the investigation team, but as an onlooker.

The investigation team had quickly interpreted the three cases, or at least the Tayama factory and the Sakurai Liquors cases, as fallout from escalating friction within Asaba's gang. While they didn't go so far as to announce their interpretation at a press conference, they did leak it to individual reporters on the police beat. The mass media took it up under headlines that competed for sensationalist effect: "Violent teens," "Sharp rise in vicious crimes by juveniles," and "Call to revise the Juvenile Protection Act"—all followed by articles that were portraits of cold-blooded criminal teens with no respect for human life.

Chikako was certainly not among the adherents to this theory. The mass media could speculate as much as they liked, but the investigation was just beginning.

It did seem, however, that the "arson squad, stay out" order from above that Shimizu had told her about had indeed been real. Captain Ito told Chikako directly that there was other work he wanted her to do.

"And what might that be?" She'd involuntarily responded as though she were interrogating him. Captain Ito looked up at Chikako's round face with a wry grin.

"Hey, don't bristle at me like that." Chikako dropped her eyes from his face to his hands while she worked to calm herself down. Rare for men of his generation, Ito always wore his wedding ring. The elegant white gold band looked almost out of place, shining on his rough hand. "I know what you're thinking and you're probably right. There has to be a connection between the latest incidents and the Arakawa case."

"Then—"

Ito raised a hand to stay her words.

"But we can't go saying that openly right now. If we bring up the revenge theory, they're just going to say, 'Okay, then what was the weapon? And if it was revenge, are you talking about one revenge seeker? Or two? How could just one or two people pull off a killing spree like that?' They'll jump all over us! Worse, they could reject it out of hand, making it harder to bring up later."

Chikako recalled her cool reception at the crime scenes the day before. And the melancholy expression of Makihara, who'd been pressing for the revenge theory all along.

"We should prepare ourselves discreetly. Let the others handle the frying pan while it's hot, and we'll collect information and watch for our chance. We'll certainly get an opportunity to step in later, so showing up to look around yesterday was a good move."

In other words, the purpose of her visit to the sites had been to introduce herself to the teams working there. Without the least intention of meddling, merely to humbly express the arson squad's interest in these cases.

Chikako eventually acknowledged his words with a nod and said, "I see. Well, what is the other case you mentioned?"

The captain opened his desk drawer and withdrew a single file in a plastic case. It wasn't an official case record folder.

He laid it on his desk and indicated it to Chikako with a nod. "This."

Chikako picked up the untitled file. Flipping through the pages she could see they were crammed with carefully printed script. It looked like a woman's writing.

"Take a close look at it, please. If possible, I'd like you to help out the detective who wrote this report. Not just because you're on the arson squad, but because she needs the advice of an experienced female detective."

Chikako sensed an undercurrent to his tone—something that was not usually there—and she looked curiously at his face. Ito glanced around, then leaned slightly forward and lowered his voice.

"It's not easy to talk about, so can you promise to listen without getting mad?"

"Hmm?"

"The detective who wrote this report is working in the juvenile section at the Tokyo Bay precinct. She's twenty-eight now and has been a plainclothes detective for barely five years. She was following in her father's footsteps when she joined the police. He was my mentor."

So that was it. Chikako smiled.

"So for you, Captain, this young detective is just like a daughter?"

Ito smiled back. "Daughter? Now that's stretching it! Let's just say she's more like a much younger sister. She's still inexperienced, but she's a go-getter. Actually this file is something she passed to me privately to get my opinion on. So putting it in your hands is exceeding my authority in a way, but—" His smile vanished, and his voice got even lower. "But what's in there is pretty interesting. It's about a series of small-scale fires, but they're similar to Arakawa and the current cases in that they're impossible. I think you'll be intrigued."

It was the middle of the night when Chikako eventually finished reading the report. It had been difficult to concentrate on it at work with so many distractions. While logically she knew what the captain had told her was probably right, she couldn't help focusing on the Tayama factory and subsequent fires.

Chikako's husband was working late, so she was alone when she got home. She spread the file out on the dining room table and prepared herself a cup of tea before settling down to read. By the time she was finished, the cup was still untouched and had gone cold. Chikako went back to the kitchen to make a fresh cup.

Yes, it was impossible.

Small fires were repeatedly breaking out around a thirteen-year-old girl living in a high-rise apartment building located in the Tokyo Bay precinct. It looked on the surface like a simple enough case. The fires always occurred where the girl was—in other words, the girl was always at the scene. There had been eighteen fires to date, and in the most recent a classmate of the girl had been taken to the hospital with burns.

This same girl, always at the scene. Pretty suspicious. But the girl continued to deny that she was starting the fires. She insisted she wasn't doing anything; the fires just suddenly "appeared."

According to the report, because the object of investigation was a minor, the Bay precinct investigator appointed to the case was handling it with kid gloves. Apparently, this was not your typical problem teenager. Her grades at school were good and she had no behavioral problems. Her family life was secure. Her father was a branch manager of a large Tokyo bank, and her mother, the daughter of a wealthy doctor, was on the board of a general hospital run by her family. The girl was their only child, and both parents were devoted to her.

Furthermore, the report continued, almost everyone who met and talked with the girl was charmed by her sweet personality and wanted to believe her. But no matter how innocent she professed to be, eighteen fires had occurred in places where she had happened to be. It was circumstantial evidence, but powerful nonetheless.

The circumstances surrounding the appearance of each and every one of the eighteen fires were itemized and recorded. The facts had been recorded with painstaking detail, and no personal speculation had managed to leak in. Chikako read through these carefully, favorably impressed with the writer. Rumors had begun to fly around the girl as the incidents continued, and, clearly labeled as speculation, these were recorded as well. How those rumors were affecting the girl and her parents was noted, too. The detective in charge was undoubtedly a conscientious police officer.

Drinking her tea, Chikako realized she was looking forward to meeting this young detective who was like a favorite daughter to Captain Ito. Michiko Kinuta was her name. What would she be like?

Chikako didn't think the worse of her for using her personal connection with Captain Ito to ask for advice—Michiko Kinuta must be at the end of her rope. Despite appearances, seemingly good people do tell lies, and the other detectives in the Bay precinct juvenile section had already decided that this girl must have started the fires. Michiko alone was anguishing over the matter as well as over another, truly alarming, aspect of these fires; something the other detectives had missed.

There had been some degree of fluctuation over the course of the eighteen fires, but as the number of incidences grew, so did the scale of the fires themselves. In this final one, in which the girl's classmate had been hospitalized, the suspect had also sustained a burn on her finger.

Would the next one be bigger still? And when would it happen? The first one had been when the girl was eleven years and four months old, and had occurred at home. They'd been continuing to occur at three-week to one-month intervals since then. The eighteenth fire had been at the start of the month, fifteen days ago. So it was possible that the nineteenth would take place in a week to ten days from now.

Chikako's husband finally returned at two in the morning. They ate dinner together and were preparing for bed when Chikako grinned to herself, realizing that Captain Ito had succeeded in piquing her interest. He might be right; it might be best for Chikako to get some distance from the Arakawa case and the three new cases. That might yield better results in the end. But her heart had refused to comply, so the captain had thrown something else her way—something really good. Chikako was thoroughly intrigued by this girl's case.

Early the next morning, Chikako called Detective Michiko Kinuta at home. That seemed like the best approach since Captain Ito had passed the report to Chikako privately.

It was barely seven-thirty, and the TV news was starting off its broadcast with updates on the investigations into the three fires. Chikako turned off the sound and watched the screen as she dialed—they were showing the front of what was left of Sakurai Liquors. Her call was answered on the first ring, in the brisk tones of someone already up and about.

"Kinuta speaking."

Her voice was both sweeter and warmer than Chikako had expected. Somehow she'd imagined there'd be a rougher, more assertive ring to it and Chikako had a silent, wry laugh at herself. Even *she* still held the unconscious assumption that there had to be something masculine about a female detective who was able to do well in the still very male bastion of the police force.

"Good morning. I'm Chikako Ishizu, from MPD." Chikako briefly introduced herself and explained that Captain Ito had passed Michiko's file down to her. Michiko seemed taken aback, and as soon as Chikako finished she rushed to apologize.

"I'm really sorry, I hadn't intended to be taking the time of someone at MPD about this, I'd just been hoping to get Un—Captain Ito's advice sometime when he had a chance. I didn't imagine when I gave it to him . . ."

Un—, she'd started to say, and then corrected herself, thought Chikako, smiling. So she must be pretty close to Ito; she'd been about to refer to him as "uncle."

"No need for apologies. To tell the truth, I decided to call you without even discussing it with Captain Ito because this case is very intriguing. I don't know if I can be of any use to you, but would you mind talking it over with me sometime?"

"Oh, of course. Thank you!" Kinuta's voice had brightened. "Any time that would fit your schedule would be fine for me. Actually, I'm off duty today . . ."

"Okay, then how about tomorrow?"

"Well, what I was thinking was that today might be better. I've got plans to spend the day with Kaori-*chan*, and that way you could meet her too."

Chikako was silent for a moment. Kaori-*chan*? Kaori Kurata was the name of the girl in the file, and Michiko had added the affectionate diminutive.

"You're meeting the same Kaori who is suspected of starting the fires? On your day off?"

"Yes," she answered flatly. Chikako suddenly realized that the real reason Michiko had approached Ito for advice was not in that report. The real problem was evidently quite different.

"Detective Kinuta, you've developed a personal relationship with Kaori Kurata?"

It wasn't rare for detectives in a juvenile section to become close to their charges with both investigation and protection in mind. Building up trust helped with criminal rehabilitation, and it tied in with crime prevention as well. But in this case it didn't feel quite right. Kaori Kurata was younger than the kids who were usually in and out of the juvenile section, and Michiko was referring to her from the very start of their conversation as a close friend or family member would. Michiko hadn't said, "I'm going to meet Kaori-*chan*," either. She'd said she was spending the *day* with her. Had she gotten herself in a bit too deep? Although Kaori Kurata was only thirteen years old, she *was* the main suspect in a string of fires.

"Does 'spending the day with her,' mean an outing just for fun?" Chikako pressed.

"You think I'm going too far, too, don't you, Detective Ishizu?" said Michiko Kinuta with a sigh. "I was prepared to hear that from Captain Ito, and I'm already in trouble about it at the precinct."

"I see . . ." said Chikako. But then she fell silent. After a few moments, Michiko spoke again with a slightly revived challenge in her tone.

"Detective Ishizu, aren't you angry? Why don't you tell me that doing it that way will never work for an investigation?"

As often happens, it was Michiko herself who was most affected by the accusation even though it had been she who had voiced it. Clearly worked up, her next words tumbled out quickly.

"I think Kaori Kurata is telling the truth. She's not setting the fires. She's not an arsonist. It's true that there have been a large number of suspicious fires, but she shouldn't be the suspect—she's the victim. I firmly believe that. What do you think, Detective Ishizu? Are you going to yell at me, or just point and laugh?"

Chikako did laugh at that, but gently.

"I don't think I can do *either* yet. I haven't met you or Kaori Kurata. And actually, I like the fact that you told me up front that you were spending the day with her, instead of trying to cover it up."

She ventured speaking from her own long experience as she continued, "But considering the contents of the file, I would guess that you are getting it pretty hard at the precinct for having this relationship with Kaori. I want you to know that even though you are taking her part, I was very impressed with your coolheaded report."

For the first time, Michiko Kinuta laughed. "Thank you very much. Now I'm looking forward to meeting you, too, Detective Ishizu."

They settled on a place to meet and hung up. Then it occurred to Chikako that Michiko might have been testing her. It must certainly have crossed her mind that Captain Ito might not take on her case himself and instead pass it on to someone less senior in his department.

With that in mind, letting that person have it all at once—"I'm off-duty today and I'm spending it with Kaori. I'm on her side. She's not the arsonist"—was pretty smart. If the person got angry or laughed her off, she wouldn't want to ask their help. Since it wasn't an official request, she could send anyone who challenged her packing. She'd probably planned her side of the conversation from the start.

Not a bad head on her shoulders.

Her expectations had risen another notch, and Chikako left home with a spring in her step.

13

Michiko Kinuta was tall. *I seem to be drawing tall people into my life these days,* mused Chikako, eyeing her from a distance.

To describe the building where Kaori Kurata lived as a high-class condominium would be an understatement. It was a stunning skyscraper. Michiko was standing in front of the huge automatic doors at the entrance. Passing through the front garden towards her, Chikako felt like she was walking though an advertisement.

"Detective Kinuta? I'm Chikako Ishizu."

The tall woman blinked and came to herself with a start, focusing on Chikako. "Oh, excuse me, Detective Ishizu. Yes, I'm Michiko Kinuta." She strode over to Chikako, smoothly offering her hand and giving her a firm handshake. "I've told Kaori that I'd be bringing along a fellow detective—" Michiko explained as they passed through the doors. But the luxury of the space on the other side of the doors caught Chikako off guard, and she didn't catch her next words.

What would you call this space? Could it be called a lobby? It was huge—Chikako's whole house could easily fit inside it. Over her head, three floors had been left open, coming together in a point at the top, so it was like stepping into an enormous glass and granite pyramid.

Chikako twirled around looking up at the ceiling like a student on a field trip to the National Diet Building. "It's beautiful, isn't it?" she murmured. Michiko, walking a few steps ahead of Chikako, stopped and smiled.

"Isn't it? The first time I came here I was so surprised I almost passed out!"

Chikako twirled once more, then transferred her gaze to the surroundings.

To the left of the entrance was a reception desk. A neatly dressed middle-aged man was at work behind it. A phone rang, and he answered it. This could easily be mistaken for a luxury hotel.

Over by the opposite wall were arrangements of red rosebuds and baby's breath on glass tables set in front of two large couches. Overlooking the couches was a mural—a tile mosaic of a gondola in a Venetian canal.

Chikako sighed—not in envy, but rather in awe. A flicker of unease caught in her chest. Was this really a place where humans—ordinary families—could live?

"Shall we go?" Michiko's voice held just the faintest suggestion of impatience. Chikako hurriedly started walking with her toward another automatic door, somewhat smaller than the one they'd just come through, and with frosted glass. Just to its left was a granite pillar about the height of a drinking fountain in a park. The top was a panel with buttons and a phone receiver.

"Automatic lock, of course," commented Chikako. Michiko nodded as she reached out for the receiver and pushed a button set apart from the others on the right.

"Hello, Kinuta here," said Michiko into the phone in that warm voice of hers. Chikako couldn't catch it clearly, but someone on the other end was saying something. It sounded like a string of numbers.

Michiko nodded several times, then said, "Yes, I've got it," and hung up. Almost simultaneously a faint hum issued from the closed door in front of them and it slid open. They passed through and found themselves in an elevator hall. There were two elevators each to their left and right, with uniformed young men in attendance.

"What floor do the Kuratas live on?"

"The top floor—the thirty-ninth," answered Michiko. "It's the penthouse, and has a separate elevator which connects directly to it." This elevator was further back, at the end of a short hallway on the right. It was much smaller than the communal elevators. Set into the wall beside it was an electric number panel.

As she pressed four numbers on the panel with a practiced air, Michiko explained, "This elevator only opens when the correct four-digit code is entered. And the code number is changed every Sunday."

So that's what the exchange just now at the intercom had been.

It was natural that they'd be careful about security in a high-class building like this, especially for the penthouse. But as Chikako followed Michiko into the small, private elevator, she considered the eight instances of fire that had broken out inside the Kurata residence, according to Michiko's report. For someone completely unconnected with the Kurata family to have started those fires, they'd have had to pass by the front desk without being challenged, then open the auto-lock, and then enter the secret code for the private elevator.

Practically speaking, you could say it was virtually impossible. Even given the benefit of the doubt, it was possible that just once, by a tremendous stroke of luck, someone could have gotten by all the barriers. But never a second or third time.

It had to be either a Kurata family member or someone close to them who could go freely in and out. By any rational estimate, that would be the widest possible circle of suspects.

Then what would be the next smallest circle? Where had the remaining ten fires occurred? Four were in a classroom, one was on the school playground, three were on the street, one in a library, and one in a hospital waiting room. Quite a scattered collection of sites. One could almost suggest they were unrelated if they ignored the fact that Kaori Kurata had been present at all ten of them.

So Kaori was at the center of the circle of reasonable suspects. The eighteen fires were either her work, or that of someone aiming at her. Setting aside the question of whether the goal was to injure the girl or to frame her as an arsonist, it still had to be the work of someone inside this circle, and this was unknown territory to Chikako. But, in other aspects, the case was beginning to take on a hue she was fairly familiar with.

Arson was a crime of place. It was different from other types of serious crime in that personality alone was not sufficient to cause it. There had to be a combination of a certain person and a specific place first, and then a final switch—motivation—had to be flipped for the behavior—fire setting—to emerge.

It wasn't just a matter of someone with a fire-setting habit being tempted by something that could be easily burned. While it was true that some locations—like an untended dump, or a building site with flammable materials heaped in a disorderly pile—beckon mentally unstable people who get a cathartic release or sexual thrill from watching fire, they were, in the end, mere locations, not *places* that had any meaning. What Chikako was thinking of was something about the atmosphere of a *place*, whether a home or public building, that triggered the act of starting a fire.

Even with arsonists who start fires to satisfy internal cravings, in close questioning it always emerged that they had picked a place for their fire based on specific details. Chikako recalled that the first case she'd been in charge of after being transferred to the arson squad involved fires set by a woman in her mid-forties. The woman's husband had been having affairs and the instability this brought to the household made the woman neurotic. Eventually their only son left home to attend a distant university. The woman was lonely, had no diversions and no strategies to help her cope. Then one day she saw a fire scene on a daytime TV drama and it gave her a sense of release. It struck her that seeing a bigger fire at closer range might give her more release. In the end, she set six small fires.

All were within two kilometers of her own home, and each was a relatively new single-family home, built within the past five years. The area had originally been developed for housing during the period of rapid growth in the seventies and eighties. As time went on, newer houses built with more modern materials and methods were mixed in with these older ones, which now looked shabby in comparison.

In questioning her, it had not been clear even to the woman herself why she had targeted only new homes. She only said things like, "I just noticed it for some reason," or, "Anywhere would have been okay—I just wanted to see a fire."

Chikako had visited the six crime scenes, and lastly had gone to see the woman's own home. Her husband had inherited it from his parents; a wooden two-story structure with a number of patchwork additions, and quite rundown. Chikako returned to the interrogation room and putting her female curiosity into play, asked the woman about it.

"It's a nice house, but pretty old, isn't it? Did you and your husband ever discuss rebuilding it?"

Finally things became clear. The woman had been saving money for years

>

for just that purpose. She'd worked a long series of minimum-wage part-time jobs, and her monthly earnings—every last yen—had gone into the bank to pay for the cost of building a new house on the family property.

"But that money—my husband spent it behind my back. My account had about five million yen, but by the time I noticed that he'd been using it, it was almost gone."

"What did he spend it on?"

"Adultery costs money, doesn't it? I guess fooling around with women is expensive."

Chikako confirmed this with the woman's husband. At that point he'd already begun divorce proceedings, and was refusing to cooperate with the investigation. He had not shown a trace of guilt, and in fact had demanded to know what was wrong with him spending his own money.

Chikako had taken another walk around the locations of the fires. All six had been minor, scorching a wall or burning old newspapers piled by the back door, and all of the homes had already been repaired and looked good as new. Gazing at those houses with their flower boxes and bay windows, Chikako could see now what the broken-spirited woman, who never raised her eyes to face Chikako in the interrogation room, had seen in the moments she set those fires.

It was unfair.

Her husband was off having fun with some girlfriend. Her son was busy enjoying his own life. She had nothing. She might have had something in the past, but she'd given up everything over her years of marriage and child-raising. Everywhere she went she was confronted with beautiful new homes symbolizing whole and happy families—everything she'd wanted but couldn't have. So she'd set them on fire. It was purifying fire, burning away what was unfair.

Even if used in crime, fire is somehow sacred. When murderers set fire to a body and the scene of their crime to conceal the traces, it is as though they hope unconsciously that everything will be purified, spiritually cleansed as though nothing had happened at all. A mistake set right. Injustice burned away. Everything returned to ash by the absolute power of fire, leaving calm nothingness in its stead.

These thoughts naturally drew Chikako's mind back to the string of "impossible" fires. One of the reasons Chikako *had* to think the Arakawa homicides and the latest incidents were revenge, retaliation, or punishment was precisely *because* the method was fire. Judgment was always painted in the colors of fire.

"Detective Ishizu, we're here."

At Michiko's voice, Chikako returned to herself with a start. The elevator had stopped and the door opened. Michiko stepped out first into a cheerful brick-colored tile hallway in front of a solid-looking oak door. She pressed the intercom next to the door and a voice immediately answered.

"Good morning! Come in please, it's open."

Chikako quietly took a deep breath.

Michiko opened the door. "Hello—"

Before she had finished her greeting, something yellow came flying out from the shadow behind the door, attaching itself to her. The momentum of it carried her back two or three steps, but laughing, she caught herself and the yellow blur and came to a halt. "Kaori-*chan!*"

"Did I surprise you?"

Caught tightly in Michiko's arms was a girl who only came up to Michiko's chest. She wore a soft canary-colored sweater and denim mini-skirt.

"You're late!"

"Oh, I'm sorry. But only by about fifteen minutes, right?"

"No, more!" The girl solemnly examined the watch on her wrist. "Eighteen minutes!"

Michiko rearranged her face into an expression of exaggerated shock. "Oh my, I'm *so* sorry. *Please* forgive us!"

Then the girl noticed Chikako's presence. Chikako was still half-outside the door, taking in the scene of the girl hugging Michiko and gamboling around her like a puppy. Still with both arms around Michiko's waist, Kaori addressed Chikako.

"Who are you?" Then, more sharply, "What did you come here for?"

Chikako had been smiling, but the girl's questions were voiced with such an accusatory ring that the smile froze on her face.

"Miss Kinuta, who is this?" the girl repeated. Michiko hurriedly straightened up, prying the girl's arms from around her waist and turning to face Chikako.

"Oh, forgive me! Detective Ishizu, this is Kaori Kurata," said Michiko, placing her hands on Kaori's shoulders.

"Hello, I'm Chikako Ishizu—it's nice to meet you." Chikako tried smiling again and greeted her.

The girl's expression, however, did not change. Still staring at Chikako and sidling back towards Michiko, she demanded again, "What is *she* here for?"

Michiko Kinuta seemed used to this kind of reaction from the girl. Patting her gently on the shoulders, she said, "That's not the way we greet guests. First of all, I'll introduce you. Detective Ishizu is one of my role models on the force. We're doing some work together now, so I wanted to introduce her to you, and that's why we both came today—"

Kaori blinked and then her piercing shrieks began to echo from the spacious ceiling of this elegant entrance hall.

"No! Go away! I don't want you here! Go away! *Go away!"* Her voice hit Chikako like a thousand needles. It was rare to get a rejection *this* direct and flat-out.

After throwing her entire body into shouting at Chikako, Kaori whirled around and dashed into the hall leading away from the entrance. She flung herself against a pair of elaborately carved double doors at the far end, and disappeared behind them.

"Kaori-*chan*—" Clearly shaken, Michiko's cheek was twitching. "I'm terribly sorry about this, Detective Ishizu."

Chikako tried to reassure her. "It's okay; don't worry about it. She probably has had a lot of bad experiences with police while being questioned about the fires."

"Yes . . . actually she's really uncomfortable with strangers, too."

There were beads of sweat on the bridge of Michiko's nose. Though she looked calm and seemed intelligent, her inexperience showed, thought Chikako. Being a detective meant, naturally, that one ran into a lot of detestable people. Giving in to hurt feelings and wounded pride could prevent one from getting any work done at all.

But even bearing that in mind, this situation was unexpected. This was the first time Kaori Kurata and Chikako had met, and they hadn't had a conversation to speak of. Why the sudden attack?

An apron-clad woman emerged at a trot through the double doors behind which Kaori had disappeared. Were this an ordinary home, this stylish looking woman in her forties would be the mother, but—

"Good morning, Miss Kinuta, thank you for coming." The woman bowed slightly while taking in Chikako's presence as well. Her demeanor didn't quite fit that of the woman of the house. "Excuse me, but did something happen just now with Miss Kaori?"

So she was the housekeeper.

"I'm sorry, we seem to have upset her," said Michiko, looking chagrined. "And this is . . . ?"

Chikako offered her name, but then Michiko recovered enough to recapture the conversation. "To tell the truth, Detective Ishizu is from the arson squad at police headquarters. Detective Ishizu, this is Fusako Eguchi. She takes care of the Kurata household."

After exchanging greetings, Chikako asked her, "Does Kaori often explode like that?"

Fusako shook her head adamantly. "Never! If anything, we usually think Miss Kaori is too quiet."

There was strong emphasis on the "Miss" and the "too quiet." Her expression was unassuming, but the tilt of her head, the set of her mouth, and the look in her eyes all had blame written in them. *You made Miss Kaori angry.*

"Well, let's leave her alone for a little while and check in on her a bit later," Michiko suggested affably. "Could we just wait in the living room?"

Fusako's glance shifted momentarily to Chikako, then she answered, "Yes, I'm sorry to keep you standing here. Please do come in."

Chikako, perfectly unperturbed, asked, "And Kaori?"

"Miss Kaori ran into her room and has closed the door."

"Kaori's room is upstairs—this is the mezzanine level," added Michiko by way of explanation. By that she could mean: *so she won't be showing her face soon,* intending to soothe Chikako; or she might be trying to restrain her: *so please don't try to pull her out just yet.*

"Well, then yes, let's sit down," Chikako answered, resolutely prodding Fusako to get a move on. *My purpose in coming here is to inquire into eighteen suspicious small fires and investigate who caused them. I am not a private tutor, nor am I a school teacher on a home visit. There's no reason to get all flustered over a child going into a sulk.*

Kaori could certainly have been hurt and developed an aversion to detectives from being investigated and grilled about the fires, and that was too bad. However, for what Chikako had to do now, they'd have to get over that handicap, and she and Kaori Kurata—the person most directly connected with the eighteen fires—would have to build just enough of a trusting relationship to proceed. This was hardly the time to go into a timorous flutter.

Chikako and Michiko walked into what looked like a Mediterranean resort hotel. To their right was the staircase which she supposed led to Kaori's room. It progressed upward in a stately curve, with a banister. Then in front of them was the living room. It was huge—maybe three times the size Chikako's living room, and with a high ceiling, too. Across the room from them was a picture window, and outside was the lawn of the penthouse garden, the expanse of which could once again hold an entire small house. This was what luxury penthouses were like, but even so . . .

Within the room all was neat and clean, and a glass table placed next to the wall near them was polished to a shine that put Chikako's windows at home to shame; it reflected Michiko's and Chikako's faces like a mirror as they passed. The table held a vase of arranged flowers that artfully brought out the cheerful colors of the room. Inviting them to sit down, Fusako disappeared toward the kitchen—well, Chikako guessed that it might be the direction of the kitchen—and while she was gone Chikako took another look at the flowers. They were artificial, but their elegance made clear that they were by no means inexpensive.

Michiko had settled on a love seat halfway across the room with its back to the window. The way she was seated suggested to Chikako that this was the place she always sat when she came, but perhaps thrown off balance by Kaori's tantrum and suddenly unsure of how to distance herself from Chikako, she looked uncomfortable and sat examining her fingernails in silence.

As for Chikako, the vast scale and sumptuous surroundings were taking their toll and she was a little overwhelmed. In the end she settled lightly on an armchair with a view of both the stairs and the double doors they'd come through.

Fusako Eguchi returned carrying some refreshments on a large silver tray. Just like a hotel. Chikako tried to envision the daily life of the parents and child living here, but had to give up—she couldn't imagine anything other than a holiday.

Fusako set out a teapot and delicate cups on the table.

"Cleaning up must have been a lot of trouble," Chikako began.

Fusako lifted her head politely from the tea. "Pardon?" She didn't seem to understand Chikako's meaning.

Chikako continued. "Well, according to the records, you've had eight fires in this home in less than two years. Later on I'd like to see where each was and hear what was burned, but just looking around now I can't see any traces of fire damage at all. I was thinking you must have put a lot of effort into refurnishing and repairs."

Fusako's face remained composed, but Chikako gathered that she was angry when she set a cup of tea in front of Chikako with a rude clatter. Upsetting Kaori had obviously been an unforgivable faux pas.

A little queen. And another example of a place with that atmosphere of attraction.

"None of the fires were any size to speak of," Fusako replied with politeness that was clearly forced. "So cleaning up was really no trouble."

"Detective Ishizu," Michiko cut in, "I believe I noted the precise locations and wrote descriptions of each fire in the report."

Chikako smiled brightly, doing her utmost to stay in cheerful, chatty matron mode. "Yes, you did. But since I'm lucky enough to be here now and have the chance to meet Ms. Eguchi, who's in charge of taking care of everything here, I'd like to hear about them from her directly."

Michiko dug in her heels. "The most recent fire did not take place here. It occurred in the school classroom."

"Yes, that's true, isn't it? And Kaori was burned that time, fifteen days ago," Chikako returned quietly. "And guessing from the cycle, we can expect the nineteenth fire to occur between a week to ten days from now—and it's because we're worried about that possibility that we are here."

It was a hint to Michiko that it was time to get to work.

"I see . . . yes, you have a point." Michiko looked crestfallen.

Chikako was reaching the limit of her patience. Unbelievable. She'd expected this woman to be smart, although they had just met and she shouldn't have jumped to conclusions. How could someone who had seemed so composed have been thrown like that by a little girl's tantrum?

"Shall we check in on Miss Kaori?" Fusako was directing the question to Michiko. "You were planning to go to a piano concert together, then have lunch nearby, as I recall?"

"Yes." Michiko glanced at her watch. "But since we came early, we still have time."

"Yes, but Miss Kaori told me she wanted you to help her decide what to wear," noted Fusako.

"And that's why I had planned on just introducing Detective Ishizu to her."

Chikako pretended not to notice the obvious hints in their conversation and cut in, "Today is a weekday. Isn't Kaori supposed to be at school?"

"Today . . . she's off from school," Michiko answered hurriedly, as if to spare Fusako the chore.

"Even though she's not sick?"

"As I wrote in my report, unpleasant rumors have been circulating at school and she's been having a tough time. Some days Kaori says she just can't face going."

"Miss Kaori doesn't go to one of the local schools." Fusako broke in knowledgeably, looking happy to have something to add. "She attends the Essence Academy junior high. The philosophy there is to support learning in a free atmosphere, and to value individuality—"

"Oh really?" Chikako smiled again. It looked like Fusako was intent on continuing along this vein, so Chikako moved to sidestep her with a quick retreat. "I see, so classical music appreciation is an acceptable alternative educational experience." Chikako lifted her cup of tea. "This smells delicious." Drinking some, she found that though the smell was indeed nice, the tea was tepid. "Well, Ms. Eguchi . . ."

Blocked from resuming their conversation, Michiko and Fusako exchanged a discomfited look.

"Yes?"

"How about if you and I have a chat together? We can let Detective Kinuta take care of Kaori. That was the original plan anyway, wasn't it?"

Fusako, visibly nervous, glanced toward Michiko in search of assistance.

"I won't take much of your time—about an hour will do. How about . . . I know. Since Kaori seems bothered by me, let's us go out first, and then after Detective Kinuta and Kaori leave, we can come back here."

"But . . . ah . . . alone? Detective Ishizu, your authority . . . is that—"

"Officially, no. But the series of suspicious fires is continuing, and people are starting to get hurt. The contents of Detective Kinuta's report are too serious to ignore. Considering that the investigation so far has shed no light on the matter, I would certainly appreciate your cooperation now. Of course, I intend to ask the same cooperation from Kaori's parents and teacher as well."

By now Michiko Kinuta must be regretting—deeply, deeply regretting—that she'd made that private request for assistance to "Uncle" Ito who'd made so much of her as a child. And sure enough, there were beads of sweat on the bridge of Michiko's nose.

"Ah, I see, well, um—" The ending to Fusako's indecisive sentence was drowned out by a low *whooomph*. In this room, right next to her.

Chikako turned her head toward the sound in surprise and blinked in an instinctive reaction—to shield herself from the inconceivable. Fusako dropped the silver tray. Michiko's teacup landed on its saucer with a crash. Chikako leaped to her feet, away from the soft armchair.

The vase of artificial flowers on the glass table was ablaze. The gorgeous bouquet was reincarnating as huge red blooms of fire, and flaming sparks flew toward Chikako like stinging pollen, as the contents of the vase burned with flames high enough to scorch the ceiling.

14

Chikako acted quickly. Fusako was frozen in place next to the silver tray she had dropped, so Chikako shook her arm to get her attention.

"Where's the fire extinguisher?"

Fusako gaped at her, uncomprehending. "Fire extinguisher?"

Chikako shook her arm again, harder. "Yes. Where is it?" Fusako finally seemed to come to her senses and ran through the double doors, with Chikako on her heels. Fusako hurried into a large hall, turned left and went through another set of double doors into another hall. She stopped in front of what looked like a shelf of keepsakes, pulled out a small fire extinguisher from the shadows and hastily began to fumble with it.

Chikako wordlessly snatched it from her hands and returned to the living room, yanking out the safety pin on the way. The flowers in the vase were still burning, but the red-tongued flames were no longer licking at the ceiling. While there were some soot marks on it, the ceiling had not caught fire. The paint had clearly been chosen with fire-resistance in mind.

She calmly aimed the nozzle of the extinguisher at the vase and the foam flew out with a strong hiss, dousing the flames on contact. It took less than a minute for the chemical smell of the foam to fill the room, completely overpowering the smoke and flames.

Chikako continued spraying, keeping the nozzle trained on the vase and moving in closer until she was able to spray the last of the foam directly into its mouth. Only the wire stems of the artificial flowers were left in the vase. The flowers were gone, transformed into ashes and soot dissolving in the foam of the extinguisher.

Chikako could see that the partially-melted flower stems were made of several strands of wire twisted together to make them at least five millimeters thick, sturdy enough to support those gorgeous artificial blooms. To have melted these in such a short time meant that the temperature must have been extremely high.

During her first training lectures when she'd been assigned to the arson squad, they had set fire to a great number of materials to learn the smells each gave off when burning. Naturally, in the experiments they hadn't included toxic substances, so it had been things like paper, wood, cotton and hemp cloth, and some building materials. All had surprisingly distinct odors.

The smell this vase of flowers had given off had been of burning paper and heat, nothing else. Chikako couldn't smell any accelerant, but paper burning without it did not in her experience produce the high temperatures that this fire apparently had. She regretted not having examined the flowers more closely earlier.

It crossed her mind that she'd faced the same question just a few days ago in the drastically different circumstances at the Tayama factory, when she'd discovered that the steel shelf next to one of the carbonized bodies had melted. When she thought about it, the matter of high temperatures was an unanswered question in all of these arson-homicide cases.

It had to be a coincidence, but it was a strange one.

The extinguisher foam had lost its bubbles and the liquid it had been reduced to was overflowing the vase. The empty extinguisher was so light that Chikako dangled it from one hand as she turned to the others in the living room. "Everyone okay?"

Fusako and Michiko were huddled together, standing just behind the armchair Chikako had been sitting in before. With them was Kaori, who'd come downstairs unnoticed and was now clinging tightly to Michiko.

All three were looking at Chikako. Their expressions seemed to be reproaching her for committing some horrible violence.

But the one Chikako focused on, concentrating, trying to read what was in her eyes, was Kaori. The gaze of those black eyes seemed to pierce right through Chikako. "Are you okay?" Chikako asked her. "You weren't scared, were you? The fire's out, so there's nothing to be afraid of now."

Her arms still wrapped around Michiko, Kaori abruptly turned her face away.

"My head hurts," she said in a small voice. It sounded like she was on the verge of tears.

"Detective Ishizu," said Michiko, with her arm around Kaori's slender shoulders. "I'm going to have to report this to the precinct."

"Yes, that made it the nineteenth fire, didn't it?"

"Right," she said, nodding. She licked her lips nervously, obviously searching for the right words. "I didn't tell my colleagues that I asked Uncle Ito for his advice. So if you're here, Detective Ishizu . . . " she trailed off and licked her lips again.

Chikako understood, and didn't contradict her. To ease the strained atmosphere—as far as would be reasonable under the circumstances—she smiled and said, "Good point. I think I'll leave, then. But Ms. Eguchi—"

Fusako jumped, startled.

"I'd like to come back to talk with you some other time. I'll give you a call and I'd appreciate your cooperation."

Fusako looked to Michiko before answering, but Michiko, probably deliberately, was looking down, stroking Kaori's hair. Fusako mumbled something noncommittal that would give an initial impression of being affirmative but which could later be reinterpreted as negative. Chikako did not bother to wait around and listen. She quickly got her things together and headed down the elevator.

Walking out of the building and through the garden in front of it, she saw a single, plain-looking sedan pulling up. It had to be from Michiko's precinct. A young man about Michiko's age was driving, and there wasn't anyone else with him. Chikako did not slacken her speed as she walked past it. He must be Kaori's second-favorite police officer after Michiko. Considering the current circumstances, there was no way Michiko would call in a colleague who'd further displease the girl. And considering the speed with which he'd come flying over, he and Michiko had to be on pretty good terms. He could even be her boyfriend, come to think of it. She'd bet a slice of cake tonight on that, she decided, and chuckled.

The closest station was Tsukiji, on the Hibiya line. She'd come by taxi so she hadn't really noticed, but getting to the station on foot was quite a trek.

When they'd planned that apartment building, they must have assumed that none of their prospective tenants would be from the masses of Tokyo train commuters.

The walk calmed her down and when she spotted a small café in sight of Tsukiji Honganji temple, she slipped inside. She wanted to collect her thoughts and plan her next moves before returning to MPD and reporting to Captain Ito about today's events.

She took a window seat and while she was ordering coffee from the waitress her cell phone rang. The thing was useless in her handbag, so she always carried it inside her jacket. The waitress gave her a look as she pulled it out.

"Detective Ishizu?" It was Makihara. Chikako thought it had to be either fate or divine intervention—she'd just been absently thinking of him.

"Are you telepathic?" she demanded in all seriousness. "I was just thinking of calling you."

"Did something happen? Or was it that nothing's happening and you've got time on your hands?"

Was it only banter or was there was a little sting in that? A bell went off in the back of her mind. "Where are you right now? Are you at MPD?"

She'd nailed it. "How'd you know that?" Makihara retorted.

"You came to visit me, and someone in the office told you that I'm not on the Tayama case anymore, right? It must look like I lost interest overnight, dropped it, and took off in a totally different direction. And you're none too pleased."

There was a pause. "Am I really that easy to read?"

"No, it's just the situation that's so clear."

The waitress was bringing over Chikako's coffee; Chikako lowered her voice. "Listen, I'll explain why I've been shifted onto another case. And I just had a really interesting experience that I want to tell you about . . ."

A short time later, Makihara listened, perfectly still, as Chikako related the details of the private request for support on the Kaori Kurata case, and what had transpired. He didn't even change expression or make a sound—he was so quiet in fact that, had a tape recorder been set on the table, anyone listening to it later would have assumed Chikako was talking to herself. He remained silent even after Chikako finished. She took a sip of her now luke-warm coffee and prompted him. "So, what do you think?"

Makihara finished his tea—black, with no milk or sugar, then lit up a cigarette. When he finally answered, he looked at her with his eyes clouded, but not just from smoke.

"When you ask me what I think, which part are you asking about? Do you want to know how I think the Kurata family fires were started? Or are you asking who I think the perpetrator might be?"

Chikako burst out laughing. Makihara had reminded her of her gentle, unassuming collie, but he had a chip on his shoulder, too.

"Either or both would be fine," Chikako replied politely. "I still don't have that much experience in arson investigation. Frankly, it was unnerving to see something burst into flames like that right in front of me. I have no idea how it could have started."

Makihara stubbed out his cigarette. "But you know who did it. It couldn't be anyone else."

Chikako decided they might as well be direct with each other. "You mean Kaori?"

"Of course."

"Well, she's the prime suspect and I thought the most likely one, but after seeing the fire break out, I just don't know."

Makihara lit a new cigarette, and Chikako continued. "If it is Kaori, then she must have developed an ingenious method for starting fires by remote control, and she has to be very skilled at using it. It leaves no evidence of the method or trace of the device, and furthermore, that fire was hot enough to melt wire. Can a thirteen-year-old girl do that? It just doesn't seem likely."

"If you take a wider view, it's not unlikely at all," said Makihara. "But, of course when I say things like this, everyone on the force thinks I'm insane."

Examining Makihara's face as he sat across from her and tossed this out, Chikako intuitively understood that he wanted her to ask him why people thought he was so strange, and to assure him that she didn't agree. Chikako smiled at him.

"Hey, don't sulk with me. It's just a waste of time. Thanks to my husband and son, I'm immune." Chikako raised her hand to ask the waitress for a refill of her coffee. Makihara's mouth snapped shut, and a long line of ash from the end of his cigarette crumbled and fell off; it looked, out of the corner of Chikako's eye, like the chip had fallen off his shoulder.

"So please tell me what you're thinking," Chikako continued. "I don't plan on being shocked whatever it is, and I know you want to tell me anyway."

Makihara sighed.

"During the investigation of the Arakawa homicides, I told them what I thought. They just laughed and told me I was crazy, and that I'd better get a grip or they'd kick me off the case. So I've been watching my step ever since."

"Well, then we won't get anywhere," said Chikako composedly. "And I'm not in any position to kick you off anything, anyway. All you have to resolve if you are going to share your opinion here is whether you can deal with the totally trivial risk that one middle-aged female colleague named Chikako Ishizu will think you're insane after all. So there's not much to lose—go on and tell me."

Makihara froze, staring at Chikako, then burst out laughing in spite of himself. Chikako laughed with him, then quickly returned to the matter at hand. "Okay, what was the theory you expressed to the investigation team?"

This time there was a pause not because he was hesitating, but because he was enunciating it slowly and clearly. "Pyrokinesis."

"Pyro—?"

"The ability to start fires by willpower."

Chikako blinked. Come to think of it, he'd used this word when they'd first met.

Makihara continued. "Being able to set anything—organic or inorganic—on fire at will, simply by concentrating. Not just being able to start fires, but to instantly produce temperatures high enough to melt steel." The image of the melted steel shelf in that factory floated through Chikako's mind again.

"I'm positive that the person behind both the Arakawa homicides and these new arson-homicide cases possesses this ability. And this person is extremely rare among those with the ability, because he or she can control it almost perfectly, and has the ability to judge distance and aim almost without fail." Makihara gave a little shrug and added, "And this Kaori

Kurata you've come across sounds like another, but one who is still immature. So what do you think? You said that nothing would surprise you, but you're looking pretty surprised after all."

Chikako looked down. Yes, she was surprised. She couldn't believe she was hearing this—and hearing it said in all seriousness—from the mouth of a police detective.

Makihara went quiet and his expression said, "Well, I told you so." From the corner of her downcast eyes, Chikako watched as he drew a new cigarette out, then, perhaps in irritation, crumpled up the empty packet. She noticed that his fingers were long and slender, like a woman's. It was a sign of a high-strung personality. The conviction settled on her that the problem was not just with his opinions, but with his character.

Come to think of it, he was downright childish. If he pulled this kind of attention-getting stunt with male colleagues or superiors, it was no wonder they avoided him. On the other hand, women probably found him attractive. Amused, Chikako smiled again as she lifted her eyes and asked, "Detective Makihara, why do you believe in the existence of an incredible paranormal ability like that?"

His eyebrows flew up. "You mean, why do I believe in such a ridiculous thing?"

"No, that's not what I said. Listen, please. I said, 'incredible paranormal ability.' I didn't say 'ridiculous.' If the power that you are speaking of actually exists, and people who can use it really do exist, it would not be ridiculous at all—it would be terrifying."

Makihara was listening, watching Chikako's face. His eyes looked wary, suspicious that Chikako was just outwardly going along with him while laughing at him inside.

"So tell me," she continued. "When you offered this theory, your colleagues at the precinct and the Arakawa homicides investigation team all wanted to know why, too, didn't they?

Makihara snorted. "No, they never got that far. They left it at 'get a grip and don't read so much science fiction'."

She certainly understood their reaction. But she wasn't throwing questions at him now just for show. Somehow, she sensed, Makihara was *driven* to talk about this. And that would explain his impatience and his quick leaps to irritation, too. Today he'd gone all the way to MPD to see her and had been angry when he'd learned she was already on another case. The flip side was that it showed how much his hopes were pinned on her. No matter how much he was laughed at, he'd sunk his teeth into these horrible, bizarre homicides and couldn't let go of them—or his preposterous theory.

"Look, I don't think you're stupid, and I'm not making fun of you. But it *is* hard for me to believe this pyrokinesis theory. So I'm just asking you a straightforward question: why do you believe in it?" Chikako pressed on. "You don't believe things just because someone tells you they happened; that's what children do. I know, I just told you that I saw fire erupt in front of my eyes where there'd been none, but that for me is a basis for nothing— either about the fire or about Kaori. Yes, I saw a fire that started strangely, but it isn't enough to make me believe in pyrokinesis. We're limited by our five senses, and eyes, especially, are easily fooled. There's got to be more to something than just having seen it. There's something else that makes you believe so strongly."

Makihara's eyes lost their focus and swam in space for a split second.

When Chikako had first become a plainclothes detective, she'd been mentored by a senior detective who had a reputation as a master interrogator. Every precinct had one or two who earned the nickname "Mind Reader" for their interrogation skills. Most were older male detectives who had seen a lot of the world and this man was no exception. Also typical of men who'd seen it all, he was kind to underdogs and he'd been an ally to Chikako, the only woman on the team. Of all he had taught her, she always remembered one thing in particular.

Once in a while, Ishizu, the eyes of the suspect sitting across from you in the interrogation room will swim for a moment. It's not like the shifty eyes when they've been caught in a contradiction, or when they're adding lies to more lies. They'll just lose focus for a split second.

What it means is that something they've shut up inside their heads that they don't want to remember has suddenly come back to them. Vividly. So for a moment their attention is yanked toward it, and their eyes swim. It's something you've got to learn to recognize.

For some suspects, the memory has something to do with the details of the crime. But with others, it could be a memory of being abused by a stepfather, or of a terrifying accident. It doesn't necessarily mean that they have committed a crime—but the memory could be an important key to a deeper understanding of that suspect. So, when it happens, remember what you were talking about or what was going on when it happened. It could give you a better handle on the case.

Chikako had never forgotten this. It hadn't earned her the reputation of "Mind Reader" in the interrogation room, but it had helped her countless times.

Now was no exception. Chikako did not miss the moment that Makihara's vision was suddenly pulled inside, and she watched as he hurriedly averted his eyes from what he saw there, shut it away again and returned his focus to Chikako.

What did Makihara remember just now? What were we talking about just now? Pyrokinesis. *Could it be . . . ?*

"Makihara," Chikako demanded, "you don't have that kind of power yourself, do you?" Makihara looked as though she'd thrown water in his face. Ash crumbled from the cigarette he held between his fingers. Chikako leaned forward, now asking seriously, "Is that it? Is that why you can say so certainly that pyrokinesis exists?"

Makihara looked directly in Chikako's eyes—and burst out laughing.

"Oh, okay," Chikako laughed, too, and let out her breath. "So it's not that?"

The waitress had been taking note of them, craning her neck to see them better. She grabbed up a pitcher of ice water and started to walk in their direction.

"It's not that, huh?" Chikako repeated for confirmation, and this time Makihara shook his head.

"No, I don't have that power."

"Okay, then maybe someone close to you?"

This time Makihara jumped as though she'd poked him. *That arrow hit pretty close to the mark*, thought Chikako.

The waitress looked from Chikako to Makihara. She poured some more water in their glasses, as slowly as she could it seemed, and then took her time in moving away.

"My son likes reading science fiction novels," explained Chikako. "And movies, too; he's built up a quite a video collection. So it's not that I've never heard of things like ESP or supernatural powers—I probably know a little more than the average middle-aged lady."

"How old is your son?" asked Makihara. She might be mistaken, but he looked greatly relieved at this change of subject and his shoulders seemed to relax.

"He's twenty. He's in college in Hiroshima, so I only get to see him at the New Year. Boys are such a bore that way." Chikako laughed, then took a sip of her water. "Makihara, you just remembered something, didn't you?"

Silence.

"Something somehow related to all this? At least that's what I thought a moment ago. Have you had something happen to you personally? Something to do with this pyrokinesis?"

"Personally . . ." Makihara muttered, half in reply, half, it seemed, to himself.

"Yes. You have, haven't you? And just now—didn't you recall it?"

Makihara asked with a half-smile, "And are you a mind reader?"

"No, no, not at all. It's a technique someone taught me once."

Makihara abruptly reached for the check and stood up. "Let's leave."

"But we're not finished talking, are we?"

"I'd rather not continue here. Being a detective, wouldn't you rather see where it happened?"

Makihara drove towards northwest Tokyo, mostly in taciturn silence. Whatever Chikako asked, he'd just say, "Let's get there first."

The roads were crowded, and it took almost an hour. When he said, "This is it," and stopped the car, they had turned right off the Mejiro highway by the Toyotama overpass, and were about five minutes from Sakuradai.

It was a quiet, mostly residential area. Near them a sign read, "School Zone." To their left was a small park. It was surrounded entirely by trees, but the leaves had fallen and through the bare branches they could see the varicolored sweaters and jackets of children as they played.

Makihara stepped over the low, cement block wall, cut across the planted area and headed toward the swings. Chikako, who couldn't hop over the wall as easily as Makihara, detoured to the entrance and then followed him. Some schoolchildren were swinging high enough to make Chikako nervous as she listened to the chains squeaking. Makihara stopped near them and thrust his hands into his coat pockets. Chikako caught up with him. "Is this where it happened?"

Makihara looked at her and nodded. "This is where I grew up. Our house was about a five-minute walk from here. This park was built when I was little, and we played here all the time. It's a lot fancier now, but these swings are still in the same place and the trees and flowerbeds are, too." There was a bench nearby and Makihara indicated it with his chin. "That bench has been here all along."

It looked like he was finally going to answer Chikako's question. It was cold, but Chikako sat down on the bench anyway.

"Exactly twenty years ago now, I was in junior high—fourteen years old. It was the end of the year, December thirteenth. I was in the middle of exams."

It didn't sound like he was drawing up a distant memory so much as reading aloud from a case record.

"It was probably past six in the evening. Since it was winter, the sun had already set and it was dark. All the kids had gone home. But Tsutomu was there, swinging."

"Tsutomu?"

"Yeah, my little brother. He was in second grade."

"So small."

They could hear the children on the swings shrieking as they pumped vigorously in the wind. Makihara, who had been staring off toward them, looked down at Chikako. "He was my half-brother. My mother died soon after I was born. My father raised me alone for years, but about the time I started school, he met someone and they married. She was my younger brother's mother."

Looking cold, Makihara hunched his shoulders, shook his head a little, and continued. "My stepmother and I didn't follow the typical pattern—it was the opposite, in fact. Maybe she didn't want me to feel hurt or isolated, but she tried almost too hard to be good to me . . . and was too strict with her own son, my brother, instead. So by second grade, Tsutomu was already a real problem child."

That day, Tsutomu had come home from school, got into mischief and broke something. My stepmother lost her temper and really laid into him. Tsutomu ran off somewhere.

"She said to just leave him and let him come home when he felt like it, but I could tell she was really worried, so I went out looking for him. A little kid like that didn't have a lot of places to go, so it wasn't hard to find him here in the park, all wound up and blowing off steam, standing and swinging as hard as he could."

"He spotted me coming to get him, so he swung up even higher and then jumped off and started running as fast as he could. I was calling something to him like, 'It's dark out here! Time to come home!' and he was yelling back, 'I hate you! Go away!' as he ran. He was a fast little kid and was getting way ahead of me. Then, over there, where the sandbox is now—"

Chikako squinted against the cold wind and followed Makihara's gaze. The half frozen sandbox was completely deserted.

"Back then, there was a little slide there. Tsutomu was going to run under it to get away, but he stopped suddenly—it looked like he was surprised, and he said something. I was running after him so I couldn't hear very well, but it sounded like he was calling someone by name."

"He had a friend there, maybe?"

Chikako had asked casually, but Makihara's expression darkened. "I don't know if it was a friend or not, and I still don't know. There was someone there—hiding under the slide—let's just leave it at that for now."

Makihara's gaze rested on the sandbox, but Chikako knew he was seeing the long-gone slide. She felt a chill creeping into her heart. The significance of his words—*let's go see where it happened*—had not been lost on her and it looked like he was about to describe something related to pyrokinesis. She had a feeling that it wasn't going to be good. What happens to a small, unruly boy in an unstable relationship with his mother . . . ?

"Tsutomu stopped and said something," Makihara resumed. "I was less than ten meters from him at that point. Since he'd stopped, I thought I had a chance to catch him, so I sped up and yelled to him, 'Come on home! Mom's worried . . .'"

The children were still swinging. Chikako heard their happy voices, but it was getting colder and colder.

Still standing with his eyes fixed on the sandbox, Makihara went on,

"There was a low sound, *whooomph*, like an explosion, and Tsutomu went up in flames."

Chikako saw him shudder. People didn't usually shudder like that in a wind-whipped park. They'd shiver, maybe, but this was more like the kind of shudder you'd make if you came upon a warm fire in a bitterly cold, frozen place.

There was no fire here now, though—at least to Chikako's eyes. The only fire that existed was the one in Makihara's memory. He was seeing his little brother burning again, now, just in front of him—and that was the source of the shudder.

"I had no idea where the fire had come from. One second there was none; the next, his whole body was on fire. That's how it looked. Then, just for a second he was standing still—I remember his arms were outstretched. And he looked down at himself, like he was wondering what was happening. Like when someone's repairing their broken bike, and they suddenly see that while they were concentrating on the job they somehow got themselves covered in machine oil—that happens sometimes, right? Especially with kids."

"Yes, it happens . . ." Chikako answered gently.

"It was just like that. 'Hey, whoops, how'd I get so much oil all over me?' He was just surprised and wondering, 'Hey, where'd all the fire come from?' That's the way he was looking at his arms and the rest of his body. Then—"

Makihara's voice had begun to shake a little and he broke off for a moment. "Then he started screaming. By then I was right next to him so I could see his scream come out of his mouth. I don't mean metaphorically— I mean I really saw his scream. Tsutomu opened his mouth and flames came out, like a dragon in a movie. And then he started flapping around, trying to shake off the fire. Or get away from it."

The fourteen-year-old Makihara had been frozen to the spot when his brother screamed. All he could do was call out his brother's name—*Tsutomu!*

"Tsutomu saw me. He looked at me but his eyes were moving like they wanted to run away from his head. Not just his eyes—his arms and legs—it looked like every part of him was trying to break free and run off in every direction."

He began to run, arms outstretched, lurching towards his big brother. "I began to back up. Tsutomu was coming to me for help, but I was about to run away. Tsutomu saw that, and he knew. He stopped and he just screamed my name, over and over.

"The fire had burnt him inside—I could see that behind his eyes and inside his mouth were all black. Fire was pouring from his fingertips. He held his arms out to me and then his mouth moved—'*Help me!*'"

Makihara shuddered again. Chikako had gotten up from the bench and was standing just behind him. She could see that the skin of his neck exposed above his collar was raised with goose bumps.

"Then he fell. Right at my feet," continued Makihara, his eyes on the ground.

Protecting herself from the cold, Chikako had folded her arms and pulled up her collar as she stood next to Makihara. Unnoticed, the swings had come to a stop. The children who had been so determined to fly had gone off somewhere. It was quiet. The happy shouts were gone, the sandbox remained deserted, and only the freezing wind whipped by Chikako's ears. It made a thin wailing sound, like a child's scream.

"When Tsutomu collapsed, I finally started trying to put out the fire. I was hitting him all over. Partway through I thought to take my shirt off and tried to beat the fire out with that, too. But it was already too late. Tsutomu was burned through."

"You know, telling it, it seems like it took ages, but it can't have been more than ten or twenty seconds," Chikako said. "So your reaction wasn't slow at all. You probably just ran up to your brother and tried your best to put the fire out. It's a kind of a mental illusion and it happens to everyone— when they recall it later, they think they were terribly slow."

She wasn't just saying the first thing that came into her head in an attempt to comfort him. Time truly does slow down in the middle of an accident or other emergency situation. It isn't that time itself is prolonged, it's that the information-processing rate of the brain speeds up to double or triple its usual speed. That's why the senses sharpen, perception clears, and memories of the scene are unusually vivid. But the body can't keep up with the brain; it can only move as usual. So people who survive an emergency often agonize over how they were incredibly awkward, useless, and slow when they recall the details of that moment, even long afterwards. While it's extremely painful, it's by no means rare.

"I kept hitting him to put out the fire, but by then it was just his remains. My brother was gone," Makihara resumed, his voice devoid of life. "Now I was the one yelling for all I was worth. While I was hitting at him like that, the flames died down and were just sputtering and smoking, and then I heard someone shouting from a ways off. Probably someone passing by the park had seen signs of the fire, so now two or three adults were by the park fence and calling over to me, 'Hey, are you all right? What happened?' I couldn't talk or even breathe, and I was shaking so badly. Tears were running down my face and my eyes were just barely open. Later on I found that all my eyelashes had burned off."

Makihara rubbed his hands over his face, looking exhausted.

"But I could hear. Someone was crying near me—someone who wasn't me."

Makihara raised his head and pointed toward the sandbox. "I said there was a small slide over there, right? And my brother was going to run under it to get away, when he caught on fire?"

"Yes, I remember."

"I was on the ground next to what was left of Tsutomu. From there I could see under the slide, by the ladder. There was a little girl about Tsutomu's age crouched down under there."

There were some lights in the park, but it was well after sundown and in the shadow of the slide, Makihara couldn't really see her face. What he could see was that she was wearing a canary yellow sweater, that her hands were hiding her face—and that she was crying. She was sobbing, convulsively shaking her head from side to side.

"I tried to get up. I was going to go over to the girl, but I was too unsteady. I think I called to her, 'Are you okay? You aren't hurt, are you?' Something like that. I thought she was crying because she'd been scared by the fire."

But the little girl stood up with such surprising swiftness that her skirt flew out around her. Her face was pretty but crumpled in tears. She turned her stricken face to him and looked at Makihara for a moment, then she looked back at the still smoldering remains of Tsutomu.

"I'm sorry," she said. It was barely a whisper. "I said to leave me alone but he kept picking on me. But I'm sorry, I'm sorry for burning him. I'm sorry, I'm so sorry . . ." And then she ran. It took Makihara several seconds to realize that she'd run not toward the voices of the approaching adults, and not for help, but clearly *away*.

"When I came to my senses, she was already out of sight," said Makihara. It was as if he could see her footprints even now—there was no hesitation in the path his eyes traced as they followed the route the girl had run twenty years ago.

"Then the adults were here and they called an ambulance. The police came, my parents came running . . ." Makihara's eyes finally left the route the little girl had taken, and returned to Chikako. He grimaced.

"At first my parents thought I'd gone mad, I guess."

"Why?"

"I was saying, 'A little girl set Tsutomu on fire, a little girl burnt Tsutomu, we've got to find that little girl . . . ' and I wouldn't give up on it."

"The people who came running to you didn't see her?"

"No such luck."

"But you saw her. And you heard her say, 'I'm sorry for burning him.'"

"Yes."

"The adults didn't believe you?"

Makihara lifted his chin almost imperceptibly as he recalled aloud, "Eighty-two percent of Tsutomu's body was covered with third-degree burns. Not just his outer skin—his esophagus and windpipe were burned, too. His body looked just like someone who had committed suicide by self-immolation. But there was one obvious difference—"

"There was no accelerant, right?" Chikako supplied. "That seems to be the point we keep running up against."

Makihara nodded. "There wasn't any trace of gasoline or kerosene on Tsutomu. He'd been wearing cotton jeans and underwear, and an acrylic sweater and, as you know, none of those reach such high temperatures anyway."

Makihara shook his head, apparently clearing it enough by that motion to recall that he was outside and cold, and he scrunched his neck down into his collar. "The thinking ran something along the lines of, 'There's no accelerant, and even though this was a little boy, to burn a living human body through like that is simply not possible without something like a very large flamethrower. This poor teenager is saying that a child about the same age as his little brother did this and that he heard the little girl say *I'm sorry*, and run away from the scene of her crime in tears. It's so sad, he saw his brother burn to death, and he's lost his mind.'"

"But still they should have made an effort to search for the girl. Did they?" asked Chikako. "First of all, she was a witness. And she said something important: *I said to leave me alone but he kept picking on me.* You said that even from your point of view as his older brother that he was a handful, right? That little girl could have been in his class and have been someone that Tsutomu was giving a hard time. Somehow—on purpose or not would be another matter—she could have set him on fire."

Chikako's breath was white in the cold air and she continued indignantly, "She was in the shadow under the slide. Tsutomu was running and about to duck under it. Then, he saw her hiding there. Tsutomu was surprised, thinking, *what's she doing here?* If she was someone he was always picking on, then all the more so . . . so he stopped running. He may have said something to her. Then, in the next instant, he was on fire—right? The probability that the little girl knew something was well over one hundred percent!"

Chikako looked up at Makihara for a reaction, but his eyes were closed.

"They did try a sort of search," he said quietly. "They looked for a girl about Tsutomu's age. And they had me look at pictures of all the girls at Tsutomu's school, and check pictures of girls from other schools, too. But she wasn't there. The girl I saw wasn't in any of the pictures. It's possible that I ended up getting confused because there were so many photos, but at any rate, I wasn't able to identify her.

"So next it was, 'Oh, the mysterious girl isn't there? Well, I guess it's because she wasn't there in the first place. His story sounded pretty weird anyway. A little girl was apologizing for burning him? Yeah, *right.* So he's saying this girl was packing a flamethrower in a park? To incinerate a bully? Give me a break. It's all in his imagination.'"

Makihara sounded like he was reading from the program of a ceremony he didn't want to attend. "And though I knew that was what they were beginning to think, all I could do was just stand by and watch. Even my parents believed I was unhinged by the shock.

"Then the rest of the adults decided that I was lying. The school teachers, the police, the fire department. And that's what they told my parents. My parents were appalled. 'Our boy, lying? Making something up? Why? And why would you say that? This is our eldest son, the one who's so level-headed. He's always been so mature. Why would he make up such a crazy story and then stick to it like this?' Those questions led naturally to the given conclusion."

Chikako couldn't bear to hear it from his mouth, so she cut him off and finished for him. "They suspected that you might have set him on fire."

Makihara paused a fraction of a second, then said, "Yes."

Now his breath turned white in the cold air, too. The whole time he had been talking, his breath hadn't been visible. It was as though in the telling his body temperature had dropped, and now that he'd finished it had reverted to normal. When Makihara told the story of his brother, he died again, too, thought Chikako, and now he was returning from death to life.

"After Tsutomu died, my father and stepmother stopped laughing," Makihara said. "It was as if it would be a kind of betrayal to him if I did something funny, or I brought home some story and the three of us laughed together."

Chikako thought about that stepmother who'd resolved so firmly not to hurt the feelings of her stepson that she'd tended to overcompensate by being too hard on her own son instead. She'd lost her child, but had to live with her stepson, who was suspected of killing him. How could she manage that household or make any kind of family life?

"I got into a high school that had a dorm and left home. I didn't even go home during summer or winter breaks. Once I'd left, it was too hard to go back—I was scared, and bitter."

"So, your parents . . ."

"My father died when I was twenty-five. He had a cerebral hemorrhage and never regained consciousness. I hadn't seen him for ten years, and now it was too late. We couldn't talk. My stepmother—"

Makihara hesitated slightly. "We talked after my father's funeral. I knew that we might never meet again, so before we went our separate ways, I asked her to tell me anything she'd been holding back but wanted to say."

Chikako asked calmly, "And what did she say?"

Most likely no effort would be necessary to recall this—it would be engraved on his heart, but Makihara paused to think a moment. Perhaps to steady himself.

"She asked me, 'Did you become a policeman to atone for what you did back then?'"

Chikako was silent.

"I told her no, because I hadn't done what she thought I had. After that she had nothing more to say."

15

That evening, Chikako Ishizu soaked in a warm bath, running what Makihara had said to her in the park through her head again and again.

That was no normal fire. My brother didn't catch on fire by any usual method.

Pyrokinesis. He had spent his youth searching for that word. He told her the names of the books he had read, all the people he had visited, what they'd told him, and what he'd had to beg them to tell him. This was not a world that Chikako was familiar with, but she could see that Makihara was sincere. There were times, though, when there was a dangerously fuzzy line between sincerity and insanity.

Although their numbers are few, there are people with pyrokinetic powers. In the evening shadow of the slide in the park . . .

I don't mind if you tell me you don't believe it. But this is a wonderful opportunity. Take it and observe Kaori very carefully. She's got the ability. I'm one hundred percent sure of it. If you get to know Kaori Kurata, Detective Ishizu, you'll have to stop laughing at what I have to say.

A child who could emit fire strong enough to carbonize a human being, without using any kind of fire starter.

Chikako shook her head, then washed her face.

What had happened to Makihara's brother was terrible, and sad. It was such a tragic experience that Makihara had been possessed by it. He was clearly being dragged by the heels through life by the death of his brother.

Pyrokinesis?

Did the girl in the shadow of the slide set Makihara's younger brother on fire?

It was ludicrous.

All right, she'd give him the benefit of the doubt. Let's say that there really was such a thing as pyrokinesis. Let's even say that twenty years ago the girl in the shadow of the slide had pyrokinetic powers. Why did she have to burn the boy to death? Did he bully her? Did he threaten her? Even so, she could have just flung a handful of sand at him. She could have screamed for help. No matter what kind of power she had, she didn't have to set him on fire.

I said to leave me alone but he kept picking on me. But I'm sorry, I'm sorry for burning him. I'm sorry.

Isn't that what the girl had said? It sounded pretty farfetched. Even a child would understand that the punishment did not fit the provocation. And if it was something she'd done intentionally, why would she apologize like that?

It's pure fantasy. There's no way Makihara's story could be true.

Chikako got out of the bath and was drinking some cold barley tea when her husband Noriyuki came home. It was after midnight and his face was red. He smelled of alcohol—his breath made Chikako wince. She wondered if something good had happened at work because he seemed to be in a great mood. He said he was thirsty, took Chikako's glass out of her hand and gulped the tea down. Then he dropped into the chair at the table opposite Chikako and said he wanted to eat *ochazuke*—rice and savory toppings with green tea poured on top.

Chikako went into a lecture on excessive drinking and acting like a slob, but in her heart she was smiling at his good humor. She quickly and efficiently prepared his snack, boiling water and cutting up some pickles to go with it. She wanted to tell him how lucky it was for him that she had been taken off the investigation of the multiple homicides. She would never have been at home if she were involved.

Noriyuki wolfed down his *ochazuke*, then picked up the hot tea she had set in front of him and pulled the ashtray on the table closer. He took out a pack of cigarettes and put one in his mouth.

Chikako watched Noriyuki using his lighter. He was drunk and that made him clumsy. The lighter must have been low on fluid, too, and the tip of the cigarette tilted up and down as he moved his hands. He couldn't get it to light.

Pyrokinesis.

Chikako had a sudden thought. Pyrokinesis meant that she'd be able to sit across the table from her husband and light his cigarette without moving her hands. All she would have to do was concentrate on the tip of it for a second or two.

A tiny flame sputtered from the lighter. He took a deep pull. Chikako stood up and began clearing off the table.

Chikako was sensitive to detergent, so she put on rubber gloves that came up to her elbows and began washing the dishes. As she did, she continued to think.

It wouldn't be any problem if it just meant lighting cigarettes. Pyrokinesis could be useful, especially outdoors on windy days. But a person who had such an ability would not necessarily limit themselves to small acts of kindness. They would have the capacity to burn to death anyone who did the least little thing to displease them. That was what pyrokinesis would mean to someone. One could respond to teasing or bullying by simply setting the culprit on fire.

Her husband was feeling good tonight. He hummed to himself as he read the evening paper, and Chikako knew that if she didn't watch him, he would fall asleep in his chair.

She knew, however, that he hadn't necessarily been in a good mood all day long. She knew that he'd probably had his feet trampled in packed trains, encountered rude waitresses, had to be pleasant to disagreeable clients, and had at least a few moments of outright exasperation. That was the way it went.

We just put up with it. We put up with it because that sort of thing always happens. It is how we become adults. If we got angry and lashed out at others over every little thing, not only would we never fit into society, we'd end up wasting our own lives.

But what if you didn't have to put up with anything? What if you were capable of instantaneous retaliation? And what if you could get revenge without anyone ever knowing who had done it?

That woman in the train who stepped on your foot with her high heel. She knew she had done it, but hadn't apologized, and it made you mad. She's getting off the train, mincing along with a stuck-up wiggle to her butt.

All you need to do is concentrate on her expensive perm. Keep looking. Focus. And her hair goes up in flames.

Boy, that felt good!

Whoever crossed a person with such power would immediately pay for it.

"Hey, the water's running!" Noriyuki's voice brought Chikako back to the present. She had been standing there thinking while water gushed out of the faucet.

"I'm going to take a bath and go to bed." Her husband stood up unsteadily.

"Are you okay? You're still pretty drunk."

"I'm not that drunk!"

"The bath has probably cooled off, so it'll have to be heated up again."

"Don't worry about it. I'll do it myself. Go on to bed, you look tired."

Chikako watched her husband weave happily off to the bath, and then went back to her thoughts. If you had the power to start fire, what about heating water? It would be downright convenient, not to mention cheap, to be able to heat a bath to a perfect forty degrees Celsius without having to turn on a switch or even use gas.

Chikako had to laugh. She had begun this train of thought on a purely professional level, but had ended up off on this silly tangent. *I guess it's impossible for me to understand what Makihara feels or to accept what he was trying to tell me.*

Chikako turned off the light in the kitchen and headed for the bedroom. As she slipped between the sheets, she realized that it was just as her husband had said, she was much more tired than she'd thought.

Steam filled the bathroom.

Several days had already passed since Junko had had the chance to wield her power at full capacity, and she could feel her energy beginning to build up inside again.

Her body was also healing. The gunshot wound was still painful, but fortunately it was not infected. The loss of blood made her feel somewhat anemic, and the ceiling twisted around in a half circle every time she got up out of bed, but even that was beginning to settle down.

Junko sensed that it was the power inside of her that was setting the pace for her recovery. It was like a separate living entity that had independently made up its mind that she was going to heal.

Junko could feel that the power wanted to get out. It wanted to be put to use. It had been a long time since Junko had wreaked destruction the way she had the other day, letting her power flow without restraint, but the power had gotten a taste of it and wanted more.

It was urging Junko on.

She could no longer use the abandoned factory to try to appease it. Tayama had become the area with the highest concentration of reporters in Japan. It would even be dangerous to use her power by canals or in parks. She couldn't risk even the slimmest chance that someone might see her or take her picture.

The only thing left for her to do was simply to devote herself to boiling water. She filled her bath to the brim with cold water and let her energy pour into it. It didn't take long for the tiny bathroom to turn into a sauna.

She wiped the sweat off her face and left the bathroom. Her bathrobe was damp. She went to open the window to let in some fresh air.

The instant she reached to open the window, the phone rang. As she moved to pick it up, pain shot through her wounded shoulder. Junko paused for a second, glanced at her shoulder and then her arm, and then took the receiver with her other hand.

"This is Junko Aoki, right? Are you free to talk now?"

Suddenly Junko had the feeling that the pain she had just felt in her shoulder had been telling her something.

"Who is this?" Junko asked, tightening her grip on the phone. It was slippery from all the hot steam coming out of the bathroom.

"I can't just come out and give you my name." It was a man with a gentle, relaxed voice. He didn't sound young. It was the voice of someone who understood his own power and the responsibility it brought with it. Junko thought he sounded like a doctor. She had not been to see one in years, but the doctors she remembered all sounded like that.

Don't worry, Junko. Your mother will be fine.

It's time to notify your mother's family and friends and tell them about her illness. I'll do my best for her, of course, but her heart is getting weaker.

She remembered those voices.

"Hello, are you still there?" the man on the phone said, pulling her out of her reverie. "I'm calling to tell you about the Guardians."

She was sure she had heard something like that recently . . . that's right, it was that other call. Junko's voice unconsciously rose a little as she remembered.

"I got a call recently from some young guy, and he used that word. He was saying something about how he wasn't supposed to be calling me yet."

The man sounded startled—and displeased.

"That rash little . . . He already contacted you?"

"Do you have something to do with him? He said, 'We're impressed with the way you work.' What did he mean by that? What is this 'guardian' business you're talking about?'"

"It's the name of our organization."

"That doesn't tell me anything. I don't know who 'we' is or what your group does."

"That's true." Junko could hear a smile in his voice. "That's why I'm calling, because we'd like to meet you. Would you be interested in meeting us?"

"Why exactly should I meet you and your group?" Junko felt as though she was being played along and asked skeptically, "Are you trying to sell me something? Is this a pyramid scheme?"

Now the caller laughed out loud. His voice became fainter—Junko could tell he had moved the receiver away from his mouth.

"What are you laughing about? I'm asking a straightforward question."

"I apologize." The caller was still holding back a chuckle as he brought the receiver back to his mouth. "I know that you won't want to come meet us just because we call you up one day and ask you to. Today I'd like to give you a present. Try it out and see if you like it. I'll call again in, let's see, a few days."

"What are you talking about?"

The caller ignored the irritation in Junko's voice and said, "Hitoshi Kano." Junko's eyes widened. "Excuse me?"

"I'll give you Hitoshi Kano's address. He's the young man you've been looking for. He's twenty now, a legal adult. He's got a driver's license, and he's into snowboarding these days. Every weekend, he puts his snowboard in the carrier on his car and heads for the mountains. With his friends."

His friends. Junko closed her eyes. Hitoshi Kano. What sort of friends would he be hanging out with?

"There's more. There was an election in his district last month to fill an open seat in the Diet. I don't know if he voted, but he could have if he wanted to. Boy, that hit me hard. The right to vote, the duty and privilege of every citizen in Japan. He has it! Talk about equality and tolerance, huh? Our country gives the right to vote to this conscience-less scum, this unrepentant murderer."

Junko spoke without even thinking.

"Give me his address."

"Of course I will."

Junko quickly wrote down the address and telephone number he gave her. She could feel exultation growing inside her. She'd been looking for Hitoshi Kano for ages, and had been chagrined that he was still on the loose. Despite this good news, however, a doubt lingered at this sudden offer of information.

"How did you get Kano's address? And why are you giving it to me? How did you know I was looking for him?"

She could hear yet another chuckle on the other end of the line.

"We know all about you. We're comrades, working for the same cause."

"The same cause?"

"And our best wishes go with you for success—not that we have any worries, with your abilities. And since you're so pleased with this present, and we're so sure you'll know what to do with it, we've got another one waiting for you when you're finished."

Junko leaned forward, closer to the phone. She knew it wouldn't bring her physically any closer to her caller, but she couldn't help herself.

"What are you going to tell me? Who next?"

"News of Kazuki Tada." With that, the caller hung up. Junko stood there with the phone in one hand and her memo pad in the other. She felt as though she'd been abandoned on a street corner.

Hitoshi Kano. Three years ago he had been an unemployed seventeen-year-old living in Nakano Ward, Tokyo. He'd been one of Masaki Kogure's gang. Far from being a leader, his main job had been running errands for the others. His personality was a warped combination of resentment at his status in the gang and abject cruelty towards anyone weaker than himself.

Now he was twenty—an adult. So he was into snowboarding, was he? And he had a driver's license?

Who was he planning to drag into that car of his next? Junko's cheeks felt hot and her temples throbbed. When she got angry, the energy inside her would gather momentum. If she tried releasing it just a little, the chances of it getting out of hand were too high, so she kept it under tight control, closing off its outlet, and she paid for it with migraine headaches.

Junko went back into the bathroom. She stripped down to her underwear and sat on the edge of the tub. Once again, she turned on the faucet and let cold water pour into it, pouring her energy in, too. By the time the bath was full the water was hot, and she automatically reached out to pull the plug to let it drain, then repeated the process. This took care of the raw energy, but she had no outlet for her emotions—just turning water into steam wasn't satisfying.

It was too late to do anything tonight. She would take action tomorrow. Even though she knew this was the only reasonable thing to do, her mind was already whirling and she couldn't stop it. Hitoshi Kano. She had found him and now she would see him take his last breath.

Junko had only ever seen him once, and it was from a distance, but she had noted that his only outstanding features were his flat nose and crooked teeth.

Years had passed since several high school girls had been murdered around Tokyo. The girls had become targets only because they were unlucky enough to be walking alone. They were snatched off the street and taken to lonely mountain roads or deserted lakesides. In the car on the way, they were beaten and tortured. When they arrived at their "destination," the girls would be tossed out of the car and told they were free to run away. By that time they would have been stripped of their shoes and most of their clothes. The thugs would tell them, "This is what we call 'Life or Death Tag.' If you can escape from us, you'll live."

The girls would run with every ounce of strength they had left. The gang chased after them in the car. They were careful to release the girls in places they'd chosen in advance, where there were no thickets or groves they could hide in. It was no more than a foxhunt, and the girls were run over and killed. Their bodies were either left like used-up rags or taken somewhere else and abandoned.

After the third killing, the police finally put out a dragnet and started an investigation. They had their eye on a single group of juvenile delinquents that they had learned about from a chance clue let drop by a boy brought in for questioning on another case. That their only tip, no more than a rumor really, came from a delinquent under fourteen would haunt them afterwards, but at that stage they needed to act on any clue, no matter how small.

The investigation began. The crimes were horrendous, but all of the suspects were minors, and the investigation could not be conducted aggressively. The police were further hampered by the lack of material evidence. Then there was a leak and the mass media got hold of it.

Soon after, sixteen-year-old Masaki Kogure, the prime suspect, held a press conference to announce that he was planning to sue the police department. He claimed to be innocent of any crime and had no idea why he was under suspicion. He said that the police had not only thrown his personal life into confusion but had purposely leaked his identity, making him easy fodder for the mass media.

Masaki Kogure had a kind of precocious charisma, a slick tongue and a smart, confident way of carrying himself. He catapulted to celebrity and became the darling of daytime TV. He was featured not only on afternoon tabloid-style chat shows, but even on prime-time entertainment variety programs. Junko had seen him getting the teen-idol treatment a number of times. He wrote a semi-autobiographical novel titled *A Cry of Protest from the Soul of Rebel Youth,* and he told anyone and everyone that it was his dream to personally produce the movie version of it.

There was no hard evidence but plenty that was circumstantial. There was enough verbal testimony to fill a library. The media hyped Kogure on one hand while publicizing the leaks from the police on the other. Public opinion was divided.

In the end, the police had been unable to press charges against either Masaki Kogure or any of the members of his gang.

And that was where I came in.

That was why Junko had gone to see Kazuki Tada, the elder brother of the third victim. His sister's name was Yukie, and she'd been a beautiful girl.

If the law couldn't put away a monster like Masaki Kogure, some other means had to be found. That was why Junko thought she might be useful to Kazuki Tada—in the role of a loaded gun.

She could help him get revenge; they could execute Kogure. It seemed preordained that she knew Tada already because they worked in the same company. In early fall of that year, she and Kazuki Tada put together a plan to go after Masaki Kogure. They had followed him at a distance, and all she had to do was aim her power at him from the passenger seat of Tada's car.

Junko watched as Kogure's hair, shirt, and skin caught on fire, and he screamed and fell to the ground, rolling to put out the flames. But then Kazuki Tada changed his mind. At the last moment, just before she could finish Kogure off, Tada had driven off with Junko, away from the scene. He said that he didn't want to stain their hands with murder, making them no better than Kogure.

Junko could not understand. How could they ever be the same as Kogure? Tada had never tortured someone to death nor enjoyed killing for its own sake. Executing Masaki Kogure, who had done these things, was a sacred duty. But Kazuki Tada refused.

Junko left Tada, and continued the pursuit on her own. It took some time, but after Junko finally executed Masaki Kogure, in what was known to the public as the Arakawa riverside murders, she went to see Kazuki Tada. She wanted to report that the job was done. By the time she reached him one rainy, foggy night, Tada had already figured it out. He told her to stop her pursuit of Kogure's gang, but she had no intention of abandoning her mission and, disheartened, she had left him in the rain.

That was the last time she had seen him. She had continued her search for the other gang members alone. Kogure had been her main target and, with him out of the way, it was their turn. It was not too difficult to figure out who they were. Kogure had mentioned many of his friends in interviews and in his so-called autobiography. Junko did some investigative work, and hired a detective agency to do the rest. She eventually identified the whole group.

The shock of Kogure's grisly murder, however, had spread though the gang like wildfire. When speculation went around that it had been revenge for the high school girl murders, the gang members began to make their escapes. They moved to new homes, left Tokyo, and used aliases. Junko's hunt became more difficult.

Still, she had managed to hunt down the nineteen-year-old youth who was another one of the ringleaders, as well as the eighteen-year-old who acted as the driver, and she had taken care of them both. The former she had burned along with his entire house. The fire was labeled "suspicious." The youth's parents, who had been out at the time, put on a grand funeral for their son. Junko had attended, dressed as a mourner. As she listened to the glowing eulogy the father gave for his son, Junko wished she had finished off the parents, too. She knew that three different boys had testified to police, independently of the others, that they had heard this paragon of virtue brag, almost howling with laughter, about how he had tied up the first victim of their murder spree, a sixteen-year-old girl, and stabbed her in the eyes with an ice pick.

As for the gang's driver, Junko had set his car on fire. In flames, the car had continued to run until it hit a utility pole. The car had been totaled, but, miraculously, the driver had survived. As far as Junko knew, he still clung tenaciously to life—as a vegetable.

Now, only Hitoshi Kano was left.

This cunning ape of a young man had moved and was able to live completely free of his past. Junko knew what he had done to the girls he had kidnapped, and she knew what he had done to other victims of his. She knew everything. Before killing Kogure's co-leader, she had used her power to break his legs to keep him from escaping, and had then interrogated him.

Sobbing, he had confessed everything; he admitted all their crimes. Not only had they killed the high school girls, they had also committed crimes against other women that had never surfaced. In every single case, the cruelest acts had been carried out by Hitoshi Kano, the one who always came along for the ride and who sat with his finger up his nose, waiting impatiently for his turn to torture the victims.

Junko refused to consider her duty to the murdered girls completed until she got rid of this son of a bitch.

And now, she'd finally found him.

Guardians. Protectors. Junko closed her eyes and thought. When that man on the phone said "we," did he mean a group, all of whom had powers like hers? If that was the case, who—or what—were they protecting?

It saddened Junko that she couldn't protect anyone. If some horrible evil drew near, she could attack it head on. Unfortunately, though, the world was full of evil, and Junko could only be in one place at a time. She could not even move instantly to wherever she was needed. The only thing she could do was to set out after a tragedy occurred to get rid of the monster who had caused it.

She ended up staying in the bathroom that night until the early hours. She was still hot when she finally climbed into bed, and it took her a long time to get to sleep.

When she closed her eyes, it was not Hitoshi Kano's face that she saw but Kazuki Tada's. That was strange. She thought she had no feelings left for him. She had been attracted to him: he was diligent and sensitive, and she had to admit that she had offered to serve as his "gun" because she had liked him.

But everything was different now. He hadn't been able to understand her, but that was not unreasonable. They were from different worlds. He couldn't accept Junko. And he had said it was more important to him that he not be a murderer than it was to avenge his little sister.

Why did that man who called himself a Guardian think it would be a gift to her to hear news of Kazuki Tada? Junko didn't want to see him. There'd be no point.

It was almost dawn before she fell into a light doze. It was not clear whether she was sleeping or awake; the only thing she was aware of was her exhaustion and inability to move.

Then she dreamed. It was a nightmare about something that had happened many years ago when she was still a child. She had set someone on fire accidentally and was apologizing in tears, *I'm sorry!* There was a small boy in the center of a ball of flames, and he was dancing around in pain as his own body burned. Junko could see his eyes opened wide in fear.

There had been someone else there, too. The person held out his hand to the burning boy and was shouting something. He—yes, it was another boy—was reeling with terror and screaming. Then he was crying. But he noticed Junko and tried to run after her. Junko ran away as fast as she could. *I'm sorry. I'm sorry. I'll never do it again. Leave me alone!*

She woke up completely then.

Why had that old nightmare returned again after so many years? It was an awful memory, one she'd shut far away in the back of her mind. Her pajamas clung damply to her skin, and she could feel sweat trickling down between her breasts.

She got out of bed and pulled the curtains back. The day was beginning to break. Junko shook her head to get rid of the dream and set her mouth tightly. Another day of battle had begun.

16

Shimotanaka 2-chome, Koto Ward, Yokohama. It was the first time Junko had ever been in this part of Yokohama, and although she knew nothing about it, she could tell at a glance that it was an affluent neighborhood. The address given to her by the man calling himself a "Guardian" led her to an impressive house, complete with white walls and red Western-type tiles on the roof. She wondered if this was what you would call Spanish style. The area was lush with trees and other greenery. Each house was on a large plot of land, and many of them had extensive lawns and gardens within the walls that enclosed their property. It was not yet noon, and there were no people or cars out on the street.

Junko was wearing blue jeans and an old, warm jacket, along with a well-worn pair of high top sneakers. She had tied her hair up casually, and she hadn't bothered with make-up. She'd left her apartment ready for battle. Looking like this around here, though, she was bound to attract attention. Anybody passing by would know instantly that she had blown in from somewhere else. Not only that, but she had a map in her hand. She hoped that she looked like a quiet college student who had wandered by mistake into prime real estate while walking around looking for a cheap apartment.

The real question was, what was Hitoshi Kano doing in a place like this?

As far as Junko could recall, he wasn't from a well-to-do family. In the phony autobiography Masaki Kogure had written, Hitoshi Kano appeared as "K." According to the book, the two had met late one night on a street in Shibuya. They hadn't had a cent between them, so they picked up some teenage girls who happened by, fleeced them of their money, and took them off to a cheap hotel. When they got there, the girls had noticed a scar K had gotten from a beating by his father, and it scared them away.

"Both K and I were children who were tired of the friction between ourselves and our parents. I was under pressure from my successful father, and K's father was the lowest of the low, someone who beat his son."

The book had said something like that, though it wasn't like the book had been written by Kogure himself. A ghostwriter must have taken down and organized his verbal ramblings, so it wasn't a book to take seriously—half-truths mixed liberally with out-and-out lies. But if K were Hitoshi Kano, and he had actually come from such an affluent neighborhood, chances are he would have held a better position in Kogure's gang. Whether or not his father had actually abused him, it was difficult to imagine Hitoshi Kano as the son of a wealthy family.

The "Guardian" had let her know Kano's current address and that he was enjoying his lifestyle. He hadn't told her, however, how he had gotten there. Masaki Kogure had become a kind of star, and the atrocities his group had committed had become more and more vague in the public memory. Eventually, society had forgotten about these crimes which nobody had confessed to. What sort of changes had Hitoshi Kano undergone since then?

I'll just have to catch him and ask him myself.

Junko looked up at the colored glass imitation of an old-fashioned gas lamp over the front gate. This was the main entrance. The two-meter high wrought iron gate kept Junko from going any farther. To the side of the gate was a nameplate, with the family name written in fashionable, cursive lettering: Kinoshita. Unlike some nameplates, it did not list the names of family members, making it impossible for Junko to get any sense of who lived there. Beyond the gate was a garden with an expansive lawn. It was obviously well-cared for. There was not a fallen leaf in sight, and a softly curving gravel drive led to the house.

The wall that surrounded the property had a brick façade. When Junko scratched at it with the tip of her finger, powder came off. She could easily knock it down with her power—it wasn't solidly-built.

Kinoshita. Junko wondered if it was the home of Hitoshi Kano's maternal grandparents. Or had his mother divorced his father and remarried? Or was he living with a foster family?

Junko turned right at the main entrance and began to walk around the property. At the point where the wall met the next-door neighbor's lot and turned inward, there was another wall with only enough room for a cat to get through. Junko turned back, headed towards the entrance again, and continued walking past it to the left. At the west end of the property there was a service entrance with an intercom buzzer next to it. Junko tried opening it, but it was locked. Looking through the metal slats, she saw that it had a latch-style lock. She pushed her fingers through the slats and lifted it open.

Now what should she do? To be honest, she had no idea that the house would be so difficult to approach. With most homes, all you had to do was walk once around them to get an idea of whether anyone was home, and it was easy to pretend to be conducting a survey or making door-to-door sales and just ring the door bell. But if she pressed this intercom buzzer, she was bound to be answered by a servant. She wanted to avoid having to ask for Kano by name. After she dispatched him, naturally the police would come. They would find out that a woman had been here asking for the victim right before he was murdered, and then they'd be able to get a description of her.

Hmm. Victim? Junko hated the idea of referring to Hiroshi Kano as a victim, even when thinking to herself. It seemed such an insult to the real victims.

What would the police do? She had thought about this after she had taken out Masaki Kogure, while watching the news of the Arakawa killings on TV. The police were bound to realize that the Masaki Kogure who had been killed was *the* Masaki Kogure. They would naturally link his murder to his past. And when they thought about it, would they ask themselves whether he was truly a victim?

Probably because she was thinking about the police, she was suddenly struck by a thought. *The Guardians.* If the Guardians were like Junko, they too would have to be careful to stay under the radar of the police, even if they didn't go as far as considering the police their enemies. Had the Guardians ever been pursued by the police before? Exactly what sort of activities were they involved in?

Once again, Junko felt overwhelmed with doubts and confusion, and she took a few steps back. She looked up once again at the Spanish-style house. *Does Hitoshi Kano really live here?* She had been elated to have information about him thrown her way after her own fruitless search. Now she realized that she might have gotten carried away. *Is this a trick?*

She thought about leaving and calling the Kinoshita's telephone number. If she didn't make sure that Kano lived here she might be inviting danger.

Still trying to decide, she heard a car lightly hitting its horn. Looking around, she could see in the distance a small red car coming her way. Junko hurriedly dropped her head and began studying the map in her hand. Once more she was a college student looking for an apartment.

The red car stopped in front of the wall surrounding the Kinoshita property. Junko lifted her head and pretended to be checking the address against the map. At the same time, she checked to see what the car was doing. It was a Mini Cooper, and it was stopping much too long for its driver to just be checking nobody was in the crosswalk. With the map still in her hand, Junko turned her back to the service entrance and began walking away from the red car—she didn't want its driver to see her face.

Then she heard the horn again behind her. It was the driver of the Mini Cooper. It never occurred to Junko that the honking was for her, so she just kept walking. But then she heard the voice of a young woman calling her.

"Excuse me! Hey!"

Junko looked to the right and to the left. There was nobody else. There was not another person in sight.

"Hey! You!"

Junko finally realized the woman was calling her, and cautiously turned around.

The driver was very young, probably just out of high school. She was dressed in a sweater the same shade as the car and was leaning out the Mini Cooper's window, waving at Junko. She'd parked by the service entrance.

"Look, are you here to see Hitoshi by any chance?"

Junko was too taken aback to respond immediately. The girl seemed bright and cheery, and as light on her feet as a little bird as she hopped out of the car and walked quickly over to Junko. Junko caught a whiff of liberally-applied perfume.

"You're trying to get into this house, right?" The girl jerked her thumb confidently toward the Kinoshita residence. "Won't the maid answer?"

Junko was startled to realize that, through no effort of her own, the dice had rolled in her favor.

"Oh yes, you're right," replied Junko. "But it's such a big house, I just lost my nerve. So is this really where Hitoshi Kano lives?"

"That's right," the girl smiled. "Everyone is surprised at first. But there's nothing to worry about. I'm going to see Hitoshi, too. I'll take you."

The girl swept ahead of Junko, opened the gate, and walked right in. Junko plucked up her courage and followed.

As they stepped into the garden with its winter-brown grass, they could hear the faint sound of music. It sounded like a classical melody.

"Just as I thought," the girl said turning back to Junko and then waving in the direction of the music. "The old man here likes listening to classical music. The maid likes it too, and she's hard of hearing, so when there's a CD playing, she can't hear when someone calls on the intercom."

The girl obviously knew where she was going. She wasn't heading for the main entrance but around to the back of the house.

As they got closer to the house, Junko began to see a number of extensions had been made on it, and that was why it was so large. The girl was heading for one of those additions.

"This is where we go in."

The girl pointed to an entrance partially hidden behind some trees planted around the house. It was a simple, functional door that looked more like an emergency exit. A pair of men's sneakers, covered in mud, had been left outside. Junko felt her heart begin to beat faster.

"Is this where he lives?"

"That's right."

Maybe Kano's mother was the Kinoshita's live-in maid and he had a room with her in the servant's quarters. Before she could ask, however, the girl began to explain.

"Hitoshi's mother got a divorce about two years ago. She moved around for a while, but they finally took her in here. And then Hitoshi came to live with her."

"It says 'Kinoshita' on the sign at the front gate . . ."

"That's the name of the man of the house. He's married to Hitoshi's mother's sister."

So that explained it. Hitoshi Kano was living off his aunt.

"It's a regular mansion."

"Yeah, they're *rich*." The girl sounded like she was bragging about her own circumstances. "Hitoshi is finally having some luck."

When they reached the door, Junko hesitated.

"Uh, I don't want to sound nosy, but you and Hitoshi are . . . ?"

"Oh, sorry, I skipped that part. I'm Hitoshi's friend. And I'm a member of Circle S, too, so you've come at just the right time. Who introduced you?"

Introduced? Circle S?

Junko was speechless, so the girl continued helpfully. "Hmm, was it Hashiguchi? Really enthusiastic, but kind of pushy? You probably didn't really want to come, did you? But you don't have to worry. Circle S doesn't sell anything weird, and they always pay you back. I'm sure the initial payment seems kind of high, but if you bring friends into it, you'll make it all back in about three months."

After finishing her quick little speech, she kicked the sneakers out of the way and opened the door, calling out, "Hitoshi! I'm coming in! You'd better not still be in bed! Come on, get up, there's a new member for you!"

The door opened into a roomy studio apartment. The wood flooring was still new, and the papered walls and ceiling were perfectly white. The room itself, however, was a complete mess. It looked like a disaster area.

Dirty laundry was piled high in one corner. The pile appeared to be moving, and then the head of a young man poked out. Junko quietly gasped, and then turned sharply to make sure her companion had not noticed her reaction. The girl, however, had already left her side. She ran straight for the guy in the pile of laundry and leaped on top of him.

"I knew you were still in bed! Do you know what time it is?"

It was about eleven. Junko took a good look at the sleepy face of the young man. She had to stand hard on her right foot with her left one to keep herself in check as she stared at the two of them, wrestling like kittens.

That face. That man. There was no mistake: it was Hitoshi Kano. The Guardians had given her accurate information.

"We don't want to force you into anything. You can go home and think about it before you make your decision. We don't do hard sales."

So saying, Hitoshi Kano took a bunch of pamphlets and catalogs off the cluttered table and handed them to Junko.

She then spent the next hour listening to the two of them. Circle S was the name of their sham import company—a pyramid scheme. They gave a long spiel on its many virtues, but it was clearly not an aboveboard business. They sold health food supplements and cosmetics, but it was not clear what any of the products were supposed to do. Junko wouldn't have bet even a hair that had already fallen out of her head on the veracity of their claim that it was the exclusive agent in Japan for some major American corporation.

Gathering from what the two of them said, however, Circle S was having a fair amount of success. She guessed it meant that there were lots of young people willing to trick their friends into forking out money as long as it meant they themselves would profit.

Junko hadn't realized that swindlers and murderers were made of the same stuff. Ever since Hitoshi Kano had been taken in by his wealthy aunt, he must have quit squeezing the life's blood out of people in favor of squeezing the money out of them. Life in the wealthy Kinoshita household had evidently planted a new craving in the heart of this cunning, cruel, and selfish youth. Junko guessed that he'd decided that as fun as killing was, it would never make him rich.

Kano and his girlfriend were convinced that Junko had come at the introduction of Hashiguchi, another one of their members. They were totally off guard, not even asking for any kind of identification. Junko gave them the first name that popped into her head, talked as little as possible, and left them to draw their own conclusions. There was no doubt that they saw Junko as a naïve girl come lately to the big city, and not awfully bright either. In other words, she was perfect for their purposes. An easy mark. They were sure to get money out of her with just a little smooth talk.

Hitoshi Kano, despite his crumpled T-shirt and chinos, had grown up quite a bit since the time Junko had seen him. He had dyed his hair brown and cut it short in the fashion of strong-man movie stars. He had a shiny pierced earring in his left ear, and his personality was much more sophisticated than Masaki Kogure's portrayal in his so-called autobiography.

The room was uncomfortably warm, and the girl eventually took off her sweater, revealing a short-sleeved pullover underneath. She had not introduced herself, but Kano was calling her "Hikari."

"If you agree to the conditions for joining, put your seal and signature here. You can bring it back here or mail it in."

Hitoshi Kano gave her a bright, engaging smile. He seemed like such a nice young man.

"You can pay the initial fee of two hundred thousand yen into this bank account or bring it with the application. If you bring it in cash, I'll give you a receipt and your member's card on the spot, but you've probably got to go to work, right? I know Hashiguchi can be a real slave driver."

Junko gathered from what they said that this Hashiguchi was a member in his thirties who ran a restaurant. He made money on the side by bringing in new members to Circle S, probably those in a subordinate position to him, like suppliers or employees anxious to keep their jobs. Both Kano and Hikari assumed that Junko was one of his waitresses.

Junko had already made up her mind. She wanted to finish off Hitoshi Kano here in this studio apartment. She could do it without anyone else in the house noticing anything. The only problem was this Hikari. Junko was grateful to her for helping her get inside. She wanted to avoid killing her if possible.

On the other hand, she didn't appreciate being made a mark and she didn't think much of Hikari for her obvious intention to scam Junko. Where had the money for her designer sweater and brand-new Mini Cooper come from? It had been conned from others, hadn't it? That wasn't something that sat well with Junko.

Hikari was obviously in love with Kano, and Junko was sure she had no idea of his past. Maybe Junko owed it to her to let her know just what kind of person he was. But if Hikari witnessed what she planned to do next, Junko would not be able to let her get away. It would be much too dangerous.

She couldn't decide what to do. Her temples began to ache, reminding her that her power was looking for a way out. It had no trouble at all making a decision: it wanted the target that was right there in front of her, and it was not at all influenced by the human hesitations of Junko's heart.

Junko had spent years learning to control her power. After that evening in the park when she had burned that little boy to death, she had worked on her control, and the number of accidents had decreased remarkably. That was how she had grown into an adult. She was certain that she was in control; that the power was in her possession.

Since the incident at the abandoned factory in Tayama, however, she was beginning to have flickers of doubt. Especially at times like this. *I don't want to kill her, but the power does. Who is making the decisions here? Me, or the power?*

How many people had Junko burned at the factory, the coffee shop, and then the liquor store? It hadn't even been twenty-four hours.

At the time it had been right. It had been a rescue mission, and all her battles had been to exterminate evil. Junko had been certain that she was the one in control. But now, looking back, her certainty began to waver. *Had I really wanted to do all that? Was that really what I had hoped for?*

Then with a chill, she recalled the dream she'd had the night she had visited the abandoned factory. The dream had ended with Junko seeing flames rushing up her own arm. She'd woken up with an aftertaste of horror and had had to immediately scramble about checking her pajamas, her blankets and her mattress for fire. At the time she had wondered, *Could my technique for controlling the power be slipping?*

Was that the truth? Or on the other hand, maybe her technique was the same as it had always been. Maybe it was the power itself growing larger, more clever, and more independent. And maybe while she was in action, still unaware of this, it dulled her consciousness of the carnage she was wreaking? It might be why she'd recently been so quick to judge someone as her opponent in battle, too.

The power was like a guard dog that had grown, learned, and could occasionally outwit its own master. And it knew this. It knew it could drag Junko around whenever it felt like it, but for now it remained chained up.

"Hey!"

Junko heard a voice from far away. She blinked. The finger that had been rubbing her temple stopped.

"Are you okay? You look pale." Hitoshi Kano leaned towards her, looking into her face. Junko quickly drew back. He was less than a meter from her, and he looked ready to come closer. She was afraid that if he touched her, or even breathed on her, that her power would leap right out and destroy him. The timing was still not right for that.

"I'm sorry. I just sort of drifted off."

Hitoshi Kano smiled. "Short on sleep?"

"Maybe."

"Hashiguchi wears his employees out. I've got just the vitamins for you. I'll give you a sample. Some of our members say the vitamins help you look even better than the cosmetics do."

His voice was gently coaxing. Junko shivered with revulsion but managed a weak smile.

"Hitoshi can never let a cute girl go by," Hikari grumbled and hit him on the back. "You want to be nice to them all. It really bugs me."

"There's nothing for you to get angry about," Hitoshi retorted.

"No, of course not. I do apologize!" Hikari lifted her nose to the ceiling and stood up. "I'm going to see your uncle. I've got to take his order for that vegetable vitamin mix."

"Does he order a lot?" Hitoshi asked.

"Half a dozen at a time. Pretty good, huh?"

"That ought to set you up pretty well!"

Hikari laughed in reply, and put her shoes on. "Sure does!" She turned around to face Junko. "I'll take you to the station, so wait till I get back. And that way Hitoshi can get you filled in on more of the details."

Hikari hurried out, and Junko could hear her footsteps on the garden stones as she headed toward the main house. The door closed slowly behind her on its own, finally shutting with a click.

They were alone.

The trap was set.

Junko's mind was now completely clear.

Junko the machine was now switched on.

"Look—" Hitoshi had started easing back up to Junko. Junko turned to look him straight in the eye.

"How did it feel to stick an ice pick into a girl's eyes?" she asked.

Hitoshi Kano's eyes widened. Junko noticed that he had a tiny black mole to the side of his left eye.

Now that's exactly where I would stick an ice pick in him. It's like God put that on his face so I'd know the spot. An eye for an eye, and a tooth for a tooth.

"What are you talking about?" Hitoshi Kano's voice was tight.

"You know exactly what I'm talking about." Junko smiled. This time it was a real smile. "It's what you did. It's too late to say you didn't do anything. I've heard all about it from your friends."

Hitoshi Kano, still sitting on the floor, began to creep backwards.

You fool! If you're going to try to escape, stand up and run. Run and never look back! Run for your life.

But I'll still be right behind you.

"I've been looking for you. All this time."

As she spoke, Hitoshi Kano's face broke out in flames.

Junko heard footsteps on the garden path again. She was in the doorway putting on her shoes when she noticed that Hikari was on her way back. The room was stifling and the burnt smell overwhelming. Well, it would be. Junko herself was used to the smell and didn't even notice it anymore.

Hikari's footsteps were light. Junko paused in the doorway, listening to them. Junko the machine was still switched on. It would be very easy to invite Hikari back inside and watch her hair go up in flames.

Looking back inside, in the very place where Hitoshi Kano had sat— alive—not more than ten minutes ago, she could see a mounded heap of slightly soiled blankets. Junko had used them to cover up the charred remains of Hitoshi Kano, now burnt black. Otherwise the messy room was the same as it had been when she arrived. None of the furniture or anything else in the room was burned; there were just bits of ash scattered over the little table, and the spot where Hitoshi Kano had fallen was slightly blackened.

Junko stepped outside. She closed the door securely. Hikari finally noticed her and stopped in surprise.

"Leaving so soon?"

Junko nodded wordlessly.

"What do you think? Are you planning to join up? Hitoshi's a qualified Circle S sales trainer, so I bet his explanation was a lot easier to follow than mine."

Junko didn't budge from in front of the door, so Hikari just stood there chatting. Her smile was as friendly as before, but her eyes flitted back and forth from Junko to the door, signaling Junko to move out of the way and let her get by.

"I want to go home now," Junko finally spoke. "You said you'd give me a lift?"

"Sure, I'll take you, but would you wait just a minute? I have to give Hitoshi this order form." A piece of paper was fluttering in her hand. "Hitoshi's uncle bought a bunch of expensive vitamin packages. He said Hitoshi's always getting spending money off him, so the commission for this whole order should go to my account instead of his."

Hikari was trying to support her explanation by waving the order form for emphasis. Junko watched her coolly, and thought she saw a flash of uncertainty cross Hikari's face. She was probably noticing a change in Junko's demeanor. Was it the glitter in her eyes? Was she speaking differently?

The switch on the killing machine still wouldn't turn off.

"Um, could you move out of the way?" Hikari said, stepping forward gingerly, as if her legs had gone to sleep. "I just need to give him this order and then I'll be ready to go."

Junko spoke hurriedly.

"But he just left."

"What?"

"He got a call from a friend, and he took off. He told me to wait here, right at the door, until you got back."

"So the door is locked?"

"Yes."

Hikari sighed in exasperation. "He's always doing that. Oh well, I'm busy today too, so I guess it's just as well. It was a girl, wasn't it?"

"I really don't know."

"It's always a girl. They're all after him. Okay, let's go." Junko wondered if Hikari made it a habit to show up at Hitoshi Kano's room whenever she felt like it. She had no trouble believing Junko's lie. In fact, the hint of uneasiness seemed to have completely disappeared. She turned right around and headed for the service entrance.

Junko would accompany her to where her Mini Cooper was parked, but she didn't plan to get in the car. She had no intention of letting Hikari take her anywhere. She would watch her go and then leave on her own. She would not kill her.

Junko believed that she would not have to kill her.

But the power wanted to kill her. Junko could feel it. The power's desire. That's why the switch wouldn't go off yet—Junko wanted it off, but the power was demanding that it stay on.

Once again Junko found herself in a swirl of doubt. Who was in charge here? Junko or her power?

Are you going to let that greedy, selfish girl live?

(Her sins are not serious enough for death.)

If she does something to cause the death of another person, will you be able to live with it?

(She's not smart enough to deliberately take a life.)

How can you overlook a woman who has anything to do with Hitoshi Kano?

(She doesn't know the truth about him.)

The power inside Junko jeered at her and grew more insistent. *Kill her! Vanquish her! Her life has no value! You are the judge. She might remember what you look like. She might tell the police about you. Just do it! Like that customer at Café Currant. Like Keiichi Asaba's mother. Turn them all into ashes and leave them behind. It's for your own safety.*

I know you want to kill her.

"Aren't you getting in?"

Junko was standing next to the red car. Hikari had her hand on the door on the driver's side, and she was looking at Junko questioningly.

Junko felt like something was swelling in her throat, and it was about to leap out of her mouth. She clenched her teeth.

"I've decided not to join Circle S."

She felt like she was fighting to get out each word.

"Really?"

"I don't think much of the system. You have to drag your friends into it. Isn't that what you've done? I don't think I'd feel right about that."

"But, I . . ."

Junko saw the uneasiness crossing Hikari's face again. It was much darker than before; it was very close to fear. "It's none of your business about me.

And why do you have such a scary look on your face?" Hikari was planning to fight back. "What's your problem? If you don't like Circle S, you don't have to join."

Junko kept her jaw clenched and looked down. She stared at the deep wine red color of the car. *I think I'll melt it. It'll look like lava.*

"Come on, say something!"

Hikari's voice was sharper. She did not realize yet that she felt any fear, so she was getting aggressive. If you're scared, you're the first to throw a punch.

"Hitoshi told you all about it, didn't he? It's not what you say—you'll make money all right, but only if you're quick enough. Not everyone will. That's the way the world works, doesn't it? There're all kinds of businesses like this. And it's not illegal. I'll tell you right now, the police and consumer organizations can't do anything about it. Stop glaring at me like that!"

Hikari was almost yelling now as she opened the car door. "There's nothing wrong with what we're doing, and I won't listen to you smear it. Nobody's making you do anything. Stupid people are stupid their whole lives. But don't blame smart people for making something of themselves!"

Hikari turned and bent to get in the car. Junko directed her words to the back of Hikari's head.

"Do you know about Hitoshi Kano's past?"

Hikari's head flew up. She looked truly and almost comically surprised.

"Hitoshi's past?"

"That's what I said."

A new expression came over Hikari's face—one Junko hadn't expected.

"What happened between you and Hitoshi?" Hikari challenged Junko, both hands on her hips. "I know what you are—an old girlfriend that he dumped. He sure didn't look like he recognized you just now. Did he just hit on you once? So you came chasing after him? Is that it?"

Junko was rattled. For Junko, having a past had never remotely meant something as simple as a relationship between a man and a woman.

"Say something!" Hikari rounded the car, back to Junko's side. Her eyes were narrowed. "Don't expect me to take this! I'm Hitoshi's—"

"Hitoshi's what?" Junko asked in a calm voice. Deep inside of her, she could hear her power clearing its throat. *Didn't I tell you? What value does her life have?*

"He's mine!" Hikari spit the words out. "So what's your problem with him?"

"Your boyfriend is a murderer." Junko folded her arms and took deep breaths to control herself. "He killed high school girls. Not just one. It was a few years ago."

Hikari stood there, chin jutting out and her legs set apart in a fighting pose. "What kind of garbage is that? Take it back!"

"It's not garbage. Check into it. You'll find out soon enough what your boyfriend and his friends did."

Hikari winced slightly.

"Hitoshi doesn't have a police record."

"That's only because there wasn't enough proof and the police couldn't arrest him. And they were all still underage at the time."

Hikari stared hard at Junko. It looked like she was thinking about something and trying to come up with something to back it up. Then she blurted out, "So what did those girls you say were murdered have to do with you?"

Junko was silent.

"What did you come here for?" Hikari demanded, still staring hard at Junko. Her eyes widened as she came up with an answer to her own question. "Did you do something to Hitoshi?"

Junko didn't answer.

"You did something to him," Hikari shrieked, leaving her car and running back toward the service entrance. "He didn't leave—you did something!"

Junko didn't try to follow her, but Hikari ran anyway. She stumbled over her own feet in her panic and almost fell. Junko willed her not to look back. *I just want to leave this place. Don't turn around!*

But Hikari did turn around. As she went through the service entrance, she turned to make sure that Junko was not chasing her and that she'd really gotten away. Junko's control was shattered by the fear and hatred in her eyes. The power triumphantly made its escape and went dancing out after Hikari.

There was a muffled sound. Hikari's hair stood up straight, and her slight body floated upwards. Her stylishly shod feet flew forward in the air. By the time they hit the ground again, they were engulfed in flames. The hot air blew on Junko's cheeks, and it was mixed with the strong perfume Hikari had been wearing. She hadn't screamed.

Junko tried to leave as slowly as she could. She wouldn't run until she got to the first corner. She counted to herself.

The area was quiet. Nobody had noticed anything strange. Now that it was still, she could hear classical music faintly wafting from the Kinoshita residence.

Junko counted to a hundred and then started running. She felt like someone was screaming but she couldn't tell if it was a real scream or the one in her heart.

17

"Quite a place isn't it? When you live in a high-rise building like this, it gets to be a lot of trouble to go out, and residents tend to stay at home. That's not a good thing for children." Chikako Ishizu spoke to Makihara, who stood silently watching the floor numbers fly by as they rode in the elevator. When she'd called him to say she'd been able to make an appointment for them to see Kaori Kurata again, he hadn't seemed too keen to go even though it had originally been his idea.

"You punched in a pass number downstairs. Does this elevator go straight to the Kurata's apartment?" Makihara finally asked as they sped past the thirtieth floor.

"That's right."

"That means outsiders can't easily get in."

"Security is tight," said Chikako. "That's why I think the fires are an inside job." She couldn't resist taking a dig at Makihara. "But I still don't believe that Kaori is starting them by willpower alone."

Makihara was silent, but he raised one eyebrow just as the elevator arrived at the thirty-ninth floor.

As they stepped out, they found Michiko Kinuta waiting for them. She had managed to set a tight little smile on her decorous face, but her anger at their visit and suspicions about their intentions were so patently obvious that Chikako couldn't help a wry smile.

When Chikako had asked to visit the Kuratas again, this time to meet Kaori's parents as well as Kaori, she had not expected them to agree so readily. She had planned to use their refusals as a way to study them, but they had caught her off guard.

When a crime involves a child or adolescent, the investigation procedure often involves something akin to counseling, something detectives were often amateurs at. One of the mistakes they often made was to force the issue—they just couldn't wait, especially in cases when it was important to do so. Chikako was afraid that she should have waited a little longer before she made a second visit.

Chikako had informed Michiko ahead of time that Makihara would be with her, explaining that he'd been involved in cases similar to this one.

Now she briefly introduced the two to each other, and they responded with the minimum of niceties. It looked like a competition for who could show the least interest in the other. Michiko immediately turned away from Makihara and addressed Chikako.

"Mr. Kurata is a very busy person, and it is impossible for him to be at home during office hours." She spoke politely, but coldly. "Mrs. Kurata is with Kaori. She heard from Kaori about what happened last time, and it has worried her terribly."

Chikako ignored Michiko's implied blame and got right down to business. "The other day when I was here, the nineteenth small fire broke out. Have there been any problems since then? A twentieth fire?"

"Not yet."

"That's good to hear. Shall we go in?"

Mrs. Kurata and her daughter were sitting together on the elegant living room couch. Kaori was leaning against her mother and the two of them clutched each other's hands tightly. This might have been the reason Mrs. Kurata did not stand when Chikako and Makihara came forward and were introduced by Michiko.

"Please come in and sit down." Her words were pleasant enough but tinged with weariness.

"I'll bring something to drink. Will coffee be acceptable?" Fusako Eguchi poked her head out briefly from the door leading to the kitchen. She soon came out pushing a cart with cups and a pot of hot coffee. She gave only the briefest of nods in response to Chikako's greetings and left the room as soon as everyone had been served. All present held their coffee cups grimly, as if it were the opening formality for a particularly difficult meeting.

Kaori was a lovely girl so Chikako had imagined that her mother would be attractive, too, but she was taken aback by just how beautiful she actually was. Chikako had never considered herself to have more than average looks, but even Michiko Kinuta, who was definitely in the "unusually attractive" category, paled before Mrs. Kurata.

Her appearance was modest and her face only lightly made up. She did not have the angular features of fashion models; the curves of her face were gentle and her eyes classically Japanese. Her face might seem too quiet and even lacking drama, somehow, for some. But Mrs. Kurata was the sort of woman that most people, male or female, would feel instinctively protective towards. Chikako suddenly understood the sympathy for the Kurata family that underlay Michiko Kinuta's reports and Fusako Eguchi's diligent care of them.

Sitting next to each other, Mrs. Kurata and Kaori looked less like parent and child than like the eldest and youngest sisters in a well-spaced family. The two shared the same translucent skin, and it was painful to see the tension that was pulling both of their faces taut.

Michiko spoke up as if she felt it was her role to break the tense silence.

"Detective Ishizu, the Kurata family is considering moving out of this apartment."

Chikako carefully hid her surprise and glanced at Makihara out of the corner of her eye. They had just discussed this possibility no more than thirty minutes ago.

They'll probably tell us they are going to move. Makihara had made the statement almost coldly. *They'll say that they want to move to get away from the arsonist stalker and that they're going to keep the address secret. If they don't try to keep up that appearance, people are going to figure them out.*

"Are you planning to go far?" Chikako asked Mrs. Kurata, who in turn looked at Michiko the way murder suspects in movies look at their lawyers while being interrogated. To be specific, she looked at Michiko's mouth. Maybe it was a secret code.

"I don't know . . ." She responded vaguely and then grabbed onto her coffee cup as if it would provide some assistance. "It's just that, with all these frightening things happening, we don't feel comfortable living here anymore. We're also thinking that a house with a garden would be better for Kaori's health."

Chikako smiled in Kaori's direction.

"I guess that means changing schools, too. Aren't you going to miss your friends?"

The girl looked away without answering. She tightened her grip on her mother's hand.

"Excuse me," said Makihara, and he stood up. He crossed the room and went straight to the spot where the vase of artificial flowers had caught fire when Chikako had been there before. Instead of flowers, a lamp with an elegant stained-glass shade now decorated the table.

"This is where the last small fire was. Am I right?" Makihara remained facing the wall as he asked the question. "Did you put a fresh coat of paint on this wall, Mrs. Kurata?"

Michiko opened her mouth to respond but looked over at Mrs. Kurata, whom Makihara had addressed. Mrs. Kurata blinked and responded in a small voice.

"Yes, that's right."

"It can't be easy having to do that after every fire. It must get expensive after a while."

"It's preferable to having anyone hurt."

"That's true. But when there was a fire at school, wasn't a student taken to the hospital? That's what it said in the report."

Mrs. Kurata was silent, as if she didn't understand what Makihara was getting at. Makihara still had his face to the wall, as though examining it.

"And you paid for the treatment?"

Michiko looked at Mrs. Kurata in surprise. Mrs. Kurata froze for an instant. Kaori continued to look down.

Chikako was startled. She wondered where Makihara had come up with that piece of information.

"You paid for the treatment. Isn't that right?" Makihara finally turned around to face Mrs. Kurata.

"Yes, we paid for it." She responded in a voice that was even smaller than before.

"Why?"

"What do you mean 'why?'"

"There was no reason to, was there? Kaori wasn't hurt, and she was a victim of the fire too, wasn't she?"

"It was because if the fire was meant to hurt Kaori, then the other child was an innocent bystander. And she was one of Kaori's friends as well."

"I see."

"And the family has little money."

"Even though they send their child to a private school?"

"The truth is that things are difficult for them."

"I see," Makihara said again, this time more to himself than in answer. His tone didn't seem sarcastic, but Chikako noticed that Mrs. Kurata pulled in her chin as if prepared to defend her actions further. Then as she glanced from Mrs. Kurata to her daughter, Chikako sucked in her breath in surprise.

Kaori had gone white as a sheet. She had been quiet and subdued, but a few seconds before her color had been good and her eyes clear. Now her eyes were clouded and glazed over, and her cheeks were devoid of all color. The girl looked ill.

What had come over her? Why was she so upset to learn that her mother had paid for her friend's medical treatment?

"Kaori?" Chikako asked uncertainly, and Makihara wheeled around and strode back to their side of the room. Standing next to Michiko's chair, he bent down to look into Kaori's face.

"It's hard to have all these strange people in and out of your house, isn't it?" His voice was so gentle he sounded like a different person.

"If you move, things will settle down. Your mother and father are doing everything they can to protect you. And we'll do what we can too to keep you safe, so don't worry."

Kaori slowly lifted her head. It was as though she was afraid something inside of her would break if she tried to move too fast. Finally, she looked Makihara straight in the face.

Makihara smiled. "By the way, what happened to that finger?"

There was a brand-new bandage on the middle finger of Kaori's right hand. It was flesh-colored, so Chikako hadn't noticed it.

"Oh, she cut her fingernail too closely," her mother answered for her. "It's because she cuts them at night—even though she knows it's bad luck."

"I see you're superstitious," Makihara said, still with a smile. "Back in the days when lighting was poor, it was easy to cut fingernails too close to the quick if you waited until after sundown. That's why they used to say if you cut your nails at night, you wouldn't outlive your parents. There's no need for such a belief anymore."

"Are you sure? I can't believe there's no meaning to it at all."

"There's also the superstition that says if you play with fire, you'll wet your bed."

Mrs. Kurata froze again. Kaori pulled her left hand out of her mother's grasp and leaned toward Makihara, staring at him. Her eyes were narrowed into slits. Chikako felt her heart begin to pound. This wasn't looking good.

Makihara didn't flinch from her gaze. He reached out in a natural way and took her right hand.

"Let me see what you did to yourself."

Just as they made contact, Kaori's eyes flew open wide, her back arched, and she opened her mouth in a soundless scream.

"Kaori?" Makihara saw the change, too. Still holding her hand, he kneeled down. Michiko jumped to her feet, about to push Makihara away from Kaori. But then Kaori let out a long, long breath, saying, *"You know."*

"Kaori? Kaori, are you all right?" Michiko reached for her, but the girl used her left hand to push her away.

"You know. I can tell," Kaori repeated eerily, gripping Makihara's hand. "Who is he? Who is that boy?" Her lips were trembling and she was gazing into space.

"Kaori?" Mrs. Kurata put her arm around Kaori, but Kaori didn't respond. Instead, she latched her free hand onto Makihara's elbow and leaned closer to him. Her grip was strong enough for Chikako to notice Makihara wince.

"Where are you?" she shouted, her voice ragged. Her eyes were bulging and her face, pale a moment ago, was flushed. "Where is he? Can I see him? Why do you know him? He's my . . . my . . ." Kaori's questions came more and more rapidly. "Tell me, *tell me!"*

The cups and hot water pot on the table seemed to shiver in sympathy, and then shattered. Mrs. Kurata put both hands up to her mouth and slid off the couch.

Makihara finally pulled himself out of Kaori's grip and held her tight. Her entire body went rigid and her limbs shook. Her eyes rolled back in her head showing only the whites, and her mouth went slack.

"Call an ambulance," pleaded Mrs. Kurata. Michiko crawled over to the phone. Chikako quickly moved objects within range of Kaori's arms and legs out of the way.

"Kaori, calm down. Everything's going to be all right. Calm down." Makihara held her, and repeated the words over and over, like a mantra. "It's all right. There's nothing here to hurt you. Calm down. Breathe in. That's the way, take another deep breath."

Kaori's breath was still rough, but she did her best to inhale deeply.

"That's right. Take another one. Good. That's the way. Nothing is going to happen. Nothing bad's going to happen."

Kaori's eyes returned to normal, but her pupils were constricted with fear. Then tears welled up and overflowed. Her head fell on Makihara's shoulder and she wept. Makihara continued to hold her, rocking her gently and patting her hair. "That's it. Everything's okay now. There's nothing to frighten you anymore."

Chikako glanced up and noticed that Michiko and Mrs. Kurata were still sitting on the floor. She realized that her own back was damp with sweat as well.

"Let's get her to the hospital to make sure nothing's wrong." Makihara spoke to Chikako over Kaori's head. Then he turned to Kaori's mother and said, "You don't want her having another seizure like that, and it wouldn't hurt to have a full check-up while she's there. Would that be all right with you, Ma'am?"

Mrs. Kurata nodded, still looking dazed. Near her feet lay the delicate white china handle of a coffee cup. It looked almost like a human ear.

"What sort of trick was that?" Chikako directed her question to Makihara's back as they passed through the automatic doors leading to the special ward. Makihara just kept walking straight ahead without answering.

Kaori Kurata had been admitted to a private hospital that was a ten-minute walk from her home. The "special ward" was not for people with particularly serious diseases; it provided luxury accommodations for wealthy patients. Each private room was furnished more comfortably than most hotels. Mrs. Kurata had wanted to take her to the hospital where she served as a director, but Chikako and Makihara insisted on finding one that was better prepared for emergencies, and Mrs. Kurata had eventually given in, choosing instead this hospital where there was a doctor she was acquainted with.

"What did Kaori mean when she shouted at you? What did she want you to tell her?"

The two of them stopped to check Kaori's room number, and Makihara glanced Chikako's way and answered casually.

"It was psychometry."

"What?"

"Psychometry. Haven't you ever heard of it?"

"Almost everything you have to say is new to me."

Makihara grinned and turned to face Chikako.

"It's another type of extrasensory perception. The ability to read lingering impressions that remain on a particular object or person. In other words, Kaori used that ability to read my memories."

Chikako sighed.

"Didn't you say that the power she had was called pyrokinesis? Now you're telling me there's something more?"

"Detective Ishizu, do you play any sports?"

"Hmm?"

"Do you exercise at all?"

Now what? Chikako wondered. "I play a little tennis."

"Did you play tennis as a student?"

"Yes. I was always quick on my feet. I started out on the track team, then I was scouted out by the tennis team."

"Exactly! That's what it means to have a certain kind of ability." Makihara laughed at the long-suffering expression on Chikako's face and tapped his temple with a finger.

"If extrasensory perception means having the ability to use parts of the brain that most humans are unable to, then you could also say that having more than one such ability is only natural. Someone who is fast can be good at tennis as well as running races—because they are quick on their feet and at following the ball. It's the same thing. It's not that unusual to have one main power and some degree of others that are connected to it in some way."

18

Chikako's incredulity must have shown on her face. Makihara laughed, shook his head, and turned back to the list of room numbers posted on the wall.

"So what I'm saying is that Kaori Kurata has a powerful pyrokinetic ability, and it seems this ability does not exist independently but coexists with a certain number of other powers."

"And one of those powers is psychometry?"

"That's right. She can read the memories of someone she comes into contact with. She's not reading thoughts, but actual memories. It's not always limited to people. It can be a physical object. In the West, some psychometrists assist police in criminal investigations. You might say this is the most common sort of psychic ability."

"But—"

Makihara found the room number, and he strode off down the corridor, the hem of his overcoat flapping behind him. Chikako had to quicken her pace to keep up with him.

"She also has a certain amount of telekinesis. You saw the coffee cups on the table shatter, didn't you?"

Now it was Chikako's turn to shake her head.

They arrived at Kaori Kurata's room. A "No Visitors" sign was hanging on the door. Makihara may have been showing respect for the sign as he took care to avoid it when he knocked on another part of the door, but then he walked right in without waiting for an answer.

The room was furnished like a large living room. Across from the leather couch, a small white bed was against the window. Kaori Kurata was sitting up in bed propped up by pillows, her mother at her side.

When Kaori saw Chikako and Makihara, her eyes grew round. Her mother jumped up to intercept them, but before she could say anything Makihara asked amiably, "Kaori, how are you feeling?"

The girl concentrated on Makihara for a moment without answering, then looked up at her mother who spoke instead.

"Please leave. My daughter is not well enough yet to talk to the police." The ends of Mrs. Kurata's words shook a little.

"We just came to see how she was doing," Chikako responded soothingly. "We wanted to make sure neither you nor Kaori were hurt."

Her gentle response seemed to confuse Mrs. Kurata. She dropped her gaze, and, clenching and unclenching her hands, asked them again to leave.

Makihara looked squarely at Mrs. Kurata.

"We're not here to talk to your daughter today. We would like to talk to you, Ma'am," he said briskly.

This seemed to distress Mrs. Kurata even more. She twisted her wrists as if wringing out an invisible towel.

"With me? What about?"

Kaori reached out a slender hand and touched her mother's arm. Mrs. Kurata's hands stopped moving, but her fingers were trembling visibly.

"Mama," Kaori spoke in a small but surprisingly firm voice. "Mama, you can trust them. It's safe to talk to them."

Chikako sucked in her breath. Makihara showed no surprise whatsoever and remained planted by the door.

"He knows. He can see. That's what I saw, so you can talk to him. Mama, we have to talk to someone. We can't keep going on like this forever."

There was no sign here of the hysterical little princess who had clung to Michiko Kinuta and screamed at Chikako. Chikako saw a healthy shine in her eyes that she had not seen previously.

"Kaori . . ." Mrs. Kurata took her daughter's hand. She seemed to be relying on the strength of her daughter instead of the other way around. Kaori turned back to Makihara. Her voice was that of a child, but it did not waver.

"Detective, you know all about people who can start fires, don't you?"

Makihara nodded silently. Next, Kaori looked at Chikako. Chikako felt her mouth go dry.

"This detective thinks I started all those fires. It's true, but I want you to know that I didn't start them on purpose and I didn't do it for fun. That's why I got mad. And that's what set the flowers in the vase on fire."

As Kaori spoke, her words came more quickly and began to tumble over each other. "That's the way it always is. I . . . I never mean to start a fire—it just happens! Sometimes it's because a person I don't like comes too close to me, or someone says something mean to me. But other times, it's nothing. If the weather's bad, or if I don't do well on a test, or if I have a stomachache. Even little things like that, and a fire happens. I can't control it!"

Mrs. Kurata put her arms around Kaori and held her head.

"You don't need to talk about this now. You should be getting some rest."

Kaori's breathing was heavy, but she closed her mouth and buried her face in her mother's arms. Mrs. Kurata gave her a strong hug, then turned back to Chikako and Makihara. Her eyes were red and there were deep lines in her cheeks. She seemed to have aged ten years right before their eyes.

"We can't talk here. My husband is coming . . . and so is the housekeeper. Let's go somewhere else."

Mrs. Kurata seemed desperately concerned that they not be observed. The three finally went, at her suggestion, out to the large hospital parking lot and got into Mrs. Kurata's car. The dark gray import still had a new-car smell. Chikako sat in the driver's seat, while Makihara and Mrs. Kurata got into the back.

"Would you mind moving the car?" Mrs. Kurata was still on edge about being seen. "Try to park where we can't be seen easily, because when my husband comes he'll be parking here, too."

"Is there some reason you don't want your husband to find us talking with you?" Mrs. Kurata did not respond immediately to Makihara's question. Her eyes glazed over as if she were preoccupied with something else, but then she slowly nodded her head.

"My husband—he doesn't understand Kaori."

"Do you mean he doesn't understand her feelings? Or her powers?"

Mrs. Kurata dropped her head.

"Both. They're the same thing."

As Chikako slowly moved the unfamiliar left-hand drive car, Mrs. Kurata pulled a handkerchief from her handbag and wiped her eyes with it.

"Is this a good spot?" Chikako tried to speak as gently as possible. "It'll be cold until the heater warms things up. Shall I get us something hot to drink?"

Mrs. Kurata declined. "No thank you. But would you have a cigarette?"

Makihara pulled a pack of cigarettes out of his coat pocket and offered it to her. Mrs. Kurata took it, but it took several tries before she was finally able to pull one out, and then a while longer before Makihara was able to light it in her trembling hands.

"Thank you." She finally took a deep drag, exhaled and then coughed a little. "I never really smoked, not until Kaori began starting all those fires."

"Did you do that so the fires would look like cigarettes you had forgotten to put out?"

"That's right." She covered her mouth and began to laugh convulsively. "It must sound stupid. Kaori starts fires at school, on the street; anywhere. But I wanted to at least make the fires that started at home look like they were my fault."

Chikako could feel her convictions beginning to crumble. This poor woman seemed completely exhausted and ready to break down at any moment. Looking at her, Chikako wanted to be able to believe everything she said. That this woman's daughter was able to start fires just by thinking about it. That she could burn things and hurt people. Chikako wanted to believe wholeheartedly that this power was causing great pain and confusion to both the mother and daughter, and that they had nowhere to turn for help.

On the other hand, Chikako's more rational side insisted that this mother and child were only encouraging each other's illusions, and that they could only be helped by a doctor specializing in such disorders. Right now, however, Chikako was unable to decide which to think, and since she could not decide whether or not to believe Mrs. Kurata, she had no idea what sort of questions she should be asking her. She recalled the second rule of the police veteran who had taught her about interrogations: never ask a question when you have no idea what sort of response you will get. So she kept her silence.

With nervous precision Mrs. Kurata stubbed her barely smoked cigarette out in the car's ashtray. Makihara watched her and then asked gently, "When was it?"

Chikako had never heard an interrogation begin in that tone of voice.

"When did you realize that your daughter had that kind of power?"

Mrs. Kurata stared sorrowfully at the broken cigarette in the ashtray. She finally responded, "I was always afraid she would have something."

"What do you mean 'always'?"

"Ever since Kaori was a baby. No, it really began when I was pregnant with her."

Chikako switched her own gaze from Mrs. Kurata to Makihara. She didn't know what Mrs. Kurata meant, but she was sure he did. When she was pregnant? Before Kaori was born? Did she mean that an unborn child was capable of setting curtains on fire?

Mrs. Kurata lifted her head and looked at Makihara. Their eyes narrowed as they studied each other's faces, as if searching for something there.

"Kaori told me that she found a memory inside your head. A memory of a little boy burning. She said that it had been started by a little girl. She said that you were still young too, and you were screaming."

Chikako recalled Kaori's seizure and the words she had wrung out one by one.

Who is he? Who is that boy?

Why do you know him?

Tell me, tell me!

"Did that little boy die?" Mrs. Kurata asked.

"Yes," Makihara responded shortly.

"He was related to you?"

"My younger brother. It happened twenty years ago. He was eight."

"I see." Mrs. Kurata lifted a hand to her face. "I'm so sorry. And you have never for a day forgotten it, have you? That was why it was so easy for Kaori to read. Kaori's ability to read memories is not that strong. It's like something that came with the other. I think maybe she reacted so dramatically because your memory hit so close to home with her."

"Because of her pyrokinesis?"

Mrs. Kurata couldn't bring herself to respond to this direct question. She put her hand back up to her forehead, half hiding her face, and continued.

"Kaori told me that you believe in her power, that it is frightening to you, and that is why we should trust you. She said that you might be able to help us and that at least you won't want to use us. That's why she said it would be safe to open up to you. It's the first time we've ever met someone like that."

Chikako, sitting in the driver's seat, knew very well that she did not meet Kaori Kurata's definition of "someone we can trust." The only reason she was here was because she happened to be with Makihara, and she felt slightly uncomfortable listening in on these delirious-sounding ramblings of Mrs. Kurata. On the other hand, she knew she was the only one able to view the situation objectively, from her perch on the fringes, so she forced herself to pay attention.

"I . . . want to believe what Kaori said. And that's why I'm going to tell you something." Mrs. Kurata said this, sighed, and rubbed her forehead hard with the palm of her hand. Then she lifted her face, the way a courageous child might do when determined to say something.

"I have some abilities, too."

Chikako was surprised, but Makihara did not move.

"And so did my mother. You probably know that these powers are inherited. I don't know if it has anything to do with gender, but in my family line the trait only appears in women."

"In what form?" asked Makihara, obviously unrattled by this revelation.

"My mother could occasionally move things, but that wasn't her main ability. She could read people with uncanny accuracy. Or more precisely, their memories." A smile warmed her face. "My mother was an emergency room nurse. She was good at her job, but that was because even when patients were brought in unconscious, all she had to do was touch them to find out what had happened. I remember it well, and my father spoke about her with great pride, too. Once a small boy was brought in by ambulance. He was unconscious, barely breathing, and he was covered in sweat. Just before he passed out, he had been vomiting and crying about stomach pain. The doctor diagnosed it as a gastrointestinal infection that children often get. But my mother had "seen" the truth when she picked the child up off the stretcher. He had eaten an entire bottle of sweetened children's aspirin. He'd thought it was candy and had poisoned himself.

"My mother was smart, so she chose her words carefully when informing the doctor, and he immediately ordered the child's stomach pumped. The boy was fine the next morning. At the time, my father was a doctor in the same hospital. When he heard the emergency-room doctor praising my mother's calm judgment, he brought home a bunch of roses for her. He told me that I had the best mother in Japan." The fond memories had wiped away some of the signs of fatigue from Mrs. Kurata's face.

"Your family runs a hospital, correct?" asked Makihara.

"Yes. My father took over a small clinic he inherited from his own father. He and my mother made it into a much larger facility. I'm sure my mother's ability was a great asset for them."

"How are your parents now?"

Mrs. Kurata shook her head sadly. "They've both passed away. That was before Kaori was born. My brother took over the hospital, and I serve on the board of directors."

"From what you've told us, your mother led a happy life with her abilities."

Mrs. Kurata nodded. "It's a rare case. But she still had to hide them even from her own family."

"So your father didn't know anything?"

"No, he didn't. And I had no idea until after I began to show signs of having powers of my own, and she told me. To this day my younger brother knows nothing. Both of his children are boys, and he will probably live his whole life with no idea. Excuse me, may I have another cigarette?"

Mrs. Kurata's hands were no longer shaking as badly as they had been. "My father and mother got along so well. I've never known another married couple to love and trust each other as deeply as they did. I'm sure that made it even more difficult for my mother to keep such a big secret from my father. But she was scared."

"Scared?"

"Yes, I'm sure she worried about whether my father's feelings towards her would change if he ever learned about what she could do. I mean, my mother could read people's memories. Are you married, Detective Makihara?"

"No."

She turned to Chikako, looking a little apologetic for having ignored her so far. "And you?"

"I have a husband, and a son in college," Chikako answered.

"Then I'm sure you can probably imagine. No matter how close a married couple is, there are always a few things you keep from each other. Respecting each other's secrets might even be one of the things that builds trust between adults. That's why my mother was worried that if she inadvertently let my father know about her powers, it could create a barrier between the two of them. It was because she loved my father so much that she couldn't tell him the truth."

Chikako said nothing, nor did Mrs. Kurata demand a response.

"When did you realize you had powers?" asked Makihara.

"When I was thirteen. The same age as Kaori is now."

"What sort of power do you have?"

Mrs. Kurata glanced around them and then spoke. "I can . . . move things . . . a little."

"Telekinesis. Your mother had that, too."

"Yes, but mine is even weaker than my mother's. There is very little I can do of my own will. When I feel strong emotion—when I'm upset, angry or shocked—things might come off the table. Chairs fall over, or glass cracks. That's about all."

"Wait a minute." Chikako broke in for the first time. "When we were at your home and Kaori was having her seizure, the coffee things shattered. Was that . . . ?"

Mrs. Kurata looked down, embarrassed. "Yes, that was me. I was taken off guard."

Chikako looked at Makihara, who blinked in surprise as he took this in.

"I thought that was Kaori's power too," he said.

"No, she used to do that but not anymore. Every once in a while she can read people's memories, but, as I said before, she's not very good at it." Mrs. Kurata paused and when she spoke again, her voice had dropped even lower. "Most of her power is concentrated on starting those fires."

Mrs. Kurata asked Chikako to move the car again. She had been talking for quite some time, and her voice was getting hoarse. Makihara got out to go buy some coffee. While he was gone, Chikako and Mrs. Kurata were divided by the tangible barrier of the front seat. They were also separated by the intangible barrier of what was accepted as possible and what was not. At any rate, they looked away from each other in silence. Mrs. Kurata finally spoke.

"You said your name was Ishizu?"

"That's right." Chikako was nervous. This beautiful woman lived in a world that was very different from hers. As far as Chikako was concerned, Mrs. Kurata could be from another planet.

"Kaori said you were different from Detective Makihara."

"If she meant that I do not believe unconditionally that it is possible to spontaneously set fires, move things, or read people's minds, then I would have to say she was right."

Mrs. Kurata laughed. "Then you must think that Kaori and I are quite a strange pair."

Chikako did not know what to say, but she forced herself to smile.

"What I do understand is that you and Kaori both need our help."

"Thank you," said Mrs. Kurata.

Her simple words touched Chikako deeply. Mrs. Kurata looked down, her clean-cut silhouette facing Chikako.

Makihara returned. He got in the car, closed the door, and asked, "Does your husband drive a midnight blue BMW?"

Mrs. Kurata's eyes widened. "Yes."

"Just now, a man driving a car like that pulled up to the entrance of the hospital, got out, and asked for Kaori's room number at the reception desk."

Mrs. Kurata's expression froze. "That must be my husband."

"Mrs. Kurata," Chikako put her hand on the seat and leaned toward her. "Does your husband frighten you?"

Makihara opened his mouth to say something, but Mrs. Kurata responded first.

"Yes, he frightens me. I'm terrified. I'm sure that he has tried a number of times to take Kaori away and leave me."

"Why?"

She looked as though she wasn't sure how to respond. Her private thoughts had finally found an outlet and they were all trying to get out at once.

Then Makihara spoke up. "Before you say any more, let's go back a little.

Your mother hid her power from your father. The first time she ever spoke about it to you was after she realized that you also had powers. How did she tell you about the abilities in your family line? Who told your mother about this power that manifests itself in the women of your family?"

"My mother said that my grandmother had told her. But my grandmother didn't have any powers herself."

"None at all?"

"That's right. Neither my grandmother nor her mother. But my great-grandmother said that her father's sister was what they used to call a *miko*— a medium. She would become possessed by a spirit and prophesy about the future. That was apparently how she made her living. But since she was so eccentric, very few people came to her, and she eked out a miserable life. Mention of her was taboo in the family, but my great-grandmother met her a few times because her father was probably secretly helping her out as she was his elder sister."

"A *miko*, hmm. Telling the future."

"I guess she had the ability to read people's memories. She spent the last ten years of her unhappy life in an asylum. She died there alone."

Mrs. Kurata sighed and continued, "My great-grandmother heard from her father that every once in a while their family produced a woman with powers like that. Her father told her to be very careful when she got married and had her own children. When she asked him what he meant by 'a woman with powers like that,' he never gave her a clear response. All he would say was that if a child were different from others, it would become evident around the time she entered adolescence, so she should keep a close eye on her daughters. He said how worried he had been about her and that he had been relieved when she showed no signs of any power. My great-grandmother remembered how serious her father had looked when he told her that."

"I see," said Makihara, nodding. "Your great-grandmother did not have any special powers. And you mother's mother was also normal. Is that correct?"

"Yes."

"So they were carriers. Then the powers appeared in your mother. Your power is not strong, but you can use it."

"Yes . . ."

"Your mother must have been very concerned when you got married that you would have the same difficulties she had."

"Yes, she was very worried."

"But you decided to get married anyway."

"Yes. At the time I felt it was the right thing to do." Mrs. Kurata frowned at her own half-hearted excuse. "And, as you know, my power was very weak. I didn't think there would be any trouble."

Mrs. Kurata had begun opening up all the drawers in her chest of secrets. There was still one drawer left, and she was holding onto its knob.

"I told my husband . . . everything. I told him about my power. It was after we had been seeing each other for about a year, when he started talking about marriage." She was pulling open the final drawer. "My husband was . . . very interested. He wanted to hear all about it. He went straight to meet my mother. My husband was already working his way up at the bank. He was so busy he hardly ever had a day off, even on Sundays. Despite this, he found the time to go and talk to my mother and then set off on his own to confirm the truth of her memories. He even hired a private investigator to look into aspects he couldn't pin down on his own." Mrs. Kurata turned to gaze absently out the car window.

"At the time, I thought this was a sign of my husband's sincerity. He told me that he wanted to understand the situation because he loved me. He was doing it so that he could understand me better. He said that there was no reason that we should break up and that he wanted to marry me. I . . ." Mrs. Kurata was unable to go on. Her eyes filled with tears. "I believed him."

Believed. She'd used the past tense.

"I was happy." She raised her head and continued, "I wouldn't have to worry about the same things my mother did. I was sure that everything would be perfect. My mother was happy for me, too.

"Soon after we married, my mother became ill and we knew she was dying. She called me to her bed and asked me to look after my younger brother. She said that if he married and had a daughter, she wanted Kurata and me to look out for her. That was how much she trusted my husband. She died in peace. I realized I was pregnant soon after the forty-nine days of mourning were over. That was Kaori." A single tear trickled down her cheek. She wiped it away with her fingertip.

"I was worried. When I learned that the child I was bearing was a girl, I was so worried I couldn't eat. I'd been lucky and had managed to find some happiness only because my power was so weak. But I didn't know how it would be for her. She might be born with enough power for both of us. When I thought about it, I wasn't sure if it would be right to carry her to term.

"My husband scolded me and assured me that we could handle whatever happened. He was overjoyed when Kaori was born. She was beautiful, even as a baby. The nurses in the hospital laughed at him because he was so proud of her."

Kaori was a healthy child. Mrs. Kurata continued to worry, but the growth of a child was something to enjoy unreservedly, and the encouragement of her husband was a great support.

"But it turned out that Kaori did have powers." Without thinking, Chikako took one of Mrs. Kurata's hands in her own.

"The first sign came when she started using a walker. She would be in her bed, and her walker would slide across the room, from one end to the other. She had a battery-operated toy rabbit that clapped a set of cymbals together. We noticed that the rabbit would move even without batteries. She had a small box of toys and I could never find it where I had put it. These were all signs of telekinesis. I was terribly disappointed, but my husband was not. He said that just because she had some power it didn't mean her future was all bleak. Then he started pushing for a second child. I was against it. I told him it would take all my energy just making sure Kaori grew up to have a normal sort of life.

"My husband watched her very closely. He seemed more interested than concerned. I should have been suspicious. At the time, though, I was sure it was just affection and didn't look for any other motivation."

Mrs. Kurata sighed deeply.

"Then two years ago, when she was eleven, Kaori had her first period. It was right after that, that she began starting fires."

The flowers burning in the vase.

"To begin with the fires were all small. The edge of the tablecloth would be scorched, the wallpaper would be tinged brown, the whiskers on a stuffed animal would melt. But it escalated to the point that my husband and I could actually see the flames.

"As her pyrokinetic powers became more pronounced, her telekinesis completely disappeared. I knew that psychic powers manifest in different people in different ways. But it was the first time I had heard of anyone starting fires. I couldn't believe that there was such a thing. One day I finally asked her about it and she told me what was happening. It didn't seem as though she was doing it consciously. And she'd begun to scare herself. Any time she becomes emotional, she starts a fire. She's a smart little girl and she's always tried to understand and do as I ask, but it's like living with a loaded gun that can go off at any time. She's grown more and more wary, and now she hardly goes out at all anymore."

Mrs. Kurata squeezed her eyes shut, then opened them and looked from Makihara to Chikako. "You must think she is a very difficult child." She directed this to Chikako. "When she likes someone, she hangs all over them. But if she dislikes a person or thinks she might grow to dislike them, she is terrified that any contact with them could set off a fire, so she tries from the start to keep a distance."

Chikako spoke up. "Today, Kaori went pale when you admitted that you paid for the medical treatment for her classmate who was injured in the fire at school. Why?"

Mrs. Kurata pressed her cheeks with her hands and her head drooped.

"I told Kaori that if she started a fire outside the house, it wasn't her fault because she didn't mean to do it, and she shouldn't tell anyone else. She might have been reluctant to follow my orders, but she did as she was told. Despite what I had said, I went to apologize to the child who was injured. That must have been a shock to her. I didn't want her to feel ashamed, so I kept it a secret from her."

"That must have been hard," said Makihara.

"I don't think it was about losing face for her," said Chikako. "I think the shock to Kaori was that you hadn't told her. I don't think it's a very good idea for you to be keeping secrets from her right now."

Mrs. Kurata looked up. As their eyes met, Chikako realized that no matter how difficult it was for her to follow the train of this discussion about extraordinary powers, there was one thing that the two of them had in common—something that Makihara was not privy to. They were both mothers.

Makihara cleared his throat.

"Who was the first person to contact the police about the suspicious fires?"

"Our housekeeper, Fusako Eguchi. I was against it, but I couldn't resist too strongly without coming under suspicion myself. In any case, fires were already breaking out at school, too. My husband, of course, was furious."

Makihara sent Chikako a meaningful look. Chikako asked before Makihara had a chance to.

"Mrs. Kurata, you mentioned that you were scared of your husband. From what you've said, you used to trust him. But now all that has changed. What happened?"

"He . . . he's really happy that Kaori has been cursed with this power. He's ecstatic."

"Why?"

"Because now she has a value for him. Kaori can be used as a weapon."

She frowned as she searched for the right words to explain.

"He belongs to some sort of organization. It's like some kind of police network. No, that's not quite it . . ."

Then her face cleared. "I know. It's a 'guard' group. That was the word he used when he told me about it."

"Who do they guard? What are they guarding them from?"

Mrs. Kurata shrugged dismissively and answered, "He said that they protect justice from imperfect laws. They execute criminals that the law fails to punish. Can you believe it?"

Makihara narrowed his eyes. "So what you're saying is that people with special powers, like Kaori, are useful to this organization?"

"That's right. That was what he had planned all along. That was what he married me for. There was never an ounce of love for me in it!"

"It's going to be all right." Chikako reached out, but Mrs. Kurata buried her face in her hands again.

"He was thrilled when Kaori began setting fires, and said that his wait had been worth it. He said that he had always wanted a child like her, and that she would become some sort of savior. Kaori could burn a hundred people to death all at once and never leave a shred of evidence. He said that it was her God-given duty to get rid of monsters, people that the world would be better off without; it was what she was born to do. What sort of father

236

would force his own child to fulfill that sort of obligation? Kaori is a human being. She's not a flamethrower and she's not a bomb! He wants her to be an assassin. He intends to have her trained to control her power and use it for the sake of his organization!"

"Mrs. Kurata?"

"I can't let him do that!"

"Mrs. Kurata, please. Try to calm down."

Kaori's mother broke down and sobbed against the seat of the car. Chikako and Makihara listened in silence. Makihara waited for her tears to subside before he spoke again.

"Has your husband told you anything about that organization? How it's structured, where it is, or who's in it?"

Mrs. Kurata wiped her eyes and raised them to look at Makihara.

"I don't know anything about it. He just insisted that there was nothing unsavory about it. The members are all respected members of society. Some are even well-known politicians and leaders of industry."

"Where do they get the funds to run their activities?"

Mrs. Kurata shook her head again.

"Do you know when your husband became a member? Did he ever mention it to you?"

"His father was a member. The organization began after World War II. The initial purpose was to secretly pass judgment on illegal activities of the occupation forces. It was just a small policing group."

This was a side of the twentieth century that had been forgotten. Japan had surrendered unconditionally, and the U.S. Army occupied the country. No matter how steadfast and uncompromising the character of General MacArthur, some individual soldiers committed crimes that Japanese laws were unable to punish. This organization was founded to rout out the evil that flourished out of reach of the law.

"Did you ever catch the name of the group?" Mrs. Kurata thought a few moments, and then shook her head again.

"I'm sorry. I might have heard it, but I was so upset when he told me about it. He told me again and again that it was no good trying to oppose them; nobody would ever believe it existed. He told me that if I let them have Kaori without a fuss, they would respect me as her mother, and that if I agreed to have another child, the organization would be grateful because that child might have powers, too."

"How dare he treat you like a baby-breeding machine!" sputtered Chikako indignantly.

"But that's what my husband had planned from the start. The only use he had for me was to give him the children he wanted. He's had a lover since right after we got married." She laughed cheerlessly. "But he told Kaori, when she started setting fires, 'Don't worry. I'm so proud of you. I love you more than anyone in the whole world.' He told her he'd do anything for her. I guess that was his idea of being a good father. He seemed to me more like a soldier vowing to take good care of his gun."

Chikako could only nod in sympathy. Then she saw a faint light in Mrs. Kurata's eye. "Now that you mention it . . ."

"What is it?"

"He did mention something. He said to Kaori that he was her protector or guardian, something like that. And that Kaori would someday be one herself."

"A protector?" asked Chikako.

"If it meant that Kaori would become a member—would that be the name of the organization?"

"Guardian," muttered Makihara. "He must have meant she'd be a guardian."

19

Sitting on the foot of her bed, Junko stared listlessly at photos of Natsuko Mita and Kenji Fujikawa as they flashed on the TV screen, bitterly recalling her battles with the Asaba gang and the events on the roof of Sakurai Liquors.

The evening news was doing a special report on the three fires, taking up unanswered questions about the gang and its final two victims.

The police premise had remained basically unchanged from the outset—that the root cause of the deaths and fires had been pre-existing tensions within the group. The conjecture ran that the trigger that night had been a disagreement over how to dispose of Fujikawa's body, but underlying that conflict had been a struggle for power within the group and a feud over the profits from selling drugs.

According to the police, "Y," a nineteen-year-old whose body was discovered at Sakurai Liquors, had been competing with Asaba for gang leadership. A photo of him was displayed on-screen, but since he was a minor the area around his eyes was obscured by a mosaic pattern, so Junko wasn't certain if she'd seen him. He might have been the one in khaki pants who'd been pointing a gun at her. She'd seen his eyeballs melt in the wave of heat she'd flung at him, and she had to hand it to the police for identifying him. But then again, it was probably not the first time they had dealt with him.

The latest police theory held that, after abducting the young couple, Asaba and some of the gang had confined Natsuko at their base at Sakurai Liquors, and had then gone to dispose of Fujikawa's body. Asaba intended to dump it in the abandoned factory, but some other members opposed him. A quarrel ensued, shots were fired, and a spark ignited methane gas which caused the explosion and fire.

Asaba alone escaped with his life and decided that he had to get rid of any opposition to his leadership then and there. He went to his supplier of black-market guns, Tsutsui, to get a more powerful weapon. The two met at Café Currant, and when it became clear that Tsutsui had failed to come through, Asaba struck him in a paroxysm of rage, breaking his neck and killing him. To destroy the evidence, he set Currant on fire, then returned to his base where, high on the rush of his killing spree, he continued to eliminate his rivals one by one, killing even his mother in his rampage, and then setting fire to Sakurai Liquors. He'd planned to escape with Natsuko as his hostage, but the fire spread faster than he'd expected and, cornered on the roof, he'd shot Natsuko and then turned the gun on himself.

Junko was impressed by the plausibility of this new scenario. She wondered, though, why the police with their chemical analysis team hadn't been able to figure out that the fires she started were different from conventional fires. Oh well.

She hadn't been able to save Fujikawa, and she'd seen Natsuko killed while she'd been trying to save her. She hadn't been the one to kill Asaba either. The feeling of defeat was still intense, leaving her with a black craving.

Who had killed Natsuko? Who had Natsuko recognized up there on the roof of Sakurai Liquors?

The TV screen was showing Natsuko's face again and there was a voice-over of an interview with a woman she had worked with. According to her story, it wasn't simply bad luck that Natsuko and Fujikawa had been caught by the Asaba gang that night. About a month before, Natsuko and this woman had gone to see a movie in Shinjuku. On their way back to the station to go home, Asaba and a couple of others had surrounded them.

"I remember their faces clearly. There were three of them. One of them was the one they call 'A.'"

Ah, A for Asaba, thought Junko.

"There were two of us, so we got up the courage to turn them down and run away. But Natsuko dropped her handbag while she was running and her things spilled out all over the road. They were still chasing us so we grabbed what we could and ran into the police station at the west exit of the station.

Then when we checked her bag, it turned out that Natsuko's train pass was missing. The policeman went back with us to look for it, but it was gone."

Natsuko had been unsettled by this, and her apprehension was justified. The next day she got a call at home from Keiichi Asaba. He had learned her name, address, and phone number from the holder she'd kept her train pass in. He began stalking her. He and some others would lie in wait for her to leave work, and Asaba would call in the middle of the night, regardless of the hour. Natsuko lived with her parents and tried to deal with the calls by having her father answer the phone, but Asaba threatened to kill her whole family if she didn't take his calls herself.

Within a week, Natsuko, out of her mind with fear, told her coworkers what was happening and asked them for advice.

So Natsuko had been targeted all along—from the moment she'd dropped her train pass. Junko felt powerlessness wash over her and her body grow heavy with it. *I'm a gun—a powerful one—but I've only got one set of ears and one set of eyes, and I'm not telepathic either.*

Junko had encountered Asaba and his buddies in the factory purely by coincidence. In a way, taking them out on the spot had been lucky. If she hadn't been there that night, she would be listening to news about the discovery of Fujikawa's body and how his girlfriend Natsuko Mita had been abducted and was missing. A few days would pass before they found her body and then ten days, or two weeks, or six months later, the police would manage to round up Asaba and the rest of his gang. But they would fail to pin a major crime on them, and the whole gang would eventually make their way back into society. And that would be when Junko began to search for them the way she had Masaki Kogure and his gang. But this time she had been lucky; in less than twenty-four hours she'd succeeded in wiping most of them out, thus saving anyone else from falling victim. But that didn't bring Fujikawa and Natsuko back—she wished she could have saved them before it was too late.

A commercial came on and Junko clicked the TV off. She looked up at the ceiling and closed her eyes. Behind her closed lids she replayed the scene of the slow, elegant way Hikari had risen into the air and then fallen to the ground, enveloped in flames, in front of the home of Hitoshi Kano.

If she could catch criminals as they began to act, she wouldn't have to go chasing after them later, and there would be less chance of secondary casualties like Hikari. It would almost be like catching early-stage cancer.

What a weakling you've become, jeered something inside Junko. *What's so bad about having killed Hikari? She was just like Asaba's mother and Tsutsui the gun dealer—a parasite. Are you saying you didn't want to kill any of them? Don't be a liar. You went after them and executed them of your own volition.*

Junko opened her eyes and murmured to the ceiling, "No, it wasn't that I wanted to kill them."

Liar! You are a powerful weapon with the ability to distinguish between targets. You have both the power and ability.

Was that true? Was it really right to think that? She had to admit that if she made mistakes in setting her targets, if it were *possible* for her to make mistakes in setting her targets, she would have to wonder *why* she had the power in the first place.

She'd always believed that she had the power because she had the competence to use it well. And furthermore, that she had the *right* to use it freely because this power had been given to her.

The phone rang.

She shook her head to banish her confusing thoughts. It wasn't good to be thinking like this. Until recently, Junko had never felt any conflict between herself and her power. Everything had always seemed simple and straightforward.

Nor did she feel she had time to spend on leisurely reflections. Her power was restored and the pain from her shoulder wound had subsided. Neither the police nor the media had picked up her trail, so she needed to get back to work. She had to find out who had shot Natsuko Mita, and make him pay the price. The case wasn't wrapped up as far as Junko was concerned.

The phone was still ringing. When she picked it up, her voice reflected her irritation. *"Yes?"*

"Hey . . ." It was a young man's voice. "Sounds like you're in a bad mood."

Junko was caught off guard. *Who was this?*

"Oh come on, did you forget me already? That's not very nice. Even after I said you were pretty?"

Now she remembered. It was *him*. The young guy, the one who'd sounded like a prank caller, who'd called right before the older man who'd told her where to find Hitoshi Kano.

"I remember you now."

"Well, *thanks*."

"What do you want?"

"That's not very friendly, sweetheart. And I was calling to congratulate you for getting rid of Hitoshi Kano."

"Hey, you weren't supposed to call me, right? The man who gave me Hitoshi Kano's address was angry about that."

"Oh, that old guy," her caller scoffed. "With a short temper like that, he really shouldn't be in management."

"He said he wanted to meet me, too."

"Oh yeah? He's just supposed to be laying the groundwork, so he didn't like it that I went ahead and contacted you first. But I don't see any point in getting all uptight about it. It's obvious that you're already one of us. By the way, did you see the news?"

Junko was silent.

Kano's death had been another one of the top stories in the news program she'd just been watching. The words "suspicious fire" and "unnatural death" had been used. There'd been a comment that the method resembled the Asaba cases, but no direct connection had yet been found. The case was "under aggressive investigation."

Her caller seemed to be reading her thoughts as he continued. "You don't have to worry about it. As usual you overdid it a bit, but the organization will make sure it gets a low profile."

"Organization?"

"I *told* you—the Guardians."

For the first time, Junko felt a stirring of interest. This was the organization that had located Hitoshi Kano. And it was an organization that could dampen police and media interest in a case.

"You know, I think I'd like to meet you."

She heard a whistle from the other end of the line.

"Happy to hear it."

"But the man who called last time said that after I took out Hitoshi Kano, he'd give me another piece of information. It was about, um, a person I knew but haven't heard from lately; he was going to tell me where that person was."

"You don't have to beat around the bush with me. Kazuki Tada, right?" laughed the young man. "Yeah, of course we'll tell you. Right now if you want."

"Really?"

"Yeah. You don't want to bother talking with the old guy again, do you? Hold on just a sec."

He put her on hold and a beautiful melody floated over the line, sounding oddly out of place. It was *Für Elise*. After a few phrases it was cut off. "Hello? Do you have something to write on?"

"Yes, I do."

He proceeded to give her an address in Shibuya. Then he had her read it back to make sure she had it right before he remarked, almost as an afterthought, "He's living with a woman."

Junko felt her insides lurch unexpectedly. She knew that he couldn't see her face, but she still felt terribly exposed. Her caller seemed to guess her reaction.

"Personally, I think you're a lot prettier, but he seems to go for the pleasingly plump type."

"That's rude!"

"Huh? I just said that you were prettier!" He switched suddenly from a teasing tone to a more serious one. "Hey, don't take it hard. That's just the way it is for us."

Junko caught both a note of consolation and real understanding in his words.

"Excuse me?"

"Only people with special abilities can understand others like themselves. Tada couldn't understand you. Even if you lived your whole lives together, he'd never understand you. That's why it's better just to forget about him."

Junko was silent, trying to make sense of what he'd said.

"Hey? Hello?" Her caller sounded alarmed. "You're not crying, are you?"

Junko finally asked in a whisper, "Who are you, really?"

"Me? I'm me."

"Don't play games with me. You're a member of the Guardians, right? What do you do for them? Are you saying that you have something, too—some unusual power?"

There was a short silence, as though he was choosing his next words carefully. "You light fires," he said. "I make people move."

"Make them move?"

"Yeah. You could say I work them like puppets. But I usually think of it as 'pushing.'"

"I don't understand."

"Well, you'll understand when you meet me." He'd returned to his former, carefree tone. "I think the reason the organization wants you to see Kazuki Tada is to let you know that he is doing fine and leading a happy, peaceful life, so that you can regain some of your confidence. They want you to see the people you've actually helped and not just the ones you've punished. Personally I don't think it's necessary."

So Kazuki Tada was leading a happy, peaceful life . . . with a woman.

"And I'm supposed to be your escort. Actually, that old guy is supposed to be telling you all this, and then I was supposed to appear on the scene after a proper introduction, but I can't wait to meet you so I'm jumping the queue."

"When I go to see Kazuki Tada, you're supposed to come and be there with me?"

"No," her caller seemed highly amused. "The main thing is for the two of us to meet, and Kazuki Tada's just being thrown in as an extra. Oh, there's another call coming in. I'm going to hang up and I'll call you back."

Junko stood there for a minute thinking, and then the phone rang again. She quickly picked it up and this time it was the voice of the polite middle-aged man who'd given her Hitoshi Kano's address. He sounded angry.

"I understand our hothead has gone and jumped the gun again. He keeps our hands full. He didn't upset you, did he?"

Junko reassured him that she was fine. "But actually I'd like to ask you something. The last time we talked, you said that we were comrades, with the same goals . . . is that right?"

"Yes, that's right."

"So, what are the Guardians?"

"Well, that's . . . well, it's probably better to meet directly and talk about it."

"The young guy just now, he's like me? He has an ability that's not . . . usual, right? So are the Guardians a group of people like that?"

Her caller paused before answering, "No, it's not really like that. People with special talents have a very important role, but their actual numbers are few. Most of us are completely ordinary. But we're all very good at what we do."

"This all seems a little farfetched, like a B-grade suspense film."

The caller chuckled in return. "You could be right."

"So maybe I should laugh this off, hang up, and just forget about it."

"You could do that. But then you'd have to live knowing you'd lost a chance to make the best possible use of your power. You may not know this, but people with special powers have life spans about twenty years shorter than average. Not only that, but your power will grow weaker with time. You've probably only got about ten good years left. After the power is gone, you could have the satisfaction of knowing that you did your best, doing the work you were born to do. We really only have your best interests in mind." This last sentence was voiced gently but firmly.

Junko was quiet. Her caller was quiet. If this was a contest of wills, then he had won.

Junko spoke quietly into the phone. "What should I do?"

"Well, let's set a time and place." Underneath his smooth tones ran an undercurrent of triumph. "Would you mind meeting that headstrong kid? He's interested in you. We are, too. It's not that we feel confident relying on him, but we think the two of you might just hit it off."

"You mean because he has a power? He said he can move people."

"He already told you *that*, too? He really doesn't know when to shut up. Well, I'd better let him explain it himself."

"And Kazuki Tada?"

"Whether or not you go see him is completely up to you."

He's leading a happy, peaceful life.

"Okay," Junko nodded, "I'll do as you suggest. Even if by some chance you are out to trap me, I'm perfectly capable of defending myself."

He laughed with pleasure. "It's nice to come across a really capable woman."

20

Chikako heard about the two new arson-homicides in Yokohama after she'd left Makihara and returned to MPD. Shimizu told her. He wasn't supposed to be involved in the three cases that had begun in Tayama, but it appeared that he was interested after all.

"It looks just the same, doesn't it? I'd like to read the coroner's report, but they probably won't let me since it's under the jurisdiction of Kanagawa police."

Chikako, exhausted, found it difficult to stay focused on what he was saying, and found herself just throwing in the occasional "Hmm . . ." and "Oh yeah?" at appropriate intervals. It wasn't that she'd lost any of her interest in those cases, but it was hard to concentrate after what she had just heard from Mrs. Kurata.

While they were walking to the station after leaving the hospital, Makihara had said that they shouldn't move immediately on the Kurata mother and daughter.

"We don't know enough about this "guardian" organization yet. I'll check a few sources."

Chikako suppressed a sigh and nodded. What kind of sources would he check? Publications dealing with psychic phenomena and conspiracy theories?

Glancing through the memos, documents, and messages piled on her desk, she noticed that Michiko Kinuta had called twice without leaving a message. Both had come in since Kaori Kurata had been taken to the hospital.

Chikako lifted her head and looked around the room but Captain Ito was nowhere to be seen. No one had asked her for her thoughts on the Kaori

Kurata case yet, and she wondered what Michiko would have to say to her favorite uncle.

Chikako's exhausted face must have made an impression on Shimizu because he brought her coffee for the first time ever.

"Hey, don't look so surprised! I was just making some for myself and there was extra, that's all!" he blustered, covering his embarrassment.

"Thanks." She took the cup and then called after him as he was leaving, "Hey, just a minute—"

"What is it?"

"Well actually, I just heard an unbelievable story and I'm wondering if someone younger, like you, would have an easier time getting a handle on it."

"What kind of story?" Shimizu looked curious.

"Well, it's about, um, super . . . ah, psychic powers, I guess . . ."

Shimizu's small eyes widened. "Huh?"

"Well, anyway, people with unusual powers. Do you think there really are people who could kill a target just by concentrating on it?"

Shimizu choked with such force that the coffee in his mouth nearly sprayed Chikako. "Good grief, Detective Ishizu! I would have thought you were old enough—I mean, that you had better sense than to talk like that!"

"So you don't believe in psychic powers at all?"

"No way," Shimizu dismissed it with finality. "It's all just lies, illusions, and sleight of hand. At any rate, that kind of garbage isn't something adults—especially we police—should take seriously."

"Okay then. Well . . . what if, for example, I'm feeling put out at you laughing in my face just now and I stared really hard at you, and your hair caught on fire?"

Shimizu looked as though he was losing patience. "This isn't a Stephen King novel. Would you lay off ?"

He wheeled around and stalked off. Chikako felt her shoulders droop. *That would be the typical reaction after all, wouldn't it?* she thought to herself.

The phone on her desk began to ring. Thinking it might be Michiko Kinuta, she picked it up immediately.

It was Sergeant Kinugasa. It had been less than a week since he'd suggested she meet Makihara at Arakawa precinct, but it seemed like it had been ages ago.

Happily, the armed robbery-homicide case that had been tying him up in Akabane had been resolved the day before. Chikako offered her congratulations.

He thanked her, then asked, "By the way, were you able to meet up with Detective Makihara?"

"Yes, I did meet him."

"What did you think? Was he any use to you?"

Chikako was apologetic. "Well, that has turned out to be a moot point. I've been completely removed from the Tayama case and no longer require any assistance he could offer."

She explained what had happened, and Sergeant Kinugasa seemed surprised and dismayed at this turn of events.

"That was rather sudden," he growled.

"Yes, but there are three sites involved now, so they probably want detectives with more experience."

"Well, I can't understand it. But I think in the long run meeting Detective Makihara won't have been a waste of time for you."

Chikako was confused. Obviously everyone else he worked with considered Makihara more of a puzzle than an asset, and frankly Chikako was inclined to agree. What had inspired Sergeant Kinugasa's apparent confidence in him?

"Detective Makihara is quite a character, isn't he?" ventured Chikako indirectly. "He shared some stimulating theories . . ."

Sergeant Kinugasa laughed. "He told you about his firestarter theory?"

"And you knew about that, of course."

"Oh, yeah. It's probably a reflection of his childhood trauma. Did he tell you about his younger brother burning to death?"

"Yes, indeed."

"He's never gotten over that. But still, he's a sharp guy. I'm hoping that through his work, he'll find some kind of solution to that obsession of his."

"I hope so, too."

Before he hung up, Kinugasa said he would come by MPD the next day and would see her then. Chikako set the receiver down only to have it ring again. This time it was Michiko Kinuta.

"I'm sorry—I've had two messages from you. You didn't make it to the hospital to see Kaori?"

Michiko was all wrought up, and her voice was a few notches higher than usual. "When I reported in to the precinct, they called me back in."

"Oh, is that what happened?"

"Detective Ishizu, they've taken me off the case."

"What?"

"I've been ordered off Kaori's case. I've been assigned to one that's completely unrelated. My boss said that I—I've been sucked in too far by Kaori and have lost the ability to grasp the situation objectively."

"Detective Kinuta, try to calm down."

"I'm being replaced by an officer who has always considered Kaori guilty of starting the fires. He's never even met her! He says that it's only a matter of time until Kaori is hauled off to a juvenile reformatory." Michiko was obviously close to tears.

Chikako's head started to ache.

21

I already know what you look like, so I'll find you—and dress up, will you? It's our first date after all.

The young guy on the phone had come out with this line, but Junko dressed in jeans with a black sweater and rubber-soled boots for walking— running, if it came to that. Her wallet and other essentials she put in a waist pouch, and slipping on a short black-checked coat, she left her apartment.

She wasn't all that nervous. As she'd told the older man on the phone, there was no need for her to be on guard to go meet someone for the first time. Her wardrobe, however, was another thing altogether. Years of tracking and combat had whittled out any embellishments.

The meeting place she'd been directed to was the main lobby of a newly completed high-rise hotel in Shinjuku. The spacious lobby was dominated by a towering Christmas tree. Junko paused, looking up at it in surprise. It wasn't exactly that she'd forgotten that it was the holiday season; it was more that Christmas, New Year's, and even the summer holidays had ceased to have much meaning in her solitary life.

Comfortable looking armchairs formed an enormous ring around the Christmas tree and all the seats were filled. Junko looked around, but there wasn't a single spot open. Were *all* these people meeting someone here?

It had been a long time since she had been out in a crowded place like this. It was stiflingly hot and she felt almost dizzy. She tugged off her coat and slung it over her arm as she began to circle the Christmas tree. Since he was supposed to find her, there was no need to stay in one place craning her neck looking for him.

She'd only talked with him on the phone, but she had already developed a dislike for the young man she was about to meet. Or, more precisely, she was confident that when she did meet him, she wouldn't like him. As she'd dressed and prepared to go out, she'd thought sardonically that he was bound to be one of those conceited lightweights she detested; the kind who assumed that any woman he approached would fall all over herself to please him.

But—does he really have a special power? He'd said he could make people move. Like puppets. Did he do it by exerting control over a person's mind and feelings? Was such a trick possible? Junko grinned wryly to herself and shifted her hold on her coat. "Trick" wasn't really a fair thing to say, coming from her.

Someone tapped her lightly on the shoulder. She turned and found a young man blocking her path. His stiffly gelled hair was dyed light brown and his grin stretched from ear to ear.

"Hi there! You here alone?"

Junko looked him over carefully. It took a couple of seconds to decide that his voice wasn't the one she had heard on the phone and that this was a different person. He was obviously looking to pick up a girl, and those two seconds of hesitation were enough to swell his confidence.

"You know, I've been stood up and I'm all alone under this romantic Christmas tree. So what do you think—how about we go to a movie or something?"

"I'm—"

"Oh, you don't have to tell me your name. Oh wait—I'll guess it."

Junko rolled her eyes in exasperation, but the guy paid no attention and began to rattle off women's names. Spit was practically flying from his mouth in his enthusiasm. She shook her head and backed up a step, but he continued, undeterred. "If you'd like to go somewhere for tea instead, I know a great place. There's this little café that never advertises, and big producers go there to meet with actresses, you know, 'cause there are all these studios around here."

Junko tried to wave him away and move past him, but he grabbed her by the shoulder.

"Hey, don't blow me off like that. I was just being friendly because you looked lonely!"

He suddenly made a gurgling sound, though his smile was still pasted to his face. Junko froze. His eyes rolled back in his head and his lower jaw worked convulsively. She glimpsed his tongue jerking inside his mouth. Junko took a step backwards, her hand over her mouth.

The hand that had been on her shoulder was now in mid-air, slowly forming a gun-shaped fist with only the pointer finger extended. His other arm was pinned to his side. His eyes rolled forward again and now he stared in horror at his raised finger as it moved slowly towards his face. He was unable to speak, making only a gagging sound as his finger headed straight for his right eye. As it reached his eyelashes, Junko finally found her own voice and said firmly, *"Stop it right now!"*

Immediately, his arm dropped limply to his side. His whole body went limp, too, and he would have fallen, but someone caught him from behind.

"Hey, you all right, man? You get all spiffed up and then fall on the floor. And right in front of a girl, too? Not cool at all." The man who had caught him tossed him aside. Then he turned to Junko with a smile.

"Sorry to keep you waiting."

Junko recognized the voice of her mystery caller.

"I was only three minutes late and someone was hitting on you already— sorry about that, princess."

"What was that just now?"

He raised his eyebrows in mock misunderstanding.

"Yeah, what *was* that? A guy in from the sticks, all dolled up for the girls, but it didn't come off at all. Did you notice his hair? He looked like a rooster!"

They were in a coffee shop on the second floor of the hotel, sitting at a table by the railing closely overlooking the Christmas tree.

Junko set her coffee cup down, hard. "Don't play around with me. You know I'm not talking about that guy. I'm asking about the trick you just pulled."

"Trick?" He pretended not to understand. He leaned over toward the tree and said, "Hey, even up close like this the snow on the tree looks real. It can't be cotton—what do you think it is?"

He was about a head taller than Junko, and very thin. She thought he was about her age—maybe a year or two younger. He wore chinos with a thick wool shirt under a black leather jacket. The leather of his loafers looked soft and expensive, like the rest of his wardrobe. But his wide, open smile and his hair, dyed fashionably brown and brushing his shoulders, made him look like a student. A rich family's spoiled son?

The coffee shop was even more crowded than the lobby downstairs. The end of the year was supposed to be a busy time at work; what were all these people doing out on a weekday afternoon?

Junko lowered her voice and hissed, "Just now, was that the 'push' you were talking about—being able to make someone move? He was under your control, wasn't he? You were going to make him poke out his own eye. Is that what you can do?"

Her companion was looking at her without a flicker in his innocent smile. He scooted over a seat to sit directly across from her, and when she made a discomfited gesture he said, "It's easier to talk close up, isn't it? And you have beautiful skin."

"Come *off* it!" Junko smacked the table in frustration. A man in a suit at the nearest table raised his eyes to look at them, and Junko's companion gave him a nod in apology.

"Sorry—I just offended the lady here."

The man looked away with a frown.

Junko sighed. This was futile. She didn't know how to handle this situation. He was irritating her beyond belief and yet she had just the slightest urge to laugh—which made him all the more infuriating.

"This seems like a waste of time."

"Really? But there's plenty of time."

"For you maybe."

"What time is it now?"

Junko checked her watch. "Three-fifteen."

"Then I've got eight hours and forty-five minutes until tonight's mission."

"Mission?"

"Yeah. There's this pitiful man in his thirties who can't get along without periodically interfering with little girls. I'll be relieving him of his animal instincts."

Junko sat up straight and stared at him. She leaned toward him over the table so she could speak in a lowered voice. He leaned forward, too.

"What do you mean by that?"

"You mean what exactly does it involve?"

"Yes."

"Easy. Make him get a good grip on a cleaver, and give him a push—cut it off."

"Cut . . . what?"

"Hey, that's not for your delicate ears, sweetheart."

"That's what the Guardians do?"

"In America, there are some states where castration is a legal punishment for the worst sex offenders."

Junko bent her head even closer to his and lowered her voice still further. "But isn't that too cruel?"

"What's wrong with it? If you take the long view, it's helping him." Another sunny smile lit his face. "I like whispering up close with you like this."

Junko jerked upright. He laughed.

"You know, you haven't even asked me my name yet. No interest at all?"

"None whatsoever."

"Now *that* is cruel."

"I'm leaving." Junko picked up her coat.

"Don't you want to go see Kazuki Tada?"

Junko fixed him with an angry stare. "You seem to be laboring under the impression that there was something between us, and there wasn't."

This time her companion made a gun shape with his own hand, aimed it at Junko and fired. "You're a liar. Bam!"

"Whatever."

Junko moved to get up but unexpectedly she felt a slight tingling at the nape of her neck. Then her forehead suddenly got burning hot, the heat spreading between her temples. Her field of vision went hazy and the point between her eyes ached.

One of Junko's hands flew up to her face and pressed against her cheek. The other arm went limp and her coat fell to the floor. Then, pulled by an invisible hand, she landed back down in her chair. Her feet bounced up in rebound.

She looked across the table. The young man's eyes were on Junko and his head was cocked slightly to one side, but his eyes were out of focus. There were a few beads of sweat on the ridge of his nose. She smelled something. A familiar smell.

Burning.

Junko gasped, sucking in air and blinking hard to pull herself back to full consciousness. She snatched up the glass of iced water in front of her and doused him around the collar. He reeled as though he'd been punched and came back to himself with a snap. His eyes refocused on hers.

People at the surrounding tables were looking at them, startled. Junko froze with the empty glass still in her hand and sat down stiffly. Her other hand clenched in a fist.

The front of his shirt was dripping wet. He reached out and removed the empty glass from Junko's hand and placed it on the table, and then put his hand over Junko's fist.

"It's okay," he said softly. "It's okay." They were looking directly into each other's eyes. One by one he pulled the fingers of her fist open, and then he gripped her hand tightly. Junko didn't brush it away.

Somewhere deep inside, her heart started dancing.

"Just now, were you 'pushing' me?"

"Yes."

"I . . . I didn't intend to use my power. It just happened."

"I know."

Still holding Junko's hand, he used his free hand to retrieve Junko's coat from under the table, setting it next to him.

"The collar of your shirt is scorched."

"I didn't get burned," he said, loosening the collar. "It's just uncomfortable because it's wet, that's all."

"Why . . . ?"

"It must be a kind of defensive wall." He'd suddenly turned serious and sounded like an academic. "You have some resistance to being invaded from outside by another power. You make an instant counterattack."

"So when you 'pushed' me, I tried to set you on fire?"

"Looks like it. I'd say that match was a draw." He grinned. "By the way, do you still not want to know anything about me?"

Junko felt some of her defenses drop. Her shoulders relaxed and she said, "Will you introduce yourself? Oh, but first—"

"What is it?"

"*Would* you let go of my hand?"

His name was Koichi Kido. "Pretty bland, huh? Aren't you disappointed?"

Rather than feeling disappointed, Junko was thinking of a strange coincidence. An ad for a business magazine had caught her eye on the train coming here. The latest issue had a feature on the factions doing battle within the Kido Corporation, the largest manufacturer of office machines in Japan. The name Kido wasn't commonplace, but it wasn't all that rare either. Junko wouldn't have made the connection with Koichi except that he had such an air of wealth about him.

She'd also just caught a glimpse of a Lirico watch on Koichi's wrist. It was an Italian brand and was enjoying a boom in popularity during its import debut in Japan. Junko knew that the company importing them was a subsidiary of the Kido Corporation. The watches were not cheap and their import was restricted, so scarcity value had driven up their popularity as well.

"Is your father the president of Kido Corporation?"

His eyes widened. "How'd you know that?"

Koichi Kido looked impressed as she explained, and he ran his eyes over Junko's face. "You're quick."

"Hitoshi Kano wanted a Lirico." She'd been so revolted to find fresh evidence of his greed when he'd shown her a catalog for them that she'd tossed it on his body to burn with him.

Koichi Kido's eyes narrowed. "Speaking of which, I think the news said there were two bodies found at Kano's place."

Junko nodded. "His girlfriend was with him. I didn't want to kill her."

Is that really true, is that what you really thought? Wasn't it the opposite? sneered the voice inside her head.

Koichi shrugged. "It happens. There was nothing you could do about it. Noncombatants sometimes get caught up in the crossfire. That's the way war is."

"War?"

"Yeah."

Junko fixed him with a level gaze. "Tell me about the Guardians."

In a low voice he told her about the organization, its goals, and what it did. It took her full concentration to catch everything amid the chatter and background noise of the coffee shop. When he'd finished filling her in he lifted his coffee cup only to find it empty. He called the waitress over to ask for a refill, and as they waited for it, Junko stared pensively into her own empty cup, trying to process what she'd just heard.

"Did all that make sense?"

Junko looked up at him, still frowning. "When did you join the organization?"

"When I was fifteen."

"So young?"

"Well, my dad's a member. I'm the third generation. My grandfather was actually the first. My dad joined the Guardians because he didn't want to go against my grandfather. He never made much of an impression, but I think he worked hard on the financing side of it."

"Financing?"

"Yeah. No organization can move without money."

"So it was formed just after the war and since then financiers, logistics supervisors, and operatives have all worked together in secret?"

"Exactly."

"And nobody has ever been suspicious or threatened to expose it?"

"It's not all that difficult to arrange."

"I can't believe that. Even though you consider your work to be executions, it looks like murder, and the police do investigate, don't they? And doesn't the media pick up on it?"

"That's why we always make sure it doesn't look like murder. Our executions look like accidents or suicides." He grinned. "That's what makes me a *very* valuable member. You saw how that guy looked like he was going to poke his own eye out. And we have members in the police force and the media who make some accommodation for us."

"No—I don't believe it!"

"Why are you so surprised? You weren't so surprised that heads of big corporations were members."

"The police are different!"

"No they aren't. However it's not the police or the media who have the power in this country. It's the business world. When they pull strings for us we can do almost anything. But the police are a big help, too."

His hand was in a pistol shape again and he pointed at Junko in mock warning. "If you still don't believe me, I'll give you an actual example. Before you cleaned up Masaki Kogure at the Arakawa riverside, you tried once and failed, right? At Hibiya Park."

It was true. Kazuki Tada had been with her that time.

"You set Masaki Kogure on fire and were about to kill him. But just when you had him, someone stopped you. Kazuki Tada, who'd probably asked you to do it, lost his nerve and drove off with you still in the passenger seat."

"It wasn't that he was scared."

"Whatever you say. But you'd already started releasing your power and couldn't fully control it. So the car you and Tada were in nearly caught fire. Tada drove into a gas station and the attendants there hosed it down."

In fact, that was exactly what had happened.

"The police aren't as slow as you think. When Masaki Kogure was hospitalized with serious burns, they questioned people in the area. The gas station you and Kazuki Tada stopped at was in that area, and naturally they got statements from the attendants. 'Yes, Officer, that was the day, and we couldn't see what started the fire, but the seat was really smoking. The people in the car didn't seem injured, but they took off in a big hurry as soon as the fire was out. It was a man and a woman. Yeah, I thought there was something funny about them and that's why I took down the number on their license plate . . .'"

Koichi Kido leaned back in his chair with his arms crossed, observing Junko closely as his words sank in. Junko, sitting there, felt her bones going cold. *Such little details . . . at the time it never occurred to her to notice such little details . . .*

"But neither you nor Kazuki Tada were traced," Koichi Kido continued. "The police didn't question Tada or even check his car for signs of fire damage. Do you know why not?"

Junko raised a hand to cover her eyes.

"That was the work of our members on the police force. Because they were in a position to cover up your little accident."

"*Members?* How many are there?"

"The police are a big organization."

Junko raised her eyes to look at him. "I guess I really owe you one, don't I?"

"But we're not demanding that you cooperate with us because of that." He smiled, revealing white teeth. "It was just thanks to that little error of yours that the Guardians became aware of your existence. That was when we began searching for you. But you're good at covering your tracks. After the Arakawa killings we thought we had you. But you disappeared *again* and the Guardian leaders were beside themselves. Then when the Tayama thing came up, we thought it might be our last chance."

Without really thinking Junko responded simply, "It's because I don't have any baggage, being alone. I can just go anywhere. I'm not like you, surrounded by a huge, wealthy family, you know."

"I live alone."

"But your father pays your rent, doesn't he? You're his successor. You've got the kanji character for 'one' in your name; you've got to be the eldest son."

For the first time something cold flitted across his eyes. *He's angry,* thought Junko.

"I'm not his successor," he answered evenly. "You're right that I'm the eldest son, but my younger brother is going to take over the company. It's because he doesn't have a power like me."

Junko listened in silence.

"I think it was when I was thirteen or so that my grandfather figured me out. Until then I didn't really understand my power myself, so I hid it. But my grandfather was overjoyed. 'You're going to be a soldier for the Guardians!' he said. And that was how my future was decided. So no one complained when I dropped out of high school and they just smiled indulgently and looked on when I didn't bother finding work. I'm only on my grandfather's payroll for appearances' sake."

Junko started to say something, but he cut her off. "So yes, I am the son of a wealthy family, and you might not be able to stand me, but I think it would be a mistake to discount everything I say because of it. I didn't think you'd be that one-sided, but maybe you're just like other girls, huh?"

"No, I'm not like other girls," Junko shot back.

Koichi looked at her steadily.

Junko finally relaxed and smiled at him. "I guess in the same way you're not just a rich playboy."

Koichi paused an instant, then grinned back. "That's the first time you've smiled."

"Oh?"

"Okay, let's go."

"To see Kazuki Tada?"

Koichi dropped his eyes to his watch, then shook his head. "No, he's working so he won't be home till after six. It's still too early."

"Then where are we going?"

Koichi laughed and stood up, pulling her up by her hand.

"Shopping."

22

It didn't seem so much like generosity as a wanton waste of money.

"I can't believe this. Are you planning to buy everything in the store?"

"Of course not. Wearing that much stuff at once wouldn't look cool. Now will you shut up for a second so I can figure out a combination that'll look good?"

At first Koichi had said that he wanted to get a new shirt because the one he was wearing was sopping wet and uncomfortable. But in fact he'd brought her to a boutique near the hotel that sold only women's clothes. The shop's name was in Italian, and the prices were as exclusive as the designs.

The elegant proprietress of the boutique looked perfectly at home in one of the shop's brightly colored Italian wool suits. Her face broke into a smile when she saw Koichi, and she hurried over to greet them. Koichi stood behind Junko with his hands on her shoulders and an expression of mock exasperation.

"Would you do something with her?"

The proprietress was pleased to take over. Junko tried to protest, but it was too late. Before she knew what was happening she had been shoved into a fitting room and stripped down to her underwear. One thing after another was brought in for her to try on—suits, dresses, slacks and sweaters. As soon as she had something on, the proprietress pulled her out so that she and Koichi could look her over in the full-length mirror, before pushing her back into the fitting room to try on more.

"Look, I can't afford any of these things so there's no point in this!"

The proprietress responded to Junko's protest with amusement.

"It's all right, Mr. Kido is paying for everything."

"But there's no reason for him to do this for me!"

"He's always enjoyed giving gifts to his friends. There's no need to worry. And besides, a change of clothing will make you look so much more attractive. It's such a shame when someone with your natural beauty doesn't dress up a bit."

After settling on a large array of purchases, she and Koichi continued to confer and debate over what to dress Junko in before they left the shop. They finally settled on a sweater in a beautiful deep blue and close-fitting slacks that showed off the shape of her legs. Junko's boots, with their worn-down soles, had disappeared somewhere and had been replaced by a pair of knee-length boots in soft suede. Without pause, the proprietress continued on to Junko's hair, which had not been cut in quite a while. She braided it and then handed her a hat the same color as the sweater.

"Now don't pull it down too far. There! You look lovely."

"Not bad," said Koichi, rubbing his chin, with the air of a man supervising the tune-up of his favorite car. "How about a little make-up?"

"Just a moment . . ." the proprietress bustled toward the back room. Junko waited until she disappeared and then turned to glare at Koichi.

"What do you think you're doing?" she hissed.

"You look great," he grinned back, unperturbed.

"I'm not a mannequin!"

"If we're going to see Kazuki Tada, don't you want to look gorgeous? Don't you want him to have at least a moment of regret at having let you get away?"

Junko would have liked to punch him, but just then the proprietress returned with a tube of pink lipstick. "With your complexion, this is all you need. Perfect!" she said as she stepped back to view her handiwork.

Koichi made an exaggerated bow and said to Junko, "Well then, shall we be on our way?"

Back in the hotel parking lot, Junko growled as she fastened her seatbelt. "Don't think I'm going to forget this."

Koichi let out a hoot of laughter. "Look, I'm begging you, don't burn that shop down. The owner imports everything herself and most of her things can't be bought anywhere else in Japan."

"You're too much, you know."

He turned to her in surprise. "What do you mean? You look so much better now."

"Pushing a person around like that . . ."

"Yeah, but that's what I do for a living, remember?"

Junko sucked in her breath and snapped her mouth shut. Koichi was concentrating on backing his car out of the narrow parking space and his eyes were focused on the rearview mirror.

I burn people, thought Junko, *and he moves them around like toy soldiers.*

Junko had expected Koichi's car to be a flashy foreign import, but it was a practical domestic four-wheel drive. It looked like he'd been driving it around for a long time judging by the little spots of rust she could see here and there on the body. The tires were just slightly larger than normal and it felt as though they were riding higher than other cars.

"Bet you didn't expect me to be driving such a wreck?" Koichi teased her as they were pulling out.

"It's not a wreck, but it doesn't seem like your style."

"Yeah, but it's the best thing for mountain roads and snow. When I'm not working I stay out of the city, so my car has to be practical."

"So you have a vacation home?"

"Well, not just one. Actually when I called you the other day it was from Lake Kawaguchi. It's already below freezing there and everything's frozen solid—the lake, the roads . . ."

Traffic was heavy. It was stop and start, start and stop. The mountain of shopping bags piled in the back rustled together.

"Where in Shibuya did you say Kazuki Tada lived?"

"Sangubashi," answered Koichi shortly.

"With a woman, right?"

"For a while now."

"And they're lovers?"

"Well, at least we can rule out her being his mother or younger sister, since they're both dead."

"Stop it."

Koichi may have noticed the change in Junko's voice, because he apologized immediately. "Sorry."

They were silent for a while in the midst of the traffic jam.

"His little sister's name was Yukie," Junko told him. "And she was beautiful."

"You saw a picture of her?"

"Yes, I asked Tada to show me some."

She'd seen many, but the one she remembered most clearly was a picture from a kindergarten play. Yukie was costumed and dancing. Her little hands were spread out like Japanese maple leaves and her face was lifted as she sang something.

"Do you have a younger sister?" Junko asked.

"No, I don't."

"For an older brother, I think a little sister is special in a way that's different from a lover or wife."

"That's probably true."

They rode together in silence for about ten minutes. Eventually they got through the traffic jam and the car moved faster.

Hanging in front of Junko on the passenger's side was a funny-faced clown wearing a polka-dot suit and a red hat. There was a bee on the clown's big round nose and the clown was looking at it cross-eyed.

Her eyes still on the bouncing clown, Junko said quietly, "I don't understand."

Koichi didn't answer, but glanced over at her.

Junko continued. "I tried asking them. Before burning them I always tried asking them. 'Why did you do such a horrible thing to Yukie? How could you be so cruel? Did you forget that she was human, just like you?'"

Koichi quietly asked in return, "What did they say?"

Junko slowly shook her head. "They didn't answer. They just begged me not to kill them."

"None of them said anything?"

"Not one." Junko looked at him. "Come to think of it Masaki Kogure was a little different."

"What did he say?"

"He asked me, 'Why do you care? What's it got to do with you? I can't even remember what happened anymore.' And I could see from his face that he was telling the truth.

"It was like approaching some guy at a bus stop on his way home from a day of work and saying, 'Excuse me, but this morning when you were getting on the bus, you stepped on an ant.' 'Oh? Did I? I had no idea. And who made you the spokesman for all the ants anyway?'"

"Begging for their lives," muttered Koichi, with his hands still on the steering wheel. "I've never had that. I've heard screams. Lots of screams."

"Screams?"

"Yeah. *What's happening to me?*-type screams. I think it was about two years ago, there was a guy I was pushing into a machine, a grinder, while it was on, the blade scraping around and around. He was a rapist. His methods were slick, and he'd been getting away with it for years. So I was perfectly comfortable with what I was doing."

Junko was silent, watching the side of his face.

"He was under my control, strolling along, getting closer to the grinder, just like he was heading off to the bathroom. I pushed him over and past the safety bar. Just below him the grinder's blade was whirling around, and I pushed him a little more. He took another step, so his feet were almost off that final ledge. Then I pushed him a little more, to bend him forward about forty-five degrees. And then I quit; I just pulled back. It was the first time I ever did that."

Koichi cleared his throat. "The guy came to his senses, but he couldn't catch his balance. He screamed like crazy as he fell in. He kept screaming for about ten seconds as the blade sliced him into pieces."

"What did he say?"

"He was pretty incoherent—but it sounded like total surprise. *What is this? Why is this happening to me?*

"Ever since then, when I've got them pushed to the point of no return, I pull back so I can hear what they say when they know they're going to die. It's the same as you, I want to know."

"Do you ever get any answers?"

Koichi yanked the corners of his mouth into a smile. "I realized that all they ever do is ask questions. *Why me?* They completely forget about what they've done to deserve it."

"So they don't feel any regrets, any sense of guilt? No self-hatred?"

"None," he said conclusively. "I've finally decided that they're just one variety of human being—a horrible one without any conscience at all. But there are other varieties out there, too. I'm here, you're here—we're their opposites."

Koichi glanced over at the swaying clown. "I bet you think that's a strange thing to have in my car. I found it in a local crafts shop in the Tateshina Highlands. We went up there to ski when the snow was deep, and I bought it on the way home. My friends laughed, 'Why buy a thing like that in a place like this?' But it has a special meaning for me. I'd had a job to do while I was up there and I bought it after I finished."

"Who was the target?"

"There was this woman who'd set up in a resort hotel and had been scamming for a long time. She was old enough to know better but she'd pulled off more crimes than she had wrinkles on her face—and that was saying something. When I told her why I was there, she tried everything to get me on her side. The original aim wasn't execution; it was just to break her spirit. Which was why I was in charge . . ."

"What happened?"

"Who knows? She's still listed as missing."

Junko reached out to gently restrain the clown that kept on dancing with the big bee on his nose.

"If it looks like a bee is about to sting you, it's normal to swat it away or kill it, isn't it? It's the natural response," said Koichi. "If you don't do anything, it's just a matter of time until you get stung. Anyone who feels sorry for it and just leaves it on his nose is no smarter than a clown."

Junko released the clown. He bounced around on the elastic strap looking for all the world like someone frantically attempting to get rid of a bee.

Koichi was right. If you're about to be stung by something poisonous you should strike it down, whether it's an insect or a human being.

"We'll be there in about ten minutes."

Koichi announced this in such a cheerful tone that Junko let her thoughts go unspoken. *I understand what you're saying. I think you're right. But I'm beginning to lose confidence in myself. It might be because I did too much killing in so short a time. It might be because the smell of blood has filtered into my pores.*

You and I, are we really the opposite of that horrible variety of human being? Or are we closer to them than we think?

Kazuki Tada lived in one of a row of newly-built town houses. The exteriors looked almost like dollhouses, designed to appeal to young women and newly married couples. Koichi drove by slowly so that Junko could check the nameplates hanging on each door from the car window. She unbuckled her seat belt to lean forward and see better.

Kazuki Tada's name was on the third door of the second building. So was another name—a woman's: Miki Tanigawa.

"Apparently she was living here first. He moved in with her, not the other way around."

"How do you know so much? Have the Guardians been watching him all along?"

"Well, yeah."

"Why?"

"That's obvious, isn't it? There was a good chance that you'd contact him. After your attempted execution of Masaki Kogure in Hibiya Park, you and Tada went your separate ways for a while. But we knew that someday, one of you might try to contact the other again. And like I said, you're very good at disappearing. He was the only lead we had to you."

"I did go see him once," Junko said, her eyes still resting on the name-plate. "He was still living in his old place."

The entrance to Tada's house was tidy and there was an evening paper in the mail slot of the white front door. There were no lights on, inside or out, but Junko could see that floral patterned lace curtains were hanging behind the lattice grating on the shoulder-high window next to the door. When he lived alone, there hadn't been any curtains like that. Junko wondered if he still displayed the picture of his little sister in his new home with this woman.

"What did you go there for?"

"It was right after I got rid of Kogure at Arakawa."

"In other words, you went to report it, right? That you'd carried out the revenge?" Koichi stepped on the gas pedal. "Looks like they're not home yet. Let's go around the block once and come back."

The dashboard clock showed that it was past seven-thirty. Koichi seemed to read her mind and replied to her unspoken question. "They both work."

"Tada still works at Toho Paper, right?"

"No, he quit soon after your Arakawa executions. Now he works in accounts at a small advertising firm in Shinjuku."

"I wonder why he quit?"

"Who knows? Could have been shock after you killed Masaki Kogure and the others."

"But why quit his job over it?"

"Don't get mad at me. It just seemed that he lost his equilibrium for a while. It was probably in reaction to his mother's death, too."

They drove slowly around the block and just as they were getting back, they could see two figures walking together in their direction. Koichi took a breath and muttered, "There they are."

Junko kept her eyes on the two. She could already see their clothes and expressions, and they were still coming closer. Koichi cut his engine and turned off the lights.

Neither of them seemed to take note of an unfamiliar car parked in front of their house. They were deep in conversation and didn't look around as they wound their familiar way home.

Outwardly, Kazuki Tada looked the same. He had the same haircut and his walk was easily recognizable. He was even wearing a white coat over his suit that Junko remembered. In one hand he carried a briefcase, and a bulging supermarket bag hung from the other. She could see something green poking out of the top of the bag. He looked like a family man.

He was smiling, and the smile too was the same one that Junko remembered. *But he didn't smile much with me*, Junko thought absently.

The evening was chilling fast. The woman was wearing a long wool coat and comfortable boots. It was the season to be warmly clothed, and looking at her from the front, Junko hadn't noticed. Under the street lamp though, when the woman turned slightly, laughing in response to something Tada had said, Junko saw that she was pregnant.

Junko felt something shattering inside of her. Something like the first thin ice of winter, the sheer kind you can see through and watch fish swimming underneath.

"It looks like she's expecting," Junko said in a small voice. "You knew, didn't you?"

"Yeah," Koichi said. "But I didn't know how to tell you."

Words swirled around inside Junko and fought with each other to be the first out. She sat staring steadily ahead and waited for the battle to come to a natural conclusion.

Finally in an even smaller voice, she said, "Idiot."

Koichi remained silent rather than asking the even more idiotic question of who she meant by that.

Kazuki Tada and his girlfriend were at the door of their home now. Looking more carefully, Junko could see that Tada was also carrying her handbag for her. She searched in it for her keys and pulled the newspaper from the slot as she opened the door. They disappeared inside and a light went on in the window.

"How long do you think it is before the baby's due?" asked Koichi in a low voice.

"I don't know . . . but it doesn't look like it's very far off, does it?"

"It'll be here by spring then. Since he's the serious type, they'll probably get married before that."

"That's great," said Junko. The words just spilled out naturally. "They look so happy. I'm glad for him."

Koichi hadn't restarted the engine yet, and they were sitting together in the dark. By the light spilling out from the window, she could just barely make out the straight line of Koichi's nose.

"You gave him his happiness," said Koichi, still looking ahead. "Tada told you not to execute Masaki Kogure. He even interfered with you doing it. But I don't think he'd be smiling and laughing the way he is now if nothing but time had passed by, if you hadn't wiped Masaki Kogure off the face of the earth and avenged Yukie's horrible death. In a way, his life was cut off midway, too. You gave him back his life and helped him get it back on track."

Koichi turned the ignition forcefully and started the engine. Junko sat in silence. She felt like she might cry, but her eyes were dry. It wasn't that she was sad so much as just plain lonely.

Koichi launched into a tuneless song. "We're the bachelor firefighters. You rescue a pretty maiden from a blazing building, and she says 'I owe my life to you!' And then her sweetie comes a-running, and in tears and hugs off they go a-flying. And you—off you go a-home all alone. Your house's a-dark and the stove's got not a spark and your kitty comes a-calling, *mew!* for food."

Junko burst out laughing. "What *is* that? And did you know you're tone-deaf?"

"Yeah, I know."

With a growl of the engine, his car started to move. Just then Junko, absently looking at the town house window, saw the lace curtains flutter open and Kazuki Tada's face peer out.

He'd probably looked out for no special reason either, maybe he'd just heard the sound of a car engine in front of his home. But through the two panes of glass and the space separating them, his eyes met Junko's.

Perhaps it was the light of recognition in Junko's eyes that illuminated her place in his memory. Had Junko been looking away, he might not have recognized her. Or would he? At any rate, his eyes opened wide in surprise and she could see his mouth moving as the car pulled away from the curb.

Junko looked back, feeling her heart being pulled towards that window receding in the distance. But suddenly the door burst open and Kazuki Tada flew out, running barefoot. He yelled something, and started chasing after them. She couldn't catch his words over the sound of the engine. Through the rear window he looked like the hero in a silent movie, gesturing wildly and pelting after them down the nighttime street. Junko was the sole audience, her hands gripping the seat as she watched.

Ahead of them a railroad crossing came into view. The red crossing signals were flashing, and the warning bells were clanging. The black and yellow striped bar started to descend to block their way.

Koichi floored the gas pedal. Junko could hear the sound of the bar brush against the top of the car as they flew across the tracks and came down with a jolt.

Junko was still turned around in her seat, looking back. Tada had stopped on the other side of the tracks, unable to chase them further. He was shouting something—it could have been Junko's name. Then the train swept past, wiping Tada from view. The roar filled Junko's ears.

They came up to a traffic signal as the light was changing from yellow to red. The car slid to a stop just before the crosswalk.

His eyes still fixed ahead, Koichi said, "I couldn't stop back there."

Junko turned to face ahead as well. She pulled her seatbelt into place and buckled it in with a metallic click.

"Idiot," she repeated shortly. Once again Koichi didn't ask who she meant.

Koichi drove her back to her apartment in Tayama and started to get out to carry up the shopping bags that were piled in his back seat.

"No," Junko said flatly. "Didn't I tell you that there was no reason I should be receiving presents from you?"

Koichi pointed to the sweater she was wearing. "Well, then what about that?"

"I'm going to have it cleaned and then return it."

She'd turned her back to Koichi to mount the stairs when he called after her, "Wait a minute. You forgot this—"

Junko turned to say that she hadn't forgotten anything when a black suede coat flew at her. Reflexively she caught it; the price tag was still attached.

"I'll call you tomorrow," Koichi said, and shut the car door. Junko stood still and watched until he drove around the corner and disappeared from sight. Even though there was no reason for her to do so.

The next morning she was awakened a little after ten by the doorbell. She opened it to find a deliveryman with the pile of shopping bags from the boutique.

"Delivery for Junko Aoki," he said and helped her move the bags into her apartment.

"Idiot!" she muttered under her breath and smiled despite herself. The deliveryman looked puzzled.

She checked the return address on the label and found Koichi Kido's address and phone number. He lived in Yoyogi in what must be a high-rise—his apartment number was 3002.

Junko dragged the bags into a corner and then called the phone number. It rang seven times before he picked up, sounding sleepy. She remembered then that he'd had a mission to carry out in the middle of the night.

"Good morning," she said. "I'd like to join your organization."

23

After a long struggle with indecision, Chikako wrote her report. She included everything, down to the last details about possible fire starting and the unidentified "guardians" that Mrs. Kurata had spoken of. The essential thing, Chikako decided, was not her own ideas and impressions, but to faithfully record what everyone involved in the case was saying. The report was ten pages long, and Chikako finally finished it three days after Kaori Kurata was hospitalized.

Simply reporting the events chronologically and in detail was something she was used to. What took time was the search for objective, scientific reports and other documents about the supernatural ability to start fires in which Makihara so adamantly insisted on believing.

Chikako tried research groups at universities and even called her son to see if he knew anything. She got astonished laughter from the former, but her son seemed genuinely concerned. *Mom, are you okay? Are you sure your job isn't stressing you out?* Galling as it was, Chikako tolerated it all because, deep down, she was convinced it wasn't a laughing matter.

When she handed it in to Captain Ito, she was as nervous as the day she gave out her first ticket for a traffic violation. The request from him had been in secret, and because Michiko Kinuta was involved, she assumed he would want to take a few minutes to discuss it, so she had prepared for that, too.

But it turned out quite differently. When she arrived at work, Ito was on the phone, and only acknowledged Chikako briefly with a nod. She stood there waiting, report in hand, until he gestured with evident irritation that she leave whatever she had on his desk. Chikako got the feeling that the caller, to whom Ito was speaking with deference, was incensed about something and Ito's silent anger in response was being redirected at her. Deflated and no longer sure of the urgency she had assigned to the task, she returned to her desk.

Michiko Kinuta had been officially removed from the Kaori Kurata case. Chikako had never formally been assigned, but she knew that, personally, she wouldn't be able to just drop Kaori's case and move on. Shimizu eagerly relayed information on the rivalries and vying theories in the investigation of the arson-homicides at the Tayama factory, Café Currant, and Sakurai Liquors, but when Chikako recalled Kaori's frightened eyes and the hopeless look on her mother's face when she admitted that she too had special powers, Chikako was unable to interest herself in anything her partner had to say.

In the afternoon of that day, however, Chikako learned, much to her surprise, of a personal connection she had to the arson-homicide cases. Natsuko Mita, the young woman who'd been shot and killed at Sakurai Liquors, had apparently been stalked by Keiichi Asaba's gang for some time and had sought advice from a private group called "Stalker Hotline." A retired detective, with whom Chikako had once been quite close but had since completely lost contact, was working there.

The detective's name was Shiro Izaki, and he had been a veteran at Chikako's precinct. Just before Chikako had been transferred to MPD, he had astounded everyone by suddenly submitting his resignation. They all did their best to dissuade him, but no one could make him change his mind.

Izaki's wife had died young and he'd raised their only daughter alone. Besides being an able detective, he was also a hard-working homemaker. He'd taught Chikako how to make "Izaki-style pork miso soup," and she remembered it well. He had cited health concerns as his reason for leaving work, and no one questioned that. In the preceding six months, he'd lost a lot of weight and looked so haggard and unhappy that he had become a different person.

The day of his good-bye party, as he and Chikako headed home in a shared taxi, buried in keepsakes and huge bouquets of flowers from his friends, Izaki finally told Chikako the real reason he was leaving his job.

"This kind of thing, well, with the other guys around I just couldn't talk about it, so I kept my mouth shut."

"That sounds serious. What's wrong?"

"The truth is, Chika-*chan*," he said using the familiar form of her name, "I'm not the one who's in bad shape. It's my daughter."

"Kayoko?"

"You know she had a baby, right?"

"Of course I know."

Chikako had known Izaki's daughter, the apple of his eye, since she was about thirteen. Chikako had been invited to her wedding, and when Kayoko had produced a plump baby boy less than a year after the wedding, she'd sent her a big bouquet of sunflowers with a card. "A honeymoon baby! You're such a dutiful daughter, Kayoko. I can hardly wait to see Izaki with a grandson on his knee." Sunflowers were not often used in florist bouquets, but Chikako knew they were her favorite.

And Kayoko was just like a sunflower herself. She'd been a swimmer throughout her schooldays and had even been in the annual National Athletic Meet. Her arms and legs were muscular, she was tanned the color of golden wheat, and she had a charm that lit up the room when she smiled. Thus the news that Kayoko was not well came as a shock to Chikako.

"Is it a serious illness?"

"If it were an illness, we could do something about it, but . . ." Izaki spoke with difficulty. "It's her relationship with her husband that's bad."

Kayoko's husband was a researcher for a drug manufacturer, and they had met at the wedding of a mutual friend. In contrast to the sunflower girl, he was thin, scholarly, and delicate-looking, with eyes behind wire-framed glasses blinking as though perpetually frightened about something. Chikako had been surprised at the match, but had chalked it up to opposites attracting. Anyone could see that Kayoko was head-over-heels in love with her husband.

In the taxi that evening, though, Chikako had voiced her previous misgivings to Izaki. "Her husband seems awfully high-strung, doesn't he?"

Izaki nodded, burying his chin miserably in his chest. Although he'd probably drunk quite a lot at his farewell party, the flush from drinking had disappeared from his face.

"It was peaceful for about three months after their wedding, and then things started going wrong. By that time, Kayoko was pregnant; she probably decided it was too late to do anything. Then about six months ago, well, she couldn't take any more, she said, and came running home to me with her son in her arms."

Chikako shifted her hold on the flowers and waited for Izaki to continue.

"The scumbag beats Kayoko," he said. "Just over little things, he goes nuts and hits her. In fact, she told me he even beat her when she was pregnant. I lost it and yelled at her, 'Why didn't you come home sooner?' Then she started crying, see, and said she hadn't wanted to worry me."

"Poor thing . . ."

"Ridiculous, trivial things make him angry, she says. He doesn't like what she's fixed for dinner, or she doesn't laugh at the same things he does when they're watching television, or the bath is lukewarm, or she's too long on the phone . . ."

"But isn't Kayoko stronger than her husband? She was an athlete. She should give him a punch back. That kind of person is always weak when counterattacked."

"That's what I told her, too. But he's ready for her. To begin with, he doesn't hit with empty hands."

Chikako was appalled. "He comes at her with a weapon?"

"Yeah. He's always got a metal bat wrapped in a towel. Then when he hits Kayoko and she falls down, he ties her up with clothesline and hits her again. It's gotten worse since the baby was born; now if she doesn't do exactly what he says, he threatens to hit the kid, and he makes Kayoko hurt herself . . ."

Chikako, who tended to get carsick anyway when she'd been drinking, started to feel nauseous. "That's criminal. It's not just a domestic matter anymore."

"That's what I say, too. And Kayoko really put up with a lot. But the thing is, other than these episodes of insane violence, she says he's an incredibly nice guy. I just don't get it. His salary, all of it, goes home, and he doesn't gamble or drink. He never plays around. His reputation at work is top-notch, too—they say with his brains, he'll go far."

Chikako, hardly unfamiliar with the duplicity of human nature, couldn't help but heave a sigh.

"How about consulting the precinct's public safety division? You know they've been looking more closely at domestic violence issues, and—"

"Yeah, I thought about that too, but . . ."

"Well, why not?"

"After Kayoko came home, her father-in-law came chasing after her. He apologized and begged us on his knees to keep the thing quiet."

"That's unbelievably self-centered."

"Kayoko's mother-in-law has heart trouble, see? They're under strict orders from the doctor not to upset her in any way. If she got wind of this, it could kill her."

"Well, if that's the case, then the father-in-law should take responsibility for teaching his son to behave!"

"Yeah . . ." Izaki shook his head. "I doubt there's any point in waiting for that to happen. But anyway, I won't hand over Kayoko or my grandson again, and I've told him we'll be getting a lawyer and an immediate divorce."

So this was why Izaki looked so haggard.

"Have things started to calm down at all?"

To that question, Izaki didn't offer an answer.

If the situation were under control, he wouldn't be quitting his job, thought Chikako.

"I'm thinking of getting out of Tokyo."

"All three of you?"

"Yeah. I'm originally from Kyushu, you know. It's a distant connection, but I've still got some relatives there. Move to somewhere around Fukuoka, look for a job as a security guard or something, and the three of us can live together and take it easy. That's what I'm thinking . . ."

"That sounds like a great idea. And Kayoko can get away from the memories of everything that's happened here."

"Besides, if we stay, he comes chasing after her." Izaki said it offhandedly, but his eyes were dark. "I don't know how many times he's done it already. Coming around uninvited, bawling like a baby to try and force Kayoko to get back together with him. He'll never be violent again; he's been reborn, he says. And Kayoko falls for it. She's gone back to him twice—the first time she told me she was going, and the second time she left while I was at work."

There was no need to ask how it had worked out. Izaki's grim expression said it all, but he told her anyway.

"Both times, the bastard beat her up so badly that she ended up in the hospital."

"Oh, my God!"

"You know how they say that even Buddha forgives three times and then gets angry? Well, since then no matter what the guy says Kayoko's stopped going back to him. Even when he threatens to kill himself on our doorstep. But you know, Chika-*chan*, the scary thing is that now it's like a state of war. And a guerrilla war at that."

"What's he saying now?"

"He wants to make off with my grandson," Izaki growled. "If he manages to get the kid, Kayoko would have to go back to him, right?"

Chikako felt a chill run down her spine. "Izaki, you can't just let this go on. Even the story about the mother-in-law's heart disease sounds fishy. It would really be better to just call in the police."

Izaki looked drained. He shook his head. "It's an option, but it's the second-best strategy. First of all we'll go and try out Kyushu. I'd always thought I'd retire there, so the only difference is that it will just be ten years earlier, right?"

To Chikako it had sounded as though he was trying to convince himself that their problems would soon be solved.

So Chikako was astonished when she heard from Shimizu that this same Izaki was back in Tokyo, working for a group that consulted on stalker problems.

"Izaki wasn't directly involved with the Natsuko Mita consultation. Since he's in management, he's out and about a lot giving lectures and teaching the basics of self-defense at girls' schools and women's events."

"Is the Stalker Hotline a volunteer group?"

"No, I'm pretty sure it's a registered company."

"I wonder who's backing them?"

Shimizu looked into it and reported back, "It's actually part of a big corporation called Kanto Comprehensive Security Services. Stalker Hotline is just its nickname. In Kanto, two major security service companies hold its stock, and its charter shows that it does a lot of different things, like setting up specialized security systems for companies with lots of female employees, and corporate education to prevent sexual harassment. But it's better known by its nickname because their work on stalking has been in the news a bit. Apparently inquiries have been pouring in from all over the country."

"That really shows how many people have trouble with stalkers and the like, doesn't it?"

"Are you saying we should be taking a more active role, Detective Ishizu?"

"Yes, I am. It's no joke."

Police rarely acted before a crime was committed. It was no wonder that Izaki wound up working in an organization preventing crimes against women. It must be because of what had happened to his own daughter. But what about Kayoko? Perhaps the situation had improved enough that she could safely return to Tokyo. Or maybe she was somewhere else, remarried and with a true partner this time. How was Izaki himself doing now?

I'll go see him. There was still no response from Captain Ito. Glancing at his desk, Chikako's report looked untouched. *Why waste time waiting around here?* she thought. Putting her cell phone in her pocket, Chikako stood up.

Stalker Hotline was located in a trim twelve-story building overlooking the main intersection of central Ginza, Tokyo's high-class shopping and entertainment district. It was in room 602, on the sixth floor. The company's full name, Kanto Comprehensive Security Services, was properly displayed alongside its nickname in the row of nameplates in the building lobby.

As she neared the elevator, she saw a poster hung conspicuously on the wall just next to it. Large fluffy-looking letters designed to resemble skywriting were set against a light blue background and read:

Ladies who have come to visit Stalker Hotline, please do not give up here. We are on the 6th floor. The first consultation is free. Take courage! We will empower you!

A red-winged biplane was spilling out these letter-shaped clouds, and from the pilot's window a woman in an old-fashioned flying cap raised a balled fist to the sky. Chikako smiled. This poster was a great idea to encourage women who had made it this far but who needed another push to make it onto the elevator.

The sixth floor had a tiny hallway, no larger than a single tatami mat. In case a visitor had any lingering doubts, the single door ahead was decorated with another poster just like the one in the lobby.

Chikako opened the door and walked in. She was met by a row of desks on which were set a number of neatly-arranged boxes filled with pamphlets and a sign saying, "Please help yourself." Behind these was a partition set up to block the visitor's view of the rest of the room, but Chikako clearly heard voices and the insistent ringing of telephones.

The pamphlets were exactly what one would expect in the reception area of an organization like this: a list of clinics providing counseling for victims of crimes against women; publications on post-traumatic stress disorder; phone numbers for various public offices; and a hand-bound booklet published by women with personal experience fighting stalkers. After briefly glancing over the numerous titles and headings, she pressed an inconspicuous little bell that had been placed next to them.

Answering, "Hello! Be right with you!" in a bright voice, a young woman came out from behind the partition with some papers in hand. She was dressed in a navy blue high-necked sweater and a long wool skirt. Her hair was cropped short to show off her shiny earrings. Her cheerful welcome made Chikako feel more like she'd just popped into a neighborhood hair salon than a crisis center.

"Hello," Chikako responded just as warmly. "I haven't come for a consultation, but to call on an old friend. I heard that Shiro Izaki was working here."

"Mr. Izaki?" The young woman blinked, then broke into a smile. "Oh, you mean the vice-president."

"Mr. Izaki's the vice-president?"

"Yes, he's been a member of our staff since we opened. We call him 'Captain Shiro.'"

When he'd been a detective, Izaki had been popular with the young women in the office. It wasn't his looks so much as that he seemed so solid and reliable. Obviously, not much had changed.

"My name is Chikako Ishizu. I'm from the Tokyo Metropolitan Police Department." Chikako dug out her police ID. "Mr. Izaki and I worked together for many years. I don't have an appointment, but would it be possible for me to see him?"

A cautious expression suddenly appeared on the young woman's face. "Excuse me for asking, but is it connected with an investigation?"

"Pardon?"

"We've received a great number of visits from police officers recently . . ."

"Oh, because of Natsuko Mita, right? Thank you for your cooperation with that."

"She came here only once and was so terribly frightened that she was not able to do as we advised. Soon afterwards—only three days later—it happened. We were terribly disappointed."

"I'm so sorry."

Natsuko Mita had gotten up the courage to knock at this door, but had not had enough to take the next step. And before she could build up more, disaster had run her down.

"Oh, excuse me, I'll let him know you're here." So saying, she turned around, then turned back hurriedly, looking questioningly at Chikako. "Uh, sorry to ask again, but you're not really a reporter, are you?"

"No, I'm not."

"Your police ID is the real thing, right?"

Laughing, Chikako got it out once more and opened it for her to see. Relief spread across her face.

"I'm sorry. We've been overrun with reporters—it's been horrible. We couldn't get any work done because of the uproar."

As if reciting a speech from memory, she added, "While we're happy to be on TV to publicize our work, we've also gotten terrible coverage from some stations. We've made all the facts about the situation a matter of public record, so we are now declining to respond to further inquiries."

"That makes sense." Chikako tried to sound reassuring, and the young woman finally disappeared behind the partition.

Chikako listened to the sound of phones ringing. Tuning in more carefully to the voices answering them, she heard expressions of encouragement, interjections of agreement, and street directions, all mixed together.

"Chika-*chan*!"

A small man wearing a gray suit emerged from behind the partition. She could see at a glance that the red vest he was wearing under his suit jacket was hand knit.

"It's been a long time, hasn't it?" Shiro Izaki welcomed Chikako with open arms.

"Chika-*chan*, you haven't changed a bit!" Izaki gazed intently at Chikako over a table in a nearby café, looking pleased as he stirred the milk into his tea. "I heard that you were recruited by MPD soon after I quit. That's great."

Izaki was no longer the haggard man who had taken early retirement. He looked entirely returned to health, his slack cheeks had filled out again, and he seemed genuinely pleased to see her.

Chikako relaxed. They'd be able to talk frankly, just like they used to. When Izaki and his family had left Tokyo, they'd cut off communication with everyone they knew, not sure who or what might provide Kayoko's husband with a clue as to their whereabouts. He had promised Chikako that he would get in touch as soon as it was safe, and she had believed that he had been in Kyushu all this time. She'd needle him just a little for treating her so distantly.

"So when did you come back to Tokyo?" Chikako asked gently, after explaining the circumstances of how she came to find him.

Izaki scratched his head. "Well, it was about a year after I retired."

Chikako stopped with her coffee cup in mid-air, her eyes widening. "So soon? But you *did* go to Kyushu, didn't you?"

"Yeah. I found work there, too."

"How is Kayoko?"

Izaki stopped stirring his tea. He took the spoon out and laid it gently on the saucer.

When he looked up again, all the sparkle in his eyes was gone.

"Kayoko's dead. My grandson with her."

Chikako set her coffee cup down and eventually managed to squeeze a question past the constriction in her throat.

"What happened?"

Izaki searched the inner pocket of his suit and pulled out a Mild Seven cigarette. He'd always carried that brand around with him, but as far as Chikako knew, he'd never smoked. He'd just hold a cigarette between his fingers and fiddle with it until it snapped and the tobacco fell out.

"Did it happen in Kyushu?"

Izaki shook his head as he twisted his cigarette around. "No, they died here."

"But you weren't living here, were you?" As soon as her question was out, Chikako hit on the answer. "Oh—her husband's family's place?"

Izaki nodded defeatedly.

"How . . . ?"

Izaki told her the story. Kayoko's husband had shown up just as Izaki and his family were settling into their new home in Kyushu. It was as though he had calculated the timing.

"I was shocked. How'd he find us? I still can't figure it out. I was a *detective*, and I thought I had done my absolute best to make sure that we couldn't be followed. I was even careful to make sure the moving men kept their mouths shut."

"Some people's lips loosen for money," Chikako commiserated regretfully.

Izaki continued. Kayoko's husband had refused to sign the divorce papers. One way or another he was determined to make a new start of things, and he made daily visits to their house. Izaki recalled his grandson reaching his small hand through the gate towards his father, who was calling the boy and crying out apologies to him.

Chikako felt sick. How could the boy have so quickly forgotten the beatings he and his mother had suffered? It must have been unbearable for Kayoko and Izaki to watch.

"You never saw such a reformed character as that bastard when he came to call. You'd never imagine that he could be violent at all. Rain or shine, he'd come, pushing candy or toys through the gate to the kid, leaving with, 'See you tomorrow!' He eventually managed to persuade Kayoko to let him in and have dinner with them. When I got home from work and saw him there, I blew up. Kayoko cried, the guy cried too, and we had it out all night. Then about two weeks later, Kayoko said she wanted to go back to Tokyo *just once*—because she wanted to set things straight with his parents and then come *right* back . . .

"I said I'd go with them. But she said not to worry about it because I'd just gotten a job down there and I couldn't really take any time off yet. So, the plan was that she'd take the boy, stay just one night in a hotel, and as soon they'd talked things out, she'd come right back. When the date was set, the guy came to get them. He looked overjoyed, practically carrying Kayoko and the boy in his arms. And off they went to Tokyo together."

They left Kyushu on an early morning flight. Mother and child were supposed to return to Izaki's house in the afternoon of the next day.

"But . . . I think it was just past noon. A phone call came into work. I got on, and it was a police detective from Hachioji North precinct. That's where the guy's family's place was. It hit so hard I thought I'd die right then and there. I wanted to hang up before he said anything. But I didn't."

The detective told him that Kayoko and her little boy were dead.

"They died in the hotel they were staying in, stabbed with a knife the bastard had hidden on him. The hotel maid found them the next morning when she came to clean the room. They say Kayoko must have fought madly for her life because the room was covered in blood."

Izaki took an audible gulp. He seemed to be picking out just the essentials to tell Chikako; the rest he swallowed and sent back to the recesses of his heart.

"They told me she was stabbed twenty-six times. The coroner said he killed Kayoko first. He stabbed her in the side, then, when she fell down, he rode her horseback, stabbing her over and over. The guests in the next room heard my grandson crying; he must have been watching it happen, and his noise covered the sounds of the fight. After that, the bastard stabbed the boy once in the abdomen and once in the neck."

The police started the search for Kayoko's husband right away. The manager at the hotel reception desk remembered him from the night before. Just after midnight, he had been with his wife and son at the front desk as Kayoko got her key, and then he went up to the room with them. The manager remembered that he was holding the boy in his arms; he'd said something about seeing them to their room.

Just let me carry him that far, please! Chikako could imagine him coughing out that line. Kayoko had taken the long trip to Tokyo because she had wanted her in-laws to see her sincerity and to convince them that nothing could be done to save the marriage. No matter how deep his regrets were or how great his change of heart, Kayoko wasn't likely to have done a sudden turnaround and have consented to get back together with him, and meanwhile, heavy with humiliation and anger, he must have planned to murder her as soon as he could get her away from her protective father.

"They found him the next day," Izaki continued. "He was holed up in a city center business hotel and an employee who'd seen the news on TV recognized him. 'I'm ready to turn myself in. Will you take me to the police?' he said, and came out with the manager."

"They say he cried all the way. He said that when Kayoko had insisted on a divorce and refused to hand over his son, he had lost his will to live. He said he had planned to die with them."

Apparently there were dozens of hesitant cut-like marks on his wrists.

"Stabs his wife twenty-six times—what were those scratches supposed to mean?" Izaki laughed ironically. The cigarette in his fingers snapped just at the filter, and the shredded leaves scattered over the tabletop. There was the scent of tobacco without the smoke.

Chikako urged him to continue. "Of course, he was convicted in court, right?"

"He got thirteen years," Izaki replied. Then his voice rose a little as he appended, "*A model prisoner.* Well, he *was* a model prisoner."

Chikako looked at him quizzically.

"Ten months after he was jailed, he hung himself in the prison toilet. He cut a sheet into strips and tied them together. By that time I was already back in Tokyo, so after they buried him, I went once to see his grave."

Chikako did not ask what he did there. Instead she said, "But . . . even though it happened here, not one of us knew anything about it."

"Yeah, because the case was outside Tokyo's central wards. We didn't know anyone there, and it was a clear-cut case to begin with—they knew from the start the bastard was guilty, so an investigation team was never formed. Besides, around that time the city was in an uproar with all kinds of other big cases, so Kayoko and her boy barely even made the newspapers."

Izaki dusted the loose tobacco off his finger, and drank his cold tea.

"Forgive me, but I just haven't been able to face anyone from my police days. I didn't want to be reminded of what happened to Kayoko by talking about it with anyone who knew us before. I wasn't a father, a grandpa, or even a policeman anymore. It was like I'd become invisible, like a ghost or a shadow. So it seemed more expedient to become a totally different person."

With difficulty, Chikako finally managed to force a smile. She felt deep down that if one of them didn't smile soon, neither of them would ever be able to smile again.

"You don't look like a ghost to me," she said quietly. "At least, you look a lot better than when you left."

"That's thanks to my work now."

"Yes, I can see that. I think you were right in getting back to the same kind of work."

Izaki's face became serious. "Getting back to the same kind of work?" he returned.

"Yes. Doesn't your company, Kanto Comprehensive Security Services, have the same spirit as the police? After everything you've been through, you're still a policeman, Izaki."

"We flatter ourselves that we're more activist and aggressive in our work than the police."

He spoke with a smile, but the comment was barbed.

"So that's why the girls in the office call you 'Captain Shiro,' You're as popular as ever, I see," Chikako teased and then smiled at the flustered look on Izaki's face. "Did someone on the force introduce you for the job?" Chikako had intended it to be a casual question, but his answer was just an instant too long in coming.

"No. Since I retired, I've had no contact with the police, either retired or on active duty," Izaki said, looking restlessly into his empty cup. "So I got the job without anyone's help."

"Oh, is that so? It's not the kind of work that's usually in the 'help wanted' ads, is it? I thought maybe you had some police connection."

"No, it wasn't like that. First I was in the security company, and then I got transferred over to the subsidiary."

Chikako felt a vague sense of inconsistency in Izaki's strong denial. Police officers often found post-retirement jobs with security companies, and generally their cross-connections were strong. Relying on these connections was neither embarrassing nor rare. And furthermore, why the emphasis on not meeting anyone?

If he's not in contact with anyone, how come he knew I'd been transferred to the MPD?

Izaki was looking sideways at the check, apparently ready to leave. It looked like he was going to reach for it any second. To stall him, Chikako changed the subject.

"I hear that because of the Natsuko Mita case, you had an awful time with news reporters."

The focus of Izaki's eyes swam for an instant. Chikako's breath caught in her throat. His eyes looked just like Makihara's had when he recalled his younger brother's death. She could see that Izaki had been pulled unwillingly back to an unwelcome memory; his eyes revealed an unconscious response to a psychological wound or perhaps some kind of guilt.

But why would Izaki react so strongly to Natsuko Mita's name? Was it because they hadn't been able to save her, even though she'd made the effort to go once for a consultation? But from what Shimizu had said, it wasn't as though Izaki had been directly involved with her. He was not reacting normally for someone in his position.

"It was horrible what happened to her," Izaki said as he started to push together the scattered tobacco leaves on the tabletop. "It was Keiichi Asaba, wasn't that his name? I wish you would catch more animals like that, Detective Ishizu."

"Me, too. Preferably before they do something big."

"But, preventing crime isn't the job of the police, is it? That's the painful part."

"Touché. But I *do* think there's a line that you have to stay behind, that you shouldn't cross."

Izaki raised his eyes. "Even if innocent victims are sacrificed? Chika-*chan*, is that what you really think?"

As Chikako was about to answer, her cell phone began to ring. She clucked in annoyance as she checked the number and then cut the line without answering.

"You've got to make a call, huh?" Izaki was obviously anxious to leave. He picked up the check. "This is my treat. Next time, let's have a relaxed dinner or something. Okay?"

"Yes, definitely, let's do that," Chikako answered, getting up as well. She watched him from behind as he paid the bill. He looked relieved, as though he was now finally able to drop his guard and relax.

"Well, see you," Izaki said and waved. Chikako nodded and waved back, but she knew that there wouldn't be any invitation to dinner. She stared after him with a puzzled frown until his figure disappeared into his office building. Then, she pulled out her cell phone to call Makihara back.

"It was last night," Makihara said. He and Chikako had met at Odaiba Station on the Yurikamome monorail and were now walking quickly toward the high-rise where the Sadas lived. "He called just before, to ask if it would be all right if he came over to see them. Of course the Sadas said it would be fine. Apparently he'd been keeping an eye on their website all along, but now he needed to ask for their help."

"And what did he want?"

It had been past ten o'clock in the evening when Kazuki Tada, the elder brother of Yukie Tada, one of the high school girls murdered by Masaki Kogure, had come to see the Sadas. They had met a few years before when he came to see them after the Arakawa homicides, but despite their efforts to keep in touch, they had since lost contact with him and had no idea where he was or what he was doing. Then suddenly he came to see them of his own accord.

"He wanted them to help him find someone," said Makihara, blinking against the biting wind in his eyes. "A friend of his named Junko Aoki. She used to work with him at Toho Paper."

"Why is he looking for her? What connection does she have with the murdered high school girls?"

"I don't know. Mr. Sada said that they couldn't discuss it over the phone because it was too complicated, but he asked us to please come over as quickly as possible so we could talk face to face."

As always, the Sada's apartment was homey and welcoming.

"Come in, come in," Mrs. Sada said. Both of the Sadas were home waiting for Chikako and Makihara. Their table was piled high with books, some straight from the bookstore and some heavy-looking tomes with library covers on them. As she sat down, Chikako ran her eyes over the titles in astonishment.

Supernatural Phenomena of the World
The World You Don't Know

Taking On the Puzzling Challenge of Paranormal Phenomena
Psychic Detective
Psychic Abilities and Science
Supernatural Abilities: Current Research

Seeing Chikako's expression, the Sadas exchanged a look.

"You're surprised, aren't you?" said Mrs. Sada.

"Both of us decided to take the day off today and go around some book-stores and the library and read up a bit," said Mr. Sada.

Makihara looked over the titles as well. He didn't show a flicker of surprise; Chikako guessed it was nothing new to him.

"What's this all about?" asked Makihara.

"Well, please sit down first and I'll make us some coffee. I dare say you'll be needing a strong cup when you hear what we have to say."

Chikako couldn't care less about the coffee; she wanted to look at the books. As Mrs. Sada headed off for the kitchen, Chikako murmured, "Excuse me," and picked up the top one. There were bookmarks stuck here and there, and when she opened at one of them, her eyes fell on a bold print headline: *Pyrokinesis.*

Makihara was reading over her shoulder. Still no change in expression from him other than a glimmer of interest in his eyes.

"Junko Aoki?" Makihara muttered to himself in what seemed both a question and an answer.

"Yes, yes—that's it!" Mrs. Sada said as she brought the coffee.

Then the Sadas told their story, which was, indeed, incredible, although it was on a topic that Chikako was now more familiar with than during her last visit. Nonetheless, she was grateful for the coffee. It could even have been a bit stronger.

"It seemed like he needed to get everything off his chest," said Mrs. Sada, and then her husband picked up the story.

"We felt so sorry for Tada and yet what he was saying was so unbelievable that we couldn't do anything but listen with our mouths open. He was sitting right there crying, with his head in his hands, saying that he wished he hadn't stopped her—this girl named Junko Aoki—when she started to burn Masaki Kogure in Hibiya Park. That incident had thrown us for a loop, too, when it happened . . . Anyway, Tada was saying that if he had let her finish Masaki Kogure off that day, maybe she wouldn't have escalated to the scale she was operating on now."

"So according to Kazuki Tada, this woman named Junko Aoki is responsible for the attempted murder of Masaki Kogure in Hibiya Park, his subsequent death in Arakawa, and the recent attacks aimed at wiping out the Asaba gang?"

"That's right," the two Sadas nodded together. "Tada knew all along that they were her work because nobody else could have done it. And also, the day the Arakawa killings were reported, she came to visit him. She told him that it had taken some time, but she'd finally avenged Yukie's death. At that point the bodies had not yet been identified, but she told him that Masaki Kogure was one of them. Then she disappeared."

Chikako asked, "When Tada came to visit you before, it was just after the Arakawa incident, wasn't it?"

"Yes," they replied together.

"But at that time he didn't say anything about this Junko Aoki?"

"Nothing at all," they said, shaking their heads.

"Then why now?"

No sooner had the words left her mouth than Makihara answered.

"He feels guilty."

"Guilty?"

"Yes. It's on his conscience that he left her to do it alone."

"So what has changed since Arakawa?" Chikako asked, quickly adding, "That is, assuming this isn't some elaborately made-up story."

Makihara didn't turn a hair. "No, Kazuki Tada knew she had pyrokinesis and that she could use it. She's a walking flamethrower—a perpetually-armed assassin."

Chikako noticed that Makihara had deliberately chosen the word "assassin" rather than "murderer."

"No matter how much his conscience bothered him when Kogure was killed, he could never claim to be unhappy it had happened. But this recent string of incidents was different. Asaba's gang wasn't any less dirty or cruel than Kogure's, it's just that their crimes didn't directly affect Tada. But it must have hit him hard when he realized that after he'd left her on her own, she'd turned into a killing machine."

"But it's already been ten days since the Asaba homicides," Chikako argued. "He must have recognized her work as soon as he heard about it. Why didn't he come out with it then?"

"It was because he hadn't seen her," Makihara answered, sounding almost protective of Tada. "He's got his own life now. A lot of time has passed since the Arakawa incident. So when he saw the news of the killings in the Tayama factory he didn't get nervous right away. He was probably able to convince himself that it might not be Junko Aoki and that he shouldn't jump to conclusions."

But Tada had told the Sadas that Junko Aoki had turned up again a few days ago. He had seen her in a car in front of his house. There was no mistaking it. He ran after her but lost sight of the car. That was all it took to bring back vivid memories of what she was capable of.

"That changed everything. He couldn't lie to himself anymore. He had to face it squarely."

Mr. Sada, listening with his arms folded, grunted in agreement and added, "Even so, he told us he spent two sleepless nights thinking about it before coming to us. It's such a crazy story, he didn't know if anyone would believe him. But his fiancée was worried because he seemed so upset, and he finally decided he had to act rather than worry her more."

"His fiancée is expecting a baby," Mrs. Sada explained.

And that had brought him to the Sadas, to ask them to help him find Junko so he could beg her to stop.

"He knew he was clutching at straws, but he'd seen the message on our website saying that we'd like to talk with the person behind the Tayama fire. Since we promised to keep everything confidential, Tada thought that this Junko Aoki might possibly have contacted us."

"When he saw her in that car three nights ago and chased after it, he didn't think to memorize the license plate?"

"He didn't think of it at the time—he'd totally lost his head. He's kicking himself about it now, though."

"What's his address?" said Makihara. "And could you tell me some more about what kind of person he is? I want to go meet him and see if I can draw out anything else that might be useful."

"He's a nice young man," said Mrs. Sada.

Mr. Sada nodded in agreement, "Yes, he is. And he's not the type to lie or make things up."

Makihara snapped his notebook shut and got up. He and Chikako asked them to keep the message on their website calling for contact from the person behind the Tayama fire, and then they hurried toward the elevator.

"You're looking grim," said Chikako. "So you believe that a woman named Junko Aoki exists, that she has pyrokinesis, and that she is behind all those fires?"

"Yes, I believe it."

When the elevator arrived and they got in and the doors closed, Makihara said briskly, "What the Sadas said would be enough in itself, but I'm convinced for personal reasons, too."

"Personal reasons?"

Makihara looked up at the light. "There aren't many people with that particular ability walking around."

"Well, of course not."

"According to Kazuki Tada's story, Junko Aoki would be twenty-five or twenty-six years old now."

Chikako caught on before he finished his sentence and gasped.

"That little girl in the park who burned my brother," Makihara said, still looking at the light above him. "Assuming she grew up, she'd be the same age as Junko Aoki is now."

The elevator stopped and he strode quickly off, as if rushing towards something. Chikako hurried after him.

24

The advertising firm where Kazuki Tada worked was in an office building about a twenty-minute walk from the south exit of Shinjuku station. The office itself was small and jammed full of desks. Most of the staff were out when Chikako and Makihara arrived.

The young woman who greeted them checked a schedule board on the wall and informed them that Kazuki Tada should be back in the office within about a quarter of an hour. She asked if they wouldn't mind waiting and, without asking their names or business and with no trace of suspicion, simply invited Chikako and Makihara in. "I'm sorry we don't have a waiting room," she smiled apologetically. Chikako smiled back and asked where Tada's desk was. The young woman pointed to one, and they pulled some swivel chairs up next to it and sat down to wait.

Makihara promptly began looking around the desk, and then, setting his jaw in determination, he pulled his chair closer and began reading the papers on the desk and pulling open drawers.

"Don't do that!" Chikako scolded him quietly. "Why would there be anything you want to see in his desk?"

Makihara didn't even pause. "I wonder if he keeps anything here to remember his sister by," he muttered, more to himself than Chikako.

"Yukie?"

"I wonder if his co-workers know about his past?"

Chikako smacked him lightly on the arm. "Why would he tell them—you didn't tell everyone at Arakawa precinct about Tsutomu right off, did you?"

Without answering, Makihara proceeded to flip through a memo pad made from recycled office paper that Tada had left on his desk. There were what looked like notes on ad copy for baby formula.

"Well, that's appropriate for him right now," Makihara commented dryly as he tossed the pad back down.

The office door opened, and a large woman wearing a worn coat came in. Her eyes landed on Chikako and Makihara and she bowed reflexively. The young woman who'd received them spoke up first.

"Ms. Minami, we have some visitors for Tada."

The large woman nodded as she took off her coat, then she turned to Chikako and Makihara. "Did you have an appointment with Tada?"

"Yes," Chikako lied.

"My name is Minami," said the woman. She hung her coat over a chair and then came over to them, offering her business card. It read, "Tomoko Minami, Head of Accounts."

"Tada works under me. I'm sorry but I don't recall if we've met before . . . ?"

Her words were smooth and her manner friendly, but she was clearly on guard. Chikako sensed that although she must be older than Tada, the two of them were close and she might even know a fair bit about him.

Chikako pulled out her police ID. Minami's eyes widened, then she glanced quickly around the office. No one else had noticed. Minami pulled her chair closer to Chikako and Makihara.

"Is Tada in some kind of trouble?" she asked in a low voice.

"Not at all. There's no need to worry about anything like that."

"Is this the first time you've come to see him?"

"Yes, it is."

Minami hesitated, moistening her lips, then asked, "Have the police been watching him for some time?"

That was a strange question. Chikako asked in return, "Have other police officers been here before?"

"No," she answered shortly, looking worried. "It wasn't that, exactly . . ."

The door opened again, and two young men came in. One was muscular and tanned despite the season. In contrast, the one following him was pale, and a white coat hung on his tall, lanky frame.

Ms. Minami stood up and called the tall one over. "Tada, you have visitors."

Kazuki Tada's eyes betrayed his surprise, and his pale, exhausted face tightened with tension.

"Um, since it's a little cramped in here, shall we go somewhere nearby?" suggested Minami, reaching for her coat again. "And I don't mean to be a bother, but may I join you? I'll explain when we get there."

"Are you with the police?" were Kazuki Tada's first words to them after they sat down in a coffee shop a few doors down from the office. He had a deep, resonant voice and a handsome face. He had a trustworthy air about him, too—he was the kind of young man women would consider good husband and father material, thought Chikako.

Those attractive features, however, were currently offset by the angry suspicion on his face. She could see that his eyes were swollen and bloodshot. She recalled that the Sadas had said he'd been crying when they saw him the night before.

"We've spoken to the Sadas," Chikako began gently. "There are a number of things we'd like to hear more about directly from you. But first of all, Ms. Minami—"

Chikako looked over at her and continued. "I think we'd better hear what you wanted to tell us first. Is there something concerning Mr. Tada that's been worrying you?"

This was clearly a surprise to Tada himself. "Minami . . . ?"

"I'm sorry I didn't say anything before. I thought I might be mistaken . . ." She looked down, embarrassed.

"About what?"

The only sound came from a radio playing faintly in the back of the nearly deserted coffee shop.

"Well, it's been going on for a couple of weeks now. I've gotten the feeling that he's being tailed."

Makihara, who'd been slumped in taciturn silence, suddenly jerked upright.

"Did you actually see someone?"

"Yes. I'm usually the last person to leave the office at night. Our company president and I are the only ones with keys, and he's rarely in because he manages another business, too. So anyway, one night around the beginning of the month, I was just locking up when Tada came back. I think it was after ten."

"Yeah, that's right," Kazuki Tada nodded. "I'd forgotten something."

"So then we left together. We were walking to the station and I noticed then that someone was following us." Ms. Minami gave a slightly embarrassed smile. "I know it seems a bit strange, but even though we're not far from the center of Shinjuku, there aren't too many people walking around this neighborhood at night. I was mugged once on my way home, so at first I thought I was the one being followed."

"What did the person look like?"

"It was a man in a black coat. I don't think he was young. I couldn't see his face, but that was the impression I got."

"Was he alone?"

"Yes, at that point. But when we got to the station, we went our separate ways to get our trains home. I waved goodbye to Tada and tried to see if I could get a better look at the person who'd been behind us. Well, the station was crowded, and I saw the man take off in a hurry after Tada, trying not to lose sight of him. Then I saw another man who'd been standing on the concourse join the first one."

"Did you notice them?" Chikako asked Kazuki Tada. He shook his head.

Working in pairs to tail someone was the mark of professionals. Could the police have been watching Tada?

"Since that night, I've been noticing . . ." Minami looked down at the table again. "I didn't tell Tada, but I've been sort of keeping an eye out, and I've seen some things. Like when Tada goes out to visit a client, I check from the upstairs window and see a man in a business suit casually starting to walk after him. Or some young guy sits in front of our building listening to his Walkman, but he keeps an eye on everyone's comings and goings. And there are phone calls for Tada that always come when he's out, but the caller never leaves a name."

Chikako turned to Tada and asked again, "And you weren't aware of any of this?"

He just shook his head again.

"Did you notice anyone suspicious around your home or in your neighborhood?"

"No," he answered in a small voice.

"Actually, I thought it might be a detective agency." Minami glanced up at Kazuki Tada apologetically. "That maybe Miki's parents were investigating him."

"Miki is my fiancée. We're not married yet," Tada added, still looking down at the table. "We're living together."

"But her parents approve," interceded Minami. "And the date is set!"

"And your fiancée is pregnant?" Makihara asked, without a trace of warmth.

"Yes, she is," Tada answered gloomily.

"When's the baby due?"

"February."

"How nice."

"The doctor says it's a healthy baby girl, isn't that right? They're waiting to hold the wedding so all three of them can be in it together," Minami said, smiling brightly. She was still trying to lighten the atmosphere, but an uncomfortable silence descended over the group. "I'm sorry; I guess I'm just meddling."

"Not at all," Chikako gently reassured her. "Your information has been very helpful." Left unspoken was, *and now please be on your way.*

Minami caught the hint. She glanced at her watch and said, "I'd better get back to the office," and hurriedly gathered her things. Turning to Tada, who was still looking down, she apologized again. "When they told me they were from the police, I thought I'd better come straight out with what I had seen instead of keeping it quiet . . . and it might not mean anything anyway. I'm sorry for sticking my nose into your business."

She turned to Chikako and Makihara to explain some more. "I used to work with his fiancée. Actually, I was the one who introduced them, so . . ." Minami faltered, but Chikako smiled and nodded understandingly. "So I really am hoping for the best for them both." Minami bowed deeply and rushed out.

Silence descended again. Heavy silence that almost made it hard to breathe. To Chikako, both Makihara and Tada looked like angry boys in a sulk. She was casting about for a way to break them out of it when Makihara suddenly straightened up.

"All right." Arms still folded, he glared at Tada. "When are you going to quit protecting Junko Aoki?"

25

Kazuki Tada lifted his eyes and stared at Makihara.

"What do you mean by that?" Tada's voice shook.

"Just what I said."

"Now look—"

Makihara unfolded his arms, leaned forward, and put one of his hands on the table.

"You've got a nice life for yourself. You're about to get married and become a father. You've got a good job. You have friends who look after you. If you look for Junko Aoki, and if you try to get in her way or become involved in any way in what she's doing, it's going to mean trouble for everyone. There is nothing in this for you and you're running the risk of losing everything you have. I'm telling you to forget about Junko Aoki."

"But I . . ."

"You left her once before, right?" Makihara was intransigent. "You left her in the middle of your plans to get rid of Masaki Kogure. You retreated to safety, licked your wounds, and got the time you needed to start a new life. Meanwhile, she refused to give up until she had avenged the death of your sister. She found Kogure and executed him. You got what you wanted without having to get your hands dirty. What could be better?"

Tada lost all his color, but continued glaring at Makihara. Chikako was startled by this change in Makihara's attitude. When they had talked with the Sadas, he had been sympathetic towards Tada. She kept silent and waited to see what would come next.

Makihara smirked and went on. "But this is the important thing. You didn't ask Junko Aoki to do what she did. She was following her own instincts. That means you have no responsibility at all towards her, and no need to feel any. If you're looking for her because you think you owe her something, you are wrong."

"Are you trying to say that I . . . that I didn't care at all?" Tada finally spoke, stammering with rage. "Are you telling me I just forgot about my little sister, forgot about Junko, put my entire past into a drawer and threw away the key?"

"Isn't that right?" Makihara narrowed his eyes at Tada. "Isn't it true that you've never told your fiancée or the people you work with about what happened to your sister?"

It was a bold assumption, but it appeared to be correct. Kazuki Tada began to shake.

"You're keeping it all a secret from everyone in your life who means anything to you. When you saw Junko Aoki near your home, you panicked— the past you had so carefully locked away was right there in front of you. No longer able to hold it all inside, you went to see the Sadas. You told them everything. You told them how you were looking for Junko Aoki to try to get her to stop what she was doing. You told them that you were responsible for her turning into a killing machine. It felt good to get it out, didn't it?"

"No! You're wrong!" Tada was rigid with fury and Chikako could see that his hands were balled into fists under the table.

"No, I'm not." Makihara remained calm. "Your true intentions are completely different from what you're trying to make them out to be. You have no intention of looking for Junko Aoki. You don't plan to make her stop what she's doing. You are well aware of what you could lose and you are not going to risk that. You just thought you could get rid of some of your guilt and ease your conscience by going through the motions."

"That's not true!"

"So why did you choose the Sadas to talk to? Why didn't you go to the police? Why didn't you offer all that information to the investigation?"

"I didn't want them to catch Junko. And I knew that they wouldn't believe what I had to say anyway!"

"How are the Sadas any different? Did you think they would believe you?"

"They came to you with my story, didn't they?"

"Yes, they did. But that wasn't part of your plan. You said you wanted information from their website, hoping to use it to contact Junko Aoki. You wanted to meet her and convince her to stop her executions. Wouldn't it be convenient if you could keep her from getting caught and assuage your conscience at the same time? Two birds with one stone."

"That's going too far—"

"But if you hadn't panicked, you could have figured out how to use the Sadas website without telling them everything."

Kazuki Tada held his head in his hands, shaking it back and forth. Makihara continued.

"But you didn't even really want to do that. Junko Aoki means nothing to you now. If you really did intend to find her and stop her, you would never have abandoned her in the first place. If you had taken her seriously to start with, she might not have ended up like this. But whatever you might have been able to do when you had nothing to lose is no longer possible now that you have so much."

Kazuki Tada slowly drew himself up. He no longer had the strength to fight back. He looked like a defeated fighter dragging himself out of the ring.

"That's enough." Chikako gently stopped Makihara from going further. Then she looked at Tada. "Mr. Tada, there's something I'd like to know."

He replied despondently from between the fingers covering his face, "What more do you want to ask?"

"I heard that Junko Aoki went to see you right after the Arakawa murders. Is that true?"

"Yes."

"And after that you had no contact whatsoever with her until the other day."

"That's right."

"No calls, no letters."

"Nothing at all." Tada wiped his face with his hands and looked at Chikako. His eyes were red. "I . . . I waited to hear from her. I even went looking for her. But I couldn't find her."

"You quit the company you had been working for, right?"

"Yes."

"Why was that?"

"Junko worked there, too. That's where I met her. After those killings—the Arakawa killings, I just couldn't stay there any longer. It was my fault . . ." He swallowed hard. "It was my fault that she became a full-fledged murderer. It was because I betrayed her. I abandoned her. I couldn't escape from that, but I had to leave that company where everything reminded me of her."

Makihara was about to say something, but Chikako stopped him with a look and she spoke instead.

"The Sadas said that your life was in turmoil after that for a while."

Tada nodded and was quiet again for a few moments before continuing. "But I kept on looking for Junko."

"We heard that people saw you at the scene afterwards."

"That's right, but there was nothing to go on. Then my mother died and my father began to fall apart. I felt like I was going mad waiting around to hear something, and there wasn't a spark of hope in anything around me. So I started drinking, and spent a lot of time out on the streets."

"You've recovered nicely," said Chikako warmly. She wasn't trying to get him to talk, she just genuinely sympathized with the young man. Tada's expression, responding to her tone, softened a little.

"I got thrown in a drunk tank. My father had to come bail me out."

"Oh dear."

"While driving me home he told me he had been having dreams about my sister. In the dreams she would tell my father how worried she was about me. After that . . . I couldn't . . ." Once again Tada's voice broke.

"It must have been awful for you."

"I let my father take me home. I gave up drinking but had to be hospitalized for a while for liver problems. After I recovered I got the job I have now."

"Ms. Minami takes good care of you, doesn't she?"

"She's a good person," Tada said with feeling.

"And your fiancée, Miki—the two of you get along well?" Tada nodded as he looked out of the corner of his eye at Makihara, who continued to sit with his arms crossed, a stony expression on his face.

"Miki was the one who got me back on my feet."

Chikako nodded with a hint of a smile and asked another question. "But you've never told her about your sister?"

"No . . ."

"You don't want her to have to worry about you?"

"No, I don't."

"You don't want to be reminded of Junko Aoki."

"Yes, that's true, too."

"Your sister is free of suffering, and Kogure is no longer a threat to society. It's only natural for you to try to put some of that behind you."

Tada wiped his face again. "Until Miki got pregnant, I couldn't bring myself to consider marriage. As long as we were just seeing each other I didn't have to give her many personal details. But when it comes to marriage, the families get involved and everything has to come out."

"Even if you never said anything, your father would be bound to mention it to your wife or her parents. They'd want to know why your sister died so young."

Tada just nodded in agreement. He closed his eyes tightly. "Everything Detective Makihara said is true. I'm selfish. Maybe I just wanted to shut out memories of my sister and Junko. And shut out my true feelings, too."

"You're only human. We humans are not as strong as we'd like to think we are." Tada smiled weakly in response to Chikako's words, and his shoulders drooped. "Apart from telling her about your sister's murder and the subsequent death of Kogure, the prime suspect, it would probably be best if you didn't talk to your fiancée about Junko Aoki or any of these other things." Tada blinked in surprise. Makihara merely sighed. "I mean it," Chikako continued. "Don't talk to Miki or anyone else."

"Are you sure?"

"Oh yes. There are many things in life that are best left unsaid. I think you should just concentrate on taking care of your family. Make sure Miki has a healthy baby."

"But what about—"

"Leave Junko Aoki to us. That's our job. Can you trust us to take care of that?" Tada looked at Chikako and then at Makihara—and then back at Chikako.

"Does that mean that the police will believe what I said?"

"You mean about pyrokinesis?"

"You're not going to just laugh me off?"

Chikako had to smile.

"To tell the truth, Mr. Tada, I don't believe in the supernatural, although I can't speak for Makihara here." Makihara looked glum. "I do believe, though, that Junko Aoki is connected to these cases. Of course, we'll be in hot water if it turns out that you have an over-active imagination and have made this all up. But we'll know one way or another soon enough."

"Thank you," was Tada's simple response, and Chikako was relieved to hear it. She got out a card and, on the back, wrote down Makihara's and her cell phone numbers and her home telephone number, and handed it to Tada.

"If you do hear from Junko Aoki again, contact us no matter what time it is. Try to find out anything she'll tell you about what she has been doing and tell her you want to see her."

Tada took the card and his face became serious again. "If I call you, does that mean I'm selling Junko out?"

Chikako paused a moment as possible responses leapt to mind. She didn't believe there was more than a fifty percent chance that this Junko Aoki had pyrokinetic power, that she was using it, or that the police would actually arrest her. But before she had a chance, Makihara answered instead.

"No, it doesn't." Tada looked at Makihara, who looked back calmly. "You won't be selling her out, you'll be saving her."

Tada closed his hand over Chikako's card and then, as if finally making up his mind, put it in his pocket.

"You don't have to worry about the Sadas. We'll tell them that you were still grieving over your sister and that you just confused some fiction with reality. I'm sure the Sadas will continue to keep an eye out for you; they won't think the less of you and they won't laugh."

"Yes, I know that."

"We will, though, ask them to keep the plea up on their website for contact from the person behind this latest string of arson-homicides. Junko Aoki might see it." Thus ending their discussion, Makihara and Chikako rose to leave.

"Detective Makihara," Tada began, and Makihara sat back down again. "Everything you said was true," he continued, looking straight into Makihara's eyes. Makihara listened silently. "But there's something else I want to say. You figured me out, but you still have no idea how I feel. I'm sure you are very sharp and all . . . But to lose a member of your family, to see the person who murdered her get away with it . . . you can't imagine how badly I wanted to kill him myself. It's true that I let Junko go. I couldn't go along with her plans. But I truly wanted to kill Masaki Kogure. That's no lie, but it turned out that I didn't have the courage to do it. I just want you to know that you'll never understand how I felt then or feel now."

Makihara was silent, but Chikako could almost feel his emotions churning the air around them.

"I know how you feel," he said. "I've had the same experience." Tada's eyes widened. "I lost my younger brother and the murderer has never been found. I saw my brother die. There were no other witnesses, so I became a suspect. Finding the murderer became my only reason to live. Just like you—I wanted to catch whoever did it and make sure they got the punishment they deserved." Makihara choked on his words. "But unlike you, I never got the chance to change paths, and I've wasted half of my life."

Makihara stood up, grabbed his coat and walked out. Chikako and Tada stood there in silence for a few moments.

After parting from Tada, it took Chikako a few minutes to find Makihara. He was standing at a bus stop, smoking and talking to someone on his cell phone. He ended his call as Chikako approached.

"I was just talking to Mrs. Kurata. Kaori was released from the hospital today."

"I wonder if they're home yet."

"No. She said they would be living at a hotel in Akasaka for a while. She and Kaori. She gave me their telephone number there."

"What about their housekeeper, Ms. Eguchi?"

"Mr. Kurata had her fired."

"And Michiko Kinuta has been removed from the case. That leaves just the two of us."

Makihara put away his cell phone and stubbed out his cigarette in the ashtray at the bus stop.

"You didn't tell him," began Chikako. "You didn't tell him that you were looking for Junko Aoki and that she might be the one who killed your brother."

Makihara's shoulders sagged. "Why should I? It would just make everything more complicated for him."

"That's probably true," said Chikako as she put her hands in her pockets. "But Makihara, you haven't wasted half your life." Makihara pretended to read the information posted at the bus stop and acted like he wasn't listening to her. "You haven't wasted half your life," she repeated. "You're more than ten years younger than I am."

"That much?"

"That's right," laughed Chikako.

Makihara didn't laugh, but he turned around to face her when he replied.

"It's only natural that Tada should want to forget everything. And it's only natural that he wouldn't want the people who have helped him build his new life to know what happened in the past. That's the way it should be."

"Why do you think that?"

"I did just the opposite, and it was a terrible mistake. I was the same age as Tada when he first met Junko Aoki. There was a woman I wanted to marry, and she felt the same way about me. I told her everything—all about my brother. I didn't want to have any secrets from her. I told her I'd spend my whole life looking for my brother's murderer, and she said she'd help me. At the time, anyway," he concluded sadly. He smiled wryly.

"At the time." Chikako repeated his words and nodded.

"I guess you can imagine what happened as time went on."

"Eventually, your brother's memory came between the two of you."

"Exactly." Makihara lifted his hands and shrugged. "She told me that I was obsessed. My brother's death never left my mind, and I could only focus on finding and punishing the culprit who did it. She said that since that was the center of my life, I could never love her or hope to build a home with her or even love the children we would have. I told her I could do it, she said I couldn't—we were unable to agree." Makihara laughed dryly. "She told me that I had spent so many years looking for revenge that I had become cold." Chikako shook her head at the sadness of it, trying to keep it from settling on her shoulders. "We broke up about a year later. I was bitter for a while, but I gradually realized that she was right. That's how I know that Kazuki Tada is right, too."

"I don't know if we can assign right or wrong to either of you. Come on, let's go." Chikako adjusted her bag on her shoulder and started walking. "You've got your whole life ahead of you, but I have to admit I do feel relieved."

"Relieved? Why?"

"It doesn't sound as though you hate Junko Aoki." Chikako looked up at Makihara, and, just for an instant, thought she saw fear in his eyes.

"I don't know if I hate her or not," he answered. "And I still don't know if she's the one I'm looking for."

"I see."

"I'm sure of one thing, though," he said, his breath white in the cold. "She and I are probably very much alike."

26

"What are you doing right now?"

"Why do you want to know?"

"No special reason. I'm just curious."

"Why are you calling?"

"Don't be so cold!"

"Is it about work?"

"That's right, young lady."

"Does this mean I'm really a member of the Guardians?"

"Of course, why would you doubt that?"

"Well, I haven't been called for an interview or asked to submit any kind of application."

"As if there were such a thing! It's not like applying for a job. And you've left behind a record of your accomplishments. We're well aware of what you can do. That's why we came looking for you."

"So there's no induction ceremony?"

"You mean like the Freemasons? That might be fun, but no, there's nothing like that."

"I don't get to meet any of the other members?"

"Someday, when there's a job the two of us can't handle alone, I suppose someone will come to help us out. But not till then."

"So, I'll be working with you for the time being?"

"That's right, we're the Golden Duo."

"Somehow, I don't feel too safe with that."

"Hey, don't hurt me like that."

"So how much do *you* know about the other Guardian members?"

"Come on, sweetheart, it's too soon for you to be worrying about all that."

"Of course I'm worried. How can I get in deeper without knowing anything?"

"Hey, who was the one who said she could take care of herself?"

"How do you know about that? Have you been talking to that other man?"

"Yeah, he's my boss."

"So shouldn't I be able to meet him, too?"

"No."

"Why?"

"I'm *your* boss. You can see me, and all you have to do is follow my orders. Isn't that the way it is in companies? You don't get orders from the company president or any of the executives. You hear from your section chief."

"Yes, but when you join a company, everyone gets a welcoming speech from the company president. We know what he looks like."

"Sure, but you're being hired between speeches. Look, can you use a computer?"

"I have no idea. I've never tried."

"So you don't have one."

"I don't need one."

"Okay, let's go out and buy one. I'll be right over to pick you up."

"No, thank you."

"You're not allowed to refuse. It's an order. We're all required to have computers. Cell phones, too."

"Why?"

"So we can send each other information. We can't just send details about a target back and forth by parcel post now, can we? And we need to be able to get hold of each other at any time, too. We can send email whenever we need to and then delete it when we're done."

"Ah . . . I hadn't realized."

"I'll set the whole thing up for you and teach you how to use it. I'll be over in an hour. Wash your hair, change your clothes, and put on some make-up."

"I wouldn't go out with wet hair on such a cold day."

"You're unbelievably stubborn." Koichi Kido glared at Junko as she closed her wet umbrella and climbed into his car. "Why aren't you wearing the clothes I bought you?"

"I can't take anything I have no business receiving." Junko fastened her seatbelt. She wore an acrylic sweater she'd bought on sale, jeans, and sneakers. She had, however, tied her hair back the way the boutique owner had showed her. It was just right because her hair had grown out and was in her way.

Koichi was wearing jeans too, but Junko could tell there had been an extra zero on the price tag. He wore a natural beige fisherman's sweater, and she caught a glimpse of a shirt underneath. His long hair was tied back in a ponytail with a dark blue woven band, unlike the plain black elastic one Junko used. He looked even younger than he had the other day. It occurred to Junko that anyone seeing the two of them together would assume they were an older sister and younger brother.

Since morning, the weather had been rain mixed with sleet. It was only a week until Christmas, and it seemed to be getting colder every day. The weather report forecast good weather for the next day, but another storm front was moving towards Japan, and there was a strong possibility of a white Christmas.

The road in front of Junko's apartment building was narrow, and Koichi maneuvered carefully into the main road. While he was preoccupied with that, Junko watched the bouncing clown. As they pulled up at the first intersection, Koichi abruptly said, "Would you mind—?"

"What?"

Koichi let go of the steering wheel with his left hand, put it around Junko's neck, and pulled her towards him. He buried his face in her hair for a second and lightly rubbed the back of her neck. Then he let go and scowled.

"Why didn't you wash your hair for me?" Junko was too surprised to speak. The soft touch of his hand remained somewhere on her hairline. Her cheeks flushed with heat. "Your face is red!"

Koichi laughed as the light turned green and he pulled into the intersection. Now Junko was too furious to speak and she turned to look out the window. How could he provoke such anger and yet make her heart pound like that? Something inside her knew the answer, but she knew it would be safer to convince herself she didn't.

"Did I make you mad?" Koichi asked with a naughty grin. "Have you ever had a boyfriend?" Junko refused to respond. "I've always had lots of girlfriends," he went on. Junko began counting the drops of sleet as they hit the front window. "You should have seen all the presents I got on Valentine's Day. I went to a school that was modern for its time. It was a private co-ed junior and senior high. There weren't many girls, though."

"Oh, really?" mumbled Junko sarcastically.

Koichi ignored her lack of interest and went on. "But wouldn't you know? The one girl I really liked wouldn't have anything to do with me. When we were about fourteen, all the boys in the school were crazy about her. I was convinced it was only a matter of time before she'd notice me; I was popular too, right? But it turned out that she had set her sights on an older guy, the ace pitcher of the baseball team, the one who made all the hits, too."

Junko stopped counting the drops of sleet.

"I decided to take a direct approach and wrote her a love letter. I spent days working on it. I plagiarized classic romance novels. My mother couldn't believe that I was sitting at my desk and reading books without anyone having to tell me to. She even baked a cake!"

Junko had to laugh.

"That last night, I didn't even sleep. My final draft was a work of art. Even I was moved to tears. It was a confession of love straight from the soul. The next day, I gave it to her. Two days later, the letter came back to me in the mail. She hadn't even opened it."

Junko turned to look at Koichi. He gave her a sidelong glance and laughed again. "You'd think she could have at least read it, right? It wouldn't have hurt her to open it up and take a look."

"Well, she probably didn't feel that way."

"Really? How come?"

"She must have felt that reading the letter would somehow make her unfaithful to that other boy. Teenage girls can be old-fashioned like that."

"Hmm."

"Weren't you just as glad to know she and her boyfriend hadn't sat down and read it together?"

"That's an awful thought! Where did you get that from?"

"I'm just saying that a young girl might think like that."

What with the bad weather and people rushing around on year-end errands, traffic was at a standstill. The car crawled forward and then stopped, crawled a little farther and then stopped again. Each time it halted, the clown swung back and forth.

"It pissed me off." Koichi had a faraway look in his eyes. "So I gave her a 'push.'" Junko's smile disappeared. Koichi had told her that he was thirteen when he first realized he could control others, so he had probably not yet mastered his power when this happened.

"You overdid it?"

"I was heartbroken." Koichi still had a faint smile on his face.

"What happened?"

"We went on a date."

"You 'pushed' her to go out with you?"

"Yeah. I made her promise at school, then after school I went to her house to pick her up. I even introduced myself to her mother. As the effect wore off, I pushed her again. And again. I was afraid that if she came to herself and said she wanted to go home, there'd be trouble."

"So where did you go?"

"There were only so many places kids our age could go. We went to an art museum. I figured her parents wouldn't mind. That was part of my strategy."

They drove on in silence for a while, until Junko asked, "Did you have fun?"

Koichi responded without hesitation, "Not at all."

She'd thought as much. Junko closed her eyes. She imagined a fourteen-year-old couple holding hands and walking awkwardly down the corridor of an art museum. Adults who saw them must have thought they were adorable. But did anyone turn around to look when they'd passed, vaguely disturbed by something about them? Did they guess that they weren't really a couple, but a puppet and puppeteer?

"Then I went and threw up three times while I was walking her home."

Koichi must have used more of his power than he was capable of.

"Divine retribution?"

"Something like that." As Koichi scowled, Junko recalled how this conversation had begun. He'd wanted to know if she had ever had a boyfriend.

"I've always been alone," she said. "I've never dated anyone."

Koichi responded in a respectful tone, "I figured as much."

"Not like you with all your admirers."

"You've probably been careful to make sure no one was ever interested in you."

The words were simple, but they hit home.

"I've never even had friends. We were always moving when I was small."

She had begun using her power long before Koichi even knew he had his. As she'd toddled around when she was a baby, her parents had never been able to take their eyes off her for a second. They never knew when or where she would start a fire.

Junko told Koichi about her parents and grandparents. She told him how neither of her parents had any power, but they understood it. She told him that she thought they had always protected her because they knew they had unwittingly handed it down to her. For her part, Junko had never hated her parents for her power. She also knew that her own children or grandchildren would never bear a grudge against her—because she would never have any.

She knew that the family line of her parents and grandparents and all of her other ancestors would stop with her. She knew there was no risk of any man falling in love with a human flamethrower.

"My parents did their best to train me to control my power. But it was like trying to tame a wild animal. My emotions would get out of hand and a fire would start, and then we would have to move and I'd change schools. Teachers never knew what to do with me."

"You must have been lonely."

Junko was about to agree with him, but she said something completely different instead.

"But my parents loved me." Koichi looked at Junko for a moment, then turned back to the road. The sleet was coming down harder than ever. "Both of them sacrificed their whole lives for my sake. The usual happiness, like success in careers or making money—they gave up everything and lived just for me. When I look back now I almost can't believe it. I don't think I could do that. I could never raise such a dangerous child. But my parents never abandoned me—they took care of me until the day they died."

On the other side of the gray curtain of sleet they could see the lights of the electronics shops in Akihabara. Junko, suddenly embarrassed at the speech she had given Koichi, hastily changed the subject. "Don't tell me that secret organizations buy their equipment at the same places as everyone else?"

"Buying at these general merchandise shops makes it more difficult to trace our activities," Koichi answered with a straight face, then burst out laughing. "As if! But we do try to economize whenever possible."

It turned out that Koichi did know a lot about computers. Junko understood almost nothing of the conversations he had with sales staff as they walked around the enormous stores.

"What are you talking about?" she asked over and over.

His only response was, "I'll explain it all later."

Junko finally lost her patience. "I live in a tiny apartment—get something that won't take up too much space!"

"It won't have enough power."

"How much power do you need for email? You're not looking for something for me; you're picking out a computer *you* want!"

"Is it that obvious?"

They eventually settled on a small desktop model. Koichi put it on a cart, pushed it out to the parking lot, and loaded it into his car.

On their way back to Junko's apartment they stopped for dinner. They didn't talk about either the Guardians or themselves; instead Koichi lectured Junko on the basics of working a computer. Junko threw questions at him and his estimation of her seemed to rise and fall dramatically with each one, from "You're a genius!" to "That's totally irrelevant." Junko laughed so hard she cried. Suddenly they noticed that out the window, the sleet had turned to snow.

"It won't stick," Koichi declared.

"It looks like it might clear up," Junko added optimistically. But by the time they reached her apartment, it was snowing harder. The two of them hoisted their purchases out of the car and ran for shelter. When they were safely inside, Koichi took a critical look around.

"What are you looking at?"

"You're right. It is small."

"My sincere apologies."

"Let's move that little bookshelf over here, and we just might have enough room to set up. We should have got a computer desk for you."

"There wouldn't be any room for it," Junko retorted. "I can use the kitchen table."

"And where will you eat?"

"I always use that smaller table over there."

"What a simple life!"

Now that they had agreed on a spot, Koichi began opening boxes. Junko looked at the clock on the wall. It was already past eight.

"Are you going to set it all up tonight?"

"There's no time to lose, sweetheart. There's work to be done."

"How long's it going to take?"

"Maybe two hours." Koichi leered at her. "There's no need to worry, I'm not after your body. I'm not going to risk ending up barbecued."

"Jerk."

Koichi took over the kitchen table and got down to work, plugging in cords and pushing buttons, all the while mumbling to himself in computer jargon. Junko decided to leave him to it. She realized that she would have to put away the shopping bags full of the clothes he had bought her the other day if there was to be enough room for the computer. Koichi noticed them, too.

"You could have put them away before," he complained. "It's too late to return them, you know."

"I'm donating them to charity."

"You don't have a compliant bone in your body, do you?" he sighed. "Okay, I've got an idea. We'll have the Guardians pay for them."

"They won't do that!"

"Yes, they will. Remember, young lady, for Guardian work we need to be able to go anywhere, including high-class hotels, without looking out of place. So these clothes are a business expense."

She set to work putting them away.

It was the first time another person had ever entered her home—either this apartment or any of her previous ones. She'd never invited anyone in, not even Kazuki Tada. She had been to his place, but never the other way around. The only thing he needed to know was that she was his weapon—there was no reason for him to see his weapon's private life. Still, she might have let him in if he had asked, but he never had.

Junko stood in the doorway and watched Koichi's back as he worked. He looked relaxed and seemed to be enjoying himself, she could tell even from behind. She hardly knew him at all, but there he sat, absorbed in his work and completely at home. It was almost like they were family. Junko was not short, but Koichi was so tall that he made all her furniture look almost miniature. Junko remembered the time she worked briefly at a furniture shop. The owner told her that furniture was essentially feminine.

'When you get married and live with your husband, Miss Aoki, you'll understand what I mean,' he had declared. Did that explain how Junko was feeling right now? She wasn't sure, but she felt as though both she and the furniture had shrunk in size. And it didn't seem so bad. She looked through the curtains out the window and could see that it was still snowing hard. Cold had begun to seep through the glass.

Junko decided to make some coffee, and she went over to the sink. Fresh ground coffee was about the only luxury she allowed herself. She inhaled the delicious smell of the coffee beans as she got them out.

"That's so great!" Junko heard Koichi's voice and spun around. He sat next to the computer keyboard with his elbows on the table. "I've always dreamed of having someone make coffee for me."

"I'm not making it for you."

"You won't give an inch, will you?"

"You just get that job done."

"It's almost ready. The only job left is the tough one—teaching you how to use it."

Junko filled two large mugs with coffee and pulled up a chair next to Koichi. He began his lesson by turning on the machine. After a while, he switched chairs with Junko so she could sit in front of the screen. She thought she would have had the hang of it after his lecture at dinner, but she found it tricky even operating the mouse.

"I've seen worse," said Koichi magnanimously. "You'll get used to it." He taught her how to send and receive email and then told her it was time for the most important step. "You complained about the price of this little gadget," he said pointing to a small box connected to the computer by a cord, "but you've got to have it." There appeared to be nothing more to it than a switch and a red light.

"It's a voice verification device."

"A what?"

"It works when it hears your voice." Koichi pushed some keys and Junko saw a new display appear on the screen. "When you register, you'll be able to access email from the Guardians. But only you will be able to log on. It's security—the most important thing for a secret organization."

The screen read, "Enter password."

"Should I say some numbers?"

"No. Later I'll tell you the numbers I typed in, but this is a two-stage system. At this stage, the machine registers your voice and decides that it really is you and can safely show you your email. Pretty clever, huh?"

"So what you mean is that my voice acts as a key, is that it?"

"That's right, you have to say the password."

"How about 'Guardian?'"

Koichi shook his finger like a director chiding an actor, "Now that would be no fun at all."

"I can't think of anything else!"

"Then I'll think of one for you."

"It'd better be good."

"How about, 'I love Koichi?' *Ouch!*" he yelped, as Junko gave him a kick in the shin.

"Just be glad I'm not wearing any shoes."

Koichi rubbed his shin and then said, "All right, I thought of one a few minutes ago . . ." He turned the manual for the machine over and showed her something he'd written on it.

Junko read it. "What's it mean?"

"It's you." The screen waited patiently, continuing to show the same command. Junko hesitated. Koichi nodded, urging her on.

Finally she said, "Firestarter." The screen showed her voice as a wave, and she heard her voice come out of the speaker. "*Firestarter.*"

"Is that it?"

"That's it! Perfect."

Now the display said "Registration completed," and a new screen appeared. On a sky blue background, a small white angel was wielding a large silver sword and rising up to heaven. It looked like some kind of a religious painting.

"Welcome to the Guardian Network," said Koichi.

The snow had stopped, but a thin layer remained on the outside stairway of Junko's apartment building. Unconcerned about any danger of slipping, Koichi descended the stairs quickly, walked over to his car, and looked up at the sky.

"I wish it hadn't stopped." Clouds were scudding across the sky. The air was freezing, and Junko began to lose the feeling in her ear lobes. "Would you have let me stay if it were still snowing?"

"You saw how small my place is! You'd have to sleep in the bath. I don't even have an extra futon."

"Move somewhere bigger!"

"I'm not a spoiled rich boy!"

Koichi jangled his keys in his hand as he got them out of his pocket and looked at her with his head tilted to one side.

"You'll get paid, you know."

Junko looked around. The lights had gone out in most of the other apartments. That was only to be expected as it was past midnight. She noticed how far voices carried with snow on the ground.

"Let's not talk about that out here," she said in a lowered voice.

"You're not officially working anywhere right now, are you?" Koichi asked, more quietly.

"I'm not working officially or under the table either. For the time being." Junko moved closer to Koichi so he could hear her. Her footsteps were muffled by the snow. "I used to work in a coffee shop, but that was only part time."

"Then you'd probably better get another job like that."

"I can work?"

"Of course. The Guardians don't have missions for you every day. You can do anything as long as your hours aren't too long. It's good to keep up appearances, too. But, you know . . ." Koichi grinned and put his hand on Junko's shoulder. "I'd appreciate it if you didn't work somewhere that made me worry."

Junko looked up into Koichi's face.

"Why? Because we're partners?"

Koichi also turned serious and answered in kind. "That's right."

They looked at each other for a while longer. Finally Junko pulled the corners of her mouth upwards into a smile, just the way Koichi did.

"In that case, fine," she concluded shortly. But Koichi didn't smile. He continued to look deeply into Junko's eyes. They stood there looking at each other, their breath white in the deserted, snowy street, almost as though they were turning to stone.

Suddenly Koichi leaned down and embraced Junko. Junko didn't push him away. Instead she rested her head on the thick sweater covering his shoulder. He had looked so thin, but when he held her she realized that he was more solid than he'd appeared. She felt his chin on her hair and then his lips. Junko's mind went completely blank. She only knew that she was shaking, though she was neither cold nor afraid.

Then from the stillness in her mind a single thought surfaced and she said, "You're lonely, aren't you?"

Koichi started in surprise.

"I know because I've always been lonely, too." Junko pushed gently at his shoulders and looked up at him. His eyes seemed darker than before. Her next words came out in a rush. "But please understand that I will never give my heart to anyone until we have killed someone together. Until we have been in the same place and our hands have been dirtied *together*." Koichi's eyes narrowed, and he reached out to touch Junko's cheek and wipe away a tear she had not realized was there.

"I'm not the same as Kazuki Tada," Koichi said, his breath cold as ice. "And don't forget—what we do is not murder."

"What do you call it, then?"

Koichi's smile finally returned. "Delivering justice." He held Junko's face in both of his hands, touched his forehead to hers, and closed his eyes. Junko closed her eyes, too. It was almost like they were praying together, though she didn't know for what or to whom they could be praying.

"Good night." Koichi lifted his face, smiled, and headed towards his car. "You'd better get back inside before you catch a cold." He opened the car door, got in, and started the engine. He did not turn back again to look at

Junko, but she stood and watched until she could no longer see his tail-lights.

Now, for the first time, she truly felt as though the Guardians had become real to her. She sensed with her whole being that she'd stepped into a place from which she could no longer turn back.

27

Out in the garden pruning away the dead leaves and branches that had been ruined by the snow and sleet the day before, Chikako heard the phone ring inside the house. She ran into the kitchen and picked up her cell phone, which she had set on the kitchen counter. It was Michiko Kinuta. She had calmed down since their previous conversation but was obviously still troubled. Chikako encouraged her to come over and talk about it.

"It's not that far to my place, you know."

"Are you sure you don't mind?"

"I'm taking a day off today; I've been ordered to use some of my vacation time."

Michiko said she'd be there in about an hour and hung up. Chikako finished her household chores and then went to a local bakery to get a cake to serve her guest. She still hadn't heard from Kazuki Tada. She was concerned that his pregnant fiancée may have become suspicious about his confusion over Junko Aoki. It wouldn't do for her to be out in the bad weather following him around.

Makihara seemed convinced that Junko Aoki would try to contact Tada, but Chikako was now fairly certain that she would not. The two had failed in their bid as partners in crime, and now that Junko had found out that Tada was engaged and soon to become a father, she was bound to keep her distance from him.

If Junko Aoki was, as she had claimed to Tada, a champion of justice who was out to avenge the death of his sister and, at the same time, ease his suffering, there was a good chance that she would understand that she was no longer needed by him, and would not jeopardize his only chance of happiness.

On the other hand, Tada was their only connection with Junko Aoki. If they let him go, Makihara would lose his best chance of catching her.

Chikako leaned against her kitchen sink and continued to think. Even if they arrested Junko and discovered that she really could break a person's neck with a beam of high-temperature energy, and even if she demonstrated it to them in the interrogation room, no court would ever convict her. Every once in a while someone would confess to having used a curse to murder someone. No matter how convincing the confession, though, it was still classified as an "impossible crime." You could believe what you liked, but the law would not recognize it. She knew that Makihara was well aware of all of this, but he needed to find Junko Aoki—not as a policeman, but as the brother of a boy who had been murdered. Chikako's goal, on the other hand, was more prosaic; she simply wanted to solve the case in a way that could be satisfactorily reported to her superiors.

When Michiko Kinuta finally arrived, Chikako was relieved to temporarily shelve her mental debate over supernatural powers.

Michiko looked somewhat smaller than she had the day Chikako met her. She was dispirited and her cheeks had lost color.

"Uncle Ito raked me over the coals."

Chikako had tried to put Michiko at ease by seating her in her most comfortable armchair, but Michiko had merely perched herself nervously on the edge of it.

"I don't think you were so horribly mistaken in the way you were dealing with Kaori."

While it was true that Michiko had become too involved with the Kuratas, she had still reported the suspicious fires in a completely objective way. She hadn't solved the case, but that wasn't her fault.

"Mr. Kurata went to Uncle Ito, he was so angry about me."

"Kaori's father?"

"That's right. He claimed I forgot my role as an investigator, was too lenient with Kaori, and delayed any possibility of solving the case."

Chikako was surprised to hear this.

"Does that mean he thinks Kaori started the fires?"

Michiko nodded. "He's assumed from the beginning that she was guilty."

"Well, even speaking from the standpoint of a slightly deficient parent, I've got to wonder what sort of father would suspect his daughter of a crime and bring the police into their home, demanding that they investigate the situation. If Kurata were convinced of his daughter's guilt, at least you'd think that he'd have a good long talk with her about the situation before bringing in the authorities."

"Kurata claims that it's his wife's influence. That she's the reason why they've raised such a problem child."

"Mrs. Kurata's influence?" All at once Chikako remembered everything she had heard from Mrs. Kurata about her genetically inherited powers and the mysterious "guardians."

"He didn't go into detail, but he claims his wife is heavily into mysticism and that it's behind the marital problems they've been having for years. Mr. Kurata is planning to divorce his wife and take custody of Kaori so that he can get her away from her mother's influence."

Chikako recalled Mrs. Kurata's tear-streaked face and said, "I'm sure she'll never agree to that."

"Yes, apparently she is adamant that she'll never hand over Kaori."

Chikako realized that Michiko had had no idea of the tensions in the Kurata household until she had been called in by her uncle at the behest of Mr. Kurata. She had probably been blinded by her sympathy for Kaori. Kaori had taken to Michiko with the simple faith of a child, but she hadn't told her about her pyrokinesis, and her mother had not encouraged her to. That was what Michiko had failed to pull off, and that was why Mr. Kurata was dissatisfied with her. Chikako felt sorry for the way Michiko was obviously being used.

"Uncle Ito has been busy lately. I assume he hasn't spoken to you yet?"

"That's right. I submitted a report, but I haven't heard anything about it yet."

"I came here today to apologize to you for both Uncle Ito and myself. I'd like to ask you to forget about the Kuratas. Someone else at my department has taken over the investigation. But I appreciate the fact that you agreed to participate as an unofficial observer for someone as inexperienced as me."

The truth of the matter, thought Chikako, was that she had done nothing.

Yet. But now, before she'd even had a chance, she was losing the official pretext that could have enabled her to stay in contact with the Kurata family. She had written up a report and was deeply involved in the case, but now that Michiko Kinuta had been removed, Captain Ito was saying there was no further need for Chikako either.

Chikako was dismayed by the abrupt brush-off. But that wasn't all: thinking about it, there was more about Ito's attitude that troubled her. Chatting in the comfort of her own home, Chikako felt herself beginning to get a clearer picture of what had been happening. She knew her position in the arson squad was tenuous. She hadn't been groomed for it, nor had she been chosen for her talents; she had been promoted simply because she fit the complicated political and organizational requirements at a particular moment in time. While Chikako did the very best job she could, she was well aware that expectations of her were not high.

She had felt encouraged when Captain Ito asked for her opinion on the Arakawa homicides. She'd been still more heartened when he'd sent her to the Tayama factory with the first wave of investigators. But reflecting on it now, she realized that nothing had come of her reports on any of these cases. He'd allowed her to investigate the cases because she wanted to, but he hadn't been expecting any sort of result from her.

Once she was off the Kurata case she would go back to her usual jobs of filing papers and investigating minor fires. She knew they were important too, and she had no intention of letting them slide—but what if she asked Captain Ito for permission to continue investigating the Kuratas on her own? What would he say? No doubt he'd order her to stay away from it, claiming that it was never their case to begin with.

What had been his intention when he directed her toward this case? Was it to get her away from Tayama? He had tossed her into it only to pull her out again almost immediately. Had it all been a gesture to keep her from bothering him with her opinions and reports? No, he wouldn't go to all that trouble. It had to be something else. The Arakawa homicides and then this new series of murders. And now Kaori Kurata. How were they all connected? By pyrokinesis?

Chikako had never mentioned or even considered such a thing. That had all come from Makihara. Chikako realized with a start: it had to be Makihara.

She had been referred to him by Sergeant Kinugasa, who had been in charge of the Arakawa case. Then when she had been assigned to the Kurata case, she had unhesitatingly discussed it with Makihara. The two cases were similar, and he was the one with the knowledge—of course it was all absurd, but he knew more than Chikako could ever figure out on her own.

Both Michiko and Chikako had clearly been used as guides for Makihara. He was known as an eccentric, isolated character, and nobody he worked with recognized his abilities for what they were worth. This was the only way that he could have had anything to do with the Kurata case—which was completely out of his jurisdiction—without arousing suspicion.

For what purpose would anybody want him there?

To make him see that Kaori had pyrokinesis. If he saw that for himself, he would continue with the investigation. Makihara had spent most of his life in search of proof of pyrokinesis. If Kaori did anything or if anything should happen to her, Makihara would be there. Even if Chikako left the case, he never would. And if Makihara were deeply involved with Kaori and her family, and if what Mrs. Kurata said was true, he would eventually come in contact with the Guardians.

"Detective Ishizu?" Michiko was looking doubtfully at Chikako. Chikako blinked a few times and returned to her conversation with Michiko.

"Oh, excuse me! What was it you were saying?"

"Nothing really," Michiko looked embarrassed and smiled. "It's a little late in the game, but I was talking about how I had looked into the Kurata's affairs."

"They're very wealthy aren't they?"

"Yes, but they've also had great misfortune." The summer Mr. Kurata was ten, the family was staying at their summer home in Tateshina when they were robbed. The thieves killed his mother and made off in the family's car with her younger sister as a hostage. Her body was found three days later. The culprits were caught ten months later when they were arrested for yet another robbery in Tokyo. Of the three, one was sentenced to life imprisonment, while the other two got thirteen years each. "But the point," Michiko continued, "was that all three had multiple previous convictions for serious offenses. By all rights they should have been permanently off the streets long before they ever came across the Kuratas."

Chikako listened to the story, feeling her palms grow sweaty as she recalled what Mrs. Kurata had told her. Her father-in-law had been in the Guardians— maybe this was the reason why.

"The Kurata family has had strong police connections ever since. I heard that they've even made financial contributions. That's why Mr. Kurata felt free to go straight to Uncle Ito with his complaints. I also found out that he is vehemently opposed to any retraction of the death penalty and has published articles and even sponsored commissions in support of it. I guess he wants to make sure his opinions on law enforcement are heard."

"So that's what happened." Chikako was still deep in her own thoughts, and Michiko looked at her with a puzzled expression.

"Detective Ishizu?"

"Michiko!"

"Yes?"

"I think you should get your mind off this case and focus on your new one. Captain Ito is right; you do need to forget about the Kurata family. That's exactly what you need to do."

28

"I hope you had a nice day off yesterday." Makihara was obviously in a bad mood, and it showed in his driving. It was unusual for him to let his emotions out like that, and Chikako thought it was probably good for him. They were in Makihara's car heading for the Tower Hotel in Akasaka where Mrs. Kurata and her daughter were staying. The day before, about the same time Chikako had been talking with Michiko Kinuta, Makihara had been contacted by Fusako Eguchi, the Kurata's housekeeper. She was eager to meet Chikako and Makihara, and he'd arranged a meeting the next day in the hotel's first-floor cafeteria.

"But wasn't she fired by the Kuratas?" asked Chikako.

"She was fired by Mr. Kurata," explained Makihara. The day was clear and cold, and clouds raced across the sky. "Mrs. Kurata, however, rehired her and intends to pay her herself. Mr. Kurata knows where his wife and daughter are, but Mrs. Kurata is refusing to see him. She explained the situation to the hotel staff, and they've agreed to cooperate in keeping him away from them while divorce proceedings are under way. That means that even though he's powerful, Mr. Kurata won't be able to get into their rooms without making an embarrassing scene. So Mrs. Kurata, Kaori, and Fusako Eguchi are being left in peace for the time being."

"Is Kaori missing school?"

"For now. By the way, what were you up to yesterday?" Chikako filled him in on her visit with Michiko Kinuta. She also told him the conclusions she had reached based on their talk.

"So, you think that Captain Ito is acting suspiciously?" asked Makihara.

"I don't know what I think right now," said Chikako, shaking her head. "But I do believe that he used me to get you involved in these cases."

"And if that turned out to be true?"

"Why does he want you involved? Could he want to use you to investigate the Guardians?"

"Could be," nodded Makihara. "Or he might be a Guardian himself and trying to scout me out."

Chikako sent him a dismissive look, but inwardly she agreed.

"It would make perfect sense to have active police officers in the Guardian organization," continued Makihara. "Especially the way current laws work to the advantage of criminals."

"That's of course assuming that there is such a thing as the Guardians," Chikako reminded him. "We're still dealing with theory here."

"Yes, ma'am," grinned Makihara as he switched gears. "I was wondering. Maybe the Guardians are trying to recruit Junko Aoki?"

"Why?"

"She operates on the same premise they do. She feels a duty to go after criminals who've slipped through legal cracks. The only difference is that the Guardians can never let their presence be known. They carry out their death sentences much more subtly, making them look like accidents or suicide. Otherwise, they never would have been able to operate underground for so long. Junko Aoki, on the other hand, doesn't hold anything back or try to conceal what she's done. She takes out her victims at the first opportunity. The Guardians must know about her. And if they're aware of her powers, it would be surprising if they didn't try to recruit her as a soldier in their activities."

"Her powers—"

"Detective Ishizu," interrupted Makihara. "It is up to you whether or not you decide to believe in pyrokinesis given all of the evidence you have seen so far. But I'm telling you, *they* believe it. That's why they want Kaori. And it makes perfect sense that they would be even more interested in Junko Aoki, who has even greater powers as well as the will to fight."

Chikako nodded reluctantly. Makihara had a point.

"But we know that she committed the Arakawa homicides and the more recent series by herself—if only because they were so visible," she reasoned.

"True. And that was most likely why the Guardians would have been in a hurry to contact her. We also know, of course, that they succeeded."

"How do we know that?" asked Chikako.

"Because she went to see Kazuki Tada," Makihara replied conclusively. To Chikako's puzzled look, he explained, "Who told her where to find him? Junko Aoki has extremely strong fire-starting powers, but she's no detective. She could never have found him on her own. Not only that, but we know she went there by car. Tada was in a state of shock when he saw her, but when I questioned him closely, he recalled that she wasn't driving; he was pretty sure she had been in the passenger seat. That means that someone took her to see him."

"Are you telling me that you talked to him again?"

"Yes, I've seen him several times. He's being very cooperative. Actually I think he's relieved to finally put the matter in our hands." With one hand still on the steering wheel, Makihara took a notebook out of his breast pocket with the other. "There's a piece of paper folded in there. Take it out and look at it."

Chikako did as he said. It was a sketch of a young woman. "That's Junko Aoki," said Makihara. "Unfortunately, Tada didn't have any photos of her. He described her from memory for a police artist. This is a copy of the original, and I'll make another one for you, too."

Chikako gazed at the drawing of a quiet-looking young woman. She noticed the corners of her mouth were drawn down; she looked so sad. Her hair was in a simple style that came down to about her shoulders.

"Tada said that when he saw her, she had her hair tied back and was wearing a hat."

"What a beautiful girl," sighed Chikako.

"You'd never believe she was a monster who's killed more people than you could count on both hands, would you?" added Makihara.

"So she hasn't contacted Kazuki Tada. She hasn't responded to the website run by the Sada couple, either."

"Have you talked to the Sadas?"

"Yes, and I've also checked that site." Makihara looked startled, and Chikako had to laugh. "All right, all right. The reason I stayed home yesterday was so that I could get a computer. One of the men my husband works with has a son who teaches novices how to use computers. We asked him to help us out, and he took care of the whole thing, from purchase to set up."

This young man had arrived soon after Michiko Kinuta left, and he had spent the rest of the afternoon teaching her how to access the Internet and send and receive email. "I'd like to stay in touch with the Sadas and their activities no matter how this case turns out, so it was a good opportunity to get this done."

"I'm impressed," Makihara admitted.

"Enough about me. Do you have any more news from Kazuki Tada?"

"He gave me the names of some of the places he went with Junko Aoki while they were staking out Masaki Kogure. Some of those were places where Junko demonstrated her powers to him. She even burned a stray dog once."

Chikako looked at the picture again. *This sweet thing had been cooking up stray dogs?*

Makihara continued, "I can't just sit around waiting. She might contact him, but she might not. She might go back to places they went together, but she might not. In any case, I plan to visit them all."

"Right. I'll go along with you to help with inquiries."

"Are you sure? No one in my department will object to anything I do, but I'm sure it's different for you."

"I've still got some vacation time coming," declared Chikako. "The only thing they'll have waiting for me are women who start fires in wastebaskets when their children are failing in school or their husbands cheat on them. Nobody is going to ask me what I'm up to." She waited for Makihara to say something and looked at him out of the corner of her eye. His expression was dead serious.

"Detective Ishizu?"

"Yes?"

"I meant what I said just now."

"About what?"

"About there being Guardian members on the police force."

The Tower Hotel was coming into sight.

"Do you have any proof?"

Makihara nodded. "Do you remember when Tada talked about how he and Junko made an attempt on Masaki Kogure's life in Hibiya Park?"

"Yes. Kazuki Tada drove off with Junko before she could finish the job. But her power was out of control and she nearly burned the car they were in.

"They drove into a gas station in Ginza to put out the fire. I thought the employees had to have noticed them, so I went back there yesterday and talked to the manager. He remembered it and said it had definitely looked suspicious when they pulled in, and after they drove off in a hurry he saw a broadcast about the Hibiya Park incident on the news and called the police."

Now Chikako was confused.

"He even gave them the license number of Tada's car. Two detectives arrived on the scene in quick order, and they questioned the manager and all of the employees about what they'd seen. Then a week later, the manager heard from one of the detectives. He thanked him for their cooperation, but said they had checked into it and it had nothing to do with the Hibiya Park incident. And that was the end of it."

Makihara looked at Chikako meaningfully. "So, I went back to look at the police records."

"And?" Chikako urged him on.

"There is no record of any report from the gas station and no record of the investigation by the detectives. Nothing." Clearly still angry about the situation, Makihara turned roughly into the hotel parking lot, the wheels of the car cutting across the curb. "I can only guess the rest. It was probably the first time Junko Aoki had come to the attention of the Guardians. They must have wanted to ensure that the police wouldn't pursue her so they could get hold of someone capable of pyrokinesis for themselves."

Chikako had to admit that Makihara was beginning to make sense to her.

"If I only knew what really happened to my brother, I wouldn't care what the police did." Makihara's jaw was set in grim determination. "But that can't be the case for you." Chikako was silent as Makihara looked for a space in the underground parking garage. After he had found one, pulled in, and turned off the ignition, she spoke.

"Makihara. Do you think Tada has a good relationship with his fiancée? She doesn't know anything about any of this, does she? Do you think he's worrying her with it?"

"He told me that everything is fine between the two of them," answered Makihara.

Chikako smiled. "In that case, fine. Let's go!" She got out of the car and walked towards the hotel entrance. She heard Makihara slam the car door shut. Whether it was in frustration or elation she couldn't tell.

As Chikako and Makihara greeted the Kurata's housekeeper, Fusako Eguchi, they were surprised to see tears well up in her eyes at the sight of them. The three found a table against the wall of the cafeteria, where they huddled together in the shadow of a large decorative plant.

"How are Kaori and her mother?" asked Chikako. Fusako dabbed at her eyes with her handkerchief as she struggled to respond.

"Miss Kaori is not eating well and has lost weight, but she is sleeping well at night. Mrs. Kurata seems to feel much safer here than she did at home."

"How about the fires? Have there been any more of them?" At Makihara's question, Fusako's face brightened for the first time.

"There haven't been any since we moved to the hotel."

"That's good to hear." So Kaori was feeling more stable and at ease.

"Where are they now?"

"Miss Kaori is swimming in the hotel pool and her mother is with her." Fusako looked around, and then up at Makihara.

"Mrs. Kurata told me that she trusts you."

"She said that?"

"Yes. When I told her what I wanted to talk to you about, she urged me to go ahead and tell you. I really wanted her to be here with me, but we don't want Miss Kaori to hear, and we can't leave her by herself."

Chikako moved her chair closer to Fusako, as if trying to give her the courage to proceed. "We're anxious to hear anything you have to say to us."

"All right, then. The other day Mr. Kurata summoned me to his office, saying he had an important matter to discuss with me. When I got there, everyone had left, including his secretary. He asked me to help him get Kaori out of the hotel." Fusako paused, and then asked, "Do you know about the divorce proceedings?"

"Yes, we know. We've heard that Mrs. Kurata is hoping for a divorce."

"That's correct. She says she won't ask for anything as long as she can have sole custody of Miss Kaori."

"But Mr. Kurata wants her, too?"

"Well, he is her father, and I can understand how he feels." She was obviously finding it difficult to take sides. "I don't know anything about what happened between the two of them. I'm sure there is a great deal I don't know about. I do know that Mr. Kurata seems to love Miss Kaori as much as her mother does. He has never raised a hand to her, or even scolded her. I was the one who suggested notifying the police about the fires. Mr. Kurata was quite against it. He said that Miss Kaori was a sensitive child and that it would be better to move or change schools than to have her be surrounded by strangers asking questions."

Chikako checked for Makihara's reaction to this. He had the palms of both hands pressed together and was resting his nose against them as he listened carefully to what Fusako had to say.

"What I'm concerned about is that Mr. Kurata claims that Mrs. Kurata is ill."

"Ill?"

"Yes, he told me that she suffers from a mental disorder. He said that he's suspected all along that the fires are Mrs. Kurata's doing."

"But why would she do that?"

"He said that she wants to cast suspicion on Miss Kaori so that she'll be frightened and will isolate herself from society." Fusako looked at them both before continuing. "He said that the fact that the two of them are living in a hotel and Miss Kaori is out of school is proof."

"So he was asking you to help him free Kaori from the unhealthy love of his wife?"

Fusako nodded, apparently relieved to unburden herself. "That is correct."

"But you obviously have not done as he asked."

"I asked him to let me think about it. I told him that it would be very difficult for me to do."

"What exactly did Mr. Kurata offer you in return?"

Fusako's face went pale. "I would never—"

"Yes, I know that no bribes could tempt you to act against your conscience. That's why you told Mrs. Kurata and decided to talk to us. Am I right?"

"Yes."

"What did Mr. Kurata promise to do for you?"

"Money," her voice faded to a whisper. "Thirty million yen."

Chikako sucked in her breath. "Quite a tidy sum."

"Yes, but that wasn't all. My mother lives in a retirement home." Fusako's head drooped. "She has been there for fifteen years now, and she requires care twenty-four hours a day."

"Ms. Eguchi, do you have any other family?"

"No, I'm single. I've never even considered marriage. I have no brothers or sisters, and sole responsibility for my mother. I've lived my entire adult life for her." Fusako's expression bore the utter fatigue and loneliness of her situation. "Mr. Kurata promised me that he would find a better place for my mother. He said he would look after her for the rest of her life. He told me the thirty million yen was for me to do with as I pleased."

That much money would have given Fusako a secure future.

"Weren't you tempted to take him up on his offer?" Fusako shook her head sadly at Makihara's direct question.

"Of course I was. But I could never betray Mrs. Kurata. She has always been good to me, and I have never suffered the least unpleasantness in the Kurata household. She does not seem sick to me. She is very kind, and I've been so much less lonely since I've worked for her. It would kill her to lose her daughter, and I could never do that. I turned Mr. Kurata down."

Looking at Fusako, Chikako realized that even the most ordinary people could make the most astonishing acts of generosity when up against the hardest decisions life had to offer.

"When was that?" Chikako asked.

"Yesterday. I called to tell him." Then she described how Mr. Kurata had responded. "He said that he was deeply sorry because he had been counting on me to take care of things as peacefully and as privately as possible, but that now he would have to resort to stronger measures. His voice was so cold that it scared me. That's when I decided to tell Mrs. Kurata about it. Do you think he means to use legal force to take Miss Kaori away from her? Or is he planning some kind of trick? How can I protect the two of them?"

Makihara sat there with his eyes closed in thought. He was so still that Chikako could hear Fusako's uneven breathing.

"To negotiate a divorce, both parties hire lawyers." Makihara finally opened his eyes and began to speak. "Does Mrs. Kurata trust her lawyer?"

"Yes, I believe so. She has known him since before she got married. He took care of the legal work for her family's hospital."

"If that's the case, he will recognize any legal traps Mr. Kurata tries to lay and will know how to deal with them. And as long as Kaori prefers to stay with her mother, Mr. Kurata will have no legal recourse." After a pause he continued, "The problem is going to be any direct approaches. Such as abduction."

"Do you think he'd try that?" mused Chikako. "Mr. Kurata is a well-known and respected man."

"He could get someone to do it for him."

"Then doesn't that mean it's dangerous for them that he knows where they are staying? Would it be better for them to move somewhere else?" asked Fusako.

"Can't they go back to Mrs. Kurata's family home? That would be the safest."

Fusako looked at them sadly, "If that had been an option . . ."

Chikako finished for her. "If that had been an option, they would have gone there to start with. Is there some reason why they can't go there?"

"Her brother is planning to run for mayor . . ."

So that was the story. If she took shelter in her brother's home and her husband came running after her and made a scene, it might well result in a scandal that could harm her brother's chances at election. It would be much to Mr. Kurata's advantage if they were there.

"Then it would be better for them to stay in Tokyo," concluded Makihara. "It'll be safer for them to be somewhere where there are other people around them all the time. An isolated place would be more dangerous, especially somewhere unfamiliar."

"Should they change hotels?"

"How is the management here treating them? They understand the situation and are doing their best to ensure their safety, aren't they?"

"Yes, they have been very cooperative." Fusako turned to Chikako. "The hotel is run by a woman."

"And women tend to take care of each other," Chikako finished.

"All the more reason for them to stay here," said Makihara. "There are no guarantees that other hotels would do the same. Don't allow anyone you don't recognize to see them, and make sure they stay inside the hotel as much as possible. That will make it difficult for Kurata to make any moves on them. We, of course, will do everything we can. If anyone tries to force their way in, contact us and we will be here as quickly as possible."

Chikako nodded in agreement.

"Well then," said Fusako. "I'll have to stay on my toes."

"That's right," said Makihara. "You are their last and greatest defense. By the way, Ms. Eguchi, do you like taking pictures?" Both Fusako and Chikako looked at him questioningly.

"That's right. Can you use a camera?"

"I never travel. I don't have opportunities to take pictures."

"That doesn't matter. I'll teach you how. I'll be back in an hour and will call your room from the front desk."

"What are you going to ask her to do?" inquired Chikako.

"I'm going to give her a very small camera to take pictures of people coming in and out of the hotel. Anyone who looks suspicious or tries to get near Kaori and her mother: in the lobby, at the pool, people at the table next to them in restaurants. You should also photograph the maids and other hotel staff who enter their room. We'll know right away if there is anyone different from usual. The camera is so small that you can wear it as a pendant around your neck. If you're careful, no one will know it's a camera."

"Do you think I can do it?" Fusako looked unsure of herself and clenched and unclenched her fists as though summoning up her courage. Then she declared, "I'll just *have to* do it! I'll be like a spy!" And on that more confident note she left them. Chikako turned to Makihara.

"Do you think the Guardians will try to get close to them?"

"I'm almost certain they will. Unfortunately there is only a minute chance that we'll recognize them, but pictures might help out in the investigation."

"At any rate, we don't have many cards left to play," Chikako agreed. "While you're off buying a camera, I'll visit a few of the places Kazuki Tada went with Junko Aoki. Let me see your list."

29

When Junko got home, the computer screen announced that she had email waiting. She hung up her coat, leaned over the machine and spoke into it. "Firestarter." The display changed to the angel on the blue background, and she clicked on the email icon. She went to turn on the heat in her apartment and when she came back, photographs of three women were displayed on the screen. Next to each was a short profile.

Two were adults and one, on closer inspection, appeared to be a child. The one named Fusako Eguchi looked several years older than the age listed. Yukiko Kurata, on the other hand, was a beautiful woman who looked considerably younger than her age. The third was Kaori Kurata, Yukiko's daughter, a pretty girl of thirteen who closely resembled her mother. At the end of the profiles was a line saying that the three were currently living in the Tower Hotel in Akasaka. Junko eyebrows drew together in a frown. What sort of life could that be for a young girl?

As she read through it again, the telephone rang.

"Well, you're finally home." It was Koichi. "Where've you been? This is the fifth time I've called."

"It was crowded."

"The supermarket? Convenience store?"

"The beauty salon."

Koichi let out a whistle. "That's good to hear. Women should look their best!"

"Now that we're working together, that sort of comment is sexual harassment," Junko said, laughing.

"So we work together?"

"That's what I assumed."

"I thought we were lovers."

"I told you how I feel . . ."

"All right, all right, I remember. You can't open up to anybody who hasn't crossed that dangerous bridge with you. The Ice Princess."

He hadn't got it quite right. What she'd said was, "until you've dirtied your hands by killing someone with me." Junko was drawn up short, but she didn't let it bother her for more than an instant. She was still smiling, too. If she let everything he said bother her, they would never learn to trust each other. She wanted to believe that he was her partner—that she had finally found someone who could understand her. So she changed the subject.

"What is this email?"

"It's about our next job. Sad to say, it's not that dangerous as far as bridges go. These three are not targets."

"Thank goodness," said Junko with relief. "I don't want to go after children. You'd have to convince me this girl was some sort of evil murderer."

"You let things like that bother you?"

"Of course. Why? Don't you?"

"I couldn't do what I do if I let every little thing bother me." Koichi went back to his usual teasing tone. "You have to remember, I don't have your power of total destruction."

The smile disappeared from Junko's face, and she asked him in a low voice, "Does that mean you've killed children?"

Koichi responded too quickly. "No, I haven't."

Junko didn't believe him. She was silent as she tried to suppress the impulse to interrogate him further. Koichi tried to continue the conversation.

"Mind if I finish explaining this?"

"Go right ahead."

"Our mission is not a manhunt this time. It's more like a headhunt."

"What does that mean?"

"We're going to scout out someone to work with us."

"These three? They're going to be Guardians? I've just joined myself. How am I supposed to recruit anyone?"

"Let me start with your last question, princess. You can, and in fact you are the *best* one for the job."

"Why?"

"This thirteen-year-old girl has the same power as you." Junko was speechless for a few seconds. She looked at the photograph of Kaori. Her eyes seemed to be speaking to her. "Are you listening?" Koichi demanded.

"She can start fires, too?"

"She doesn't have anywhere near the power you do. She's more like a book of matches than a flamethrower. But she definitely has potential."

Junko put her hand up to her face.

"I've never met anyone else with the same power as I have."

"Well, congratulations. I have yet to find anyone like me."

Junko re-read Kaori's profile. She read each line carefully, looking back at Kaori's picture after each sentence. She came from a wealthy family and was well brought-up. Like Junko, she was an only child.

"So, our target is just this girl?"

"That's right."

"She's going to be a member of the Guardians?"

"That's the idea."

"And we're going to make this child go out and catch criminals with us?" Koichi laughed. "Of course not!"

Junko relaxed and responded in kind. "No, right. Of course not."

"We're not so shorthanded that we have to resort to tactics like that. Our mission is to bring her into protective custody."

Junko looked at Kaori's sad eyes again. "Protective custody? Now that you mention it, what about her father? He's not in her profile. Fusako Eguchi is the housekeeper, right? Why isn't there anything about her father?"

"He's one of us. Didn't you see that other email?"

Junko checked again. Sure enough, there was another email in the inbox.

"Let me look at it."

"It's a report of the complicated situation she is in and the way her powers appear."

The message filled the screen with small print, and Junko did her best to read through it quickly. The girl's father wanted to put his daughter under the protective custody of the Guardians. Her mother objected, had filed for divorce, and was living with her daughter at the Tower Hotel in Akasaka.

According to the document, Kaori's power had appeared within the last couple of years, and Kaori had yet to learn to control it. Suspicious fires were breaking out all around her, someone had been injured, and the police had even gotten involved.

Junko tutted. "What can her parents be thinking?"

"One reason Kaori is so unstable is because her parents don't get along. That's why she's starting all those fires."

"Somebody has to teach her how to use her power, how to control it. It's not that hard," said Junko. "It's just like learning to control your emotions. The same way you teach children who are prone to tantrums how to stay calm. It's all a matter of discipline."

"Is that what your parents did for you?"

"Yes. They taught me all sorts of things. Techniques to let off heat when I couldn't hold it in—and in ways nobody would notice. I used to use the swimming pool at school."

"And you could teach all that to Kaori, right?"

"This girl? Sure. Somebody's got to do it; otherwise it will be much too dangerous for her."

"I knew you wouldn't let us down. Mr. Kurata decided to bring in Kaori so soon because we finally connected with you. Mr. Kurata's really counting on your help."

Junko knew that she would probably be the best person to look after this girl and teach her to understand her power and the danger it brought with it.

"But you can't just teach a child by herself. The parents have to understand and be trained, too. Whatever their problems, they have to get together on this. They have to take responsibility for their daughter."

"Well, I don't think that's going to happen right away," countered Koichi.

"Why not?"

"Because, like I said, the parents are getting divorced."

"Their child has to come first."

"It's not going to work like that." Koichi sighed in exasperation. "It says right there that her mother doesn't want her involved in the Guardians, doesn't it? We'll have to separate the two for a while—until we can convince Mrs. Kurata this is the right thing to do. She's not going to agree right off that training her daughter is necessary, even if we try to explain it."

"I don't believe that! Any mother would understand that training is absolutely essential."

"Look, calm down. I understand what you're trying to say."

"How can I stay calm?" Distressed, Junko stood up with the phone receiver still in her hand. The rest of it fell off the table. "People are getting hurt! It's only a matter of time until she kills someone. Do you plan to have her kill people? She's still a child. Has anyone thought about what effect that would have on her?"

There was a small jack-in-the-box in the corner of Junko's heart. She knew it was there. And that was why she was very, very careful never to go near it. Right now, she realized, she was getting dangerously close . . . *there*—she felt the lid blow off. It had been waiting for this moment. Junko could hear a dull thud as the latch opened and out leapt a memory of a little boy who had become a ball of fire. She could feel the cold metal of the ladder of the slide in the dark park. She could taste the tears as they ran down her cheeks. The boy danced around, enveloped in flames. She could see his eyes, wide open in surprise, as they melted in the heat. She could smell his flesh as it burned. Then she could hear someone scream. *Tsutomu! Tsutomu! Somebody help! Tsutomu, what happened?*

Then she heard her own voice. *I didn't do it on purpose! I didn't mean to do it!* Junko's breathing came in uneven gasps. She was frozen to the spot, her knuckles white. The phone line was silent. Finally she heard Koichi's voice.

"Hey? Are you okay?" Koichi asked quietly. "I thought I heard something fall."

"I dropped the phone." Junko picked it up and put it back on the table. Her hands were shaking.

"So you don't set fires when you're at home alone."

"That's because I spent so much time learning to control myself when I was young." Junko took a deep breath, and deliberately closed her fists again to lock her feelings, and the shaking of her hands, back inside. "That little girl has to learn how to control her power, just like I did, so that she doesn't kill someone by mistake."

"Junko," asked Koichi, "did that happen to you when you were small?"

For a few seconds Junko couldn't decide whether to stay silent, deny it, or tell him the whole story. Finally, she chose the simplest way.

"Yes. But I don't want to talk about it."

"I understand."

Junko felt like crying. She couldn't understand what had made her feel so weak all of a sudden. She wished Koichi were there with her and not on the other end of the line. She wanted him to hold her until she stopped shaking.

"The two of us will take care of Kaori," said Koichi in an effort to comfort her. "Do you remember me telling you I've got a house by Lake Kawaguchi?"

"Yes."

"That's where we're going to take Kaori. You can train her until you're satisfied that she can handle herself. We'll stay there for a while, and we can all relax. There's nothing there right now but snow and ice. It'll be perfect for you both."

"Do we have to take her from her parents? Why can't at least her mother come, too?"

"It's a shame," said Koichi with feeling. "But if that were possible, we wouldn't have to go get her."

Junko looked at the picture of the girl and her mother again. They looked very much alike.

"Her mother is planning to kill her," said Koichi. "Then commit suicide. That's how strongly she feels about all of this. And she's tried before. If we don't move now we might be too late."

Junko tightened her grip on the receiver and nodded. "If that's the case, then I understand."

"We're going to take care of this job tomorrow night. We really don't have time, and it isn't a difficult mission. There won't be a struggle. We'll have to do some fast talking, but that's all. We should get together and discuss the details, so let's meet in a restaurant at the Tower Hotel. We can look the place over, and we'll also be meeting another Guardian member who has some background information for us."

So I'm finally going to meet another member, Junko thought with satisfaction.

"Shall I pick you up?"

"No, I'll meet you there."

All of a sudden, Koichi switched back to his usual teasing tone. "So, what did you do to your hair?"

30

After much indecision, Junko settled on a knit dress in burgundy. When she finally tried it on, it was almost embarrassingly short. She was about to look for something else when she realized she was out of time. It would have to do. She grabbed her coat and dashed out the door. Unaccustomed to dressing up, she couldn't help looking at her own reflection in the subway windows and nearly missed her stop. She had ten minutes left. The heels of her new boots clicked down the sidewalk as she hurried to the Tower Hotel. She noticed young men in business suits looking at her as she walked into the lobby, and she smiled to herself; it wasn't often that she turned heads like that.

There were a variety of restaurants on several floors. Koichi had told her to meet him at the Italian restaurant on the mezzanine level. A waiter came out to greet her but before she could give the name "Kido," she caught sight of Koichi waving her over to a table for four. He was dressed with his usual casual good taste.

"It must have been really noisy on your way over here," said Koichi, clearly in a good mood. "What with all the men whistling at you."

Junko settled in her seat and pointedly ignored his remark. As she looked away in feigned indifference, her permed hair brushed over her shoulders.

"Your hair looks great like that."

"Thanks."

"The outfit, too. So you finally felt like wearing something I bought for you."

"Like you said, it's a uniform, right? For work."

"So back in your apartment you're just plain old Junko in jeans?"

"You bet. That's the real me."

"Then I'll have to give you a nice condo as your next present so you'll want to dress up even at home." Koichi shrugged carelessly and continued, "Or you could save time and move in with me."

Junko caught the hint of seriousness underlying his joke and answered with an enigmatic smile. "So, shall we get down to work? Kaori is coming here for dinner, right?"

"They've got a reservation for six-thirty." Koichi sighed. "It can't be good for a kid to be eating out all the time."

"And when's the other Guardian member coming?"

Koichi glanced over toward the door. "He should be here by now. But it's a holiday, so it could take a while."

"A holiday?"

"December twenty-third, the Emperor's Birthday. You forgot?"

"Since I stopped working, I've lost track of the days."

"Well, you do know what tomorrow is?"

Junko laughed. "Of course! No one's going to forget Christmas Eve."

"Our first Christmas Eve together." He spread his hands in comic exasperation. "Of all days to be given a job to do—the most romantic day of the year. Talk about having a heartless boss."

The restaurant was almost full and a pleasant hubbub surrounded them. The luxurious atmosphere held hints of spices and an indefinable air of comfortable fulfillment that someone more used to these surroundings might not notice, but which an outsider could appreciate. Sitting with Koichi here, as though it were the most natural thing in the world, Junko drifted off for a moment just savoring the pleasure of it.

"What's up?" Koichi was looking at her quizzically.

"Nothing," said Junko, shaking her head. "It's just that I don't usually go to places like this—I've always lived on the cheap."

"You fit in perfectly," said Koichi. "And don't worry, you'll get used to it soon enough," he added smiling. Then suddenly his smile disappeared as he looked toward the entrance. "Look out; coming this way."

Junko stiffened. Controlling the impulse to turn around immediately, she glanced casually over her shoulder in the direction of Koichi's gaze. Some of her nervous anticipation evaporated when she saw a small middle-aged man with a friendly smile heading toward their table.

"Hi, sorry to be late," he said. "The streets were a mess."

Junko noticed that Koichi's face was rigid with tension as he looked up at the man. Why would he be so disconcerted over the arrival of a colleague?

"Mind if I sit down?" The man pulled out a chair for himself and settled into it with a heavy grunt of relief. "So our target hasn't arrived yet?"

Face still frozen in disapproval, Koichi said in a low voice, "*You're* on this job?"

"Yes, me."

"Why you?" Koichi demanded sharply. "You had nothing to do with it. I didn't hear anything about you being involved . . . why are you here?"

"The supervisor got sick," the man explained patiently. "I was the only one available on such short notice, but I've been filled in on everything so I'm all set."

"Isn't it still too soon . . . ?"

The man quickly opened his white napkin, tucking it into the front of his shirt, and answered with a smile, "There's that saying, right? When you get thrown off a horse, the most important thing is to get right back on or you never will? It's like that, see?"

"They say that about airplanes, too," Junko added, trying to alleviate the tension, although she had no idea what they were talking about.

The man looked at Junko for the first time. The wrinkles at the corners of his eyes were deep and his face was kind. If Junko's father were still alive he might have been about the same age. His suit wasn't particularly expensive, and under it he was wearing a red vest that looked hand-knit. He seemed the model of a good husband and father.

"You must be Junko."

"Yes."

"You're as beautiful as everyone's been saying."

There was nothing unpleasant in his gaze as he looked at her, yet he put Junko off balance. *He looks as though he recognizes me from somewhere—it's almost as though he's comparing that previous me with the way I look now.*

"Excuse me, but have we met somewhere before?"

There was a crash. Koichi had knocked over his aperitif glass. "I'll introduce you," Koichi said, laughing as he mopped up the spill with a napkin. "This guy is the third wheel for the job we're doing."

"At your service," the man bowed his head. "I'll do my best not to get in the way."

"If you'll just give us the information, the two of us can handle the rest on our own."

"No, the top won't go along with that, this being Junko's first time and all."

"Junko's okay," Koichi replied, still bristling with hostility. "She's a lot stronger than you."

"That's probably so." The man's eyes shifted to rest on Junko again. And again Junko sensed a reappraisal of her in his eyes.

"I'm sorry, but I didn't catch your name—"

Koichi cut Junko off. "He doesn't go by his real name the way we do. I don't know what he's so concerned about protecting, but we have to use his nickname."

"Please call me Skipper," he said.

"Doesn't fit him, does it?" snorted Koichi.

"I wouldn't say that," smiled Junko. "But if it's not too personal, would you tell me how you came by the name? Do you like the ocean? Or do you have a boat?"

"No, no, nothing like that," said the man, shaking his head.

"It's just to sound cool," Koichi interjected.

"I wasn't asking you; I was asking him!"

Skipper sent a placating smile in Koichi's direction, then turned back to Junko. "I've got a daughter and a grandson, and we live by the sea. Both of them like ships, especially my grandson."

"How old is he?"

"Four. He was the one who gave me the name. One of my friends does actually skipper a pleasure cruiser, and when he came to visit us one time, I tried on his hat. That started it with my grandson, and my daughter kept it going by saying things like, 'In our house, it's Granddaddy who's the boss, so he's the Skipper.'"

"That's a nice story."

Skipper looked down at the table. "Actually I'm no big deal, at home or anywhere else. I promised him that someday I'd buy a real boat, even if it was just a little one, so I could be a real skipper for him."

Junko kept smiling but she'd noticed that the end of his story had trailed into the past tense and suddenly felt unsure of whether she should question him further. She was also uncomfortably aware of Koichi's refusal to join in the conversation. What was he being so churlish about?

"The waiter's coming," Koichi said, sounding relieved as he turned back towards them, re-crossing his legs. Skipper, too, seemed eager to focus his attention on the menu.

They settled on a light meal with wine. Just as the waiter finished taking their order and withdrew, Koichi warned, "There they are." Looking over, Junko saw Kaori, Mrs. Kurata, and Fusako Eguchi.

"They go everywhere together like that," said Skipper, his eyes following them as they were guided toward a table in the center of the dining area. "So we'll really need you, Kido."

Junko was watching Kaori, mesmerized. She was a slight girl, somewhat wan and listless, and looked even younger than thirteen. Her pretty face lacked the animation one would expect in a girl her age.

Mrs. Kurata said something to Kaori as they sat down, and the girl's face unexpectedly lit up with a smile that seemed to shed light over the surroundings as well. Fusako Eguchi added something and the three of them laughed together. Junko couldn't hear their voices, but she could well imagine Kaori's bubbling laugh.

"They'll notice if you keep staring like that," Koichi said under his breath. Junko nodded and tore her eyes away. As they ate, Skipper, Junko and Koichi methodically went over the plan for the next day, calmly covering every detail almost as if their targets were not sitting a few meters from them.

"They're in a suite on the twenty-eighth floor, room 2825," said Skipper. "You'll begin tomorrow evening, eight-thirty. They have a reservation for six-thirty for Christmas dinner in the restaurant on the top floor. They'll probably get back to their rooms after eight. I don't think they'll be going out again, since they have the girl with them."

"Is Fusako Eguchi staying with them?"

"Yes."

"Does the hotel check visitors heading for the suites?"

"Probably not, since it'll be Christmas Eve and the staff will be busy with both visitors and overnight guests. But just to be on the safe side, let's go up in separate elevators."

"When we knock, do you think they'll just open the door?"

"That'll be my job. I look like a harmless old man." Skipper chuckled lightly. "You should know, though, that Ms. Eguchi has been consulting the police on how to protect Kaori from falling into Mr. Kurata's clutches."

Koichi's eyebrows contracted into a dark frown. "What police?"

"Well, that's the interesting part. We found out yesterday that she's been talking to a detective named Makihara from Arakawa precinct. We still don't know much about him."

"I wonder if there's a personal connection?"

"Could be. The son of a cousin or something. Apparently they met at the cafeteria here yesterday afternoon. There was another woman with them at the time, but we haven't been able to identify her. She and Makihara separated as soon as they left the hotel—she went off on the subway."

"Maybe she was a friend of Ms. Eguchi's and was introducing the detective to her?"

"That's possible. As for Makihara, he left and then came back about an hour later and asked the front desk to call Ms. Eguchi. She came down and then they went up to the suite together. When he came back down an hour later, it was with Mrs. Kurata and not Ms. Eguchi, so he must have spoken with them both."

"I've got a bad feeling about this," said Koichi, his nose wrinkling. "This is the first I've heard that the police have been poking around. I'd rather not rush into it."

"Oh, don't say that. I don't think we need to worry too much about this Detective Makihara. He can't do much on his own. The police usually don't want to get involved in divorce and custody disputes, anyway."

"After we get Kaori out of here tomorrow, then what happens?"

"Mr. Kurata and his lawyer will take care of that. There's nothing for you to worry about."

"Do you think the hotel might get suspicious?"

"Even if they did, they can't do anything."

The plan itself was simple. Skipper would get Fusako Eguchi to open the door by telling her Makihara had sent him. As soon as she opened the door,

Koichi would give her a "push." At Koichi's prompting, she'd tell Mrs. Kurata that Makihara was here on urgent business he didn't want to discuss in front of Kaori, so would Mrs. Kurata please go down to meet him in the lobby? Ms. Eguchi would promise to stay with Kaori.

Mrs. Kurata would go down. If she looked unwilling or suspicious, Koichi could give her a "push" when she came near the door. That would leave Kaori and Ms. Eguchi, now their puppet, alone in the hotel suite.

"Then we'll need Junko's help to get Kaori out safely. Junko, you'll tell her that you have the same ability she does, and that'll calm her down. Make her understand that her father's been terribly worried about her and that we've come to help her."

"That might not be so easy . . ." Junko slowly turned her head to look over at Kaori again. Kaori was pushing her food around on her plate—she didn't seem to have much appetite. Her mother was drinking wine. Fusako Eguchi was talking with Mrs. Kurata and fingering a rather unattractive pendant hanging from her neck.

"Mrs. Kurata likes to drink," Skipper muttered. "It's not just a glass or two—she's been drinking more lately."

"Aside from Kaori, what do we do about Mrs. Kurata? Do we just leave her here and take off?"

"Mr. Kurata will be waiting for her in the lobby. He'll explain to her that he's had Kaori taken into protective custody, and Mrs. Kurata will just calm down and do as he says."

Junko suddenly felt uneasy. "He won't be threatening her or hurting her, will he?"

Skipper shook his head. "Definitely not. We'll just be relieving her of the stress she's been under, that's all."

Junko looked at Skipper, then switched her gaze to Koichi. Koichi's eyebrows rose and he pulled up the corners of his mouth into a smile. "Hey princess, remember? It's like I told you. We're on the side of justice *all* the way."

Junko held his gaze for a while longer. Then, mimicking him, pulled up the corners of her own mouth into a grin. Skipper laughed. "It looks like you two get along well."

"Well, thanks for arranging our get-together," Koichi replied.

"It's good to be young," Skipper said, half to himself. "And to have lots of time."

Junko sensed that he was hurting from some loss, and it wasn't just his own youth. What was it? Could it possibly have anything to do with why he joined the Guardians?

"They're leaving."

Junko raised her eyes at Koichi's words. Kaori's mother looked a little unsteady, and Kaori's arm was around her mother's slim waist as they walked toward the exit.

Goodnight, Junko said silently to the girl. *I'll see you tomorrow. Then you won't have to be afraid of anything anymore.*

"My little sister," Junko murmured quietly.

After Skipper had left, Junko and Koichi pretended to be a couple and strolled around the hotel. They went up to the twenty-eighth floor and walked past the Kurata's door, then retreated once more to the elevator and headed up to the bar on the top floor. They settled on stools at the counter and Junko sipped a pretty-colored, sweet tasting cocktail Koichi had chosen for her, while they both munched on a bowl of nuts. He told her the name of the drink, but it escaped her immediately as their talk turned from work to lighter things. Koichi wasn't drinking because he had to drive home, but he was in high spirits and they chatted animatedly about his home, family, previous pets, and his adored Siamese cat, Vision.

"Where do you keep your cat? Your Yoyogi apartment or your house at Lake Kawaguchi?"

"She goes wherever I go. I can't leave her alone for long."

"You're so good to her."

"Hey, are you flattering me? Or just being sarcastic as usual?"

Junko threw a nut shell at him in reply.

"Vision's female, so you do have reason to be jealous. Siamese cats are so sexy."

"They have a lot of pride, don't they?"

"She's like a queen," Koichi laughed. "I'm just her servant."

"I'd like to see you waiting on a cat."

Elbows resting on the counter, Koichi looked sideways at her. "Yeah? Will you come meet her?"

Junko held onto her glass and looked in his eyes. *They're lighter than I thought*, she realized. Then her eyes lit on a pale scar, about two centimeters long, just above his right eyebrow. A souvenir from a childhood battle?

"How did you get that scar?"

Koichi touched the spot almost reflexively. "This one? Guess."

"You fell out of a tree."

"Nope, sorry. I'm a city kid. I fell off my bike."

"Slow reflexes, huh?"

Koichi laughed. "Wrong! I was flying down a hill like a streak of lightning, and then I hit some garbage cans. The neighbors went running to tell my grandfather—he'd retired by then and was home all day. He used a cane to walk, but that time he practically flew over to the mountain of garbage and pulled me out of it by the scruff of my neck. Then he laid into me but good for getting into that mess in the first place."

Junko could picture it perfectly, and doubled over laughing.

"You've gotten good at deflecting a conversation, haven't you?" Koichi added.

Junko looked down into her almost empty glass.

"Have another?" he asked.

Junko set the glass down on the counter. "No, I'd like to go somewhere else."

"Huh?"

"A place I know." Junko slid off her stool and took Koichi's hand. "It's not far from here."

Sans Pareil was right where she remembered. Through the window she could see the faces of patrons chatting and laughing, and the candles set on each table.

Junko looked up before pushing the door open. "They fixed the neon sign! When I used to come here a long time ago, the 'P' was out."

"Like a pachinko parlor on its way downhill."

Seats at the tables were full, so here too, Junko and Koichi settled on stools at the counter. He ordered espresso and Junko followed suit.

"You can have a drink if you want."

"I don't want to risk getting drunk and being taken advantage of."

Koichi looked stung. "I wouldn't do that."

They fell into silence, just like a couple who'd had a spat. *Or maybe we are a couple and we have had a spat*, thought Junko.

"I used to come here on my own a lot," Junko said quietly, looking at a flickering candle set on the counter. "I like the way they always have lots of candles here."

"It's beautiful." Koichi glanced around the restaurant. "But people don't usually come here alone, do they?"

"True. I was here with someone else once."

It looked like Koichi was slowly counting to five before he asked, "With Kazuki Tada?"

Junko nodded, still looking at the flame. She explained that she'd brought Tada there so she could show him how she could light the candles, but had ended up setting a Mercedes Benz parked on the street outside on fire. Tada had been thoroughly shocked, and she'd regretted that, but on the other hand, she'd also been proud to observe that he had looked at her differently after that.

Koichi listened without interruption or comment; his eyes had the same faraway look as Junko's. When she finished her story it was midnight. Her cup was empty and the number of patrons in the restaurant had dwindled as well.

"Hey, I wonder what that's supposed to be?" Junko said, pointing to something half-hidden behind the counter.

It was a tall candle stand. The top was shaped like a heart, and with the candles unlit it looked like a cheap backstage prop.

Koichi grinned, amused. "Aren't those the kind of candles they use at wedding receptions?"

A waiter nearby who'd overheard paused in polishing a glass and smiled at them. "That's for tomorrow."

"Why? Is there going to be a wedding here tomorrow?"

"No, it's Christmas Eve. A lot of our customers will be couples, so it'll be romantic. We use it for Valentine's Day, too."

The waiter returned to his work and Koichi said in a low voice, "Business promotion over good taste, I guess . . ."

Junko surveyed the heart-shaped candleholder and counted the candles. Twenty.

Koichi wouldn't invite her home again tonight. He'd pretended to be joking when he'd asked her to meet his cat, but Junko knew his loneliness—his thirst for companionship and his fear. She knew because it was the same for her; the long years of not knowing how to appease it, unable to hide it from herself, but compelled to watch as it grew.

She recalled how helpless and lonely she'd felt that afternoon while reading her email and listening to Koichi's voice on the phone, and how her heart had called out for him to be with her. They'd only known each other for ten days now, but there was something they shared that had nothing to do with time.

She recalled too that she'd hurt him when they first walked into Sans Pareil. And that it had been on purpose. She'd have to make the next move.

"Do you think Vision could get to like me?"

Koichi's eyes lit with disbelief. She smiled—a real smile this time—at his unfeigned surprise. "Look," she said and pointed to the candleholder. Koichi looked over and his eyes widened further. All the candles in the heart-shaped candleholder were ablaze.

"I've just got one request."

"What is it?"

"When we're alone, make me laugh." She'd meant to smile and say it lightly, but her next words were too close to the bone and her lip trembled. "But please don't laugh at me."

She felt Koichi grip her hand firmly under the counter. "Why would I do something like that? I promise."

Koichi kept his promise. In his surprisingly comfortable, homey apartment and his big, clean bed, Junko laughed, looked deep into his eyes, and when she wasn't laughing, she felt his lips on her, and under them his healthy teeth, and she discovered that besides the scar over his eyebrow, he had a number of other small scars. Koichi patiently explained the story behind each of them until they didn't seem to matter much to either of them anymore.

How many times did you fall off your bike? How many bones have you broken? How many times have you bumped your head; how many times have you ridden in an ambulance? How many times have you hurt yourself? It's incredible that you survived . . .

They were all because you were lonely. The same way I've been whittling down my heart all this time, you've been whittling down your body. Because we couldn't bear the way we were different from other people. The gifts we didn't ask for, the gifts that were forced on us, were too heavy. And no one could help us. But from now on, I'll be here for you.

At first it had been Koichi holding Junko, but as they slept it was Junko who held Koichi. Like a mother. Like love itself.

She sensed something and realized it was a rustling sound outside. Junko raised herself quietly. It was still the middle of the night. Koichi was sleeping soundly, head on his pillow. She looked around for something to put on and found his shirt lying by the foot of the bed.

Junko slipped off the bed and Vision, curled up in an armchair, opened her bright blue eyes. The cat's body was difficult to make out in the dark, but Junko turned to her and put her finger to her lips.

"Shh . . . Don't wake your master."

Junko put her arms through the sleeves of the shirt and then adjusted the blinds on the window. Just as she thought, it was snowing. For once the weather forecast had been right.

The snowflakes were big and round. It looked as though it had rained first. From this height she couldn't see the ground, but she could see that the roofs of the neighboring houses were not yet white, so it probably hadn't been long since the rain had turned to snow.

So we might have a white Christmas after all.

Junko smiled. She'd never expected the romantic associations of that phrase to have any connection to her own life. She rested her head on the window frame and watched the falling snow. It felt cold at first, but she soon forgot about it as memories, new thoughts and feelings, and images rushed pell-mell through her mind and suddenly found a focus. Tears poured down her cheeks.

"What're you doing?"

Koichi got up and wrapped his arms around her from behind. He touched his cheek to hers, then pulled back in surprise. "You're crying?"

Junko wiped her cheek with her hand. "It's nothing," she said, but the tears turned into sobs. Koichi carried her back to bed and sat next to her, holding her close until the tears stopped and she could catch her breath.

"I'm sorry." She dried her eyes on the sleeve of his shirt. She felt something soft brushing against her calves; Vision meowed.

"Look, she's worried about you, too," said Koichi. The cat meowed again as if in agreement. She jumped up and began to settle on Koichi's naked lap, but he carefully shifted her away. She kept purring and instead curled up in a ball on the bed against his back.

"It looks like we may be rivals after all."

"It's my animal magnetism."

Junko laughed, and Koichi lifted her hair away from her face, pressed her cheeks between his hands and delivered a loud kiss. "Okay, I'm hitting the switch. No more tears."

"Really?"

"Really. It's the best medicine." Still smiling, he peered questioningly into Junko's eyes. "So what was that about?"

"Really, nothing. I don't know myself. I was just thinking about all sorts of different things and suddenly I was crying."

Junko lay her head on his shoulder and remained still, enveloped in his warm male smell. Then she said, "I was thinking about someone I couldn't save."

"Who? If you don't mind my asking."

"I don't mind at all. You probably know about her from the news anyway." Junko lifted her head. "Natsuko Mita."

The only light in the bedroom came reflected off the snow and through the blinds. But the instant Koichi heard Natsuko's name, an expression she hadn't seen before flitted across his face and then was gone before she could be sure whether she'd seen it or not.

"The woman Keiichi Asaba's gang killed in the liquor store?" Koichi's tone was the same as before, and there was no trace of the expression she was no longer sure she had seen.

"Yes. She had a sweetheart. The man who was killed in the Tayama factory."

"His name was Fujikawa, right?"

"Yes. His last words were, 'Please help Natsuko.' But I failed—I didn't save her."

"You did your best."

Junko shook her head. "But the fact is, I failed, and if we'd had one more second she'd have been safe. She was shot right in front of me."

Koichi hugged Junko even tighter. "Look, you should just forget about that."

"No, I can't. I *shouldn't* forget." Junko pushed at Koichi's chest and freed herself, then grasped his arms and looked up into his eyes to explain. "I killed so many people, and in the end I still couldn't save her. And do you know what? On top of that, I don't even know who shot her. Can you believe it? I don't even know who did it."

"It must have been one of Asaba's buddies. There were a lot of guys camped out there, right?"

"That's true, but I'd killed everyone I'd seen in the place. I thought there was no one left and I took her up to the roof to escape. But someone was there, and the thing is, it was someone Natsuko recognized. 'Oh, it's you!' she said."

"So it *had* to have been one of the Asaba guys who'd been messing with her, see?" Koichi's tone was soothing and persuasive.

Junko didn't want to argue with him, and nodded. "You're probably right."

"Of course I am."

"But even so, I'd almost forgotten that I don't know for sure who killed her. Don't you think that's irresponsible? Most of Japan has forgotten them already, but I should *always* remember Natsuko and Fujikawa."

"I don't think you have to take your responsibility that far," Koichi started, but Junko shook her head adamantly. Tears were welling up in her eyes again, but she lifted her face and kept them from running down her cheeks.

"When I found her in that liquor store, in that horrible room, she looked dead. She'd been badly beaten—it was like she'd been broken. But when I told her, 'Fujikawa sent me to find you,' her face came back to life. His name was a lifeline, and she asked me if he was okay. Even in that awful place, she was worrying about him. The same way Fujikawa had grabbed my arm and begged me with his last ounce of strength to help her. Their connection was that strong." Junko paused, then continued. "I thought that I understood the pain of the victims, the pain of those who were murdered, before. So

I've been perfectly comfortable cleaning up the murderers. But now I know I was wrong—I didn't really understand anything."

Junko reached out to stroke his cheek and gently trace the scar above his eye with her fingertip. Koichi stayed perfectly still, his eyes fixed on her.

"Now I finally understand, because now there's someone important to me," she whispered. "Because there's someone I don't want to lose. Or leave. So now I finally understand Fujikawa's fear and Natsuko's pain, because now I can feel their despair as though it were mine. That's why I don't ever want to forget them."

She would find Natsuko's killer. She'd find him and make him pay. No matter who or where he was, he wouldn't escape her. She'd find him whether he ran to the ends of the earth or hid at the bottom of the sea. She'd find him and she'd show no mercy.

Junko was shaking from adrenaline and the strength of her emotions and, as Koichi held her, she could feel that his arms were shaking, too. He was with her, this would be a shared task, she thought.

I've finally become human. As she rested in Koichi Kido's arms for the remainder of the night, that one thought filled her mind. *I'm not just a weapon anymore. From here on, my battles as a human will begin.*

The snow kept falling. Christmas Eve morning opened onto a scene of pure white. A few souls, unnoticed, entered their final act. Unobserved, in perfect silence.

31

Makihara burst out laughing at the sight of Chikako outfitted in rain boots and her son's cast-off skiwear.

"How rude!" sniffed Chikako, feigning indignation as she tried to pull her right foot out of a snowdrift. The snow was nearly up to her knees and as she yanked her foot free she almost toppled over backwards from the momentum.

"Try to avoid the deep spots, will you?" Makihara offered her a hand, and Chikako took it and righted herself.

"Nice retro ski outfit."

"My son wore it when he was in junior high."

Chikako was somehow managing to walk alongside Makihara now, but the effort left her a little breathless. "It was the first skiwear we bought him. There wasn't much choice in those days—the nice looking gear the Olympic athletes wore was difficult to find and terribly expensive. We thought this would be good enough for a junior high kid, but he really gave me a hard time about it."

By daybreak on Christmas Eve the ground had been blanketed in white. The snow had stopped for now, but the sky was still heavily overcast. A milky white sky over a pristine white-covered ground: it looked beautiful and romantic, but it was a lot of trouble in a city unaccustomed to snow. Some of Tokyo's private train lines and the subways were running, but every other form of public transport was down and snow-related traffic accidents were clogging the streets and highways. With so many people trying to get to work by subway, the stations and trains were even more packed than usual.

"The forecast says there may be more snow on the way."

"Oh, I really hope not."

As they made their way along the sidewalk, they came onto a section that had been completely cleared. Chikako looked up and saw that they were in front of a coffee shop. A small man with graying hair—probably the owner—was still assiduously shoveling away nearby.

Chikako paused to catch her breath and opened her jacket to pull a map from her inside pocket. She and Makihara were on their way to visit a woman named Yoshiko Arita, and Chikako had jotted down the directions directly onto the map. They were almost there. It was a quiet, residential area about a ten-minute walk from Higashi Nakano station. They'd planned to arrive a bit earlier, but with the slippery footing they'd fallen behind schedule. It was almost eleven o'clock.

Yoshiko Arita had been one of Kazuki Tada's coworkers at Toho Paper. Apparently she had known Junko Aoki as well.

Makihara and Chikako had asked Tada to contact Toho Paper, and luckily Yoshiko was still working there, but she'd gotten married about a year earlier and was currently on maternity leave. Chikako called her at home and Yoshiko had answered, harried but cheerful, her hands full with her two-month-old baby girl.

Tada had wanted to go along with them, but Chikako had demurred. Junko Aoki hadn't had any real friends at Toho Paper, and Yoshiko was one of the few people who'd occasionally talked with her. No matter how casual the relationship between the two women, if Yoshiko had something to say that Tada didn't already know, it might be difficult for her to talk about it in front of him.

Kazuki Tada had an excellent memory and could recall places he and Junko had been together, what they'd done there, and even seemingly trivial details like the people they'd been with or had run into before their Hibiya Park attempt on Kogure's life. Makihara had made a list of all these people and places and had methodically begun to visit each. Even crossing off the people and places Chikako had visited yesterday, they were only about halfway down the list. Yoshiko Arita's name was right smack in the middle.

"This should be it."

Chikako had stopped in front of a nice-looking four-story apartment building. She heard a wet thud as a clump of snow fell from the telephone lines and hit the ground.

"When I called this morning, she sounded a little surprised that we'd actually be coming out on a day like this."

"Hmm, we'll just have to show her how hard-working the police are."

The entrance to the apartment building hadn't been shoveled at all, and Chikako nearly became mired again.

Yoshiko Arita was thirty-nine, with the rosy cheeks and cheerful smile of a new mother. She looked a little tired, probably a reflection of feeding her baby every three hours. Chikako could well recall the days of raising her only son and the standard topic of conversation when she got together with other friends in the same position: *I need more sleep!*

"I hope you didn't have a tough time getting over here." Yoshiko moved quickly about the kitchen, making coffee for them all. Chikako asked her not to go to any trouble, but Yoshiko just laughed and explained, "I need a cup myself!"

The apartment was comfortable but small, making tidying up a necessity. With all the other furniture pushed into the corners, the crib positioned in the middle of the tatami-floored room was the dominating presence. With Yoshiko's permission, Chikako peeked in at the baby, wrapped in pink and sleeping peacefully. The distinctively sweet smell of a breastfed infant gave her a pang of nostalgia.

After the freezing temperatures outside, Chikako and Makihara were grateful to be able to relax at the kitchen table over a cup of hot coffee. Yoshiko went rummaging around in a closet and finally emerged triumphantly bearing a square cookie tin. She pulled off the lid, revealing a large pile of photos.

"After Kazuki Tada called, I tried to remember what I could about Junko." Yoshiko started happily picking through the photos. "I never organized these. Oh brother! This is from a trip fifteen years ago now . . . I just saved everything in here and forgot about it."

Chikako smiled. "It'll be different with your baby's pictures—you'll get in the habit of scrapbooking those as soon as they're developed."

"Really?" Still smiling, Yoshiko glanced at Chikako. Then, extracting a somewhat larger photo, she exclaimed, "Here it is! I thought I might still have it. This is from when Kazuki Tada and Junko were both working for Toho."

Yoshiko offered it to Chikako and Makihara. Makihara accepted it.

"It's from a festival they hold every year at the men's dorm," she explained as she sat down and picked up her own mug of coffee. "It was a sort of mixer for the dorm residents. See the refreshment stands?"

About twenty young men and women were standing around signs for fried noodles and oden stew, looking as though they were having a good time.

"Were the women living in the dorm, too?"

"No, they just came to visit. Toho Paper only has dorms for single men." Yoshiko laughed. "I guess you could say it was a kind of company match-making event. Quite a few couples began dating after this festival."

Chikako located Kazuki Tada's face in the photo. He still had a boyish look about him, with warm eyes and a sweet smile. Junko Aoki had worked for the company about three years in all. It was impossible to tell because there was no date on the photo, but it was likely that this photo was taken before Yukie's murder.

"Here's Junko Aoki." Yoshiko was pointing to a slender woman standing to the far left, slightly apart from the others. "She doesn't really stand out, does she?"

She looked exactly like the portrait drawn from Kazuki Tada's memory, including the hairstyle, the thin cheeks, and the unsmiling lips.

It wasn't at all unusual for young women in their twenties to change completely in the space of a few months. Some began to glow when they fell in love or made new friends, but it was also because women at the peak of their natural beauty often enjoy experimenting with their appearance.

But Junko had done none of that. Nothing added, nothing subtracted. She'd never changed. Perhaps that was why she looked so lonely; she had no one to change for.

I wonder if it's still the same now.

When Junko had visited Kazuki Tada's place, apparently she had not been alone. She'd been in the passenger seat, so someone else had to be driving.

Had the driver been male? Could he possibly have been someone with whom Junko had shared so much of her heart that they would go together to see someone from her past—Kazuki Tada? It might well be that Junko Aoki's face no longer had this lonely look to it.

Chikako did not consider romance and marriage the only route to female happiness, but she did know that there was something about the moment you realize, "I've found someone," that changes you forever.

"Did Junko do something really awful?" Yoshiko's question was voiced hesitantly, and the expression on her friendly round face was worry rather than unease. Naturally they'd told her as little as possible, but Chikako hurried to reassure her.

"No, no, it's nothing like that."

"On the phone, Kazuki Tada sounded almost distracted with worry." Yoshiko looked down. "Junko was really quiet. She was always alone, but she seemed to like it that way, so nobody paid her much attention. We practically dragged her out to this dorm festival, but she still didn't smile or talk to anyone, so everyone left her alone."

"Would you mind if we borrow this photo?" Makihara asked.

"Not at all, go ahead. It's the only one I have with her in it. I'm sorry it doesn't show her face more clearly, but you're welcome to it anyway."

Makihara pulled out his notebook and asked Yoshiko if she recalled any places Junko frequented while she was at Toho Paper.

"Coffee shops, lunch spots, bookstores, boutiques, flower shops, dentist . . . Did you ever go anywhere for lunch together? Or go shopping at some department store sale after work? Or see a movie?"

Yoshiko Arita shook her head no to each question. "There was nothing like that, not even once. When I think about it, it was almost a miracle that she was even at this festival. She always kept to herself. She just seemed to prefer her own company. I still said hello and chatted with her about little things. Sometimes we'd walk to the station together. But that was about all."

Makihara shut his notebook and turned to Chikako, saying that he'd like to drop in at Toho Paper—there might be some old employee records that would have Junko's address from that time.

"I'm sorry, I think this must have been a waste of time for you."

Chikako patted Yoshiko on the arm and reassured her otherwise. Makihara said goodbye and exited hastily, heading toward the elevator, so Chikako and Yoshiko were left alone in the entrance.

"What's your baby's name?"

"Momoko."

"She's a darling."

"My husband named her." Yoshiko's cheeks flushed. "We married so late it's almost embarrassing, but my husband is really sweet. He adores Momoko and even washes her clothes and changes her diapers."

"That's wonderful! And what's there to be embarrassed about? There's no age limit on starting a family with someone you love."

Yoshiko nodded, smiling. "When I was single I enjoyed my work. I felt good about the way the company depended on me and I made a decent salary, too. I had a good time. But since I got married and had Momoko, looking back I realize that actually I was kind of lonely. It must have been the same with Junko. I wish I'd tried harder to be friends with her."

"Rather than brooding about that, I think it would be better to focus on your husband and baby and take care of yourself," answered Chikako.

"Thank you," said Yoshiko, and they said their goodbyes. In the background Chikako heard the beginnings of a wail. It was almost as if the baby had politely waited until her mother's guests were on their way out.

Chikako and Makihara were given access to Toho Paper's records, and they dropped by neighboring shops to see if anyone recognized Junko, but they came up empty-handed. Then they visited the area where she had lived at the time, but found nothing there, either.

"Kazuki Tada said he didn't have any luck when he came here looking for her after the Arakawa homicides."

The weight of the snow had brought down electricity lines and, with other malfunctions too, the trains were out of service most of the day. Every taxi in the city was occupied, so Chikako and Makihara were at the mercy of the subway system to get from one place to the next. Taking roundabout routes that seemed like a joke, they somehow made their way back and forth across the city.

They paused in their travels to call the Sadas and Kazuki Tada to check for news, and Fusako Eguchi to ask after Kaori and Mrs. Kurata. Otherwise they spent that Christmas Eve afternoon slipping and sliding their way around Tokyo, gradually checking off names on the list they'd gotten from Kazuki Tada. Every store in Tokyo was decorated for Christmas, complete with Christmas music that filtered out into the street. Chikako found herself in a good mood. Makihara maintained his scowl and muttered imprecations about the snow.

"Well, at least it stopped when it did," said Chikako.

The clouds overhead were as heavy as ever and there was no sign of them clearing, but the snow had not started up again. Most of the highways and main thoroughfares had been cleared of snow by now, and traffic was back to normal. That is, it was back to the usual appalling traffic jams.

By late afternoon, unsurprisingly, Chikako's legs hurt and she was twice as weary as she'd normally be.

"Shall we call it a day?" she suggested.

"Why don't you head home," responded Makihara. "There's just one more place I want to check out, but I can go on my own."

It was a restaurant in Akasaka called Sans Pareil. Chikako looked back at the list. Sans Pareil was at the top, with a check mark next to it. "But you've already been there, haven't you?"

"Yes. But that time I only had the drawing, and now we've got the photo of Junko Aoki. I'd like to try showing it to them again. I think a photo might be better for jogging people's memories."

"I'll come with you, then."

Since it was at the top of the list, it was one of the first places that had sprung to Kazuki Tada's mind. "Did Junko and Tada go there often?"

"It's where they first talked about Yukie's murder and discussed executing Masaki Kogure. The restaurant was Junko Aoki's favorite. The tables are all decorated with candles. Tada said she lit a candle to show him what she could do. But he still didn't believe her, so she burned a Benz parked outside."

Shaking her head, Chikako headed for the subway entrance.

Decorating the entrance to Sans Pareil was a live Christmas tree, taller even than Makihara. It was simply decorated with lights, and the snow on its green branches was real.

The atmosphere inside was chic, with an elegant, expansive counter. There were indeed candles flickering at every table. It was already past six in the evening, and the restaurant was getting crowded. The patrons were without exception couples spending Christmas Eve together. By the counter there was a large heart-shaped candleholder of the sort that you might see at a wedding reception. The restaurant manager must have thought it was an attractive touch, but to Chikako it was decidedly out of place in the otherwise sophisticated atmosphere.

The manager and his staff recognized Makihara's face instantly and must have groaned inwardly to have a detective visit on their busiest evening of the year. The manager grimaced openly for a moment, but quickly regained his composure, affably showing them to his office behind the kitchen. He agreed to send in the staff for individual interviews as long as the detectives kept them short. He himself, presented with both the drawing and the photo, dismissed them brusquely, saying he had no memory of this particular female customer. A number of waiters came in and said the same. It was nearing seven and Makihara and Chikako were about to give up empty-handed, when a young waiter told them that he did remember Junko.

"I was wondering whether to call you or not . . ."

He was short and had a finely featured face rather like a doll's. He couldn't be more than twenty-five, and his accent placed his upbringing somewhere far from Tokyo.

"When you came here before, Detective, you left a copy of that drawing, right?"

Makihara nodded.

"Well, I showed it to my girlfriend when I got home. She used to work here part-time, three or four years ago. Anyway, she remembered her. She says that she used to come here sometimes, by herself."

"This woman came alone?"

"That's right."

"Not coming alone and meeting someone here, but just on her own?"

"Yeah. That's why my girlfriend remembered her. You know how women remember things better than men? It can be a real pain sometimes . . ."

Chikako laughed. "You mean for you, not for her, right?"

He laughed, too. "You got me there . . ."

"And?" Makihara pressed, with evident irritation. "Is that all?"

"Um, no . . ." The young waiter scratched his head. "My girlfriend said she seemed terribly lonely, really in her own world. My girlfriend sort of jumps to conclusions about people and likes to imagine their pasts. So, back then, she decided this lady must have had some reason for coming here alone, like she used to come here with a lover but he'd died, or something like that."

"Oh . . . I see."

"So anyway, she's got a great memory. And that jogged my memory of her, too." The young man tapped the photo emphatically. "And then you know what? She came back here last night."

Makihara had been in the process of shutting his notebook to signal an end to this tedious conversation, and his eyes nearly popped out of his head.

"She *what?*"

"She was here, no mistaking her."

"Alone, as usual?"

The waiter shook his head. "No, she was with a man. They sat together at the counter and ordered espressos. They were probably only here for thirty minutes or so."

"What did the man look like?"

"I think he was rich." The waiter mentioned a brand name for the jacket he'd worn, but it meant nothing to either Chikako or Makihara. "He acted casual, like he wore that kind of thing all the time. He could have been a model. He looked really at home in it."

"How old?"

"Twenty-five or twenty-six. Long hair, the way everyone wants to have it, but most guys can't pull off."

"Just like my son!" chimed in Chikako. "He's grown it long and has it tied in the back. I tried to like it, but it just makes him look like a starving samurai. He seems to think he looks great."

"Oh yeah? I tried it, too, but my girlfriend made me cut it off."

Chikako, in her delight at finding they were on the right track, had cheerfully joined the young man on this tangent, but Makihara was clearly not amused. "Would you please keep to the point? Are you sure it was the woman in this photo?"

"Yes."

"You saw her up close and made sure?"

"Yes. I showed them to their seats. But Detective—" the young man turned to Chikako, "she'd totally transformed."

"Transformed?"

"Yeah. She'd turned into this gorgeous beauty. She looked like a totally different person from when we saw her before. Her dress was showing a lot of leg, too."

Makihara frowned. "Well, then it could well have been a different person, couldn't it?"

The waiter waved both hands in denial. "No, I'm sure, because my girlfriend and I'd been talking about her and I'd been looking at this drawing a lot. I'd been wondering why the police were looking for her, so it was on my mind."

"Maybe because you were talking about her, you saw a woman who looked similar and just thought it was her—"

Chikako cut Makihara off and asked the waiter, "What was the feeling you got about the two of them?"

"What kind of feeling . . . ?"

"Did they seem close?"

"Oh, *yeah*. They were the perfect couple. They were sitting *right* next to each other and they were holding hands when they left." He grinned knowingly. "No matter how you look at it, they weren't leaving here and then saying goodnight . . . And it was after midnight by then, anyway."

"Could you hear what they were talking about?"

He scratched his head again, regretfully.

"I couldn't get too close or they'd notice, right? The boss would have given it to me for being rude to customers. So I couldn't catch much."

"Yes, of course, there's nothing you could do about that. When they left, did you see which way they were heading?"

"No . . . but I think they came by car. When they ordered, the man said something about not drinking because
he was driving."

"Did they pay in cash?"

"Yes. It was just two espressos, after all."

Makihara was looking dubious again. The waiter, in return, was looking disappointed, as though he'd flunked an oral exam.

"A couple . . ." muttered Makihara, grimacing. "Sounds like a different person."

"Don't forget that someone took her to see Kazuki Tada's place," reminded Chikako.

"But Tada wasn't sure about that."

"I think he was."

Makihara raised one eyebrow. "Detective Ishizu, what exactly are you looking so pleased about?"

Chikako was happy because Junko Aoki had not been alone. She'd been with someone, and they'd been holding hands. Something had changed for Junko. And she probably did not look lonely anymore.

"Makihara, it isn't unusual for a young woman to completely change her appearance almost overnight. This young man could be right."

The waiter cheered visibly at this encouragement from Chikako.

"It was like she was a different person—she was practically glowing. And you know that heart-shaped candleholder we've got out there?"

"Yes, I noticed it."

"That tacky thing?" scoffed Makihara.

"Yeah, well, I think it's kind of embarrassing, too. But anyway, she was looking at it and pointing to it. It was lit up beautifully. We were supposed to be saving it for today, but for some reason it was lit when those two were sitting at the counter. Later on, the boss chewed out the counter manager for lighting it ahead of schedule, but he swore he hadn't touched it."

Chikako looked at Makihara. He'd frozen, looking hard at the young man.

"Did I say something wrong?"

"No, not at all. Don't worry about it. But do you have any idea at all where they might have headed after leaving here? You were watching them all along, weren't you?"

"Yeah, I was, but . . . well, it wasn't like I could follow them. I was supposed to be working."

"Did you happen to see the man's car?"

"No. I wish I'd thought of it then, but I didn't."

"Does this restaurant have a parking lot?"

"No, we don't. That's why everyone parks on the street and uses the parking meters."

"Were there a lot of cars parked outside last night?"

"Not especially, since it was a national holiday and just before Christmas

Eve. Maybe if I keep an eye out, they'll come back sometime," he added apologetically. "If they do I'll call you right away."

"Actually it would help more if you could write down their license number. Even if we raced over here, chances are we'd still miss them."

"Oh. Yeah."

Makihara sighed and closed his notebook. Just then the waiter perked up. "If it's the license plates of the cars parked outside last night that you want, we know those."

"You do?"

"Um, I mean, I don't know if that man's car is mixed in there with them or not, but anyway, the manager took down the license numbers of the cars parked outside."

"How do you know that?"

"Well, a while back—I guess that was a couple of years ago, too—a Mercedes parked in the street outside here caught on fire."

The one Junko Aoki had burned.

"Yes, I've heard. And?"

"Well, it was a suspicious fire, you know? It looked like arson, but they never caught the person who did it. The owner came and made trouble, putting the screws on us. He said it was our responsibility. Not that he could legally do anything about it. But it was a lot of trouble for the boss. He ended up settling with the guy and he's been neurotic about cars parked here ever since. The police told him to take down the numbers of people who park here because maybe the arsonist had come in a car himself, and he might come again. We put a camera outside the entrance for a while, too, but the customers didn't like that so we took it down. But the manager still writes down all the license numbers—the boss is really stuck in his ways, you know . . ."

Makihara leaped to his feet, his chair crashing to the floor behind him. "Get the manager in here!"

The manager's list had the license plates of all the cars parked outside Sans Pareil from their five-thirty opening to their two o'clock closing time. Junko Aoki and her boyfriend had only been in the restaurant for about thirty minutes, and had left just after midnight. Chikako and Makihara could therefore narrow the list down to the cars that had been parked out front from eleven to twelve.

Only four cars fell into that time slot. Running a check on the plates and collating against car make and model, one of the cars was clearly a company sales car. Another belonged to a lawyer whose office was near the restaurant; when they contacted him, he said he hadn't visited Sans Pareil the night before, nor had he loaned his car to anyone. From the description they had, it didn't seem likely that Junko Aoki's companion would have been driving a borrowed car anyway, so these cars could be crossed off the list.

That left two cars. Both were four-wheel drive models that were popular with young people, and both owners were men in their twenties. One was registered in Tokyo's Nerima Ward, and one, surprisingly, was registered to an address at Lake Kawaguchi. It was a resort area overlooked by Mount Fuji, with mostly lakeside vacation homes.

"Lake Kawaguchi's not really that far. I could check out both these places tonight. Why don't you go home and get some rest?" Makihara offered.

"Are you trying to get rid of me?" accused Chikako.

"Those rubber boots must be hurting by now. I can do it on my own. Besides, it's Christmas Eve."

"I'm not likely to get excited about eating Christmas cake at home with my husband at this late date. And as for Lake Kawaguchi, you can only get there by car, right? If you do the driving, I'll just stretch out my legs and relax. So let's get going."

It was about eight in the evening.

32

It was Christmas Eve. Junko Aoki spent most of the morning with her head under the covers. When she woke it was already past ten. She tried to get up, but Koichi dragged her back into bed, and they spent what was left of the morning in each other's arms.

"I'm starving," Koichi said finally, and when they checked the clock it was almost noon.

"Well, I did try to get up once," said Junko.

"You didn't look rested enough to me."

"Shame on you!" Junko hit Koichi over the head with a pillow and leaped off the bed and out of reach. Koichi laughed.

Outside, the ground was covered in snow. Koichi suggested a walk and lunch out, but Junko didn't want to go outside yet. She would have to go back to her apartment to pick up a change of clothes before their mission that night, and she wanted to stay inside feeling cozy until the last possible moment.

They put together a meal with what was in the refrigerator. It turned out that Koichi cooked for himself regularly and his kitchen was well stocked.

"I like cooking," he told Junko. "I'll make you a full-course meal tomorrow."

Junko told him that she wanted to go home before their night's work, but Koichi objected.

"You don't have to go. Don't go."

"I don't have any clothes with me."

"We'll just buy some, then."

"What a waste." Junko poked Koichi playfully on the nose. "No matter what a rich boy you are, you shouldn't be throwing money around like that."

Koichi moved around the table swiftly, catching Junko's hand and pulling her close. "I don't want you to leave. Stay with me all day—just today."

"But I'll be right back. We'll be going to stay at your house at the lake as soon as we have Kaori, won't we?"

"I know, but I've got the feeling that if you go back to your apartment, you'll forget about last night. Our spell will be broken, you'll wake up, and we'll be back to where we were before."

Junko felt a tug on her heart. She slipped onto Koichi's lap and wrapped her arms around his neck.

"That's not going to happen," she said gently.

"It will," said Koichi, shaking his head. "So don't go. Stay with me."

Junko opened her mouth to say something, but Koichi had covered her mouth with his own, and she closed her eyes and gave in to the kiss, enjoying it. But it tasted dangerously of fear, the fear of being alone and the desire to have someone there. *He's afraid*, Junko realized. Last night at Sans Pareil, Koichi had been visibly surprised when Junko had agreed to go home with him. He must have been caught off guard because she had agreed so readily.

He must have wondered, at least momentarily, if he had given her a "push" without realizing it. Junko had the power to reject his "push" and logically speaking, he knew that, too. But he'd still been afraid. It was the sort of anxiety that could only be experienced by someone who could make everyone do what he wanted. He had to live with the insecurity of wondering if the people with him were there because they wanted to be, or because he was making them stay.

"All right," said Junko. "I'll stay here. We can go out to work together." Koichi hugged her tightly, and she hugged him back. She knew that his fear couldn't be eased by words. They needed to breathe the same air, see the same things and either laugh or get angry at them together. Nothing would do but to spend time together.

And luckily this was exactly what Junko needed, too.

"Got to wash the dishes," said Junko hopping up, "and I noticed that Vision's been eyeing your lap. I don't want any conflict here, so I'll give her a turn."

They cleaned up and decided to go out shopping on foot to enjoy the snow. They blew white puffs of breath and kept each other from slipping as they walked. Neither of them felt the least bit cold.

They went as far as the south exit of Shinjuku Station and bought towels, underwear, cosmetics, and a few other things for Junko. They had so many packages that they took a taxi home.

Skipper was there waiting for them in front of Koichi's building when they arrived. He looked like a different person today. His face was pale, drawn, and set in worried lines, and his eyes showed his agitation.

"Where have you been?" he demanded, his voice shaking. "Why didn't you take your cell phone? An emergency's come up."

Koichi glanced at Junko as he walked to the entrance and began to apologize. "I'm sorry. We weren't gone more than an hour. I thought it would be okay. Look, come on in so we can talk."

"So you two were together?" Skipper asked Koichi, his eyes on Junko. For an instant his eyes lingered on her the way a man's would. She folded her arms protectively and looked away.

"It'll be faster to talk to us both at once, won't it?" said Koichi coldly.

Junko followed Koichi, and as she walked across the neatly shoveled entrance of the apartment building, she noticed something scattered on the ground. Tobacco leaves. A cigarette had been shredded. Looking up, she saw that the Skipper had a cigarette in his hand that he was halfway through pulling apart.

Now that's a strange habit.

She suddenly remembered having seen something like it before. Where was it? If it had been cigarette ash she wouldn't have given it a second thought.

"What's the matter with you? Let's go." Koichi put an arm around her shoulder, and Junko quickly moved to follow him in.

As soon as they were inside Koichi's apartment, Skipper launched into his reason for coming.

"Tonight's mission has been postponed."

"Why?"

"It's the housekeeper, Fusako Eguchi."

"The one who was talking to that Detective Makihara, right?"

"I don't know what he said to her, but she's started taking pictures of everyone who comes close to the Kuratas."

Junko had been taking off her coat, but stopped midway in surprise.

"How is she doing that?"

"Didn't you notice that strange looking pendant around her neck? That's her camera. She might have been taking pictures of the customers at the restaurant last night. There's no way of knowing whether she has any shots of the three of us."

"Who cares?" asked Junko.

"It's no good." Koichi shook his head grimly.

"Why?"

"We must never leave a trace, let alone a photograph. No matter how small the chance that we were photographed, we'll have to proceed carefully. Are you sure there's no mistake, Skipper?"

"No, I checked. She had some film developed and then I watched her put in a new roll. I'm sure she thought she was alone, but I caught her taking some test shots."

Junko asked, "Have you been watching the Kuratas all day?"

"That's right," nodded Skipper. For some reason he had a servile look on his face. "I'm not like you two. I don't have any special powers. Surveillance is about all a former detective like me is good for. I'm the lowest of the low in the Guardians."

For an instant Koichi's eyes flashed with anger. No sooner had Junko noticed it, however, than it was gone.

"Don't talk like that, Skipper," said Koichi, a smile back on his face. He patted the older man lightly on the shoulder.

"So you used to be a policeman?" asked Junko.

"That's right," Skipper said, averting his eyes from hers. "I'm a retired detective."

"Okay, we understand the situation." Koichi moved to wrap up the conversation. "We'll just have to do it another day. There's no need to get upset; this sort of thing happens all the time."

"But do you think Kaori will be all right?" Junko couldn't help worrying. "Didn't you say that her mother was considering committing suicide with her?"

Koichi grinned confidently. "It's Christmas. And then it will be New

Year's. It's the happiest time of the year for kids. I don't think a mother would kill her own child right now no matter how desperate she was. I thought this plan was too rushed from the start. Let's just wait till after the holidays."

"Kurata was in a big hurry," Skipper muttered resentfully. "He said it would be easier to get the girl while she was in the hotel."

"Look, we can do it later."

Skipper mumbled something, still looking down.

"What was that?"

"It might be someone I used to work with."

Junko and Koichi looked at each other.

"Who?"

Skipper swallowed hard. "That woman who was with Makihara and the housekeeper. Remember how we were thinking she could be a friend of hers? Well, I don't think so."

"So, is she with the police, too?"

"I talked with the previous supervisor on this job this morning, and from what he observed of the way she and Makihara were talking, I get the feeling she might be a detective as well. From the description, actually, she sounds like someone I used to work with."

Skipper wiped his mouth with his hand and tobacco leaves stuck to his lips. "And I've just seen her recently."

Koichi's eyebrows shot up. "You saw her?"

"She came to see me at work. I thought she was just coming to check up on an old friend, but . . ."

Koichi chewed on his lower lip. Standing between the two men, both seething with unspoken thoughts and disappointment, Junko was suddenly overwhelmed with a vague unease and wrapped her arms around herself again.

"Now don't lose your cool," Koichi said. "You know what a bad habit that is."

The Skipper said nothing in reply. His fingers, with bits of tobacco still stuck to them, were shaking.

"I'll see you down," said Koichi. "You should go home and get some rest.

It's Christmas Eve, after all." So saying, he and Skipper, with a defeated slump to his shoulders, headed for the elevator. Junko began putting away their purchases.

Koichi hadn't returned after ten minutes. Nor was he back after twenty. She took the tags off her towel and new clothes and folded them neatly. She washed the chopsticks and rice bowl Koichi had bought for her and put them away. Koichi was still not back.

She thought about going down to check, but she couldn't go and leave the door unlocked. Koichi finally came back as she was trying to decide what to do.

"It took quite a while to say good-bye," she commented.

"Parting is such sweet sorrow." Koichi grinned. "Let's get packed."

"What?"

"We'll go on our own." Koichi twirled his keys on his finger ebulliently. "We don't have to work now, and the news said that traffic on the Chuo Expressway has started to flow again, so we'll get there in no time. We can stay right through New Year's. It's quiet there, the air is clean, and there won't be a soul around to bother us. We can just relax and do as we please." He grinned. "We won't even have to get out of bed!"

Junko cocked her head to one side and fixed him with a look of mock skepticism.

Koichi mimicked her. "What's on your mind, princess?"

Junko grinned. "I was wondering where you keep your travel bags?"

"I'll find one for you." Koichi headed cheerfully off to a closet. Junko glanced at the clock. It was almost five.

As they drove west, the lid of dark clouds covering the night sky began to lift. They stopped on the way to stock up on food and got caught in what was left of the traffic. By the time Koichi's car had passed the sign welcoming them to Kawaguchi Lakeview resort, it was almost 8 P.M. Junko looked up through the car window and could see scattered stars twinkling in the sky. The weather was definitely improving.

"See? I told you there wouldn't be anyone here." He was right. Through the dark trees she could see the shapes of large vacation homes, but there was not a light to be seen in any of them. The only light was cast by the few streetlights. Despite the lack of inhabitants, the road had been plowed free of snow. This was not merely a housing development that had been sold and then left to the devices of the owners. The developers had clearly included ongoing maintenance as part of the package.

"During the summer, this place is full of city people escaping the heat, but there's nothing to bring them here in the winter. That's what makes it perfect for loners like me."

The whole trip Junko had enjoyed the dance of the clown with the bee on its nose, but the sudden changes in her life since the night before had begun to take their toll, and she started to feel drowsy. She opened the window to let in some cold air and it refreshed her instantly.

"Are we almost there?"

"Almost. What kind of house do you think it is?"

"A log cabin?"

"Right. How'd you guess?"

"It's just because that's what I like, that's all."

Koichi laughed. "Well then, we have the same taste. The deck on the south side overhangs the lake, and you can fish from it. I'll show you how when fishing season starts."

"I'm not going to touch any worms, thank you."

"You can use lures instead of live bait. Look! There it is—the house on the corner."

A large house made with rough hewn logs faced the dark lake, its side to the road. The roof had a much steeper angle than Junko had imagined. It reminded her of the angles on Koichi's face.

"There's a chimney!"

"And why do you think that is?"

"Because there's a fireplace."

"Excellent. A born detective!" Koichi steered the car around the bushes in front of the house and stopped at the front door. "Here we are."

When she got out of the car the cold air enveloped her entire body. It wasn't exactly unpleasant, but rather as if she had been draped with a cloth fresh from the freezer. She pursed her lips and exhaled—her breath was white.

"As a matter of fact, I designed this house myself," Koichi told her as he unlocked the front door. "I put all my childhood dreams into it. The deck over the water, the cathedral ceiling, the fireplace . . . there's an enormous attic, too."

"Do your father and grandfather have their own vacation homes?"

"They're all in warm places with natural hot springs. That's what the old people like. Oh, hey—would you take care of Vision while I get the other things out of the car?"

Junko took Koichi's precious cat in her elegant carrier out of the back seat. She started meowing as soon as she saw Junko's face.

"She's used to making these long trips; I guess she's jealous of you after all." Koichi went inside and turned on the lights and heat. They carried in their bags, stowed their things, and Koichi showed Junko around the house. Each of the rooms amazed her; they were like dreams come true. By the time they finished the tour and returned to the living room, it was warm enough to take off her coat and even her sweater. Junko loved the house and felt perfectly at home. It seemed like proof that her relationship with Koichi Kido was right, too. This house was like an extension of him.

Now that they were settled, they realized they were hungry. The two put together a simple supper of pasta and salad. Like Koichi's apartment, the kitchen was fully equipped. There was even an enormous clay pot. Koichi laughed.

"I always wanted to eat a big stew in that pot."

"It's too big for one person, isn't it?"

"Of course it is. Eating alone from it wouldn't be any fun—it would just feel forlorn. Let's use it tomorrow night!"

The question rose as far as Junko's throat—she almost asked whether he'd ever made stew in that pot with another woman. And if so, how many other women? But she didn't ask. It would be a waste of time to be jealous of the past. And no matter how many other women had come here with him, she knew she was different from them. Only she shared what she did with him.

Against one wall in the spacious living room was a TV screen about the size of the bathtub in Junko's apartment. She was more in the mood for soft music than the demanding blare of the television, but she did want to see a weather forecast and she asked Koichi if she could turn it on. He had gone into the kitchen to make some fresh coffee but called out his permission.

Junko went to turn it on, only to discover that she had no idea how. She tried to work it out for herself but eventually Koichi came out and showed her.

All at once there were resounding voices and bright colors on the screen. There must have been several speakers because Junko could feel the sound coming from overhead and behind her as well.

"What do you usually watch on this? Movies?"

"No. Actually I hardly ever watch it."

"What a waste . . ."

"There's a cable station that broadcasts plays—I watch that. I like theater."

"That makes sense somehow. I bet you were into acting when you were younger."

"How'd you know? I wrote some plays, too, at one point. They were just for practice, though. Nothing ever came of them."

"You could still write if you wanted to." Junko began flipping through the seemingly endless channels, but none of them were broadcasting news or weather. There was news on CNN, but it was not from Japan. It was nine-thirty, not the usual news hour, so Junko settled into an armchair, put her feet up and decided to see what else was on. Koichi sat with her and offered explanations of the various channels for a while, but finally gave a yawn and went to take a bath. Vision came over to her, so Junko picked her up and petted her until she settled down comfortably in her lap. Then Junko turned her attention back to the screen and flicked through the channels until she came to a music program. Leaning back in her chair, she gazed at the high ceiling, savoring the luxury of the music settling over her like a light snowfall.

She must have dozed off. When she woke with a start, Vision stirred and then resettled herself on her lap. Junko looked at the clock over the fireplace and saw that only twenty minutes had passed. The concert she had been listening to was over and now, in jarring contrast, the station was broadcasting a news program: "The Year's Top Ten Stories."

The story they were covering was none other than the series of fires caused by Junko herself. The abandoned factory in Tayama. Café Currant by the Aoto intersection. Sakurai Liquors in Yoyogi Uehara. Then photographs of Fujikawa and Natsuko filled the screen.

Junko narrowed her eyes against the glare and forced herself to watch. She still had no idea how to begin searching for the person who killed Natsuko, but it was her duty to do it, so she *had* to pay attention. She shouldn't allow herself to get lost in her own happiness.

She heard the bathroom door close and the sound of Koichi heading for the kitchen. He said something, but Junko couldn't make it out.

"What did you say?"

"I said you'll feel better after you take a bath." She heard the refrigerator opening and then what sounded like the tab being pulled on a can of beer. "What are you watching?"

"It's about my battle with the Asaba gang."

Koichi came running from the kitchen into the living room and sat down close to her on the sofa. He was wearing a bathrobe and had a towel around his neck. Rather than looking at the TV, he peered into Junko's face.

"Now why would you want to watch this?" Koichi tried to snatch the remote control out of her hand, but Junko was too quick for him. Her gaze remained fixed on the TV screen. "Come on, we're on vacation now. How can you even think about work?"

Junko didn't hear his words. He said something else, but she put up a finger to shush him. Some kind of office was being shown. It could have been a staff room in a school, or some kind of law office. Words on the screen indicated that it was the office of a private organization called Stalker Hotline. Just before she was abducted, the terrified Natsuko Mita had been there to get advice on how to deal with the gang that had been stalking her. Appropriately, behind the desks on camera, Junko could see a row of doors that must lead to small private rooms for confidential consultations.

Junko, however, was not really looking at the screen. She was listening to the off-camera voice explaining Stalker Hotline's involvement with Natsuko Mita.

"She seemed so agitated that it worried the counselor she spoke with. Since then it's been keeping us awake nights; she suffered so terribly and we were unable to save her."

More print rolled across the screen. "Kanto Comprehensive Security Services' Stalker Hotline vice-president, Shiro Izaki."

That voice.

" . . . Needless to say, the most serious issue facing us is how to protect the women who come to us; how to keep them from being attacked or murdered."

Junko had heard that voice before.

Surveillance is about all a former detective like me is good for.

I'm a retired detective.

It was Skipper's voice. He had known Natsuko Mita. Even if he hadn't been the one to counsel her, surely she'd seen him at Stalker Hotline.

Oh, it's you!

And then the gunshot.

The scene on the roof of Sakurai Liquors came flooding back. Natsuko's pale face. Her shaking shoulders. The blood that had crusted on the inside of her thighs. Her lips, cracked from beatings. Her swollen eyelids.

And . . . scattered on the concrete by the water tank, the tobacco from shredded cigarettes.

The memory hit Junko like a punch.

"That was Skipper!" Junko's shriek echoed around the high ceiling, the words shattering against the walls. The remote control slipped from her hand as she slowly shook her head back and forth, trying to dodge the other memories coming in as they pummeled her like fists.

Someone was gripping her arms. Koichi was staring into her face as though he doubted she was in her right mind. Junko gripped his arms in return.

"It was Skipper!"

"*Who* was?" demanded Koichi.

"It was Skipper who killed Natsuko Mita!"

Junko felt sick. It was too horrible, too revolting. She coughed out the words, telling Koichi what she suddenly understood.

"When I went to Sakurai Liquors to rescue Natsuko Mita, Skipper was there, too. He might have come to rescue her or he might have just been trying to find out what Asaba and his gang were up to; I don't know. He used to be a detective and he prides himself on surveillance, so it wouldn't have been hard for him to break in and stay out of sight."

Koichi let go of Junko's hands and slapped his knees in exasperation. "You're out of your mind! Why would Skipper have done something like that?"

Junko stared back at him. "Because he's a Guardian. The Guardians would have been after Asaba's gang, too. They'd probably been after them for much longer than I had."

Junko's encounter with Asaba at the factory had been an accident. She had seen what he and his gang were doing, and then she had pursued them. But there had been another accident waiting for her at Sakurai Liquors: Shiro Izaki, "Skipper," a member of the Guardians, was already there.

"He must not have known what to do when I started executing the gang. He was risking getting caught in the middle. But at the same time, he couldn't leave without figuring out who I was and what I was doing. So he climbed up to the roof and hid."

And while he watched and waited, he nervously shredded cigarettes.

"He saw Asaba come up to the roof and hide in the elevator control room, and he shot him. Or maybe he was hiding in the control room himself, waiting for a chance to escape, but he couldn't figure out my movements. Then I brought Natsuko up to the roof and found Asaba's body. He watched that and saw his chance to escape, but Natsuko spotted him."

Oh, it's you!

So he killed her.

The most important thing for a Guardian was never to leave a trace. Not only could they not reveal themselves, they had to keep their entire organization a secret. That was why Shiro Izaki could not let Natsuko Mita live; she knew his name and what he did.

It didn't make sense. He had to sacrifice the victim in order to bring down the criminal.

Sometimes noncombatants get caught in the crossfire.

Could you really rationalize sacrificing one victim in order to save a hundred others? It was unavoidable when waging a war. Junko knew that she'd done the same thing. She had killed Hitoshi Kano's girlfriend. And she had taken out the witnesses at Café Currant. Her hands were just as bloody as Izaki's.

It was what war meant. And in this war there was no front line or rear guard. With Natsuko's death, Izaki was safe and the Guardians were still secure. The Guardians could then continue secretly devoting themselves to burying many more of the worst criminals.

Junko clenched her trembling hands into fists and felt the backs of her eyes get hot. Was it really right? Was this truly justice?

Junko suddenly noticed that Koichi was no longer by her side. She looked up and glanced around, but he was gone. Junko switched off the TV, pushed Vision unceremoniously from her lap, and stood up.

She had to get back to Tokyo. She couldn't just stay here and do nothing. She would go meet Skipper and find out the truth. She wanted to know what he was thinking: whether it had been against his will, and whether or not he felt guilty about killing Natsuko.

That would lead to the truth for herself, as well.

Koichi came pelting down the stairs. He was dressed and had their coats under his arm. He'd pulled his wet hair back in a tight ponytail, and his eyes were narrowed to cold slits.

"Let's go," he said roughly. "We'll get Skipper and make him confess. Otherwise you'll never have peace of mind."

Junko nodded in agreement.

"I'll bring the car around. The main switch for the water boiler is in the backyard. Would you mind turning it off?"

"The backyard?"

Koichi pointed down the hallway. "It's just out through those French doors."

Putting on the coat he tossed her, Junko ran down the hall and opened the French doors. The cold air hit her like a slap in the face. The doors looked out over the lake and a wide snow-covered expanse sloped gently down to it. There was nothing to block her view or the bitter wind.

The tips of her nails, her fingers and her earlobes were so cold in the night air that they hurt. Leaning out through the doors, she couldn't find the main switch Koichi had mentioned. In a hurry to get going, Junko stepped outside onto the snow in her house slippers. The snow was frozen, so she didn't sink in as deeply as she'd feared.

She stepped back from the house to look at the outside wall and windows. There did not appear to be a switchboard or any other kind of switch there. The wind blowing off the lake hit her like little blades of ice. It was freezing. As she glanced back toward the lake, a stinging gust made her eyes well with tears. She wrapped her arms around herself and ran back to the French doors. She would tell Koichi that she couldn't find the switch.

Just then she saw something reflected in the glass of the half-open doors. It looked like a human form. Junko whipped around reflexively.

Koichi was standing there. He wasn't wearing a coat, and he stood firmly with his legs apart and his back to the lake. He was holding out something in his right hand. There was a bang.

Junko was blown backwards and landed on the frozen snow with a crunch. Her head was by the French doors with her legs in the direction of the lake, and her arms were spread apart as she faced the sky.

It hurts.

And she felt hot. She could feel her pulse throbbing in her chest. Then she finally realized that she had been shot.

That was what that sound was.

She couldn't move. She tried to get up but couldn't even raise her head. Where had she been shot? In the chest? In the stomach? She could feel the blood flowing out of her, but she couldn't tell where it was coming from.

She could hear the sound of tortured breathing—her own. The sound of life seeping out. Her breath was white as it rose and disappeared in the night air. Her life was leaving her body, and she couldn't drag it back.

She heard footsteps crunch over the frozen snow. Lying there, she noticed that the clouds were gone and the sky was full of stars. Stars were all she could see. From somewhere outside her field of vision she heard someone start talking to her.

"It's just like you said. Skipper is Shiro Izaki. He's the one who shot Natsuko Mita." It was Koichi. Nothing about his voice had altered.

Junko opened her mouth to reply, but her voice would not come out. She could feel blood pour out instead.

"And you guessed correctly why that unfortunate event occurred. You're a smart one." Then Koichi called out to someone else, "Isn't that right, Mr. Izaki?" Junko heard more footsteps approaching her across the snow.

Junko closed her eyes. So Skipper—Izaki—was here, too. He had come to help Koichi. To help him kill her. *No, they wouldn't consider this a killing. More like "dealing with me,"* thought Junko.

Now she understood why Koichi had taken so long to come back to his apartment when seeing off Izaki earlier that day: they had been planning this. When they had come back from shopping and found Izaki waiting for them, Junko had noticed the shredded cigarettes. Both Izaki and Koichi had realized they were in danger of her remembering the last time she had seen such a thing.

Fortunately—or not—Junko had not immediately made the connection with the shredded cigarettes at Sakurai Liquors. Koichi and Izaki, however, must have known it was only a matter of time until she did. Thinking back, Junko remembered how Koichi had acted strangely when they met Izaki at the Tower Hotel.

I didn't hear anything about you being involved . . . why are you here?

Koichi had spoken with uncharacteristic hostility. And Izaki had looked at her as though he'd seen her somewhere before. Of course. He had seen her at Sakurai Liquors.

But why had Izaki gotten involved when there was such a danger of her finding him out? Could the Guardians be that shorthanded? Or had they decided ahead of time that they didn't care if she figured out who he was?

Koichi spoke as if in reply to her question. "But, you know . . ."

Junko opened her eyes but she couldn't see where he was standing. He seemed to have moved further to her right; he sounded farther away. "I'm not killing you because you discovered Izaki's mistake."

Mistake? Is that what they considered Natsuko's murder? *A mistake?* Something you could take care of by apologizing?

Junko recalled how Natsuko's expression had suddenly brightened when she told her Fujikawa had sent her; her eyes wet with tears, her cheeks streaked from so much crying.

"I'm sorry about this." Koichi's offhand tone did not change. "But the Guardians planned to kill you from the beginning. They assigned the job to me. I was no more than a hit man, right from the start."

Junko faced the starry sky and exhaled. Her breath condensed momentarily into a frozen white cloud before dissipating. That had been her love. And now she couldn't see it anymore. It was gone.

All that was left was a question. *Why?*

"You always overdo it. Overkill is a dangerous thing for the Guardians. You could never have been any real help to us. I told you how important it is not to leave evidence, didn't I?"

"You are much too blatant when you kill." Now Izaki was speaking. "And you don't even try to cover your tracks.

"Kaori Kurata is still young. If we train her properly, there's a much greater chance that she will learn to do exactly what we tell her. That's when pyrokinesis could be useful. But you're already an adult; a finished product. You're so strong that if something goes wrong, we're all in danger."

Junko closed her eyes again. She tried to focus on where the two of them were standing, but she felt tears flowing out of the corners of her eyes. *Maybe I just want to cry,* she thought.

Junko flung out her power without knowing where it was going. She was surprised at how weak it was. It flew out into the night, but was absorbed by the frigid night air and the water in the lake. Now she understood why they had chosen this spot to kill her. They had wanted to make sure she would not be able to fight back.

"It was only natural that your targets would occasionally be the same as the Guardians'. Masaki Kogure was one. We had him cornered and were searching for a way to kill him that would look like either a natural death or an accident. Then you came along and obliterated him, turning the whole thing into front page news."

No matter how powerful the Guardians were, no matter how many police were involved, and no matter how capable they were of destroying evidence, they still had limits. The detectives in charge of investigating the carnage Junko had wrought might accidentally come across a Guardian who'd been pursuing the same target.

"And that's why we had to find you and kill you."

Junko exhaled again. Something in the center of her body had begun to ache, but the pain had apparently removed whatever it was that was keeping her from speaking.

"So why did you try to get me to like you?"

Koichi didn't reply right away. She could tell he was moving, changing his position on the snow.

"I hadn't wanted to kill you so quickly," he finally said, his voice as nonchalant as always. "We really had hoped you could help us out with Kaori Kurata. We would have brought her here tonight if it hadn't been for that ridiculous pendant camera. You would have been so happy to have that little girl in your arms. The little sister you never had. Too bad."

Junko could hear Koichi moving again. She wrung out another flash of power, but it evaporated into the sky.

"But it's like I told you. The bottom line for the organization was that if you displayed even the slightest intention to attack or even doubt a member of the Guardians, if you rebelled or second-guessed us, I was to dispose of you immediately. And that was what happened." He apologized again. "I was thinking that if you joined us and didn't give us any trouble at all, you could stay with us longer and we could have a good time together. That's why I wanted you to like me. We didn't have long, but it was fun. You know, I—I . . ."

I was lonely. She knew what he had wanted to say.

Someone had begun to weep. Junko could hear stifled sobs.

Is that me? Am I the one crying?"

No, it was Izaki. The Skipper.

Junko spoke again, to the stars.

"I—I thought . . . I thought you and I . . . understood each other."

I know you've been lonely, she wanted to cry out.

"That was a very happy misunderstanding for you, Junko," said Koichi. "But there is nothing inside me that another human can ever understand."

I understood your loneliness because I was lonely, too.

Koichi went on. "I told you about that girl I 'pushed' into going on a date with me when I was fourteen."

"Yes," answered Junko in such a small voice that only the stars could hear.

"She died two years later."

Junko heard Izaki's ragged intake of breath in the brief silence.

"She went mad because of what I had done to her mind."

I'll stay with you, Junko had promised.

"You said you couldn't give your heart to anyone until they had dirtied their hands with you by killing someone together."

Finally he had it right.

"When I found out that my first love had died because of me, I threw out the last remnants I had of human feeling. So I don't have a heart to give. I know that someone like me cannot afford to have feelings for anyone."

So she had thought they understood each other, but there had been nothing there to begin with. Yes, he could write plays. He could act, too. It had been a brilliant performance. Junko felt almost apologetic for having been the solitary audience.

Junko could see the stars blinking and hear them whispering to her. *You made a mistake, Junko. You made the wrong decision, Junko. Your judgment was off. You should have stuck to your principles.*

Junko heard them, but for some reason she did not care anymore. She wondered why.

"That's enough!" Izaki interrupted hoarsely. "Put her out of her misery. She doesn't need to know any more. Show her some mercy."

Koichi was silent. Junko listened to him walking around, settling on a position. She closed her eyes and tried to concentrate on the sound.

33

The man with the car registered in Nerima had been small and plump. As soon as Chikako and Makihara decided he was definitely not the man the waiter had seen at Sans Pareil, they headed for Lake Kawaguchi. The traffic had cleared up, so it would take them no longer than two hours to get there.

They didn't know if the man who'd been with Junko Aoki would be at his vacation home at the lake or not, but they figured that if they could somehow get inside the place they might be able to learn more about him. There would be no harm in making the trip. If by a stroke of luck he was there, they could hope for even more: Junko Aoki might be with him. That would be a wonderful Christmas present.

The way Makihara was gripping the steering wheel, he looked like a novice jockey learning to ride a horse and holding onto the reins for dear life. Chikako knew, however, what it was he was so afraid of losing a grip on, and it wasn't a horse, or the car.

It was this road. His fate. Makihara finally knew he was headed in the right direction, on this road that was leading him to Junko Aoki.

When they arrived at the log cabin-style house owned by Koichi Kido, the headlights lit up the steps to the front door. As Makihara was putting on the brakes, they saw the shadow of someone coming around from the side of the house.

What happened next seemed to be linked to the nightmare of Makihara's past by a single, direct line.

As Junko tried to focus her ears on his movements and figure out where Koichi was standing—most likely with a gun aimed at her heart—she heard the sound of a car engine. A car. It was heading this way. She could hear the sound of tires driving over the thin, crunchy layer of ice left on the road that had been cleared of snow.

"Somebody's coming," Koichi said. She could hear him treading away from her. He must have gone to see who it was.

Junko opened her eyes again to look up at the stars. They twinkled encouragement to her. *Lucky stars, lend me your power.* She mustered the strength to speak.

"Mr. . . . Izaki . . . help me."

Izaki groaned.

"Give me . . . a hand." Junko swallowed. She could taste blood. "Lift . . . me up. Please."

Izaki came closer. "Listen . . ."

"Please! Lift . . . my . . . head."

Izaki ignored her and went on. "Forgive me, please. I never, never wanted to kill anyone. I just wanted to clean up the bastards, to protect the lives of the innocent."

I know, I know. It was the same for me.

"I joined the Guardians because my daughter was murdered by a monster; my daughter and my grandson. The bastard's sentence was unbelievably light, and then he was a 'model' prisoner. When I was recruited for the Guardians they promised me they would kill him and make it look like suicide." Izaki took a shaky breath and continued. "They kept that promise. That's why I joined."

I understand completely, but I need you to help me now!

"After I became a member, I had to follow all their rules. Especially the rule about not leaving evidence behind. But I didn't want to kill Natsuko Mita. She was just an innocent victim. It's not right to kill someone just because they've seen you and can identify you." Izaki's voice was anguished. "I lost my head. There was a massacre going on that had not been in the plan; I was terrified, and I was keyed up because I'd just shot Asaba. So when Natsuko Mita called out to me, my finger just pulled the trigger by reflex.

"In that moment I was nothing more than a dirty, cowardly murderer."

Murderer? Junko had killed a lot of people. Most of them could hardly be called human beings. But it was still life that she had taken. Junko didn't think she'd been wrong, but she now wasn't sure anymore.

"I knew what Kido had been assigned to do." Izaki cleared his throat and continued. "I knew he was getting close to you so that he could get rid of you, Junko. That's why I begged the Guardian management to let me be involved in the Kaori Kurata job."

"Why?" Junko asked faintly. She was sure it wasn't so he could help her.

"I wanted you to figure out who I was," said Izaki. "I wanted you to see through me and point the finger at me. I wanted you to come after me. Then at least Kido would have to end his charade."

Well, here we are in the final act.

"I'm just a useless bastard. There's no way I can help you. We were both in this together. I'm so sorry I can't—" Choked up, Izaki began coughing in the frozen wind. "But I hated watching him fool you. It was so cruel."

Still looking at the sky, Junko smiled to herself at how selfish Skipper had been. He hadn't done anything to help her; it had just been for his own conscience. If they were going to eliminate her anyway, fooling her for another month or another year wouldn't have made any difference. As long as she was going to die, why would it have been so wrong to let her spend her final days in a beautiful dream? That wouldn't have been so bad.

Junko's head cleared as a single thought came to her. If you continued killing people, if you had the power of life and death over other humans, no matter what your purpose in killing them was, you would inexorably sink into self-centeredness. You'd always put yourself first. As though you'd become a god. And ultimately you'd begin to believe your thoughts and judgments superseded all others'. Nothing you believed could possibly be mistaken.

That's exactly the way it was with me.

"Lift my head," Junko strained to speak. "I've got to . . . Koichi . . ."

"You poor thing!" Izaki moaned. "Kido fooled you. There was no need to do it this way."

That's how it is, thought Junko, *when you know you can do something. You begin to want to do it whether you need to or not. That's what you do when you're God.*

But—he was lonely, too, and that's why he also wanted me with him, if only for a little while.

And that's why I can't leave him on his own.

"Lift my head," she said in the strongest voice she could manage. "I've got to take him with me."

Izaki came closer and leaned forward so that she could see him. Junko managed to curve her lips and smile faintly into his tear-streaked face. She wasn't sure if it really did look like a smile or not, but it seemed she managed to convey that she didn't intend to hurt him.

"If I move you, your bleeding will get worse," Izaki said.

"That doesn't matter anymore," Junko murmured.

Izaki lifted Junko's upper body. He put his arms around her back and held her up so that she could see her surroundings. There was Koichi Kido.

"Is he good with a gun?" she whispered.

"He has one for his own protection. I've seen him use it before; he knows what he's doing."

"How many bullets does he have left?"

"Five."

She would have to be careful, then. She'd have only one chance.

"The man who killed my daughter and grandson was her husband, my grandson's father," said Izaki. Junko took that as the trigger to let fly every last ounce of power she had left in her.

Makihara got out of the car, and Chikako followed suit. The frozen ground beneath her rubber boots was slippery.

The shadow they'd seen was a young man—tall and thin, with his long hair pulled back. He strolled gracefully towards them.

"Hey there, anything the matter?" he greeted them cheerily. "What's up? Low on gas? There's not another soul around, and no gas station either. Lucky you found me. Hey! I guess my being here could be your Christmas present!" He seemed not to have a care in the world.

"Are you Koichi Kido?" Makihara questioned in reply, while Chikako stood silent, looking closely at this chatterbox.

The expression on Koichi's face changed to surprise, but to Chikako it seemed feigned. Something told Chikako that he was not quite the friendly, carefree youth he was trying to portray.

"Yes, I am, but—"

Before he could say another word, Koichi Kido went up in flames.

Junko watched as Koichi was enveloped in fire. His sweater turned bright red. Blue flames leapt up his long legs, and his hair incinerated. In no more than a second, Koichi was a human torch. He lifted his arms and tried to twist his body around to look behind himself. Junko couldn't see the gun—it must have dropped on the snow. She could see each of his fingers distinctly outlined in the bright flames.

He screamed. But Junko couldn't hear. All she could hear was his voice in her head calling out to her. She could no longer feel the pain of dying or the agony of losing so much blood. She only felt Koichi's arms holding her again. Junko watched until Koichi collapsed. She could hear what was left of him fall on the snow. It was as if the snow was there to gently comfort him.

Chikako and Makihara stood rooted to the spot, staring as Koichi burned. They knew they could neither stop the fire nor help him.

Just before he fell, Chikako thought she heard him cry out, *Junko!*

Makihara ran forward. He seemed headed towards Koichi, but instead ran past him, leaving him to smolder. He ran around the side of the house and then behind, to the expanse of white snow beyond it.

Izaki loosened his hold on Junko and laid her back down on the snow.

"Don't be sad, Skipper," Junko murmured. "Thank you." *I can't punish you; we both made the same mistake, after all.*

Chikako followed Makihara. Her rubber boots pounded awkwardly and her heart pounded loudly along with them. Makihara was in danger. He shouldn't go straight in like that. He'd be the next one to burn before her eyes.

Then she saw them. The young woman lying on her back in the red-stained snow, and Shiro Izaki on his knees next to her.

Junko heard the voice of a woman. "Izaki!"

Now someone else was approaching Junko. This other person was tall enough to come between her and the stars. It was a man. But it wasn't

Koichi. He wasn't as young as Koichi. He knelt down on one knee next to her, put out a hand and gently touched her forehead.

"Are you Junko Aoki?" he asked.

Junko blinked slowly in response.

"Are you the one who burned that man?"

Junko opened her mouth and was surprised to see that she still had enough breath for it to turn white.

"Yes."

The man stroked her forehead and asked, "How did you get this injury?"

Junko heard Izaki answer from somewhere outside her field of vision.

"That guy shot her. That's why she burned him. It was only fair. *And yes, she could really do that,*" Izaki added, his voice breaking.

The man glanced at Izaki, but then quickly looked back down at Junko. He narrowed his eyes as if he were looking at something too bright to bear.

"You're going to die," he told her in a low voice. "We can't save you."

"I know," whispered Junko.

"Tell me, were the Arakawa, Tayama, Café Currant, Sakurai Liquors, and Yokohama fires all your doing?"

"Yes," said Junko and closed her eyes. "Who are you?"

"I'm a policeman," the man answered. "You have pyrokinetic powers, right?"

Junko smiled, her eyes still closed.

"So you know . . . about that sort of thing?"

He nodded. "Yes, I know a lot about it."

Here, at the very end of her life, was a policeman who knew about her. *A policeman who understands that I am—that I was—a weapon.*

"Officer," she said.

"What is it?"

"Mr. Izaki . . . he knows . . . what happened."

"Yes, I see."

"I'm a . . . a murderer."

The man just nodded, silently.

"I have . . . a favor . . . to ask."

She opened her eyes, and saw that the stars had become blurry. She didn't think it was because she had tears in her eyes.

"There's a girl . . . she has . . . the same powers I do."

"Do you mean Kaori Kurata?"

Junko strained to see his face more clearly.

"You know . . . her?"

"Yes, I do."

Junko realized that this policeman must have learned a lot while he'd been pursuing her. If that were so, she could trust him.

"Will you . . . help her?"

"Yes, I think I'll be able to do that."

"Make sure . . . she . . . doesn't turn out . . . like me." Junko sighed heavily. She knew it was the life leaving her body. Her field of vision constricted, becoming more blurry and dim.

The policeman stroked her forehead again, and she could feel him wiping away her tears.

"Did . . . he die?"

"Koichi Kido? Oh yes, he's dead."

"Check . . . again." It was getting harder to breathe. "If . . . he's not, he's suffering . . . make sure . . . he doesn't suffer."

"Don't worry."

"Officer?"

"What?"

"Who . . . are you? What's . . . your name?"

He didn't answer. He stayed where he was, bent down to Junko, stroking her forehead with his right hand and gripping her right hand firmly in his left.

Why won't you tell me your name? Junko tried to ask, but she could no longer speak.

"Goodbye," she managed softly. She thought she heard him say *Goodbye*, too, and it looked as though he said something more. It might have been *Merry Christmas*, and Junko felt that dying this way was the best present she could have received.

She couldn't see the stars anymore, but that was because she was getting closer and closer to them. Everything went dark.

34

More snow fell on the Kanto Plain after the New Year.

Chikako Ishizu put on her rubber boots once more, and headed to a park near her house. There was a lot of snow on the ground, but the sky was clear. She was almost perspiring under her heavy coat as she hurried. She had only five minutes to get there.

There he was waiting, right on time, sitting on a bench near the swings. His coat collar was turned up and he wore a scarf in which he had buried his chin. Chikako was reminded again that punctuality was a sign of a good detective.

They greeted each other and Chikako joined him on the bench. School was not yet out for the day, so there were no children playing in the snow. An old man with a dog walked along the hedge around the park.

"We can explain the deaths of Koichi Kido and Junko Aoki as a murder-suicide planned by Kido," the detective said abruptly from inside his scarf. He'd dispensed with the usual preliminary niceties. *Efficiency above all,* Chikako supposed.

"So it was a love affair gone wrong?" asked Chikako.

"That's right. And that was the truth on a certain level."

Chikako thought to herself that it was probably entirely true, from Junko Aoki's point of view.

"I still can't believe that Izaki asked me to let him contact you, back there at Lake Kawaguchi."

The detective in the scarf looked intrigued.

"Oh? Why were you surprised?"

"Because he was fingering you as a member of the Guardians."

"Well, I let him get away with it," the detective laughed mirthlessly. "It didn't matter. He was in no way harming me. We had done what we set out to do."

"What you set out to do," repeated Chikako.

"That's right. Our goal was to get rid of Junko Aoki, a dangerous woman with pyrokinetic powers."

Chikako closed her eyes. She could see Junko's face as she lay dead in the snow. In death she'd been almost paler than the snow, but still beautiful.

"Sergeant Kinugasa," Chikako asked the man in the scarf, "How long have you and Captain Ito been members of the Guardians?"

Kinugasa shrugged. He seemed to have forgotten. "I guess Ito joined before I did."

"Didn't you ever have doubts about your decision?"

Kinugasa looked at Chikako as if surprised she would ask such a question. "You mean about whether I could go along with what the Guardians did?"

"That's right."

Kinugasa sighed and leaned back on the bench, knocking off the snow piled on the back of it.

"No, I never questioned my decision."

"Never?"

"No, and you know why? Neither Ito nor I have ever had any illusions about the sort of organization it is."

Chikako was silent. She looked at his square jaw, so fitting for this man with his unyielding moral character.

"But it's a necessary evil," he continued. "We have to have an organization like this because the laws currently in place are too limited and compartmentalized. I'd be happier if we were rid of it, but we still need it. You know, Ishizu, it's not that we're Guardians within the police force so much as that we're police who tolerate the existence of the Guardians."

"For now," pressed Chikako.

"Yes, for now," said Kinugasa confidently.

"So when can we get rid of the organization?"

"When we get ideal laws and they are enforced properly."

"Does that mean laws that allow us to uniformly execute anyone who commits a violent crime?"

Kinugasa laughed. "It means laws that deal with violent offenders in a more appropriate way than they do now."

Chikako's gaze was on the ground but her voice was firm as she retorted, "What you are doing is ignoring the crosswalk and running over every pedestrian on the road—driving in places where there isn't even a road—all so you can reach your destination by the shortest possible route, no matter what the cost."

"But if you just dawdle along, even more victims get sacrificed. We might hit one pedestrian, but then save ten or a hundred others."

Chikako was quiet. Her eyes closed, her back rigid, she said, "I can't subscribe to that."

"Whatever you say," said Kinugasa with a touch of frost in his tone. "We have no intention of forcing you to join us. Either you or Makihara. You have no reason to worry, we won't harm either of you if you decide not to. We're not that childish."

"And you're not so small an operation that you have to worry about the likes of Makihara or me."

"That is correct."

They were silent for a while. The glare off the snow was stinging Chikako's eyes. She heard a dog barking somewhere in the distance.

"You wanted to get rid of Junko Aoki because she was bringing down her targets for execution in such a visible way. Is that right?"

"Yes. She operated on such a large scale, there was a risk that we'd get burned, too. Our main concern was that the attention her executions got from the media might accidentally give us away as well. We try to stay out of the media spotlight."

She'd heard the same thing from Izaki. Kido had apparently explained to Junko that it was the reason he had to kill her.

"Then why did you go to all of the trouble of involving Makihara?"

"That's simple. He's a talented young man. He was capable of finding Junko Aoki without our help, and there was a risk that he would become aware of the Guardians just as we were getting rid of her. We wanted to prevent that."

He lowered his voice and continued seriously, "There was also the problem posed by the tenacity with which Makihara adheres to his personal convictions. If Makihara discovered the Guardians after Junko Aoki was gone, and if he accused anyone, it wouldn't have mattered. Our concern was that the two of them would join forces. Junko Aoki had killed his brother; he was her victim, but temperamentally they had too much in common. They were both solitary people in search of a reason to live."

And they were both good people, Chikako added silently. She turned to Kinugasa and spoke aloud.

"This is a purely personal question. Would you set Guardian policy aside for a moment and just tell me how you feel about all of this?"

Kinugasa raised his eyebrows and wrapped his scarf more tightly around his neck.

"Do you feel any sympathy at all for Junko Aoki?" Junko hadn't asked to be born with the lethal power she had, nor had she set out to become a murderer. She had done her best to live her life with what she had, and it hadn't turned out well. But it certainly was not a life she had chosen freely for herself.

Kinugasa was silent for a long minute. Finally he answered, voice dry of emotion: "Detective Ishizu, I believe that criminals like Keiichi Asaba have a certain supernatural power of their own. Not so different from Junko Aoki."

Chikako vehemently disagreed, but she bit her tongue and forced herself to hear him out.

"Asaba and monsters like him have an unnatural ability to commit violence without being troubled by conscience. If we were at war, someone like Asaba might come in handy as long he did exactly as he was told."

How can you even think like that? How can you live with such twisted logic? Chikako clenched her hands into fists to contain herself.

"In the case of Asaba, his power was based on his lack of something that most people have. Junko Aoki had acquired something that most people do not, and that was what set her apart. But both of them were equally dangerous variations from the norm, and they both ended up as murderers."

"I don't agree," Chikako said.

"Well, I don't want to think that either," said Kinugasa, "but you can't change the facts." Chikako sensed that his voice had lost some of its conviction. "I can't tell you how much I'd like to meet someone with supernatural powers who could convince me that I'm wrong."

For a little while, the two sat on the bench together, wisps of white vapor escaping as they exhaled. They were like two machines programmed to work in opposition, ticking along in the snow.

"I'm going to travel a different road than you." Chikako finally lifted her face and spoke resolutely. "I'm not going to quit the police force."

"Nobody's asking you to."

"I heard that Izaki quit the Stalker Hotline."

"There's not much more he can do for us."

"I'm wondering whether the police could do the sort of work he was doing there."

"That's a good idea," said Kinugasa, breaking out in a smile. "I think that would be just the job for you."

"I'm surprised to hear you say that."

"Is that so? I hope you don't misunderstand me, Detective Ishizu. I have the greatest respect for those of you who choose to drive through life stopping for pedestrians. All I'm saying is that sometimes it's not enough, and that's why I believe there should also be people who can move quickly when necessary." Kinugasa stood up, obviously ready to leave, but then patted his pocket, remembering something, and turned back to Chikako.

"I wanted to give you this." He handed her an envelope in which there were several photographs. "I developed these photos taken by Fusako Eguchi."

Chikako looked at the photos. There was Izaki, and a couple was sitting with him at the same table.

"They were a good-looking pair," said Kinugasa.

"They look happy," Chikako agreed.

"They were, then. Happiness is like that. It's usually just a dot. It never stretches out into a line," Kinugasa said, a sigh mixed in with his words. "That's the way truth is, too."

He started to trudge off through the snow, but Chikako called him back.

"Sergeant Kinugasa."

He turned back to her.

"Will you give my regards to Captain Ito? You probably heard that I've been transferred."

Kinugasa acknowledged her with a silent wave, and was gone. Chikako

Ishizu decided to remain there in the park a while longer, accompanied by the radiant smile of Junko Aoki in the photo.

A phone ringing at midnight.

"Hello?"

"What do you mean by calling at this time?"

"I couldn't get hold of you before. You're never at home when I call."

"I had a lot I wanted to think about."

"All right, I understand. I would have liked to do the same myself, but I have a husband who can't boil water by himself."

"That doesn't sound like you, Detective Ishizu. Anyway, I wanted to call you, too. I've got some news for you that didn't make it into the evening papers."

"News?"

"Mr. Kurata died."

"What?"

"He and Mrs. Kurata were meeting a lawyer to take care of the final details of their divorce. A bookcase in the lawyer's waiting room fell over and crushed him to death."

"A bookcase, eh?"

"That's right. Three male paralegals came running to help, but they couldn't lift it off him."

"Why would such a large bookcase fall over, I wonder?"

"There is so much in this life that we can't explain. Mrs. Kurata was unhurt, by the way."

"I assumed as much."

"When the bookcase fell over, Mr. and Mrs. Kurata were the only ones in the room."

"As it happened."

"Yes, quite coincidentally."

"Is Mrs. Kurata taking it all right?"

"Yes, although she did seem tired."

"And Kaori?"

"She's feeling much better. Fusako Eguchi is taking good care of both of them."

"Makihara?"

"Yes, what now?"

"You'd better not quit the police force."

"What brought that up all of a sudden?"

"No matter how slowly we get things done, society needs troops like us who get the job done without running down the pedestrians."

"That's an intriguing metaphor."

"Don't laugh!"

"I'm not laughing, and I won't quit either. I've got to make a living somehow. On top of that, Junko Aoki left me with a difficult assignment."

"To make sure Kaori . . . doesn't turn out like her."

"But I can't become a full-time teacher; after all, I'm only teaching one subject." Makihara chuckled and hung up.

At the end of the month, with Kaori Kurata by the hand, Chikako visited Junko Aoki's apartment in Tayama. There were no relatives to clean out her things or handle her estate. When her landlord came crying to the police, Chikako volunteered to take care of it.

Junko Aoki had been an orderly person, and the apartment was neat and clean. Kaori looked around with great interest. She picked up and smelled the soap Junko had used; she put the sweater left hanging on the back of a kitchen chair around her own shoulders and even tried on Junko's house slippers. Chikako let Kaori do as she liked and in the meantime packed a few things into cardboard boxes. The furniture and curtains were all cheap; Chikako imagined the only thing the landlord would have been glad to accept responsibility for was the brand-new computer on the kitchen table.

As Kaori went around the room examining everything, she stopped at the bed to pick up a stuffed toy dog. She gazed at it for a while and then murmured, "She was crying."

Chikako turned around to see what she was talking about, but Kaori seemed oblivious.

"What did you just say?"

"I didn't say anything."

Chikako realized she must have seen something in the dog, the way she'd seen Makihara's memory of his brother.

"I guess I was just hearing things."

"Detective Ishizu?"

"What is it?"

"Do you think I could have this puppy?" It was a plump little dog that had seen better days. It was missing an ear and one of its eyes was hanging by a thread. It looked handmade—maybe Junko's mother had made it for her.

"Sure, go ahead," said Chikako. "Take good care of it."

"I will," said Kaori as she hugged it to herself.

Chikako finished most of the cleaning up, and the two of them went outside. Standing at the bottom of the stairway was a young woman with a pointed chin and red-dyed hair. She was holding a small bouquet of flowers. Chikako called down and asked who she was looking for.

The girl pulled at the collar of her down jacket. She frowned and answered defensively as if expecting to be turned away.

"I've come to bring flowers for the person who used to live here."

"Here?"

"Yeah. She died. Well, she was murdered. Some guy killed her and then committed suicide."

Chikako's eyes widened. "Do you mean Junko Aoki?"

"Yeah." The girl nervously ran her free hand through her hair. "I saw it on the news. They showed her picture and I recognized her, so I called up the TV station and bugged them until they gave me her address."

"I see," said Chikako. "How did you know each other, if you don't mind me asking?" Chikako introduced herself, showed her ID, and explained briefly what she was doing there. The girl did not seem to be at all surprised.

"So, you're a detective."

"That's right."

"I only met Junko once. She'd come looking for the friends—bad friends— I used to run with." She shrugged what Chikako imagined were very thin shoulders underneath her down coat. "They're dead now, too."

"You just met her that once and you came here to bring flowers for her?"

"Sure, why not? Isn't that what you do when someone dies? And she seemed kind of lonely."

"I'm sure she would be delighted with these. May I take them?"

The girl nodded and held out the flowers. "My name is Nobue Ito."

"Well, thank you very much, Nobue."

Nobue shrugged again, probably intending it as a parting gesture. She turned around to leave, but just as she did, she noticed Kaori standing behind Chikako, listening and waiting patiently. Nobue and Kaori stood and looked at each other. Nobue's face suddenly lit up.

"Officer?"

"Yes?"

"Is this Junko's little sister? No . . . wait . . . I suppose she couldn't have had a sister this young."

Before Chikako could answer, Kaori spoke up.

"That's right. She was my sister."

Nobue, impressed, looked her over once again.

"You know, you're going to be even prettier than she was. But you be careful and stay away from bad boys. There are too many of them, and they're everywhere!"

"I'll be careful," said Kaori.

Nobue left then, walking quickly away. Kaori held out a hand to Chikako, offering to take the flowers from her.

"All right then, you take care of them. Thanks." Chikako handed her the flowers and then took Kaori's empty hand in her own.

"It sure is cold!"

At the foot of the steps, Kaori stopped and turned back. She stood still for a few moments, the cold air reddening her cheeks.

"What is it?"

"I thought I heard somebody calling me." Kaori concentrated, listening in the wind, and then smiled. "No, I guess I was just hearing things."

Chikako could see Nobue's flowers reflected in Kaori's eyes. They looked like stars. Like love itself.

（英文版）クロスファイア
Crossfire

2005年10月25日　第1刷発行

著　者　宮部みゆき
訳　者　岩渕デボラ、磯崎アンナ
発行者　富田　充
発行所　講談社インターナショナル株式会社
　　　　〒112-8652 東京都文京区音羽 1-17-14
　　　　電話　03-3944-6493（編集部）
　　　　　　　03-3944-6492（営業部・業務部）
　　　　ホームページ　www.kodansha-intl.com

印刷・製本所　大日本印刷株式会社